SILENT SCREAM

SILENT SCREAM

Lynda La Plante

SIMON & SCHUSTER

London • New York • Toronto • Sydney

First published in Great Britain by Simon & Schuster UK Ltd, 2009
A CBS COMPANY

3 5 7 9 10 8 6 4 2

Simon & Schuster UK Ltd
1st Floor
222 Gray's Inn Road
London WC1X 8HB

www.simonandschuster.co.uk

Simon & Schuster Australia
Sydney

A CIP catalogue record for this book is
available from the British Library

Hardback ISBN: 978-1-8473-7545-2
Trade Paperback ISBN: 978-1-8473-7546-9

Typeset in Bembo MT by Rowland Phototypesetting Ltd, Bury St Edmunds, Suffolk
Printed and bound in Great Britain by CPI Mackays, Chatham, ME5 8TD

To my sister Gilly Titchmarsh.

Acknowledgements

My gratitude to all those who gave their valuable time to help me with research on *Silent Scream*.

Special thanks go to all my committed team at La Plante Productions: Liz Thorburn, Richard Dobbs, Noel Farragher, Sara Johnson, Hannah Gatward and in particular Cass Sutherland and Nicole Muldowney for their invaluable assistance and advice while working on this book. Many thanks also to Stephen Ross and Andrew Bennet-Smith.

I give huge thanks to my literary agent, Gill Coleridge, and all at Rogers, Coleridge & White for their constant encouragement. I am also very grateful to my publishers, Ian Chapman and Suzanne Baboneau, and to everyone at Simon & Schuster. I am very happy to be working with such a terrific company.

Chapter One

The driver was not her usual one, but as the night filming had been completed ahead of schedule, she had been released from the set in West London earlier than expected. Amanda Delany didn't mind though; all the unit drivers had become friends of the entire film company. The Mercedes drew up outside her mews house in Belgravia and she jumped out quickly. The driver made sure she was safely inside the house before he drove off. She liked that because the overhanging ivy around her front door made it possible for someone to hide there and she was cautious, although none of her fans knew her new address.

Amanda loved the little house. She had only really been in residence eight weeks, but she had purchased it eighteen months ago. The renovations and the decoration had been completed before she had moved in, and it still had the lingering smells of new carpets and paint.

She was tired, it was almost midnight, and she decided to go straight to bed, relieved that she wasn't still filming until four in the morning – which was when the night shoot usually ended. Tomorrow she would be collected mid-afternoon. They were shooting in summer and it didn't get dark until almost nine.

Amanda took a quick shower and got into her bed, new like everything else in the mews house. This was the first place that she had owned, the first time she had lived on her own, without flatmates or boyfriends. She had changed partners almost as frequently as she had filming commitments, which made perfect fodder for the tabloids. Her lovers had invariably been her co-stars and, although she was still only twenty-four years old, Amanda had broken up two marriages. Her last affair, with a famous movie star, had been very public. Amanda was one of a clutch of young, very beautiful actresses about to break into the big time, and her agent had warned her to curb her sexual exploits, or risk damaging her blossoming career.

She fell deeply asleep straight away but woke up an hour later. For a few moments she was disorientated and reached for the clock on her bedside table, wondering if she had inadvertently set the alarm. Night filming was always difficult to adjust to, and often she found it hard working through the night and catching up on sleep during the day. Had there been a change of schedule? Had it been the telephone that had woken her? Amanda threw back the duvet and went to the window to look into the mews courtyard, but it was empty.

Back in bed, she snuggled down, must have dropped off again, and then woke with a start. The scream was hideous, a scream of such agony and terror that her heart lurched with fear. She sat up listening, waiting for it to continue, waiting for something to happen. But nothing did. Terrified, she got up again to look from the window into the courtyard. She turned on the lights and went from the bedroom down the narrow hall. All was silent, and from her kitchen annexe downstairs she looked into

the back garden, a small paved square with high walls surrounding it. She wondered if it was perhaps a wounded
animal she'd heard.

Returning to her bedroom, leaving all the lights on,
she couldn't stop hearing that terrible single scream
echoing in her head. The more she thought about it, the
more certain she was that it was a woman screaming. She
recalled being cast as the victim of a serial killer in a movie
that required her to scream, and when she couldn't get
the right pitch, they had brought in another actress who
specialised in bloodcurdling screams. She remembered
when she watched the finished film how chilling the
moment had been.

Eventually she went back to sleep, aided by two
sleeping tablets. She didn't wake until mid-morning and,
brewing up fresh coffee, she wondered if it had simply
been a nightmare that had woken her.

She spent the rest of the day learning her lines in preparation for the night's filming. Her usual driver collected
her mid-afternoon to take her to the set for make-up and
hair. He apologised for not being available the previous
evening.

'This weird thing happened last night,' she said.

'Who drove you?' he asked.

'Oh, nothing to do with that. I was in bed and this
terrible scream woke me up.' She frowned and leaned
forwards. 'I don't know if it was the screaming that woke
me – you know, if it had gone on before – but it was just
one long terrible scream and it really scared me.'

'Maybe it was a cat – or one o' these urban foxes they
go on about?'

'No, no, it didn't sound like either of those. At first, I

thought it *was* maybe an animal but . . . I think it was a woman.'

'Did you call the police?'

'No, I didn't because it all went quiet and I couldn't see anyone outside or in the back garden. I just went back to bed.'

In the make-up trailer, Amanda repeated the incident to her hairdresser. She told it over again to her make-up artist and it brought forth a slew of stories from the girls about nightmares and how hard it was, working nights, to get to sleep. She told the director about how frightened she had been. His response was to joke that it would probably help her performance. They were about to shoot a scene where she was to be confronted by the arch villain, who attempts to strangle her because he knows that she can identify him.

The film was yet another version of *Gaslight*, a Victorian thriller in which a young wife is terrorised by her husband, intent on frightening her to death in order to claim her inheritance. The script had been adapted by a young writer who hoped, with the use of state-of-the-art special effects, to turn it into a successful killer chiller, its dark foreboding style in homage to *Nosferatu* and early silent horror films. The director, Julian Pike, was only twenty-seven and with just one successful art-house movie to his credit, so a lot depended on this much bigger-budget extravaganza.

The filming went well, with only a few delays. They were shooting the exterior shots in a manmade cobbled street lit by gas lamps that backed onto a massive hangar where the main set, with its remarkable reconstruction of a Victorian house, was standing. Tonight they were filming the scene where Amanda, cast as the young wife, returns from the opera with her husband and alights from the carriage to enter their house, a mocked-up exterior with pillars and three steps leading to the front door. The door could be opened but led only onto a small platform inside, five feet off the ground. With only enough room for two people on the platform, it was decided that the maid would open the door and step back quickly. An assistant would help her down, leaving enough room for the two leading actors to sweep inside. It was such a simple shot, but they had to do take after take to get it right, and Pike was losing patience.

In the next scene, Amanda is running from the house in terror. She crosses the road in an attempt to escape, tries to hail a horse-drawn Hansom cab and, failing to do so, is almost run over by a carriage. There were rain machines, and flash lighting to depict lightning; the sound of thunder would be laid on afterwards. As the fog, generated by smoke machines, became thicker, Amanda had to collide with the very man she was afraid of. Then she had to scream. Nothing went smoothly: the horses got skittish with the flash lighting; one take was ruined as the smoke machine made Amanda start coughing. There were altercations between Amanda and the uptight director. By now she was freezing cold.

The costume department were having a hard time keeping the mud off Amanda's dress, with its heavy hooped velvet skirt and boned corset, and the ringlets were dropping out of her wig. Amanda and the director then had yet another stand-up argument, both shouting at each other in front of the entire crew.

When the time came for the close-up of Amanda screaming, she was in such a bad temper, the scream sounded more like one of anger than of terror. The director yelled at her to try and do the scream she'd heard the night before. Finally he called it quits for the night, even though he knew he hadn't got the sound he wanted. He told Amanda to have a good night's sleep; she would be wanted on set for the first shot of the day and he needed her in a better mood.

Amanda, with her usual driver, did not get home until four-thirty the next morning. By this time, she was exhausted. The tight corset and heavy hooped skirt had given her backache, and she had a headache from trying to scream. She was also feeling chilled, as it had been so cold on set and the rain effects had soaked her through to the skin. She sat hunched in the back of the Mercedes on the drive home, saying little. Her driver had helped her from the car and walked her to her front door, making sure she was inside before he drove away. As he reversed, his headlights caught her opening her front door; she turned and waved to him. He was struck by her beauty. Tired as she was, with her make-up wiped off and her face pale, she had almost a translucent quality. She gave him the sweetest of smiles.

The same unit driver returned later to collect her for the end of the night shoot. They would then, thankfully, have the weekend off before returning to the usual daily schedule. It had been a long hard shoot and a few more days remained before they wrapped. The driver rang the doorbell and returned to sit in the car. He waited ten minutes. Often she would keep him outside for even longer; he was used to giving her about twenty minutes. After half an hour, he called her landline and got the answer machine. When he called her mobile phone and she didn't pick up, he rang the unit to say he was outside

Amanda's mews house but could not get any response.

The make-up and hair departments were getting impatient. It took at least two hours to do make-up and fit the wig. Then the costume designer appeared, asking for Amanda. She was to wear a very elaborate gown that required not only a corset, but they would need to hand-stitch her into it. The first assistant joined them, hoping that Amanda might have driven herself, as they still had not made contact with her at her home.

Julian Pike flew into a rage. He had a heavy schedule, but at least he would be able to start filming the only scene that did not require Amanda. Her driver was instructed to keep knocking on her door and, as the actors prepared to film the first scene, the production assistant called Amanda's agent. Concerned, the latter said she would drive herself to the mews as she had a spare key.

Two hours later, Amanda's stunt double was dressed in her costume; the director had made the decision to shoot around any close-ups, so the filming could continue. He was heard to say that they would probably be better off without the 'bitch'.

The bitch was lying naked on her new bed. Her hands were tied and her legs spread out, and the blood from multiple stab wounds had stained the sheets in hideous thick pools. Her shocked agent stood frozen as she saw the awful tableau. It was obvious that Amanda Delany had been brutally murdered. Her beautiful face was unmarked, her eyes wide open.

7

Chapter Two

DI Anna Travis had just completed her day in court. The trial had been a long-drawn-out process, but she had held up strongly against a prominent defence team. The murder trial had made headlines; the woman accused of murdering her husband was from a titled family. Lady Melena Halesbury had claimed that she was an abused wife who had shot her husband in self-defence.

Thanks to Anna's diligent enquiries, her evidence had become a strong plank for the prosecution. The victim, Lord Anthony Halesbury, was suffering from Parkinson's disease and at the time of the shooting he would have been incapable of the violent attack of which his wife accused him.

The defence team had brought in numerous medical witnesses who claimed that physical abuse *was* possible. However, the star witness, produced by Anna, was the nurse who had been hired to care for the victim. Dilys Summers asserted that the victim's right arm was virtually immobile and his hand suffered from the debilitating shakes. His wife would therefore not, as she claimed, have had to wrestle the weapon from him and in self-defence shoot him before he tried to choke her.

Anna had instigated the search for the nurse, who had been relieved of duty two months before the incident. Anna had hunted down Nurse Summers and discovered that she and the victim had been lovers and, although Summers was no longer caring for her patient at his home, they had continued to meet secretly.

Summers was able to describe Lord Halesbury's disabilities because she had seen him the day before the shooting. Contrary to his wife's statement, his illness had improved slightly, but he was still a very sick man.

The prosecution claimed that the motive for the shooting was because a divorce was imminent. The loss of her social standing and obvious wealth was enough to drive Lady Halesbury to kill. The jury took only three hours to bring in a guilty verdict.

The DCI in charge of the case took Anna aside as they packed up the incident room. A big robust man, DCI Vince Mathews was ready to retire, everyone knew it; he was also an 'old school' cop and bore no resemblance to Anna's former boss, DCS James Langton.

Detective Chief Superintendent Langton was moving up the ranks fast, hungry as ever, based now at Scotland Yard. The Mathewses of the Metropolitan Police were becoming few and far between. Mathews was an old plodder with a big family, and due to his lack of initiative, Anna had done much of the legwork on their case. The team had all been aware of it, but they liked Mathews. He was there for them and always encouraging, even if he did like to get off home early every Friday.

Mathews sat behind his untidy desk, sipping a coffee.

'It was a good result today, Travis.'

'Thank you, sir.'

'A lot of it was down to you. The Met this year have

ninety Chief Inspector posts coming up, and as you're probably aware, each CID department is allowed to put forward a certain number of Inspectors. We've got about nine places allocated to the Homicide Command and the competition will be tough because there'll be about a hundred officers applying.'

Anna shifted her weight from one foot to the other, unsure if she was hearing correctly.

'You're putting me forward, sir?'

'Correct.' He opened a drawer and took out an application form, placing it in front of her.

'Fill it out. You'll have to think hard about what you'll say when they ask how you think you would perform in the next rank. You've got to write no more than twenty lines on seven topics, covering examples of how you would deal with effective communications, planning and organisation, customer and community focus, respect for race and diversity, strategic perspective, openness to change and, last but not least, personal responsibility.'

Anna flushed, not knowing what to say.

'Well, go on, take your application home and remember, think carefully about what you are going to say. Then it's down to you, Travis. Good luck.'

'Thank you very much, sir. I really appreciate this and I'll do my best.'

'I hope you do, Travis. You've got a big future ahead of you.'

Anna thanked him again and hurried out, grinning from ear to ear. She crossed to her small office and put the application form into her briefcase. She was packed up and ready to leave. They would all be having a drink in the local pub to celebrate the end of the case, and then it would be onto the next one. She didn't mention the promotion application to anyone. Instead she enjoyed a couple of glasses of wine and then left, eager to get home.

Back at her flat, close to Tower Bridge, Anna went straight into her bedroom and chucked her briefcase onto the bed. She picked up her late father's photograph from her bedside table and kissed it.

'Daddy, I'm going up for promotion. Detective Chief Inspector . . .' Then she laughed and flopped down onto her bed, holding the photograph frame to her chest. He would have been so proud, her father, the late Detective Chief Superintendent Jack Travis. She was determined that she would work her butt off to fill in the application to the very best of her ability.

As Anna showered and washed her hair, humming, she felt so good and so positive. It had been a tedious investigation, and although the guilty verdict had been the one the team had hoped for, she was glad the case was over. Hunting down the evidence had involved painstaking enquiries and lengthy conversations with the nurse. It had never ceased to amaze Anna how complicated people's lives were. A jealous wife, a sickly husband and a homely middle-aged woman in a tragic triangle. At first Anna had not suspected that the nurse could have been anything other than a dedicated carer. Dilys was a widow in her mid-forties, rather overweight, with greying hair, and only when she spoke of the victim's kindness to her, did Anna begin to suspect there existed anything other than a professional relationship. When she eventually asked if there had been something more, the floodgates had opened. Dilys had explained how fond she had become of her patient, how admiring of the way he never complained and was at all times so charming.

Lady Halesbury, possibly suspecting something was going on, had asked Dilys to leave. It had been a terrible wrench, but the nurse had packed up her suitcase and returned to her council flat in Paddington.

'I loved him,' she told Anna. 'We loved each other. I have never known such kindness and such sweetness from a man . . .'

Anna had listened as the woman seemed to shine, her eyes bright as she explained that they had become lovers. Lord Halesbury had asked her to marry him as soon as he could get a divorce. She knew he would be an invalid, but to be in his company no matter what, would have given her the best years of her life.

Lying on her bed thinking about the case and the outcome, Anna sighed. The stout little nurse, her face shining with adoration for the dead man, and the bitter, vicious wife, who couldn't bear to lose her sick husband or his fortune; both women middle-aged and yet caught up in heated passion. The real passion in Anna's life had been with James Langton; she wondered if she would ever know or feel that passion for someone else.

Wanting a last glass of wine before bed, she uncorked a bottle of wine and sipped from her glass as she stood by the open window, looking out onto the Thames and Tower Bridge. She had not seen Langton for over eight months, though she had heard news of him and read about him in the police journals. She drained her glass and refilled it. She was suddenly depressed. Even thinking about the last time they had been together made her flush with embarrassment.

The murder enquiry they had both worked on

involved tracking down an infamous drug dealer, Alexander Fitzpatrick. During the enquiry, Anna had met Damien Nolan, husband of a woman who eventually became a major part of the investigation. Anna had found Damien attractive from the moment she had met him, and when he was excluded from the case, she had foolishly agreed to see him. She knew at the time that she was being unprofessional, that Damien would possibly be called as a witness for his wife's defence, yet she had ignored her own doubts and agreed to meet him. They had met on three different occasions before they went back to her flat and slept together. He was sexy, he was attractive and he was a very experienced lover. In some ways Anna felt her relationship with him freed her from the hold Langton had over her. Even in part knowing she was being foolish made their illicit dates exciting.

Damien was intelligent, amusing and she really enjoyed his company. He had made *her* feel attractive – sexy even. It wasn't love, she knew that; it was something she had never experienced before – a kind of lust. Anna had few friends and even fewer lovers, James Langton being the most recent and the most important in her life. Having Damien, being with him, had helped her confidence. He had bought her sexy underwear, encouraged her to dress in a more flattering way, and even suggested a new hairstyle.

Anna never kept the hair appointment. On the day she was going, Langton turned up on her doorstep. It was early on a Monday morning, three weeks before the trial was due to take place. She was nervous at seeing him and he didn't make it easy for her. He refused her offer of coffee, saying he wasn't there for a social meeting. Tossing his coat onto the sofa, he lit a cigarette and she passed him an ashtray. From the way he was behaving she knew something was wrong.

'OK, I won't beat about the bush, Anna. Are you seeing Damien Nolan?'

'Yes.'

'Then fucking stop it, you stupid girl. One, he's involved in the entire investigation, two, he'll be called by the defence and three, it is fucking unprofessional.'

She couldn't look at him.

'You having sex with him?'

'None of your business.'

'It *is* my business, Anna. I am leading the case, and to have one of my officers screwing a possible suspect . . .'

'He hasn't been charged with anything.'

'Jesus Christ, Anna, his wife has and he'll be asked to give evidence. What you are doing is crass stupidity, let alone insubordination. I could have you disciplined – which would result in you being demoted or possibly kicked out. I can't believe you would not only be so unprofessional, but what the fuck are you doing with that prick?'

She wanted to say, 'Having great sex,' but all she ended up doing was bursting into tears.

'End it now and I'll not mention it again, you hear me?'

'Yes.'

'Good, then do it – and if I hear you are still seeing him, having any kind of relationship with him, then you will pay a high price.'

He picked up his coat and walked to the front door.

'Don't think I wanted to come here and tear a strip off you. There is nothing personal in this, you understand what I am saying?'

'Yes.'

'Good. Then no more is to be said.'

'Thank you.'

As he glared at her, she felt as if his dark eyes were boring into her head.

'Yeah, you should thank me, because I won't let a whisper of this get out. You've got a bright future and you almost blew it.'

She hung her head like a schoolgirl and he walked out, slamming the door behind him.

She had not seen Damien Nolan since then. She had been on tenterhooks during his wife's trial, hoping he would not be called to take the stand. He wasn't, but he did show up in court. Anna had kept her face turned away from him, never meeting his quizzical looks. Damien's wife was sentenced to twelve years for attempting to pervert the course of justice, assisting an offender, and possessing Class A drugs with the intent to supply. Five years were added for assisting Fitzpatrick's escape. He had never been caught and his whereabouts remained unknown. The failure to bring him to justice sat heavily on everyone involved in the lengthy investigation, and especially on Langton. Fitzpatrick had been so audacious that Langton knew he had lost. It was one of the few cases with no closure for him, and it had infuriated him.

Anna was asleep when the phone rang. She checked the time: four-thirty in the morning. It was DCI Mathews and he was not a happy man.

'You heard of Amanda Delany?'

Travis was still half-asleep, so made no reply.

'Movie actress – well, she was; she's been found dead.

16

I don't have any facts and I'm on my way there, so you join me as soon as possible.'

Anna drove herself to Amanda Delany's mews house in no time at all at that hour of the day. Mathews greeted her with a sigh, gesturing for her to get into a forensic protection suit, like the one he was already wearing.

'She's in the bedroom.'

Anna followed him along a narrow hall and up the stairs. She could see the forensic team at work with specialist lighting equipment set up. As she reached the open bedroom door, Mathews nudged her.

'It's not that big a room and I want them to get on with it as fast as possible, so just check around. I'll be downstairs in the kitchen. I've already got officers making cursory house-to-house enquiries.'

Anna inched further into the bedroom, moving slowly around the bed to view the body. It lay in a spreadeagled pose. Anna was struck by the actress's beauty, which even in death was astonishing. Her wide blue eyes were open, and it looked as if someone had carefully arranged her silky blonde hair to spread out across the pillow. Her duvet had been removed and bagged, Anna was told.

A masked forensic officer turned towards Anna. 'You know who she is?'

'Was . . . Yes, I do. There's been a lot of press about her recently.'

'Be even more now!'

As if on cue, there was a flash of cameras from the press photographers gathered outside.

Mathews appeared and signalled to Anna. 'Body warm and stiff. Dead for between three to eight hours. Not a lot we can do here, and as it's such a cramped space, I'll be back at the incident room.'

There were more flashes of cameras, accompanied by shouts as the press started asking for an update. Anna remained in the bedroom doorway as Mathews went outside to give a statement to the press. He said little, bar the fact that the victim was a white female, aged in her mid-twenties. They were treating her death as suspicious.

Anna remained at the mews for another hour but there was little for her to do, apart from feeling as if she was in the way. No weapon had been found at the scene; neither the locks on the front nor the back doors were damaged. Amanda's boxes of jewellery seemed undisturbed, and five thousand pounds in cash was found hidden in a drawer with her underwear. The police made it a priority to seize her handbag and were searching for her mobile phone to check for calls and messages sent and received.

By the time Anna arrived at the incident room, set up in nearby Pimlico, it was almost 10 a.m. Amanda's body, identified by her agent, had been taken to the mortuary. The pathologist would start work as soon as he got in. The number of knife wounds visible on her torso made it clear how she had been killed, but not until they had the pathology report could they surmise whether she had been raped before she was murdered.

It was DCS Langton who had assigned Mathews to the Delany case and instructed him to retain the team who had worked on the Halesbury case. The team now regrouped and waited for instructions. Anna had written up her findings on the board: as nothing appeared to have been stolen, nor did the mews look as if it had been broken into, it seemed very possible that Amanda knew her assailant.

So far, the team had only the basic facts. Forensic would take their time; they were still at the victim's house and would be there for at least two or three weeks. The team would be forced to wait for the autopsy report. Mathews sent four of them along with a Detective Sergeant to organise and supervise POLSA, Police Search Advisors, to search for the weapon. They would continue a detailed house-to-house enquiry within the small mews courtyard to discover if any resident saw or heard anything suspicious. Amanda's parents had been contacted. They lived in the South of France, but prepared to return as soon as they could.

Mathews slurped his beaker of coffee.

'What we need is a motive for the murder. Nothing appears to be stolen and there's no damage to the property or forced entry, so at present the motive does not appear to be robbery.' He held up a large coloured day-to-day calendar they had removed from Amanda's kitchen; it contained very little personal information. He also had a small leather-bound address book.

'Amanda Delany listed her pick-up times for her current filming, costume-fittings, wig-fittings and so on, but there are no details in it of her private life. It's possible the killer was someone she knew. We'll need to draw up lists of her friends, current and ex-boyfriends, work associates, and the contractor and workmen who did the refurbishments to her house as they could have kept hold of spare keys. We also need to question everyone she was working with, as they would possibly have been the last people to see her alive.'

Half an hour later, at the end of Mathews's briefing, the duty manager began passing out to the team their priorities. Copies of the calendar and address book had been made and pages were handed around so they could begin questioning everyone listed. Mathews signalled for Anna to join him in his office. He wanted her to prepare a full intelligence victim file on Amanda's life, and start by interviewing Amanda's agent who was arriving any moment.

'This is a bloody pain in the arse,' he muttered, checking the time. 'I was hoping for a few weeks' annual leave. I also have a feeling that this is going to be a pressured investigation. The press office is already inundated.'

'She was pretty famous,' Anna observed.

'I wouldn't have known her if I fell over her.'

'Maybe her films are more for teenagers, but she had a high profile. She got a break starring in a successful movie straight out of drama school.'

'She's not gonna get any more breaks, Travis, but I hope to Christ we do, and can wrap this up as fast as possible. We'll have Jimmy Langton on our backs – and you know what he's like. I'd put money on it he'll be very "present" because he'll love the publicity. And I'm warning everyone that we're going to get a shedload of it.'

He paused, as if realising he was repeating himself. He didn't even notice how Anna flinched on hearing Langton's name. Changing the subject, she asked who would be partnering her. Mathews sighed.

'It's not usual for me to delegate a specific partner, but I can allocate a DS to be the case officer and bring in another DI.' He passed over an internal list of officers. 'Your choice. You can take your pick, and if there's anyone here that you liked working with, then—'

'To be honest, sir, you and I both know that I had to do a lot of the legwork on our last case and as you've said, this one is going to be under the spotlight. I really appreciate you suggesting me for promotion and would have liked, or sort of expected, to get a few weeks off to prepare.'

'What?'

'Is it possible for you to replace me?'

'No.'

Anna felt irritated. 'In that case, sir, I'd like to be working alongside an experienced DI or DS.'

She was trying to be diplomatic. She'd not found any of the present team to be really talented or prepared to work the long hours she herself had put in.

'Leave it with me and I'll call you.'

'Thank you, sir.'

Andrea Lesser was waiting in an interview room. She was an attractive woman in her early forties, wearing little make-up, dressed head to toe in Prada: grey skirt, grey cashmere sweater and a neat jacket that she had draped over a chair. She owned one of the biggest theatrical agencies in London.

'Thank you so much for agreeing to come in,' Anna said as she sat down opposite. She offered water but Miss Lesser shook her head.

'I'd just like to get this over with as soon as possible. I'm still in shock.'

'It must be very distressing for you. You knew Miss Delany well?'

'Yes, I've been Amanda's agent since she left drama school. Have you any idea what happened, who could have done this?'

'Not at the moment, which is why it is imperative I get as much detail as possible about her recent movements.'

'I wouldn't say I was a close friend — I mean, my relationship with her was business. I knew her, but not on a social level — by that I mean . . . Oh God! I can't think straight!'

'You knew her well enough to have her house keys.'

'Yes, she did depend on me. I had the keys to check that the building work on her new house was done to her satisfaction. She only moved in a couple of months ago. I had to make sure the interior designer was not going over budget and all the right furniture was delivered . . .' She sighed.

'Which is probably more than what an agent is normally required to do?' Anna said kindly.

'Well, yes, it *was* a lot of extra work for me but Amanda was an important client and, with her being so young, I suppose I did more for her than most actors I represent. To be honest, I did resent it a little, but there was no one else.'

'What about her family?'

'She didn't really get along with them, partly due to the bad publicity she'd had recently. Her parents are very straightlaced, and found the tabloid hounding distressing.'

'Did Amanda?'

'Did she what?'

'Feel hounded?'

'She did, but much of it was her own doing.'

'In what way?'

Andrea Lesser hesitated. She started tapping her foot.

'Amanda was rather promiscuous, and with well-known actors, so obviously the newspapers were interested.'

'Can you give me a list of her past friendships?'

'It's a long one, but yes, of course. In fact, a few days ago I'd warned her to behave herself, but she assured me that she wasn't seeing anyone and was concentrating on the filming. Whether or not she had started dating someone from her current movie, I wasn't aware.'

'When you last talked to her, did she mention that anyone was being troublesome?'

'Troublesome? No. She was very excited about moving into her new house as it was the first home she had owned. She was looking forward to being on her own for a while. She used to rent a flat, or move in with various boyfriends.'

Andrea Lesser opened her handbag and took out a tissue.

'I just can't believe what has happened,' she said, dabbing her eyes. 'I really can't continue, I'm sorry. I'll have so much to deal with at my office.'

Anna checked her watch. Perhaps she should end the interview. She sensed that the agent had a lot more to tell her about her client and asked if she would remain at the station until she had drawn up a list of Amanda's previous boyfriends and any other useful contacts Andrea Lesser could recall, including the builders, decorator and designer for her house.

Anna left her with Barbara, one of the female DCs, and went into the incident room. Mathews was standing by the incident board, studying the numerous pictures of Amanda that had been pinned up. He turned to Anna as she joined him and then looked past her.

'Ah, you're here. Let me introduce you to DI Anna Travis.'

Anna turned round to see a tall, blond, rangy man wearing a worn tweed suit and tie at half-mast.

'This is DI Simon Dunn. I've brought him on board to help with the investigation.' Mathews gave Anna a brief sideways look. 'You wanted someone with experience, well . . . you got him.'

Simon Dunn shook her hand. He had steely blue eyes and looked in need of a shave.

'Twisted my arm, he did. I was just about to go on a sailing holiday.' His voice was deep and his handshake so firm she felt her fingers crushed.

Mathews gave them the job of contacting everyone connected with the film unit, suggesting they speak first with the director.

Finding an empty office, Anna gave Simon a brief rundown on what she had been told by Andrea Lesser. He listened without interruption, looking down the list of the film crew Mathews had given them, then commented, 'We've got a lot of interviewing to do. Christ knows how many on this list will be of any interest, but we'll have to eliminate as we go along. Take a look and let me organise some coffee.'

Anna couldn't believe it. At least seventy-five names, even those of the caterers, were on the list. She looked up as Simon leaned in at the doorway.

'Forgot to ask how you take it.'

'White, no sugar. Have you counted how many people we're supposed to interview?'

'Yeah. We'll start at the top and work our way down. By the way, that list doesn't include the artists.' He disappeared as Anna sighed.

They were still counting the names as they drove in Simon's convertible Saab to the film unit in Ealing. The car was in immaculate condition and Anna noted that it had low mileage, considering it was an old model.

'You don't use this very often,' she said, tapping the polished wood dashboard.

'Nope, odd weekends but my usual banger is in the garage. This is my baby, fast as hell, a classic and turbo-charged, not that I've had the hood down too often this summer.'

Anna sat back as they continued on their way. Simon was easygoing with a wide friendly smile. She liked him and wondered if they were going to work well together. She would know soon enough as they drove into the production base of the film unit, a massive ramshackle building with trailers parked side by side. There were also the electricians' wagons, prop wagons and a large catering van with a tent erected beside it, with tables and chairs where the artists could have their meals.

He left the car in the area where the unit drivers' four Mercedes, a Range Rover and a Jaguar were parked. The drivers, sitting near the catering van smoking, looked on with interest as Anna and Simon walked towards them.

'We need to speak to Mr Mike Reynolds,' Simon said.

One of the drivers pointed to a side door. 'Production staff are in offices through there.'

Reynolds's office was in a dingy section of the rundown building.

'Come in, please sit down, and I'll get some coffee ordered.'

Reynolds was in his early thirties, wearing a tank top, jeans and leather boots. His desk was piled high with scripts. Simon had suggested to Anna that he would be the best person to give them a rundown of who was who in the film unit.

'We are all stunned by what has happened to Amanda, so if there is anything I can do to help your enquiries . . .'

'What is your job exactly?' Simon asked.

Reynolds smiled. 'I'm the line producer, which means I'm the producer's right-hand man. I make sure everything is running smoothly.'

'So who would have worked out the call sheet for the day and night filming?' Simon queried.

'That would be our first and second assistant directors. We have production assistants who type up the call sheets, arrange for drivers, and the second assistant director gets the artists on the set ready for work.'

'How did you get along with Amanda?' This was Anna, leaning forward slightly in her chair.

'Well, it's my job to get along with everyone. I didn't know her outside work – probably not attractive enough for her to be interested in.' He gave a soft laugh. 'She wasn't too difficult to handle, unlike some stars I've worked with. She was reasonably professional and didn't show up late, but she could take up valuable time when we were shooting.'

'How do you mean?'

'Well, she didn't always like her wig or costume and she would throw a tantrum or two, but it never lasted too long. She was very young and I knew she had a reputation for being a bit headstrong, so I made a point of being diplomatic with her and any problems we did have were soon sorted out.'

'We'll need the names of the drivers she used.'

'I have them ready for you. They're all here at the base if you need to talk to them.'

'Did you know if Amanda was seeing anyone from the unit?'

'You mean on a personal level?'

'Yes.'

'Not really and, to be honest, she wouldn't have had that much time as we had a very heavy schedule. I didn't hear any rumours that she was friendly with any of the actors. But as I didn't know her socially, I wouldn't have been aware if she was seeing anyone on her days off or entertaining anyone in her trailer.'

'We'll need to have access to her trailer,' Simon pointed out.

'I was told you wanted to, but have you any idea how long it will be, before someone else can move into it? Only we are re-shooting her scenes and there are things in there we may need to use.'

'As long as necessary. We'll also require a trailer for our use, as we have two more officers joining us, and we'll need somewhere we can debrief together at the end of the day.'

'Sure, I'll see what I can set up.'

'Have you replaced her?' Anna asked.

'Not yet, officially. We're waiting to hear about the insurance situation. In the meantime, we're using her double. Thankfully we only have another five days' filming, so I doubt if we'll re-shoot all the scenes we have in the can . . . we'll shoot around her.'

Reynolds's radio bleeped and he excused himself to answer the call in the corridor outside his office.

Simon glanced at Anna. 'They don't waste time, do they? Already replaced her,' he observed.

A balding man appeared at the door, wearing a heavy Puffa jacket and jeans with suede loafers.

'Aiden Brook, producer,' he said, holding out his hand. 'This is disastrous. None of us can take in what

27

has happened and as the producer it's a nightmare. I am just stunned. I was looking at the dailies in my office and thinking how lovely she was when I was told. I would have been here to take you round, but I've had the backers onto me. I've no need to tell you what this means to the movie. Without Amanda, it's inconceivable that we can continue, but I have to do what I can to salvage . . .'

He looked them both in the eye. 'Do you mind if I leave you with Mike Reynolds, as I've got meetings to sort this all out. I'll be in the production trailer.' He paused. 'Do you know who killed her?'

'Not yet,' Anna said.

'Dear God, I've a daughter her age – twenty-four – thankfully not in the business. That's all I could think of when I was told, my daughter. First thing I did was call her to make sure she was safe, but now, it's really hit home.'

'Where were you?' Simon asked.

'You mean, after we finished filming here?'

'Yes.'

'Well, I stayed on to look at some of the rushes the editor had knitted together. We were worried about a stunt from the previous night. We worked for about an hour after we stopped filming, then I went home to Chiswick. Crashed out – night shooting takes the stuffing out of you. My driver is Tony. He took me home and brought me back . . .'

Brook went to the door, saying, 'Feel free to have lunch or whatever you need. Now if you'll excuse me . . .'

Reynolds returned and passed over some sheets of paper.

'These are lists of the entire crew. It's a good day to

interview them as we're filming up on the next floor. If you want to see the set, I can get someone to show you around the place. It's a Victorian Scotland Yard set, really terrific, probably miles apart from the kind of place you're used to working in. Nothing high tech about it, just battered old typewriters and an ancient telephone system. Our main location is in a hangar half an hour's drive away, but this here is the main unit base.'

'Who on the list you've given us would Amanda Delany have been on friendly terms with?' Simon asked.

'Start with the star actors. I don't think anyone from the crew was that friendly. Maybe her driver Harry James could give you more information.'

Anna and Simon followed Reynolds into the corridor. His radio bleeped again; he was wanted on the set. He agreed to them having a chat to the other staff in the production offices as long as they avoided going on set during filming.

'He's very helpful,' Anna remarked as Reynolds hurried off.

'You know, this is going to be a long day and I think we should divide up this list between us, along with the other two officers.' Simon looked at his watch. 'They break for lunch at one, so I'll meet you out by the catering truck.'

Anna suggested she take costume and make-up first while he checked out the unit drivers.

'OK, I'll finish in here and see you later.' Simon tapped on one of the production office doors. Anna left the building and walked out into the main yard, heading for the make-up and costume trailers.

★

Anna was surprised how large and comfortable it was in the make-up department. There were four big leather chairs with roll-back head and foot rests. Each section had a mirrored unit with extra lighting, and rows of make-up, with Carmen rollers and hair straighteners and wig stands, were crammed into each separate space. There was only one girl inside the trailer and she was making herself a coffee from a cappuccino machine. She turned as Anna entered and introduced herself as Cynthia Miller.

'Did you make up Amanda?' Anna asked.

'No, I'm doing all the extras. You'll need to talk to Carol, but she's on set at the moment.'

'How did you find her?'

'Amanda? She was always friendly to me, though sometimes she could get Carol pretty frazzled.'

'Was she seeing anyone from the film unit, do you know?'

'Outside of work? No, I'm sure she wasn't.'

'Did she ever talk about being worried about any-one?'

'No, though the last time . . .' Cynthia hesitated. 'It was the last night she was here, the night before it happened. She told us she'd been woken by a terrible scream. She was quite shook up about it; she said she was sure it was a woman screaming, but didn't see anything or hear any more apart from that one scream.'

'Did she report it to the police?'

'No, I don't think so, but she said it was very scary.'

The trailer door banged open, and a voice said, 'There's a police officer asking questions.'

'Carol . . .' Cynthia indicated Anna and her colleague stopped in the doorway.

'Oh, sorry. Is it OK if I come in?'

Anna swivelled around in her chair.

'Hi. I'm Carol Maynard.' Carol was in her late thirties, attractive, if a little overweight.

'Do you need to ask me anything,' she went on, 'only I'll have to go back onto the set in a minute.'

Anna watched Carol unpin a moustache from one of the wig stands and place it neatly between two tissues.

'Actor sweats like a pig so his 'tache keeps getting unstuck.'

Cynthia seemed a little edgy as she reminded Carol about the scream that Amanda Delany had heard the night before she was murdered.

'Oh yeah, Amanda was really upset – said it sounded like a woman being tortured.'

Anna kept watching Carol as she selected different pots of foundation and rouge.

'Do you know if she was seeing anyone on a personal level from the film unit?' she asked her.

'Surprisingly no, she wasn't. I don't mean that to sound bitchy, but she was well-known for starting up affairs with her leading actors, or any good-looking guy for that matter. She put herself about a bit, but—'

'There's not much choice on this movie,' Cynthia interjected.

'It's a small cast,' Carol said, glancing at Cynthia as if warning her to keep quiet. 'The leading actor's older than her usual conquests and he plays for the other side. The big star is the lovely Rupert Mitchell; he's not being called today though. We know he and Amanda were once an item but he's back with his wife, and Rupert and Amanda seemed to have no hard feelings, wouldn't you agree, Cynthia?'

'Yes, they got along.'

'What about the extras?' Anna enquired.

'I doubt Amanda would have been interested in any of them. We've had a very tight schedule on this film and as she was carrying so many scenes, I don't think she'd have had the time.'

'It's quite lucky – well, that's not really the right way to put it, but most of her big scenes have been shot so they are trying to get away with filming her stunt double Emma, and hopefully using some of the close-ups left over from the other scenes,' Cynthia observed as she sipped her coffee.

'Emma's very good.' Carol then glanced over to Cynthia, instructing her, 'You should do a check of the police incident room. They've more extras in the scene and they just had a coffee break, so there'll be dripping moustaches and sideburns.'

'OK.' Cynthia smiled at Anna as she collected her make-up bag and left the trailer.

Anna remained silent, staring at herself in the mirror, while Carol busied herself cleaning brushes.

'Did you like her?' Anna asked softly. 'You were her make-up artist, correct?'

'Yes, I've worked for her before. In fact, she got me this job as she asked for me.'

'So you got on well?'

'She could try my patience sometimes, but she was better than some I've had to work with. She always knew what she wanted, and on this film I had to have a few words because it's a period drama. She wanted heavy eye make-up which obviously wasn't right, but in the end she settled down.'

'So she wasn't seeing anyone from this film outside work?'

'No, as I told you. Unlike the last movie I worked on with her.'

'She was having an affair then?'

'Yes, with her co-star Scott Myers. I'm not telling stories out of school, it was in all the papers. He left his wife and three kids for her. I asked her when we started this film, you know, was she still with Scott? She flicked her pretty little hands, saying that the kids had become a pain and she couldn't stand having to see them at week-ends. Unbelievable! She wreaks havoc, causes no end of heartbreak and then just dismisses the fact that Scott had left his wife, who by the way had attempted suicide, and the children who were caught in the middle of all the drama.'

Carol suddenly stopped and looked at Anna in the mirror, saying, 'Shit, I sound like such a bitch, and as if I think Scott could be jealous or a possible suspect, but I honestly didn't mean it to come out that way. He's a gorgeous guy, really sweet, and he's now back with his wife. I think Amanda went from Scott to Rupert, but don't quote me. And then after them it was Colin O'Dell . . .'

'The Irish actor who starred in *Broken Dreams*?'

'Yeah, he was her latest conquest – but again, don't quote me, for God's sake.'

Anna smiled, as if dismissing what Carol had said. She'd already jotted down Scott Myers's name in her notebook; now she added Colin O'Dell.

'You didn't really like her then?'

Carol shook her head and began to stack her make-up bag with a vengeance.

'Part of my job was to get on OK with her, but I didn't have to like her – and you're making me feel guilty that I didn't. She could be a right pain in the arse and she could badmouth me in front of the whole crew, but I just had to swallow whatever she said to me because if I didn't, I'd be out of a job!'

The trailer door opened and Cynthia re-appeared, saying, 'Carol, they're about to do a take.'

'Shit, I'm out of here.'

Anna watched her snatch up her bag and hurry out, squeezing past Cynthia who came back in and plonked herself down on one of the chairs.

'Director's having one of his turns; he's such a control freak.' She picked up a brush and started brushing her hair, then caught Anna looking at her and dropped it back into the holder.

'Did Carol tell you any more about the scream . . . ?' she asked.

Simon was standing with the unit drivers, finishing up questioning one and turning towards another sitting having a quiet smoke in his Mercedes. The windows were open and Simon crouched down by the car.

'You are Anthony James, correct?'

'Yes, sir. Everyone calls me Tony.'

Simon introduced himself and Tony opened the car door and got out, tossing his cigarette aside.

'I really want to talk to you about the last time you drove Amanda Delany,' Simon said as they fetched tea and sat down in the catering tent.

'Yeah, right – be the night before she was murdered. I wasn't her usual driver, I drove her 'cos they broke early so her own driver was doin' another job – not moonlightin', nothin' like that – he was just drivin' another actor from the cast.' Tony sipped his drink at the Formica-topped table. 'So I done the job for him.

34

She wasn't due to break until around three-thirty in the morning, but the director finished her scenes early.'

'So you weren't expecting to drive her home?'

'No, I just told you. She had her own driver – well, she thought he was her own but the company hires all of us. It's a star thing, you know. They insist on their own car and driver.'

Tony was in his mid-thirties, quite handsome with bright blue eyes. A combover job of his fine blond hair showed he was not happy with the balding process. He was well-dressed in a grey suit with a pristine white shirt and green tie.

'Tell me about the night you drove Amanda home,' Simon asked.

Tony shrugged. He had little to say. She'd appeared very tired and told him not to get out when they reached her mews.

'I watched her go in – you know, for safety – and then I backed out of the mews and returned to the set. That was the last time I saw her.'

In the costume trailer Anna was talking to Joanna Villiers, a pleasant, rosy-faced woman who had shown her the heavy costumes and corset worn by Amanda. She explained how difficult it had been drawing in the corset and how hard Amanda had found the weight of the hooped skirt to handle.

'She was such a tiny, thin thing. We got her waist down to nineteen inches in the corset.'

'Had Amanda said anything about being worried or frightened by anyone?' Anna asked.

'She told us about a disturbed night she'd had, waking up, hearing someone screaming; said it was terrifying –

35

sounded as if someone was being tortured. That was the night before . . .'

Amanda Delany's 'personal' driver, Harry James, turned out to be Tony's elder brother, handsome like him but with a thick head of snow-white hair. He was very outspoken and showed no sign of distress regarding Amanda's murder. He told Simon that he had never really liked her, as she could be a 'right bitch'. He was eager to explain the relationship between the star and driver, how very often, due to the actors screwing around, they made life difficult for the driver whose sole job was to get them to the set on time.

'By screwing around, Mr James, do you mean that in a literal sense?'

'Listen, if they don't get into the car, we wait. We've always got about half an hour to sit kicking our heels until they show, but sometimes it's a lot longer than that. You ring their doorbell, you call them on the phone, they gotta be on set and it's down to us to make sure they get there. It's not always easy though. One actor, I hadda go round the clubs to find him and pour him into the car, and Amanda could be a right pain in the arse too.'

'I'm really only interested in the last time you went to collect her for work – if you saw anything, heard anything suspicious.'

'No, nothing. I drove up to her mews, on time, rang the doorbell and waited a good while, and then panic set in as she didn't come out. I called her landline, her mobile and got no answer, and then I called the set as I was getting really concerned.'

Simon asked if he had ever, during the filming, taken

Amanda elsewhere, to someone else's home, or if he knew whether she was seeing anyone from the film unit.

'No, not on this film.'

'You've worked with Amanda before?'

'Yes, although I wouldn't call it working with her exactly. I was a unit driver on two movies she was cast in.'

'So you knew her well?'

'I was her driver; I wouldn't say I knew her. I made it a point to be pleasant to her, we all did, but as for what goes on in the car . . . well, you turn a blind eye. That's the rule of the game – see nothing, hear nothing, say nothing. Like the three wise monkeys, we are.'

'So when you were her driver on the previous film?'

'She wasn't livin' in the mews, she shared a flat in Maida Vale. But I didn't always collect her from there; she often stayed over at one of the other actors' place.'

Harry stopped to light a cigarette. 'I'm not telling stories,' he said quietly. 'It was common knowledge she put it about a bit.'

'How do you mean?'

'I can't make it any plainer. She was quite a naughty girl; at one point she was hopping between actors. It was a pain in the butt for me because I was never sure where I was picking her up from.'

'Can you give me their names?'

'It was in all the papers.'

'That's as maybe, but if you'd just give me their names,' Simon persisted.

Harry puffed on his cigarette. 'You want all of them?'

'Yes.'

'Like I said, she put it about a bit, but on this film she was behaving herself. I think someone had words with her – you know, warning her about bad press, and two of the blokes were married so there was quite a lot of paparazzi doggin' her . . .'

'Just the names, please.'

In the costume trailer, Anna was getting a similar story from Joanna Villiers. She too had worked on a previous film with Amanda, when the press had been hounding the girl about her relationship with Scott Myers. But Joanna assured Anna that on the present film Amanda had behaved herself. Like Harry James, she was certain that the actress had been ordered to curtail her sexual exploits.

'Maybe the director warned her, I don't know, he's such a control freak. I do know they had some stand-up rows. He's really shocked everyone by not delaying filming and just carrying on, using Amanda's stand-in. We all felt he should have waited, but he was adamant that he had no other option but to continue or we'd have had to shut the film down.'

'These rows between him and Amanda, what were they about?'

'Sometimes she didn't know her lines or was late on set and held up filming. Julian's got a terrible temper, but she gave as good as she got. She had quite a foul mouth on her.'

'Give me an example.'

Joanna sighed and opened a bottle of water. 'One time she couldn't stop giggling and the rain machine was making her wig uncurl and she was demanding to go back to her trailer. He yelled at her and told her to get her act together, and she just told him to fuck off.'

'Did she leave the set?'

'Yes, she did. In the end, he had to eat humble pie and go and persuade her to come back to work. They had a right shouting match – everyone could hear it. Then she came back on the set about fifteen minutes later, all sweet smiles.'

'So they didn't have a very good relationship?'

'He's the director – kings they are, but he's got a nasty side to him. Sometimes I've felt like walking because he comes in here and throws his weight about – ranting on that this or that isn't right.'

'How did he react to Amanda's death?'

'All of us were shaken, but I was told he just kicked out at his desk and swore, then asked to be left alone. Whether or not he felt anything, I wouldn't know – but like I said, he didn't waste any time on grief. We were straight back to work.'

'Did you know that Amanda once had an affair with Rupert Mitchell?'

'Oh yes, we all knew that, but it wasn't ongoing and they didn't make it obvious. In fact, she said to me that finishing with him was good because in the script he plays her husband who wants to kill her. Apparently, he's back with his wife.'

'What about Colin O'Dell?'

Joanna rolled her eyes. 'He gets his leg over anything in a skirt – well, that's what I've been told about him. I've never worked with him but I'd like to!'

'You get anything of interest?' Anna asked Simon when she rejoined him in the catering tent.

Simon nodded, flicking through his notebook. 'The victim was screwing a lot of men, not on this film, but we'll need to question them all.' He gestured across to the

James brothers, who were sitting smoking a few tables away. 'Those are her drivers – Harry and Tony James.'

'You been told about the scream she heard the night before last?'

'Yes. We'll need to check it out. I've contacted the station to make enquiries to see if anything was reported.'

Anna looked up to see Mike Reynolds heading over to them. As he reached their table, a thin-faced young man wearing a creased shirt, jeans and trainers, called out to him.

'That's the boss, excuse me,' Mike said.

Anna and Simon watched as he conferred with Julian Pike, who wafted his hand in irritation and, turning his back on them, headed towards a row of small office trailers, Mike Reynolds in pursuit.

Anna was so intent on watching them, she jumped when her shoulder was tapped.

'You're the police, aren't you?'

Anna turned. Standing directly behind her was a very pretty blonde girl.

'I'm Emma Field, Amanda's stand-in – well, I was. Do you need to talk to me?'

Anna hesitated, unprepared, then said, 'Yes, I would like to ask you a few questions. When was the last time you saw Amanda?'

'Two days ago. I was standing in for the lighting and she was sitting in a chair by the set. She was looking for her mobile. I sat with her for a while and then she was called. Anyway, I was about to come out here for a cigarette and I saw her phone. Her long skirt had hidden it – it was just by her chair.'

Emma dug into her pocket and handed the phone to Anna.

'I meant to take it to her trailer, but then I was called as they were setting up lights for the interior.'

Anna looked at the phone; the battery was dead.

'I went over to the make-up trailer later to give it to her, but she'd already left. They said I should keep it until the next day, so I did and . . .' She bowed her head, mumbling, 'It's so awful, I can't believe it.'

Simon smiled at the nervous girl. 'You've taken over her part, haven't you?'

'Not really. I'm being filmed in long shot, but luckily her costume fits . . .' At that moment, the call boy appeared with his radio and waved over to her. Emma apologised; she was needed for rehearsal.

As she hurried away, Anna checked the phone again. 'I'll get this over to the technical support unit to check out her call lists,' she said.

Simon was distracted. 'She was very pretty. I wouldn't mind working on one of these movies,' he commented. 'Big break for her, isn't it, the stand-in, but I doubt that'd be a motive.'

Anna was truly amazed when she stepped from behind the blackout curtain into a massive scenery build of a Victorian incident room at Scotland Yard. Mike Reynolds led her towards Julian Pike, the director, who was standing with his back to her, thumbing through a script.

'Boss, this is DI Anna Travis.'

Pike turned and gave her a tight smile. Anna could feel his nervous energy. He had piercing eyes and his long, bony fingers twitched. There was an elastic band around his wrist and he slipped it off, twanging it between his fingers.

'You want to sit down?' he asked.

'If you don't mind,' she replied.

Pike sat and crossed his long legs, one foot twitching up and down, his hands constantly playing with the elastic band.

'Did you get on with Amanda?' she asked, taking out her notebook.

'Of course I did – everybody did. She could be difficult, but she was a professional and the rushes we have are good. Thankfully her bulk scenes were already shot.'

'I've been told you had a few arguments?'

'Really? Well, by that you probably mean when I had to talk to her firmly about how she was interpreting the scenes. She was playing a very nervous and sheltered young heiress, and obviously Amanda was neither, so sometimes she would appear too modern – in her gestures, her delivery, et cetera, but I didn't have any actual arguments with her. I admired her – she was very strong-minded.'

'Did you have a close relationship with her?'

Pike gave a short barking laugh and pushed his glasses up onto his head.

'If you are trying to find out if I was having sex with her, you couldn't be more wrong. I was directing her; it was a professional relationship and nothing more.' He snapped the elastic band.

'Had you ever had a relationship with her before this film?'

'Christ, no, but I'm certain you'll have a list of men who did – not that I think she was involved with anyone here. Her agent had given her a good talking-to about behaving herself, as the last thing we wanted was any scandal . . . not that it wouldn't be good publicity eventually, but to have press hanging around the set would have been intrusive. It took me all my time making her concentrate.'

'You've replaced her?'

He recrossed his legs and leaned forward.

'Listen, I know a lot of the crew don't like the fact that we have kept the cameras rolling, but I have backers and producers eager to get the movie finished.' He stood up then, saying, 'Now, is there anything else you want to ask me, only I should get started as we're almost ready to go with the next scene.'

'Did you like Amanda?'

For the first time, Pike became still.

'Did I *like* her?' he repeated.

'Yes.'

'I cast her, Detective Travis, I admired her, and she was a very beautiful young woman. This is tragic and, to be honest, I've not really allowed myself to think about what happened to her.'

'Would you know of anyone who would have had a grievance against her?'

Pike sighed in irritation.

'Maybe one or other of the boyfriends she dumped, maybe even one of the wives they left to be with her, but whether any one of them would have done this terrible thing is beyond my comprehension. She was twenty-four years old, with a big career ahead of her, and she was an astonishingly beautiful girl, cut down in the prime of her life and her career.'

There was a sudden flurry of activity, actors returning to the set ready for the filming, lighting technicians hovering. Pike got up from the chair, dismissing Anna.

'Could I ask you one more thing?' she said, jumping up and following him.

'Yes,' he hissed.

'Did Amanda say anything to you about hearing someone screaming in the night?'

He turned towards her, his face pinched with impatience.

'She mentioned it, but I didn't give it much attention. I said something like . . . oh, I can't remember, but I think it was that she should use it for the sequence we were shooting. I wanted to hear her really screaming. Now, if you'll excuse me . . .'

'But she was obviously distressed, wasn't she?'

'Listen, Detective, Amanda could get distressed if her costume was too tight, but whether or not it had any connection to what happened, I really couldn't say. Now, I have to get back to work.'

'You suspect someone from the unit killed her?' Simon asked Anna as they walked towards his car.

Anna got into the passenger seat, slamming the door shut. Simon winced as he sat beside her, closing his own door more carefully.

'I think . . .' She hesitated. 'One of them knows a lot more than I was able to uncover. Which one, I don't know – but I'm not through here. Something doesn't sit right, apart from their lack of genuine grief, and I didn't like the director.'

'Julian Pike? Was it just a personal reaction or did you get something else?' Simon asked.

'There's just something about him. He's a cold fish. And he doesn't really have an alibi, does he – since he drove himself home.'

They continued their journey in silence for a while
and then Simon hit the steering wheel in frustration,
muttering, 'Fucking traffic! This bloody congestion
charge just makes it worse.'

'What do *you* think about the scream Amanda claimed
to have heard?' Anna asked.

'Christ knows. You keep going back to that.'

'I know, it just bothers me. She gets to the set and tells
everyone how much it had affected her, but she didn't
call the police.'

They eventually drove into the station car park and
headed into the incident room. Phones were ringing
nonstop as Anna threaded her way through the booths
towards her small glass-fronted office.

As soon as Mathews saw Anna, he signalled for her to
join him.

'The TV coverage is kicking in – they're showing
clippings of her films and they're impatient for an arrest.
So far, we have no suspect. Unless . . .' He peered at
Anna.

'We've come up empty-handed. No one we interviewed on the set appears to have a motive, and in most
cases they were either working or had alibis, so the team
will have to run checks on them all. Have we been given
a closer time-frame for her death?'

'Not come through yet, but they'll be finishing up the
post mortem some time soon.' Mathews sighed, then
glanced at his watch. 'We'd better have a briefing and
see what else, if anything, we've got. With such a high-
profile case, we'll be getting a lot of media attention.
You think we should go for an interview on one of the
TV crime shows?'

'I suppose so, but right now we've not really pieced

together her last known movements, apart from being dropped off at home by the unit driver.'

'You question him?'

'Yes, Simon did. His name is Harry James. He didn't see anything suspicious and waited until Amanda let herself into the mews house before he drove off. He returned to the film set and had another actor to drive home.'

'What about this scream?'

'Er, no one seems to have any concrete details, apart from the fact that she told a lot of people about it. She didn't report it at the time though, and apparently the team has found no one or anything connected to it in the area of the mews.'

'You get on and write up your report. I'll be out in half an hour, then I've got to get off home.'

'Yes, sir.'

A few minutes later, Mathews tapped on the window of her office, holding up the front-page coverage in the *Evening Standard*.

MOVIE STAR'S MURDER. WHO KILLED AMANDA?

Anna wasn't surprised to find, fifteen minutes later, as the team gathered for the briefing, that Mathews had already gone home. Simon waited for everyone to assemble.

'OK, the Guv has had to leave so it's down to me to gather all the information we've got so far.'

He turned to the board. Alongside the photographs of Amanda from various films were the tragic shots showing how her body was discovered. None of the neighbours in the mews itself and the properties backing onto Amanda's house had heard or seen anything suspicious.

Nothing, as yet, had come in from forensics or the pathology labs to help ascertain the exact time of her murder. They had no weapon.

'It was a brutal killing,' Simon stressed. 'Look at the way her body was found and then look at what we've got – fuck all. We have no suspect, we haven't found anyone so far who saw anything suspicious, and no one we've interviewed knows of anyone with a grudge against the victim.'

'Bar the ex-wives of some of her boyfriends,' Barbara the blonde DC interjected. 'Seems like Amanda got her rocks off, shagging married stars and one in particular.' She held up a newspaper. 'Scott Myers's wife is also an actress, also pretty attractive. She's been in the news over the past year, accusing Amanda of stealing her husband and persuading him to leave her and their three kids – all under seven, by the way.'

Barbara returned to her desk and picked up more copies of newspaper cuttings.

'Fiona Myers is quoted in the *News of the World* last year as saying that Amanda was like an over-sexed bitch on heat and that she needed a bucket of water chucked over her to cool her down. She said if she ever saw her, she'd be the one to chuck it.'

Suddenly Mathews returned and signalled to Anna to join him.

'I was in the car park,' he said. 'They've brought her parents here. Can you talk to them, because I've got to go. They're downstairs.'

It was never easy to confront parents in these circumstances. Anna wished she had someone with her, but she braced herself and walked into the reception.

Chapter Three

M r and Mrs Delany were waiting patiently. Carmen Delany was a very attractive woman, well-groomed and smartly dressed like her husband. They didn't appear to be the emotionally distraught couple that Anna had expected; rather they were calm and poised as they sat beside each other in one of the incident rooms.

'First let me give you my sincere condolences,' Anna said, and offered them tea or coffee. They declined both.

There was an awkward pause as Anna prepared herself for what she should say next, and neither spoke.

'We are waiting for the post-mortem report to assist in our enquiry, but I want to assure you we're endeavouring to get a result as soon as possible. If I could just ask you some questions, that might help us get to know more about Amanda.'

Still neither said a word. Anna found it unnerving as they sat so calmly, their eyes on her, waiting.

'Firstly, could you give me any reason why someone might have a grudge against your daughter?'

'Grudge?' Mrs Delany repeated quietly.

'Anyone who might have had a reason to harm your daughter?'

'Harm her?' This was Mark Delany, his voice soft but chilling.

'Yes. We need to question everyone Amanda knew and find out if there was someone who had been frightening her, or maybe stalking her. Is there anyone you can think of who would have been . . . jealous, angry?'

'My daughter, we have been told, was brutally murdered. I don't see how describing anyone's jealousy or anger would be a motive for them to kill her.'

'It's possible, Mr Delany, that you may not have been aware of how intensely someone felt about her. If there is anyone you recall meeting or hearing Amanda talk about, I would really appreciate knowing about them.'

Anna felt her words tumbling over each other, she was so nervous. The Delanys' reaction to whatever she said was just not normal, unless they were both in shock – but they didn't appear to be nor were they showing the usual signs of that.

Anna waited. They looked at each other and then returned their almost expressionless eyes to her.

'I can think of no one we met who would want to harm Amanda.' Mr Delany had a thin mouth; his words were clipped and said without any emotion.

'What about you, Mrs Delany?' Anna asked.

'No one, but you have to understand that we saw very little of her over the past five years.'

'Was this lack of contact due to Amanda's filming commitments?'

They made no reply.

'Or was there a problem between you as a family?'

Again no response.

'Did you have some kind of argument, Mr Delany?'

'Argument?' The thin mouth shut tightly.

'Yes, perhaps a falling-out. Your daughter was very famous and I'm surprised that you didn't see her often.'

'We travel and don't reside in London any more.' Mr Delany crossed his legs, and with bony fingers plucked at the immaculate crease in his trousers.

Anna stood up and asked if they would excuse her for a moment. She hurried into the incident room, where Simon was finishing up the briefing, and asked for his help.

'He's a frosty, tight-lipped man and she seems almost afraid to speak, so what I suggest is, as a ploy to separate them, I'll tell them we need to take background statements as standard procedure. I'll say I don't want to keep them any longer than necessary in their time of grief, and so on. You take Mr Delany and leave *her* to me.'

In the interview room Simon was charming, expressed his condolences, then asked to speak to Mr Delany alone. The man didn't like it but agreed to accompany Simon, who explained to him that he wanted to discuss some photographs, but didn't wish to upset Mrs Delany. In his office, Simon set out the pictures of the rooms in Amanda's house, and asked Mr Delany if he could tell if there was anything missing or unusual. No, came the answer. He had only been there briefly after Amanda had bought it, and before it had been refurbished.

Meanwhile, Anna tried to coax more information from Mrs Delany. At first the woman was unforthcoming, constantly looking to the door for the return of her husband. Amanda had left home very young, she said, just a few weeks after her sixteenth birthday, as she had won a coveted place at the Royal Academy of Dramatic Arts. They had been very proud of her and were hopeful that she would become a well-respected actress. Mrs Delany mentioned that they used to be frequent theatregoers, especially to the National or Royal Shakespeare Theatre. Amanda had rented a room in some friends' house in St John's Wood and seemed very happy, but eventually insisted on moving out and into a flat with other students.

There was a long pause as Mrs Delany looked again to the door, either hoping for her husband's return, or fearful that she was saying too much. Anna reassured her that this was all helpful as she needed to build up a complete background of her daughter. Mrs Delany gave her names of two students that she remembered, but couldn't recall any others. To begin with, she said, Amanda was doing well, and then it all became difficult.

'What do you mean?' Anna pressed her.

'She became very awkward, rude, and her father was furious, as he'd given her a bank account and a credit card and she started running up debts. No matter what he said to her, she just carried on spending and then . . .'

Anna waited as Mrs Delany chewed at her lips in agitation.

'She stole some things from Harrods and we had to go and sort it all out. Thankfully it was never reported and for a while she behaved herself. Her career seemed to take off and . . .'

Again, Anna had to wait as she saw Mrs Delany trying to control herself. Her manicured fingernails gleamed with bright red polish; diamonds glittered on her wedding finger.

'She got into trouble and we had to travel from France to sort it out, and this time it was dreadful. She had fallen pregnant and had had an abortion that nearly killed her.

52

She was bleeding internally, and if we hadn't rushed her to hospital, she would have died. As it was, she destroyed any hope of ever having children, and poor Mark had to pay a great deal of money to a surgeon to get her fixed up and released. After that, he virtually refused to see Amanda; she was so ungrateful and all the money she was earning she squandered and wouldn't let her father look after it. We didn't know what to do with her. There was no possibility she could come home with us to France – not that she would have wanted to. She went back to living in some awful place until her mews house was ready to move into, and we didn't really speak much to her again . . . Well, her father didn't.'

Anna had made a few discreet notes, but didn't want to distract Mrs Delany or put her off.

'She got into cocaine, so I came to see her and asked her to go into rehab, which she did. I booked her into the Drury Clinic and paid – she never even said thank you. Then when she was released, she got a good part in a film and her career really took off.'

'You must have felt very proud of her success.'

It was at this moment that Mr Delany walked in, Simon behind him, pulling an apologetic face at Anna.

'I was just saying how proud you both must have been, when Amanda's career became so successful,' said Anna.

'Having hordes of photographers tracking us down, invading our privacy and making life hell for us, made it very hard for us to be able to say unequivocally how proud we were. The scandals she created made our lives a nightmare, and disgusted us both. By now you have to have realised that even in death, our daughter has made us a spectacle. We have been phoned at all hours of the day and night, and there are television cameras outside our hotel, which I would really like to return to and then leave as soon as possible. There is nothing we can tell you that would give you any clues as to why Amanda was murdered. Tragic as it is, we just want to get on with our lives *in peace*.'

As Delany gripped his wife by her elbow, helping her to stand, for the first time there was some real emotion in his face.

Anna watched them from one of the station's windows. Mr Delany was hurrying his wife to a waiting Mercedes, their driver ready to help them inside. Mrs Delany was sobbing as she got into the back of the car, Mr Delany slamming the doors shut to sit in the front beside their driver.

Anna turned to Simon, commenting, 'Well, at least she's weeping. I have never met a couple like them, so hateful, arrogant and in denial that they could have had anything to do with why Amanda was so estranged from them. I know I would be; he was really horrible.'

Simon nodded. 'It was hard to keep him with me any longer. He'd only been to her mews house once before it was done up. Apart from that, he said he hadn't spoken to her or seen her since she was in rehab.'

'That's odd.' Anna frowned. 'His wife said that *she* was the one who arranged the rehab. Did he say if his wife was with him when he went to visit her?'

'No, just that that was the last time he had been with her.'

Anna went back to her office feeling depressed. Whether it was due to the experience of interviewing two very bitter and cold parents, or because she couldn't help but feel for the dead girl, she wasn't sure. She knew that shock and grief often made loved ones react in strange ways that could even be construed as suspicious. She could understand why Amanda had been so promiscuous; that what she was desperately looking for was love. She wondered if someone Amanda had thought loved her had killed her. Packing up to leave for the night, Anna made a note in her diary to check when Amanda was at the Drury and see whether she had had any visitors while she was at the clinic.

Suddenly thoughtful, Anna tapped her diary with her pen and went into the incident room. Checking on the board the items removed from the dead girl's home, she saw that the calendar from the kitchen was listed, but there was no mention of a diary. This didn't feel right: with such a hectic lifestyle, let alone work commitments, Amanda was certain to have kept some kind of a diary. Also, as a well-known actress, surely she would have had some kind of blog or a website, even a fan page, but to date they had found nothing.

She put in a call to Andrea Lesser, Amanda's theatrical agent. The answer machine was on so she left a message asking her to call back. By now it was almost eight o'clock and Anna felt tired. It had been a long day with poor results, and she was eager to get home, have a shower and an early night to start refreshed in the morning.

Chapter Four

Anna was in the incident room early the next morning and had written up her interview with Amanda's parents. She had also listed the interviews to be arranged by DC Joan Falkland with Amanda's three ex-lovers – Scott Myers, Rupert Mitchell and Colin O'Dell.

Simon joined her in her office and asked if she wanted him along to the interviews. He grinned, adding that he was certain she wouldn't, as half the females in the station were panting over Scott Myers, never mind Colin O'Dell.

'Depends on what you've lined up,' Anna responded tetchily. 'Whatever you have is priority because, as yet, Joan hasn't confirmed exactly when I am to meet them, and Colin O'Dell is filming in Dublin.'

'I want to go over to forensics and push them a bit. We should have the post-mortem results in this morning. I wouldn't mind finishing up the interviews with the rest of the cast and crew and then we can decide who to eliminate from the case.'

Anna cocked her head to one side. 'I'm sure you'll find some reason to question Amanda's pretty little blonde stand-in again.'

'No, I won't.' Simon was on the defensive. 'I'll want

to ask everyone what they know about the people listed on Amanda's mobile phone, plus we've found a few text messages and—'

Anna interrupted him. 'I haven't seen that report; it's not up on the board.'

'Because, sweetheart, I've only just had the information from technical support.'

Anna was really tetchy now. She hated being patronised and was also starting to dislike Simon; he was so self-assured and even though they were the same rank, she constantly felt as if he was belittling her. Her desk phone rang. It was the switchboard: Andrea Lesser was on the line.

'Excuse me,' she said coldly to Simon and he walked out. 'Miss Lesser, thank you for returning my call.'

The agent was certain that Amanda had to have possessed some sort of a diary. Her agency used to send her appointments by e-mail, often marking out for the week where she was to be, who would be her drivers, and about film premières she was to attend and so forth. Andrea Lesser agreed to send Anna copies of these dates, but reminded her that some of it would be very private and should not be made public. Anna assured her that the information would be held at the station.

'She was invited to virtually the opening of an envelope,' Andrea Lesser continued, 'so she must have kept some kind of record. Then there were all her boyfriends. I know she kept a couple or more on the go at the same time.'

Anna then put in a call to the station's press office to make sure they sent her press coverage of Amanda going back as far as they could. Next, she asked Barbara to

Google Amanda and print off all the articles she could find. When she asked if the laptop removed from Amanda's home had been checked out, Barbara rolled her eyes.

'Not yet. The lab has got it and they'll be processing all the data.'

'Check the e-mails.'

Barbara gave a sarcastic gasp. 'Oh right, as if we wouldn't do that.'

'It should have been done by now, so put some pressure on whoever is dealing with it.'

'Yes, Ma'am.'

Anna walked away as Barbara called over to Joan, 'Get them to hurry the laptop details over to us, will you, Joan?'

The other DC shrugged and picked up her desk phone. 'Simon said he was gonna talk to them, but if you insist . . .'

'Yeah, Simon says a lot of things', Anna interjected, 'but he doesn't get them done!'

Joan waited until Anna was out of earshot. She was a dowdy, thin-faced woman in her late thirties, who had never married but lived in hope, unlike Barbara, who was married to a plumber and had two children. They worked well together and neither particularly liked Anna, perhaps because, unlike them, she never gossiped and very rarely joined them in the local pub for a drink after work.

'You know what she's got me doing?' she said.

Barbara shook her head.

'She's only had me line up appointments with Rupert Mitchell and Scott Myers.'

Barbara whistled. 'Both of them?'

'Yes, and that's not all. She's planning to fly to Dublin to meet Colin O'Dell as he's filming over there.'

'Shit! She's got all three of them. I was hoping they might be brought in, especially Rupert Mitchell. He's a real looker . . .'

The famous Drury Clinic was located close to Richmond Park. Anna had made an appointment with the consultant registrar who admitted all the patients, but was told that he could not possibly divulge any of their patients' private medical records. Moreover, the psychiatrist who had been dealing with Amanda's case was no longer working there. Dr Eamon Suchet had moved to a practice elsewhere; Anna was given his forwarding address. When she called to make an appointment, his secretary said he would be available either within the hour or first thing the next morning.

Anna arrived at the Harley Street practice in time to see him that morning. She was surprised how young Suchet was. He was charming, explaining that his private practice ran from the Harley Street address, but he was also attached to a clinic in Tooting. He told her how distressed he had been when he had read about Amanda's murder. When he mentioned patient confidentiality Anna stressed that all she wanted was to establish certain details about Amanda's background.

'She was brutally murdered, and if there is anything that will help us track down her killer, then I am asking that you assist my enquiry.'

'Well, it was some time ago . . .'

'You said you were very distressed by her death. Did she continue to see you after she left the Drury?'

'Not lately. Amanda was a hard patient to forget. I

followed her career so she was often in my thoughts. I admired the fact that she had made such a success of herself.'

'Her mother booked her into the clinic, didn't she?'

'Yes, I believe so, but I only had one short interview with her parents.'

'Was she addicted to cocaine?' Anna asked.

'She *used* cocaine, but I wouldn't say she was an addict. Her problems were more psychological.' He hesitated, adding: 'I feel very uncomfortable discussing her case.'

'Surely not, if it can help us find her killer? Right now we have no suspects and very little evidence to help us move the enquiry forward. Do you recall who visited her?' Anna persisted.

'Yes, only because they were quite well-known, now even more so. They were the actors Scott Myers and Rupert Mitchell, and her agent, but I don't recall her name. Amanda was only in residence for four weeks, then she left, and with it being a private clinic, we couldn't stop her. She agreed to continue seeing me as a private patient.'

'Here?'

'No, I didn't have this practice then, so she said she would book appointments with me at the Drury whenever she felt she needed help – if that is the best word to describe it. She made three appointments but never kept them. I left a couple of months later. I did contact her, via my secretary, to give a forwarding address and let her know that if she wished to see me I was always available, but I never saw her again.'

Anna opened her notebook. 'When you describe her symptoms as not being drug-related but psychological, what exactly do you mean?'

Suchet sipped from a glass of water.

'Amanda had been through a bad termination and it resulted in her being unable to conceive a child. She had been hospitalised with internal bleeding and subsequently her doctors performed a hysterectomy. Tragic for a girl so young. I think her parents had played a major part in persuading her to come into the Drury. She was using cocaine and binge drinking, but as I said before, she was not an addict and had tended to use cocaine on a social level rather than being dependant on it. But what she had begun doing was self-mutilation. Her arms and her thighs were covered in small abrasions. Self-mutilation is a cry for help, and only by inflicting pain upon themselves do victims feel they are in many ways "alive". The secrecy of self-injury and the pain of it relieve the fact that they feel unworthy and have little self-confidence and even less—'

'I'm sorry,' Anna said, interrupting him, 'but if Amanda felt unworthy, with no confidence and low self-esteem, how could just four weeks be enough for her to recover from these debilitating symptoms and become a high-profile actress so swiftly after her stay in the Drury?'

'She had been reasonably successful before she was admitted, but I never said that she was fully recovered, probably the contrary. But she was admitted as a private patient, she was never sectioned and therefore could leave whenever she wished to.'

'Did she ever tell you who the father of the baby was?'

He shook his head.

'Was it either of the actors you said visited her?'

'I doubt it.'

'Did she ever mention anyone when you were with her? You must have talked about it?'

'We did. Amanda was raped, Detective Travis.'

'What?'

'That was what she eventually told me, but by whom I have no idea.'

'Did she report it?'

'If she did, she never mentioned it to me.'

'But surely she must have! She gave you no hint of who it could have been?'

'Detective Travis, if Amanda did report it, then it must be on police files. It took a number of sessions before she admitted to me that she'd had a termination, then another session before she broke down and told me she was unable to have any children. It wasn't until shortly before she left the clinic that she admitted to having been raped. As I said to you, I was more concerned with her mental state than any addiction problems. Amanda was a very damaged soul and I felt that she did require further treatment, which is why I tried to persuade her to come to see me after she left the Drury.'

'You said earlier that your secretary contacted her. Are you now saying that you personally talked to her?'

'No, I did not. It was my secretary. When I said persuade, it would have been unethical for me to approach her personally, but Julie, my secretary, did, I think, call twice. Then, as I said earlier, Amanda made appointments but never turned up.'

'When she called to make an appointment, did you speak to her?'

'No.'

'Even though you have said she was a damaged soul and didn't turn up for appointments, you never made any approach to see her.'

'No, I did not.'

Anna jotted down a few notes and then looked up.

'Did you find her attractive?' she asked.

He shook his head. 'You know, I think I can see where you are going or trying to go with your questions. I did not have any kind of relationship with her, bar a professional one. Yes, she was an exceptionally attractive young girl and she was also a very needy one. I felt concerned for her mental stability, although she made great steps forward at the Drury in such a short time, and was willing to listen and take advice. To my mind though, she was on very shaky ground and I felt that it would be only a matter of time before she broke down or began self-harming again, if she didn't have professional help. I wanted to give it, but as I have already said, Amanda chose not to keep her appointments.'

'It must have been strange for you, to see how successful she was becoming.'

'It wasn't strange at all. I have said how attractive she was; in fact, Amanda was exceptionally beautiful, like a rare creature. I think her acting talents were also very well-honed and she was capable of hiding her feelings and giving a very good performance of normality, but her protective shell was very thin and could, I estimated, crack open at any time . . .'

'Knowing this, why didn't you persist in trying to see her?'

He shook his head. 'Impossible. It was her own choice to come and see me or not, and she chose not to. Perhaps her successful career helped her self-esteem.'

'The two visitors, other than her parents, to the clinic, were Scott Myers and Rupert Mitchell?'

'I believe so. Now, I'm sorry to have to stop you there but I have a patient. If there is anything else?'

Anna stood up and put her notebook away.

'You've been very helpful, thank you.'

As Suchet ushered her to the door, he asked her if she had met with Amanda's parents.

'Yes, I did, and I found them pretty unhelpful.'

'Ah, well, there you have it. The father in particular is a very cold, unemotional man and seemed more concerned with his own well-being rather than his daughter's. His wife appears to be a little afraid of him and both were exceedingly concerned by the adverse publicity their daughter was creating.'

'They live abroad?'

'Yes, which is the reason they gave for never coming to see her.'

As Anna passed through the reception, a young girl was sitting there with a woman she guessed was her mother. The girl was skeletal thin, with lank, blonde hair and when she glanced at Anna, her eyes were like a frightened fawn's, with deep dark circles beneath. Julie told the couple that Dr Suchet could now see them and she took them into the corridor, leading the way up to his surgery.

'Did you ever meet Amanda Delany?' Anna asked Julie when she returned moments later.

'No, but I knew who she was and I'm aware of what has happened. It's just awful. Dr Suchet was quite concerned about her and asked me on two occasions to make appointments for her to come in and see him.'

'But she never did?'

'Not to my knowledge. I forwarded a bill to her for cancellation fees, but whether or not she saw Dr Suchet at his main clinic I wouldn't really know. I handle the patients here for private consultation and he's only here three days a week.'

65

'Thank you, I appreciate you talking to me.' Anna hesitated and then asked, 'Did she pay the cancellation fee?'

'No, she didn't.'

Anna returned to her car to find the meter was just about to run out and a traffic warden was hovering. As she started the engine, she thought about the interview with Suchet. Something niggled at her, not that she could define what it was exactly. Julie, his secretary, had repeated that she had contacted Amanda twice, exactly as Suchet had said, but Anna was unsure if she believed either of them.

Returning to the station, Anna marked up her interview on the board and underlined the names of Scott Myers and Rupert Mitchell as visiting Amanda at the clinic. On the desk in her office was a stack of newspaper clippings for her to wade through. She couldn't believe just how many there were, so she took off her jacket, fetched a mug of coffee and settled down to reading.

'Raped! Christ, have you run it through to see if it was reported?'

Anna was updating Simon on her meeting with Suchet. 'It wasn't,' she replied, 'and she never disclosed to Suchet who the father of her aborted child was.'

'Whatever, it doesn't really move us forward with any new evidence as to who killed her.'

'Unless it was Myers or Mitchell. Also, where is Amanda's diary? I'm certain she would have had one, so's her agent. We get anyone to tell us if anything else is missing from her house?'

'Nope, unless we contact the guy who refurbished it,

see if he can recall anything. We're also still waiting on the lab to give us all the data off her laptop.'

'Maybe read up on these before we get to see anyone else.' Anna passed him some newspaper clippings.

Simon flipped through them, shaking his head.

'She was so beautiful and, my, did she get out and about. There's one photo after another of her leaving nightclubs and being poured into taxis.'

'Yes, I've seen them.' Anna watched him nonchalantly licking his finger and flipping over one cutting after another. 'Did you get anything of interest from the rest of the film crew?' she asked.

'No, and they're "wrapping" as they say in the industry, or is it "a wrap"? I dunno, there were lots of trailers moving out. Strange existence when you think about it, all working in a tight-knit community and living in each other's pockets for months on end, and then they all pack up and wait for the next job. Or not in some cases.'

Anna leafed through the rest of the cuttings.

'Let's hope we get something from this afternoon. Has the post-mortem report come in yet?'

'Nope, and forensic are dragging their heels. Maybe we should go over there . . .'

'I thought you were going this morning?'

Simon walked to her office door. 'I wanted to finish up at the film set before they all disappeared.'

'I'll get a sandwich and then we can go to forensic together.'

'OK by me. Say in an hour?'

Anna agreed and he shut her door. She still felt annoyed by him.

After selecting the cuttings she wanted to work on, she went up to the canteen and ordered a toasted cheese sandwich and fruit to take back to her office. She had no sooner sat down when Mathews rang to have a word with her. She decided not to take her sandwich in with her even though she was feeling really hungry.

Mathews was sitting behind his desk cleaning his nails. He looked up when she entered.

'This is bloody going nowhere. I'm getting a lot of flak from the powers that be that want a result to feed to the press, but as far as I can see, we've got fuck all.'

'It's looking that way,' Anna agreed.

'We've got to come up with something soon. We still don't have a motive, a suspect or the weapon.'

'I'm going over to Lambeth to the pathologist and then onto forensics – maybe they'll have something for us.'

Mathews sighed and put away his nail scissors in a small leather case.

'Has Simon got anything for us?' he asked.

'He's only just back from the film unit. I'll give the designer who worked on Amanda's house a call and see if he can give us anything, or maybe know if anything is missing from the property.'

'Right, well, we certainly need something. And fast.'

Anna picked up her office phone to check if Joan had arranged the meetings with the three actors. She was not amused when Joan offered to tag along.

'Just sort out the meetings, please. Have we anything in from the victim's laptop?'

'Yes, they're sending over details as we speak. Apparently they found a lot of poetry.'

'Pardon?'

'That's what they said. Seems the victim wrote poetry,

68

files of it. Anyway, as soon as it's here I'll get it copied for you.'

Gowned up, Anna and Simon entered the mortuary where the pathologist Dr Ada De Silva, a petite Iranian woman, was waiting. Amanda's body was draped in green sheeting and De Silva was standing by the light boxes with a clipboard. She motioned for them to join her.

'I'm sorry that this has taken longer than usual, but I'm still waiting on the blood tests. The victim received multiple stabs. Many of the wounds are superficial, apart from the one to the right breast. This one penetrated her heart and resulted in her death. The blade was double-sided and about fourteen centimetres long. As you can see, the wound to her breast has a linear bruise to either side of it. This was probably caused by the hilt guard of the weapon, which suggests a Commando-style knife.' De Silva showed the heavy bruising on Amanda's thighs. 'Because of the bruising, both externally and internally, it's possible that the victim had been raped. The forensic lab is testing for semen and condom lubricants.'

De Silva turned to look at the shrouded body, then back to the blow-up pictures.

'Your victim had breast implants, and the right one was punctured by the knife. She was very underweight. Her height was almost five feet seven and a half, but she weighed only six stone and five pounds. I would say she had suffered from anorexia for some time, since her skin tone is very poor and dry. Further internal examination showed that she had undergone a total hysterectomy. Her fallopian tubes were removed, which could have occurred after a botched abortion. Whoever had done the operation performed amateur work. The poor child must have been in agony and for a considerable time.' The pathologist sighed, shaking her head.

Crossing to the body, she lifted a corner of the sheeting to show puncture marks between the toes.

'The blood and urine tests will give more detail but I would say she had been using heroin, not recently though, perhaps a month or so before she was killed. The injection site seems old due to yellowish bruising around it. I've recommended testing her hair for a clearer history of drug abuse. She had recently snorted cocaine, as there was a residue of powder still in her right nostril and crustation around both nostrils. Again, I will have confirmation from the toxicology report, but along with the hair sample it's going to take at least ninety days for the results. Now we get to her arms.'

De Silva lifted the sheet and held out Amanda's right arm. She showed numerous self-inflicted small scars running up the inside of her forearm. It was the same picture on her left arm. They had no skin or blood from beneath her fingernails, and all her false nails were intact. One had been removed to show that the nails beneath were bitten down to the quick. The false nails were short and unvarnished, but very good quality.

De Silva estimated that Amanda had been dead for at least twelve hours because the body had been discovered in the afternoon and rigor mortis had set in.

Lastly, she lifted the sheet away from Amanda's face. She was, even in death, beautiful, with high cheekbones, a small pert nose and eyes set wide apart. De Silva directed them to look at a bruise above her right ear. She was preparing brain tests, as Amanda could possibly have been unconscious when the knife wounds were inflicted, which would explain why there were no defence marks.

De Silva covered the body and gave directions to a lab assistant to wheel out the gurney to the freezer section.

'That's it,' she said, as she took off her rubber gloves. 'It's a wretched case and astonishing to think that this poor child was the envy of so many teenagers. The reality is, she was a shell of a woman, yet still managed to maintain her ethereal beauty. I doubt if she would have been able to retain her looks for much longer without medical assistance, as she was dehydrated and even her teeth were becoming loose.'

Anna and Simon thanked her and headed over to the forensic department. Neither said anything, but both had been affected by De Silva's report. By the time they got to the forensic section, it was almost four-thirty.

Anna entered behind Simon and paused as she caught sight of Pete Jenkins, the forensic scientist she had met when she had worked on the Fitzpatrick case, seated at a bench with a microscope. He looked up and smiled at Anna.

'Hi there, how are you?'

'I'm fine, thank you. This is DI Simon Dunn who's working with me on the Delany case.'

Pete shook Simon's hand and then eased off his stool. 'We don't have much for you, I'm afraid.'

He headed towards a long trestle table covered in brown paper. There lay a silk nightdress in pale oyster pink. Yellow marker pen circles showed the knife entry wounds; it was heavily stained.

'She was wearing this, nothing else.'

Pete gestured to the sheets and pillowcases. They had found no other hair samples, only Amanda's, but from the sheets they had raised different DNA profiles from two semen stains. Neither could be traced on the National

Database. Pete had numerous bath towels and face cloths and a section of carpet brought from Amanda's house, but all the bloodstains belonged to her.

'We can bring in more garments from her wardrobe but I can't see that it will help. From her laundry bag, we've taken two more pillowcases smeared with make-up, but no other DNA or unknown source fibres. We have some of her underwear which is being tested for DNA to match with the sheets.'

Pete glanced at Anna. She had made notes, interested in the results of the vaginal, anal and mouth swabs checking for semen due to signs of sexual assault on the body.

'Our movie star put it about a bit and we found this under her bed.' Pete showed them a tinfoil wrap and said it was crack cocaine. They had also found a glass pipe in a box, with two small rocks of crack cocaine.

'Did anyone bring in a diary?' Anna asked. 'It's just we think she kept one, but so far we haven't found it.'

Pete shook his head. They had done a thorough search of the mews house, and the numerous fingerprints found there were being checked through the database. Most were Amanda's, but as yet there was no match for any of the others. He showed them a mug of what looked like residue of black coffee, but it was Marmite. They had siphoned it off from the mug at the scene and submitted it separately so that they could examine the mug for saliva and prints.

'Her fridge had a half-empty jar of it, a bunch of grapes and some bottles of water, nothing else. The mug has her fingerprints on it, no one else's and the kitchen was clean, didn't look used. Even her microwave still had the plastic wrap around the plate inside.'

Anna nodded and crossed to two large albums. These were leather-bound, but only one had photographs inside. She opened it to see some very lovely face shots of Amanda, but no other family or social snapshots.

'Why have you got these?' she asked.

Pete shrugged and suggested they had been brought in to check out fingerprints.

'They should be taken to the station,' she said brusquely.

'Apparently she had only recently moved into the house, which is why it's so devoid of fingerprints and so tidy. Lot of carpet fluff everywhere, but that's because the carpets were new. I would say her killer would have a lot of carpet fibres over him, but he wasn't wearing anything that shed. There must have been a real tussle on the bed where she was stabbed. Oh . . .' Pete paused and looked along the table, then walked to the far side. In a small plastic bag was a tiny gold cross and a few links of a broken chain.

'We found this caught between the top and bottom sheet. It's a crucifix but the chain has been snapped. I don't know if it belonged to Amanda, but it would be good to find out, because if it wasn't hers it could be the killer's and she snapped it off when she was attacked. We've checked for skin cells but no luck.'

Anna inspected the small cross; it didn't look the type worn by a man. It was plain and quite heavy, with an eighteen carat gold mark printed on the back. The chain links were also gold.

'Can I take this?' She would look through all Amanda's photographs to see if she was wearing it.

Pete nodded, asking her to sign it out. Simon was staring at the bloodstained sheets.

'There was no sign of a break-in, was there?' He looked at Pete.

'No. There was no damage to the front or back door. Last but not least, we have the victim's handbag.'

The bag was good designer leather with a matching purse inside containing eight pounds in coins. A wallet had two hundred and fifty pounds in it, all in fifties. There was a compact, comb and lipstick and a credit-card holder with numerous credit cards and membership cards for nightclubs and a health club. Anna said that checks had been made on Amanda's accounts to see if any withdrawals had been made, but there had been none to date since her murder.

'So robbery wasn't the motive, but then we can't even be sure about that, as we don't know what might be missing,' Simon murmured and looked at Anna. 'Let's take these and double-check the clubs, et cetera.'

Anna nodded then glanced at the clock on the wall. 'We should get going.'

Simon headed out first and Pete moved closer to Anna.

'How's things with you?' he asked.

'Fine, working away, you know.'

'Maybe catch up with dinner one night?'

'Yes, maybe.'

'Still the same old Anna. I didn't get a chance to speak to you after the trial and I hear that Langton is still seething about losing Fitzpatrick, but you can't win 'em all.'

'No, you can't.'

'I reckon he'll surface one day.'

'Do you?'

'Don't you?'

She shook her head. 'No. Fitzpatrick got away with enough money to hide out for a long time. I don't think he'd risk coming back to the UK.'

'Maybe not, and like I said, you can't win 'em all. Do you have a suspect for Amanda Delany?'

'No.'

Pete shook his head, turning back to look at the trestle table.

'That's bad news. There's a lot of media coverage. I'd say it had to be someone she knew, let himself in . . .'

'We have no motive or any information about any-one stalking or harassing her. She was in the middle of shooting a movie.'

'Maybe she pissed off one of her boyfriends,' Pete suggested.

'Well, we're making enquiries.'

He laughed softly then mimicked her. '"Making enquiries" . . . good luck to you. If I get anything to help you, I'll be in touch.'

'Thanks, Pete.' Her mobile rang.

Simon was standing impatiently by her Mini.

'What took you so long?' he said.

'Just chatting. I've worked with Pete before. Listen, I just got a call from the guy who redesigned her house. He said he'd meet us there.' She bleeped open the car and Simon got in next to her. When she started the engine, he slapped the dashboard with the flat of his hand.

'Jesus Christ, you know we have nothing, nor does your friend Pete have anything for us. Some bastard walked into her house, knifed her to death and walked out without leaving a single thread or hair or . . . it's mind-blowing.'

Anna drove out of the car park and into heavy traffic heading north across the river.

'I suppose we have that cross,' Simon sighed. 'We need to find out if it was Amanda's or . . .' he said it under his breath '. . . the killer's.'

He leaned back.

'I'd put money on it that it's hers. What man walks around with that kind of thing round his neck now-adays? Tacky medallions, yes, or plain gold chains, but crucifixes? No way.'

'What if her killer was a woman?'

'Impossible.'

'Why do you say that?'

Simon asked rudely if she had listened to what De Silva had said. The pathologist was certain that Amanda had been raped; the fact that there was no semen inside her body was because the killer wore a condom.

'They could have used some kind of instrument,' Anna argued.

'Yeah, like a brass dildo.'

'If De Silva finds evidence from the brain scans that Amanda was unconscious whilst being raped and then knifed, it could have been done by a woman.'

'I disagree,' Simon retorted. 'It doesn't fit a female pattern.'

They drove on in silence for a few moments before Anna gave him a sidelong look.

'What exactly in your mind is a female pattern?' she enquired.

He glanced at her and folded his arms.

'They don't go armed with a Commando knife, they don't stab their victim repeatedly and they don't *rape* them. Unless you think they wore a strap-on dildo

76

and . . . oh look, I don't fucking know. It just doesn't feel as if a woman would do what was done to that poor kid.'

'Who in your mind *would* do it, then?'

'Someone racked with jealousy, someone she'd turned down, someone who didn't feel they were good enough or she'd made feel that way, someone she'd used and then dumped, someone full of anger. Also, I think, someone not able to mix in her circles. The more famous she got, the more out of reach she became, but I'm damned sure it's someone who knew her.'

A new Mercedes convertible was parking up outside Amanda's mews house. Getting out was a tall elegant man, at least six feet four, tanned and good-looking, wearing a snazzy striped blazer, open-necked shirt and grey flannel trousers.

'He looks like he's gonna play cricket. What a prat,' Simon snapped.

'That's got to be Maurice Sutton,' Anna observed. 'He's from Sutton and Hargreaves interior designers.'

'You met him before?'

'No, but I recognise him from their brochure. He's quite well-known.'

She got out of the car and smiled at Sutton. He turned towards her.

'Detective Travis?' He had a deep resonant voice.

'Yes, that's me, and this is Detective Simon Dunn.'

Sutton nodded to Simon and looked over at the house. A uniformed officer was on duty outside and there were yellow scene-of-crime ribbons across the front door.

'Are we going inside?' he asked.

Anna nodded. The three entered the narrow hall one behind the other. Sutton was head and shoulders above both Anna and Simon.

'Oh my God, this is so sad,' Sutton said quietly. He looked around the small hallway as Anna gestured for them to go into the drawing room. The perfectly proportioned room, with its cream walls and matching carpet, looked immaculate. The soft tan leather sofa and chairs were complemented by matching cushions. Cleverly positioned mirrors made the room feel larger. The inlaid coffee-table had a deep blue glass bowl and glossy magazines stacked on it. There were three paintings on the walls, a number of candlesticks on the shelving and nothing else. Spartan and almost austere, the room was still very comfortable and belied its size. Sutton sat in the easy chair and Anna on the sofa, but Simon remained standing.

'Is there anything in this room you think is missing?' he asked.

Sutton gave a slow glance around the room. 'Well, I've not been here for about eight or nine weeks . . . but no, it looks exactly as I left it.'

'Do you have a set of keys?'

'Er, no. I did, of course – but I handed them back to Amanda's agent, Miss Lesser.'

They eventually moved to a small room Amanda must have used as an office. There were fitted bookshelves and a desk with a leather office chair and again, little else. No books; even the desk drawers were empty. Sutton said it was just as he had left it. Even the new green carpet had no scuffmarks.

'She wanted this room kept very simple,' he explained. 'She was going to get a computer; as you can see, everything is wired and ready. The desk lamp is about the only thing she must have bought. It's not one that I supplied.'

On one of the shelves was a big stack of scripts, some

still in brown envelopes with dates written on yellow Post-it notes and handwritten memos from Andrea Lesser.

'As far as I can recall, most of the scripts were here,' Sutton said, looking around. 'I remember her agent telling me Amanda was supposed to read them. They're all offers of work.'

Anna asked Sutton if he had met Andrea Lesser frequently.

'Yes, she was overseeing the rebuilding and refurbishing and would come by to check on deliveries and progress.'

They went into the newly fitted kitchen, which looked as if it had barely been used.

'I don't think Amanda ever cooked, but she asked for all this high-tech equipment,' Sutton pointed out. 'There's a small laundry room over here.'

They then checked the dining room with its French windows leading into the small walled garden. According to Sutton, nothing had been moved or changed or was missing. The small box bedroom was done out in soft peach tones, with matching headboard, drapes and cushions on the single bed, the white carpet thick with fluff. The fitted wardrobes were empty, as were all the drawers of the small dressing-table.

As they headed to the master suite, Sutton paused. 'Is this where it happened?'

Anna nodded and stood back for him to go in ahead of her and Simon. The king-sized bed with its decorative headboard had been stripped, the pillows, sheet, duvet and mattress removed. Sections of the bloodstained carpet had been cut out. Sutton stood close to the bed, shaking his head.

'Amanda was really only interested in this room. She chose the colour scheme and the linen, even the cushion covers. The walls are lined with Japanese silk, very expensive, the drapes too.'

Anna slid back the mirrored wardrobe doors to reveal a mass of clothes. There were four mirrored compartments, one containing racks of shoes from floor to ceiling, another with sweaters of every shade, carefully folded and stacked according to their colour. There was a rack of blouses, evening on one side, day on the other; Anna could see by the labels that they were all very expensive designer and couture garments.

A massive square mirror ran the length of the wall above the bedhead. The two bedside tables had crystal lamps and cut-glass bowls full of fake velvet and silk flowers. There was a hidden dressing room, and behind one wall of mirrors was a dressing-table, an old theatrical type with light bulbs on three sides. The carpet in the bedroom was very scuffed and there were a lot of fluff balls. It showed the imprint of their feet as they moved around the markings left by the forensic teams. Anna asked Sutton to look over the dressing-table. She switched on the lights; they were so bright she wanted to shade her eyes.

There were drawers filled with make-up and hair-pieces. They opened up to sit flat either side of the dressing table. Wigs, hairbands and fake-tan bottles were jumbled together with bottles of different scents. There were drawers filled with sexy lace underwear, and on top of the dressing-table was a large leather jewel case, containing rows of rings, gold bracelets, numerous pearl necklaces, gold chains and lockets – a genuine treasure trove.

'Are these real stones?'

Sutton glanced at the many rings and shrugged. 'I'm not sure. I never saw her wearing any jewellery really.'

'What about a gold cross? Did you ever see her wearing a crucifix?' Simon interjected.

'No, no, I don't think I ever did.' Sutton turned to look at the stripped bed and frowned. Neither Anna nor Simon spoke, waiting as if they both knew he'd remembered something.

'Did you find a toy floppy-eared rabbit? It was very worn and she, I mean Amanda, used to have it propped up on her pillow. Apparently it was always with her.'

'How do you know?'

Sutton turned, looking confused. 'What do you mean?'

'How did you know it was always on her pillow? From what you've said to us, you hadn't been here since you finished the decorations.'

This was Simon again. Anna noted a frown pass over Sutton's handsome face.

'I don't think I said that. What I did say was I hadn't been here for about eight weeks. The last time I came here I was with Andrea Lesser to check over any snags, and I remember seeing the toy on her pillow. Miss Lesser said that it went everywhere with Amanda and she always slept with it beside her. It was like a child's comfort blanket.'

'This was when you gave over the house keys?'

'That is correct, but to be certain you should check with Miss Lesser.'

Simon looked to Anna. 'Did she say if anything was missing?'

Anna shook her head, more intent on seeing if there was anything more to gain from Sutton. He was staring at his own reflection in the large mirror, as if recalling being with Amanda.

'She was child-like. When I first met her here, she was very excited. This was quite a rundown property . . .'

He gestured around the bedroom.

'To create such a large bedroom, we knocked through two walls and I extended further by a couple of feet into the garden. This was to create as much natural light as possible. Amanda wanted the mirrored wardrobes – in fact, she insisted on them. Not to my taste, but she was the client.'

'How much did it all cost?'

Again, this was Simon. Anna knew that they could easily find out the exact amount from Miss Lesser; it somehow felt wrong to question Sutton about it. Thankfully, he didn't seem concerned.

'The house was gutted and we had to do extensive work to get rid of a lot of structural problems. It's a very small property, but I think the outcome was around four hundred thousand – and that was without the fabrics and furnishings. I would say the total would be somewhere in the region of three quarters of a million pounds.'

Simon whistled and Sutton gave him a raised eyebrow.

'You think that's expensive? Well, when you consider the property is now worth over three million and was bought for seven hundred and fifty thousand, it was an exceptionally good investment. Don't think when I say Miss Delany was child-like that she didn't pay close attention to all the accounts. She was an astute business-woman and bought this place at auction.'

'But didn't Miss Lesser oversee everything?' Anna asked as they walked from the bedroom.

Sutton gave a wry smile. 'Miss Lesser was Amanda's

agent and she was earning vast sums of money from her, but I sensed that she didn't like having to check over all the merchandise. Whatever Amanda wanted, she got, and Miss Lesser's job was to see that she got it, and at a good price.'

'Did they have a good relationship?'

Again Sutton gave that wry smile. 'Little Amanda was her golden goose, so she made very sure they had a good relationship. She did not want to lose her client and nor did I, for that matter.'

They let themselves out and crossed to their parked cars.

'Thank you for coming to meet us here,' Anna said, shaking Sutton's hand.

'I wish I could say it was a pleasure, but we're here under very tragic circumstances,' he responded.

Anna watched Sutton drive off in his Mercedes before she reversed and headed out of the mews. Simon sat beside her, his mood obvious.

'Well, that didn't give us much,' he said grumpily.

'On the contrary, I think we got more of an insight into our victim for one, and we now know that along with her diary, her cuddly toy is missing.'

'Terrific. So what are you saying?'

'That maybe the killer stole both these items. The diary I can understand, but not the cuddly toy. That is odd. I mean, why take it unless it meant something to him?'

It was after seven in the evening when they returned to the station. The incident room was quiet with only the night staff working. Apart from a few details regarding the files taken from Amanda's laptop, there were no new items written up on the incident board.

Anna sat in her office and felt weary. Not that it had been a particularly hard day's work; it was piecing together their victim's background that made her feel depressed. She felt compassion for the girl with her anorexia, her drug-taking and damaged skinny body; then to be murdered at just twenty-four years of age was wretched. Anna was only twenty-nine but by comparison she felt so much older. It was as if their victim had hardly lived. After finishing her reports, she was preparing to leave when she saw on her desk a file from Joan Falkland with a typed note attached.

Copies of the files from Victim Amanda Delany's laptop – more to come. I've also made a CD copy for you to use on your own computer.

Anna flipped open the folder. It contained printed sheets from the various files, listing each one by name and date. She slipped the CD into her briefcase, then finished the evening's work by marking up her notes on the incident board. She'd catch up on reading the files from the laptop at home, but as Joan had not underlined any passages or remarked on anything of interest connected to the case, she didn't feel there was any immediate urgency.

Anna didn't get home until after nine. Unlike the Amandas of this world who would probably be getting ready to go out clubbing, she had a shower, made an omelette and, too tired to continue working, went straight to bed. She set her alarm for six the next morning, intending to work at home before going into the station.

Chapter Five

It was a wonder to Anna the next morning how such a delicate, confused and tortured creature could not only be phenomenally successful but very rich and, as Sutton had said, very much in charge of her finances. It felt as if she was investigating two women, instead of just one young girl. With so many physical ailments, Anna wondered how on earth Amanda Delany had got herself out of bed each day to work on the film set.

She jotted down a list of things that bothered her: the two missing items – the toy rabbit and the rest of the gold crucifix chain – and she underlined them both. Tapping her teeth with the pencil, she then wrote down the three names, Scott Myers, Rupert Mitchell and Colin O'Dell. She paused, then wrote Fiona Myers's name down too and underlined it. She flopped back onto her pillow, trying to fathom out what else was niggling away at her. She couldn't quite get it to surface, then she remembered something. Getting up, she went into her sitting room, opening her desk drawers in search of an old notebook. Thumbing through it, certain that she was correct, she went back to her previous case – the murder of Lord Halesbury.

There it was. The nurse, Dilys Summers, had first met

Lord Halesbury when she was working as a nurse at the Drury Clinic, She had left the clinic to work privately for His Lordship. Summers must have been at the Drury around the same time as Amanda Delany.

Anna added Dilys Summers to the list of people she wished to interview. By this time it was after seven and she still hadn't checked the files copied from the laptop. Dressing quickly, she took the file into her kitchen to read while she ate breakfast. Flipping through pages of childish jottings, some diets and some awful poetry, she sighed.

> *My life is full of dreams.*
> *When they are fulfilled*
> *And nothing appears as it seems*
> *You start to wonder*
> *Why bother with dreams?*
>
> *Loving someone all the time*
> *is only trying to find*
> *that certain someone*
> *who is just kind.*

Anna shook her head. There were pages and pages of these trite poems. Headings at the top of the page read *Too Much Too Soon*, *Screwing My Life Up*, and then there were further odd lines, some misspelled: *It's not all agony, Hiding behind the screen, Not all just up to now.* There were whole pages of these one-liners; Anna couldn't make out what they meant. Were they, perhaps, the first line of a poem or just random thoughts?

She checked the time: it was almost eight and she had to leave for work. Then she caught sight of an almost-full page of neatly typed manuscript, bearing the words at the top: *Chapter One*. Anna whistled to herself. She couldn't help becoming interested, not by what was written on the page itself but by the heading. Was Amanda Delany writing a book about her life? If this was so, then perhaps the previous one-liners had not been poetry but titles for a book. She would ask Joan to check the dates from the laptop as to when the files had been written, and she'd read the material just as soon as she got a quiet moment.

It had taken DC Joan Falkland another slew of phone calls from agents to personal assistants, but she had two appointments for Anna, one with Scott Myers and the other with Colin O'Dell, who had agreed to be interviewed in Dublin where he was filming. Barbara had contacted Rupert Mitchell and he too had consented to see Anna.

'Good, arrange for me to meet him after I return from Dublin and, Barbara, can you do me a favour? I want you to get a magnifying glass and start checking all the news coverage and photographs of Amanda and whoever she was with, to see if anyone is wearing a gold crucifix like the one we found at her house. I also want to take photographs of it with me.'

Barbara glanced at Joan, and as Anna moved away, she muttered under her breath, 'Great! She gets to meet all the movie stars and I get to sit with an effing magnifying glass all day.'

Barbara did have the grace to blush as Anna returned and overheard her remark, but Anna didn't even bother reacting to it. Instead she leaned on the side of Joan's desk.

'One more thing I need you to do is to get me the rest of the files from the victim's laptop. Can you include on all of them the dates they were written? Also, can you check with the costume department on Amanda's last film, to see if she wore the crucifix?'

'They're being copied up right now.'

'Good. Get them to my office before I leave.'

'Yes, Ma'am, and I'll check on the crucifix.'

This time, Joan didn't look at Barbara but began to arrange Anna's appointment with Rupert Mitchell.

DCI Mathews gave a briefing at nine that morning. As the team gathered, it became clear that they were no further along with the investigation. Anna brought up the two items she sensed were important, the missing toy rabbit and the gold crucifix, and said that she would be interviewing three people she felt might help with their enquiry. DCI Mathews asked that they get a clear view of Amanda's financial state. So far, they had not considered that it might have a connection to her murder, but after Simon had revealed how much the house was worth and that Amanda's earnings ran into millions, the Guv wanted a full investigation.

Just before Anna left to meet with Scott Myers, Joan received a call from his personal assistant to say that he would not be at his flat, but at home with his wife and their children. Even better; Anna wanted very much to meet Fiona Myers. Joan had also arranged a flight to Dublin at lunchtime, leaving from Heathrow and returning this evening. From there, Anna would be able to drive to Rupert Mitchell's home in Kingston. Lastly, she handed Anna the rest of the file taken from Amanda's laptop.

Anna made no mention of wanting to meet up with Dilys Summers or her possible connection with Amanda when she worked at the Drury. Nor did she mention her hunch that Amanda had possibly been writing a book; she needed to find out if it was a reality or just the young girl's fantasy. She was about to call Andrea Lesser when Mathews walked into her office.

'It's flatlining, isn't it?' he said glumly, then sat down heavily in her desk chair. 'I've just had bloody Chief Superintendent Langton on the phone and he gave me an earful. There's more coverage in this morning's papers and we're gonna have to give a press release, but saying what? That we've fuck all!'

Anna was eager to leave, even more so as she knew that if they didn't bring in a result soon, Langton would be breathing down their necks.

'I've got to go and see him.' Mathews gave her a bilious look. 'You got any gut feeling about this?'

'No, sir, I haven't, but as I said in the briefing, I really do think the murder is connected to someone she knew. I suppose it'll be a process of elimination.'

'Right. They've got pictures of the cross ready for the press release. It wasn't hers, was it?'

'We're not sure. Simon is checking with her agent, Andrea Lesser, but if we find that it wasn't the victim's but could have been the killer's and there is a press release on it, then we risk alerting the killer to get rid of any connection. I think it would be best to keep it quiet and for us to simply ask everyone we interview if they recall Amanda wearing any kind of pendant as we believe some of her jewellery could have been stolen. If we get a positive recall, we can ask whoever to describe it.'

Mathews stood up and sighed, plodding to the door. Then he paused.

'OK, no press release on the crucifix. I want closure on this one. I'm about to retire, and as you know, I've got a reputation for tying things up. Mind you, *he* lost out on his last case, didn't he? So it happens to the best of us.'

'Let's hope we have a productive day.' Anna wished he'd leave.

'I bloody hope we get something.' Then he was gone.

A few minutes later, Anna left the station herself. The last thing she wanted was to be confronted with Langton, but if they didn't get a break in the enquiry, she knew he would be coming into the station. Simon was also heading into the car park and she caught up with him.

'Did you call Miss Lesser about the crucifix?'

'Not yet, she wasn't in her office. Seems they don't start work until ten so I'll call her later. Did you get the lists of the last calls Amanda made? We've taken them off her mobile.'

'No, I didn't.'

He opened his briefcase. 'Here you go. I've got copies. We'll also need to get DNA swabs from the actors associated with her as well as fingerprints from everyone you've lined up to see today, so we can eliminate them.'

Anna hesitated, about to mention the book, but decided against it until she had spoken to Andrea Lesser personally. Her competitive nature was surfacing – a bad trait, she knew. She wanted to be the one who cracked open the case, not Simon Dunn.

Scott Myers lived in a substantial property backing onto Hampstead Heath. It was well-maintained with a small front garden and stone steps leading up to an imposing front door with stained glass panels. A Volvo hatchback pulled up and parked, and the driver tooted the horn. Anna turned and waited as a slim, dark-haired woman got out carrying two large, eco-friendly grocery bags.

'Are you from the police?' she called out.

'Yes, I am DI Anna Travis. You must be Fiona Myers. Do you need a hand?'

'Good God no, this is a very light load. Could you just get the front-door key out of my pocket and open the front door though?'

Fiona had a heart-shaped face with big, dark brown eyes. Her hair was cut in a fringe and just above her ears, giving her an elfin look. She was very slender and as Anna opened the front door she hopped over the mat into the hall.

'Be careful, that brass thingy on the door is a bit loose. I keep meaning to get it fixed but haven't got round to it. Come on in.'

She headed down a wide hallway, cluttered with scooters and roller skates.

'You mind coming into the kitchen? Then I can unload.'

Anna followed her into a huge kitchen, lined with pine cabinets and with a big stripped-pine kitchen table in the middle. The fridge was covered in spelling magnets and there was a bright red Aga.

Fiona dumped the bags down. She crossed to open a dishwasher and muttered, 'Bloody thing, it has a mind of its own. You switch it on and then it does nothing, then about an hour later it springs into life. I've asked the bloke to come out and sort it, but . . .'

Anna sat on a stool at the table, as Fiona began to put away the groceries.

'Is your husband here, Mrs Myers?'

'No, but he will be. He's taken Sadie to the dentist. She must have wiggled her baby teeth with grubby fingers and now she's got a gum infection. It's all because her twin brother's lost more than she has so he's had the tooth fairy visit more than she has. Do you want a coffee?'

'Yes, if you're having one, thank you.'

Fiona moved like a dancer around the kitchen, fetching mugs and coffee and occasionally kicking the dishwasher. She chattered on, excusing the fact it was instant coffee, but one of the kids had broken the percolator. At last she brought over the coffee, but instead of sitting down, immediately jumped up to fetch a biscuit tin, banging it down on the table.

'They're rather kiddies' selections of gingerbread men and Oreos, but do help yourself.'

'Thank you.'

There was a pause as Fiona spooned in sugar and then got up again to fetch a jug of milk. Anna said nothing, waiting for her to calm down.

'I know why you're here,' Fiona said suddenly. She got up yet again and went over to a stack of newspapers; she picked up a *Daily Mail* and held it out. There was a picture of Amanda on the front page.

'I was reading this earlier. It's two days' old. Have you read it?'

'Yes, I have,' Anna said quietly.

'Yes, I suppose you would have. Terrible, very sad. Do you know when her funeral is going to be?'

'No, I'm sorry I don't.'

'I wouldn't go and I don't think Scott will either. We've had enough stinko press and she'd probably turn in her grave if she knew I was there. But who knows, I might change my mind.'

Fiona sipped her coffee and rested her chin on her hand. 'Why do you want to see Scott?'

'I also wanted to talk to you.'

'Me?'

'Yes. You knew Amanda well, didn't you?'

'Because she had carnal knowledge of my husband, didn't mean that I knew her. She'd been here numerous times, but it was just, you know, friendly dinners with some of the film people Scott was working with. I'd cook up a big pot of chilli and open lots of wine.'

'It must have been very difficult for you.'

Fiona dropped her cookie-friendly act and stared hard at Anna. After a moment she turned away.

'Well, it wasn't very pleasant. I mean, I've got over it now, but it was a horrible time. She used to call him here, had this simpering little voice. I felt sorry for her, but that was before I knew what was going on. She always looked as if she was going to keel over she was so thin, but man, she could drink like a fish, hardly ever ate anything. She would down glass after glass; I don't know how she could stand up. I couldn't believe it, of all the women, she would be the one. But she was so needy and men always fall for that act, don't they?'

'It must have been very difficult for you.'

'You already said that once! And yes, it was. It can't be easy for anyone when their husband walks out, and especially when it's front-page news before I was even told he was intending to run after her. I have three children under seven and it was stressful enough even when he was living here because of all his work commitments. Having the fucking press camping out on my doorstep was a bloody nightmare for me and the kids.'

'Did you see Amanda over this time?'

'You must be joking. If she'd come here I would have scratched her eyes out!' She sighed and then laughed. 'I must sound like a suspect and to be honest, I'd have liked to throttle her. In some ways, when I knew what had happened to her, I even thought she got what she deserved, but in reality . . . It's sad, she was so young.'

'I have to ask you this, Fiona. Where were you at the time of Amanda's murder?'

Fiona looked startled and then said that she had been at home with her children and the nanny.

'Did you ever see Amanda wearing this?' Anna showed her the photograph of the gold cross.

'Is it a crucifix?'

'Yes, gold, with a gold chain.'

Fiona stared at the photograph and then passed it back.

'I doubt she would wear something like that,' she commented. 'In fact, I don't ever recall her wearing jewellery. She was always in skimpy T-shirts and mini-skirts – you know, showing off the skeleton frame. She had her tits done, I think, as they stood up like ice-cream cones.'

'When was the last time you saw her?'

Fiona took her coffee cup to the sink and rinsed it out.

'Maybe a few months ago. I was at a nightclub and she was there with Colin O'Dell and she smiled and waved at me as if nothing had ever happened between us. It made me so furious, but I didn't go and pour a glass of wine over her, which I would have liked to do. I just turned my back.'

'Was your husband still seeing her?'

She returned to the table.

'I doubt it. She dumped him and he was in a real state and guess whose shoulder he came back to cry on – *mine*! Mindblowing, isn't it? He walks out, leaves me and the kids, and tells all the press he's never been so in love and that he wanted to marry her, and then . . . expects me to welcome him back with open arms. Men!'

'Is he living back with you now?'

'No, he fucking isn't. He comes and goes with the excuse of seeing the kids. We've got a parents' day at school tomorrow so that's why he's here. We are not back together and we won't be – ever. I can't forgive what he put us all through and he knows it; it's over. He was the love of my life. Shit, I'm only thirty-two and we'd been together since we met at drama school, and the bastard does that to me. I gave up my career for him and the kids and he leaves me for that little nymphomaniac.'

As if on cue, the front door opened and slammed shut. Fiona looked nervous.

'Oh shit. Look, don't tell him I've been sounding off about her, will you? He gets so uptight.' She crossed to the door and shouted, 'I'm in here with . . .' She turned to Anna and pulled a face, hurrying out of the kitchen.

Anna could hear a low murmur of voices from the hallway and then in strode Scott Myers. He was very tall with floppy dark hair parted in the middle. In real life he was not as attractive as the films and photographs Anna had seen of him. He was dressed in jeans and sneakers with a stained T-shirt and a leather jacket slung round his shoulders.

'Sorry I'm late, I got held up. My daughter had to see a dentist and then I had to take her to school. I'm Scott Myers.' He held out his hand.

'I'm Detective Anna Travis.' Anna shook his hand.

'Right. Have you had coffee?'

'Yes, thank you.'

'You mind if I brew a mug up, I'm desperate. Having a howling child terrified of sitting in the dentist chair doesn't make for an easy morning, but thankfully all's well and hopefully the antibiotics will solve the problem. She prods her baby teeth, trying to loosen them for tooth-fairy cash!'

Anna smiled. He was as talkative as his wife, with a cultured voice and easygoing manner. He chucked off his leather jacket and placed the kettle on the Aga as he prepared his coffee. He constantly ran his fingers through his hair, tossing it back from his face, explaining that it was driving him mad but he was filming a Byronic costume movie and playing the part of Shelley. Anna smiled. It was rather good casting as he had a sort of poetic look, more pre-Raphaelite, and a good tight, muscular frame, but at the same time was slender. He was comfortable in the kitchen, aware of where everything was, and as soon as he had made his coffee he closed the kitchen door and sat at the table opposite Anna.

'I'm sorry, what did you say your name was?'

'Anna Travis.'

'Ah yes, well, I apologise again, Anna, for keeping you waiting. No doubt my wife has entertained you?'

'She was very kind.'

'I am sure she was, and probably called me everything under the sun. She can really let off steam. Unfortunately, to everyone else she comes across as lovely, which can be a tad irritating.' He grinned.

Anna watched as he opened the biscuit tin and munched one of the gingerbread men, dipping it into his coffee. He then patted his pockets and took out a pack of cigarettes.

'You mind?'

Even if Anna had, she doubted he would have taken any notice as he lit up straight away.

'She won't let me in front of the kids.' He exhaled, left the table again to fetch an ashtray and then sat down. His mood almost visibly changed.

'Well, let's get down to the reason why you are here, Detective Travis.'

Anna explained how she was trying to get to know Amanda in an attempt to piece together her last hours. If there was anything he could add or help them with, she would be most grateful. Myers said nothing as he flicked the ash of his cigarette into the ashtray.

She opened her briefcase and took out the list of calls from Amanda's mobile phone.

'I see from Amanda's phone records that she called you the night before she died.'

Myers shrugged.

'Can you tell me if there was anything in your conversation with her that might have led you to believe someone was frightening her or threatening her?'

Still he remained silent.

'What did you talk about?'

Myers sighed and ran his fingers through his hair, tossing his head back.

'It was a brief call, one of many as she kept on calling me, which was hard to deal with as I didn't really have anything to say to her. She broke it off with me, made me look a right idiot and yet kept on ringing me here or at my flat, even at work. It was starting to get me really pissed. It was always the same. "Hi, it's me . . ." She'd ask how I was, if I was missing her, say that she was missing me and could we meet up just for a friendly drink. It was ridiculous. I'd left my wife for her, wanted to set up home with her, I was besotted with her – and it wasn't until she told me she'd met someone else, that I really took a long hard look at what I'd done and it made me angry. I thought I was in love with her, I felt she needed me. She was a sort of combination of child and bitch. Fiona was having a hard time with the press and they were hounding me, then it all blew up in my face.'

'So the last time you spoke to her was . . . ?'

'The night before it happened,' he said quietly.

'Can you tell me where you were at the time Amanda was murdered?'

'I can tell you exactly. I was doing some voiceovers for my last movie in a studio in the West End the evening before. I didn't finish until quite late, then a few of us went to have a drink and I went home after that.'

'And the last time you spoke to her, she just said she wanted to meet up with you?'

'More or less, but she also said that she'd had a big row with her current director and hated him, and then she went on to tell me how many movie parts she'd been offered. I didn't say much bar the fact that as I was filming I doubted if I could see her and I suggested she call her new boyfriend.'

'Who was?'

'I dunno. I think she left me for Rupert Mitchell. Before that, she was with Colin O'Dell and so she could have easily been screwing someone else. I think she was high – well, she usually was when she called, but as I just said, I didn't really give her much time and I hung up.'

Anna opened her notebook.

'I wouldn't wish on any living soul what has happened, it's sick and it's terrible, but I can't even feel all that much as she put me through hell, and to be honest I started to thank God it was over between us.'

'Did she ever mention that she was writing a book?'

'A book?'

'Yes.'

He laughed. Anything was possible, but he doubted it. She wasn't the brightest of creatures and he suggested she might have been dyslexic, as he had had to help her read some of the scripts she had been offered.

'You went to visit her when she was in the Drury?'

Myers nodded and then smiled. 'Good heavens, you have done your homework. That was a long time ago, but yes, I did. She had been really ill, that's what she told me, and she was painfully thin and snorting cocaine like a hoover, so it was no surprise to me when she called from the clinic to say she was there on a detox programme.'

'Did you know she had been pregnant?'

He straightened and then stubbed his cigarette out.

'Wasn't mine. We always used protection and she never told me about any pregnancy.'

'She had had an abortion.'

Again, he shrugged.

'I didn't know anything about that. In fact, when I did see her at the Drury, she was in great spirits and said she was feeling really terrific.'

'Did you know that Colin O'Dell was also visiting her?'

'I suppose she was just tossing up which one of us she'd start up with. She did like anyone with a bit of fame and Colin had just done this big movie in Hollywood. At the time I didn't pay that much attention. It wasn't until she had left the Drury that we started being serious, or maybe I should say *I* started to be serious. To leave my kids and Fiona was a very emotional time for me.'

When Anna showed him the photograph of the gold crucifix, he was certain he had never seen Amanda wearing it.

'Did you ever go to her mews house?'

He ran his fingers through his hair again. 'Once, just after she'd moved in – but it was only for about fifteen minutes. I had an early call the following morning and by this time I didn't want to get into any further involvement with her.'

'Did you know she used crack cocaine?'

Myers nodded and lit another cigarette.

'Do you recall seeing a stuffed child's toy at her home, a rabbit?' Anna kept the questions coming.

He smiled. 'You mean her Bugs Bunny?'

'I haven't seen it, but all we know is there was usually a rabbit she slept with.'

'She certainly fucked like one,' he laughed.

'It's missing,' Anna said quietly and he straightened out.

'Sorry, that was unnecessary. She used it as a place to stash her drugs – it had a zipper up its back. I think she'd had it since she was a kid; it was worn and had lost most of its fuzz and it only had one glass eye left. She did keep it on her bed and she did sleep with it.'

'Do you know of anyone who would have had a reason to kill her?'

Myers let the smoke drift from his mouth and shook his head.

'I might have sounded really callous, but I went through hell for her. I arranged a flat for us. I had the press on my tail day and night, but I really believed she was special and in some freakish way she was. She was so beautiful and she was fun, and even with all her physical problems, like her anorexia, she was a ball of energy. The sex with her was what made me so overpowered by her, I suppose, and at the same time she was this needy child. She made you want to protect her, take care of her, but just as we were about to move in together she became this real tough bitch. It was as if she changed into a different person. I couldn't get through to her, and even when I said what I had done to be with her, she just laughed. She said she'd never asked me to leave Fiona . . . she suggested I go back and sort it out. Christ, sort it out! I'll tell you, I wanted to kill her, but instead I went to Romania to make a movie there and, thank Christ, got her out of my system.'

He stood up to indicate the meeting was over and Anna put away her notebook. As he opened the kitchen door, Fiona flew at him in such a fury that she almost knocked him off his feet.

'Got her out of your system, you fucking liar!'

She kicked out at him and he grabbed her wrists, pushing her away, at the same time apologising to Anna. But Fiona was hard to restrain. Anna felt it best she side-step them both and head for the front door. It would not be a good time to question Myers or his hysterical wife further. She had just reached her car when a flustered Myers hurried towards her.

'I'm sorry about that, but you can see it's obvious we won't be getting back together. Fiona really needs some therapy to deal with her anger.'

Anna gave a nod to him as if agreeing. Just as she was opening the car door, she turned to him.

, 'One more thing. Did you have a key to Amanda's new home?'

He stepped back, shaking his head.

'No, no, I did not. We'd already broken up by the time she moved there. I told you this.'

'Yes, of course.'

'I'll tell you who you should be talking to – the druggies she used to share a flat with. I wouldn't trust any one of them.'

Anna knew that a couple of officers were interviewing Amanda's ex-flatmates that morning. As she shut the car door, she mentioned that an officer would be contacting the Myerses to book an appointment for both him and Fiona to have their fingerprints taken and for him to agree to give a DNA Buccal swab.

'You must be joking.'

'I'm afraid not. It's just for elimination purposes.'

'Fine, whenever. I'll tell Fiona.'

He remained standing on the pavement, watching her drive off before he returned to the house and to his irate wife. What Anna couldn't witness was the continuation of the row between them, only this time Scott Myers didn't come off worse. He slapped Fiona so hard she crumpled into a heap, sobbing, then he dragged her up by her hair and punched her in the chest. All the while he was shouting at her, so angry his face was puce with rage.

'You get the house, you get enough money to live in luxury and I pay for everything, but you still have to make me look like a total bastard!'

Fiona pushed him away from her and rubbed her swollen cheek.

'Yeah, and I'll go on doing it. It's a pity she didn't stay

long enough to see what you are really like. Now get out, *get out and leave me alone.*'

Scott looked at her with disgust. 'That's all I want to do, Fiona, leave you well alone.'

She glared at him. 'And don't think you can waltz in and see the kids when you want. They don't want to see you and I'm not going to let them see you.'

Scott controlled his temper, picking up his jacket.

'I have visitation rights and I will see them when the court gives them to me. If you try and stop me, I'll cut off every penny.'

She followed him to the front door, still spoiling for a fight, but he brushed her aside.

'I'll call the press,' she threatened. 'I'll tell them you beat me up.'

He sighed, clenching his fists.

'I wouldn't do that. Remember we have a witness to your craziness, a bloody policewoman. Just go and get some help. I'll probably have to pay for that as well, but this can't go on, Fiona.'

He was standing on the front doorstep, shrugging on his jacket. Fiona Myers slammed the door so hard, the two glass panels shook and for a second he thought they'd shatter.

Returning to his car, Scott sat for a while trying to calm down. He was about to switch on the engine when he paused, removing the keys. Easing off the Yale front-door key to Amanda Delany's mews house, he kept it in the palm of his right hand as he started the engine and drove off. Shortly after, he lowered his driving window and tossed the key out into the road.

★

Anna decided to go straight to Heathrow, even though she would be early for her flight to Dublin. She put in a call to the station to check that Amanda's ex-flatmates were indeed being interviewed that morning. She was told that it was on Simon Dunn's call sheet and he was taking Barbara. She then put in a call to Andrea Lesser to ask if Amanda had been approached by publishers to write a book. The agent was not available. Anna asked her secretary to call her on her mobile as soon as she was free.

Passing one of the newspaper stands at the airport, Anna collected all the papers to see what further coverage the murder case had had, knowing they would be under pressure to put out a press release very soon. The question was: what could they release? They still had no suspect and as yet no motive for the murder, apart from the fact that Amanda was promiscuous and caused a lot of heartbreak and tension, as Anna had just witnessed. But would any of the people listed as being her lovers really have a motive to kill her, especially as the main threesome were all well-known actors with substantial careers? After the interview with Fiona and Scott Myers, Anna doubted that Myers was guilty, but she nevertheless resolved to check out his alibi.

The basement flat in Maida Vale was part of a large detached house which, judging by the rows of bells beside the front door, was divided up into flats and studio apartments. Simon and Barbara moved down the litter-strewn stairs outside to the basement and rang the doorbell there. It didn't work so Simon knocked hard and waited. It was another five minutes before there was any sound from inside the flat. Bolts were drawn back and the door was opened by a scruffy boy in bare feet, wearing dirty jeans. Simon showed his ID and they followed the kid down a dingy hallway into a room with sofas and chairs covered in garish orange fabric. The curtains were hanging off the rails and partly drawn. The carpet was stained and the room smelled of tobacco and hash; ashtrays were piled high with cigarette stubs, and dirty coffee mugs were propped around the room. It was hard to believe that Amanda had ever lived there.

The boy introduced himself as Dan Hutchins; he was a film extra who had been to drama school with Amanda, but hadn't completed the course. Amanda had had a room in the flat and they shared the rent with two other actresses, Felicity Turner and Jeannie Bale, who still lived there but were sleeping off a late night. Dan had not seen Amanda for at least two or three months.

'She would only drop in here when she left one of her blokes. She kept some stuff here, but then she got a new place of her own and so we'd not seen her.'

Simon let the boy talk on, asking only a few pertinent questions. Barbara asked if he had got along with Amanda and he replied that everyone always did. She was generous and often covered the whole rent when they ran out of cash. He also admitted to being on methadone, as he was a heroin addict.

Then Felicity wandered in, wrapping a dirty towelling dressing-gown around her skinny frame. She was very shaky and sat hunched on the sofa, clutching her knees. Her badly bitten fingernails were painted black. Her hair needed washing and her face, devoid of make-up, looked blotchy. She explained that she was an actress, but like Dan, mostly worked as an extra. She hadn't gone to drama school and had met Amanda through Dan. Felicity was nervous and constantly dragging at a lock of her hair. She too had an alibi for the time of the murder: she had stayed with her cousin in Esher because she was being booked into a rehab centre. She was addicted to crack cocaine, and desperate to clean her act up and get back to what she really wanted, to become a serious actress.

Simon listened impatiently as Barbara coaxed from the girl as much as she could. She concurred with Dan: as soon as Amanda had a new boyfriend, she'd move out. She often paid their rent for them and helped them with groceries. Amanda would give the girls her cast-off clothes and was always very generous because she knew how lucky she was and that all they needed was a break. Felicity said that Amanda was a really kind, lovely person whom they all loved, and she broke down crying as she said they would all miss her. Tapping his foot, Simon asked if they would wake the third occupant, Jeannie Bale.

Barbara looked up in surprise when Jeannie Bale entered. She was blonde, very pretty, with thick, wavy hair, and had on tight jeans and a skimpy top. She was wearing make-up and looked fresh compared to the other two. Seating herself pertly on the edge of the sofa, as if she was auditioning, she explained that she had been to drama school with Amanda.

'Are you working at the moment?' Simon was more interested in Jeannie than in the other two flatmates.

'I'm up for a big commercial,' she said, flicking her hair back.

'Where were you around the time of Amanda's murder?'

Barbara was making notes and watched the girl cross and recross her long legs.

'Well, I've been thinking about it because we were all so stunned by what has happened. We got really depressed and we couldn't stop crying because Amanda was such a good friend to us. She really tried to help us all and she was always seeing if we had enough money for the rent and food and stuff like that.'

'Did you know any of her friends?'

Jeannie did a strange twist of her body.

'No, she never brought them back here really, unless . . . well, I'll be honest, we sometimes scored gear for her, you know?'

'Gear?' Simon said briskly.

'Yeah, cocaine sometimes. I mean, we're not dealing or anything like that, but Dan knows a lot of people. Maybe I shouldn't be saying this, but Amanda liked the odd joint and stuff.'

'What about the heavier gear like heroin?'

'Oh no, she wouldn't touch that, none of us do that. It's just recreational gear like a bit of a spliff or coke.'

'How about crack cocaine?'

Jeannie licked her lips. 'I dunno, I've never had that. I have to keep fit for my work and I'm always going for auditions so I look after myself.'

'Amanda didn't?'

Jeannie looked at Barbara and did the same wriggling motion with her body.

'You mean her anorexia? Well, we knew she had that, 'cos when she did live here, she was always chucking up or starving herself, and sometimes watching her eat a teeny slice of toast used to drive us nuts. She'd scrape the butter off and then nibble at it for ages.'

'When was the last time you saw her?' Barbara asked gently.

Jeannie chewed at her lips. 'Be quite some time ago 'cos she bought a house and then was living with Rupert Mitchell on and off before she left here, or was it Scott Myers? I dunno which one, she used to have a lot of famous boyfriends.'

'But she didn't bring them back here?'

'No.' Jeannie stared at the floor and then sat up straight. 'I think she didn't want to, like, introduce us. Well, me more than the others.'

'Why you?'

Jeannie shrugged and then smiled.

'We were both up for the same part, in the film called *Rock Baby* that made her famous, and it came down to me and Amanda. I was tested first – in fact, my agent thought I'd got it, and then Amanda went up for it. I've never got to the bottom of how it happened because at that time she didn't have an agent. Anyway, next I hear she is being tested for the same role and . . .'

Jeannie gave a long sigh and then leaned forward, lifting her index finger and thumb half an inch apart.

'I was this close. It could have been me, but Amanda got the part and the rest is history. She never stopped working after that, and she got Andrea Lesser, the top agent, to look after her. I couldn't even get through the door at that agency.'

Barbara reflected how many years must have passed since the film test, yet the girl talked of it as if it had happened only a few weeks ago. She felt for the girl, who carefully avoided showing them any jealousy. There had to have been a great deal.

'Didn't that make it difficult living here with her,

especially since she had become so famous?' Simon probed.

'Not really. We made it up and she did always say how much better an actress I was than her. I just needed a break.' She looked away and then said in a strange voice, 'Sick, really. Now she's dead I may get it!'

Simon had heard enough. He asked if they could see Amanda's room and Jeannie sprang to her feet. She was using it now, but they could look around if they wanted.

It was thankfully cleaner than the sitting room, with just a single bed and an array of theatrical posters stuck all over the walls. Photographs of Jeannie were pinned up, and stacks of magazines and DVDs were crowded onto an overflowing bookcase next to a TV set and stereo.

'She left her things here for me, like some of her clothes and her shoes. We were the same size.' Jeannie opened a wardrobe and showed off the racks of clothes and shoes.

'When she died, where were you?' Simon asked as he looked over the room. She had not answered the question earlier.

Jeannie said she was working, doing a promo film for a German company. It was Barbara who spotted some of the so-called glamour photographs; it was probably more a small cheap porno film than any kind of promotional work. Jeannie moved quickly to cover them up, but by now they had both seen enough and just wanted to leave the squalid basement flat. Dan and Felicity were standing in the dingy hall. Barbara asked if they had ever seen Amanda wearing a gold crucifix and showed them the photograph. Neither could recall seeing it. When Simon asked about the stuffed rabbit, it was Dan who remembered that Amanda always had it on her pillow.

'It was sort of a kid's thing. I think her dad had given it to her and she took it everywhere, and when she left to stay with anyone else, she always had it with her.'

Felicity asked about the funeral arrangements. Barbara said that they had not had confirmation of when her body would be released for burial, but was sure that when her parents arranged the funeral, they would let them all know.

'I doubt it,' said Jeannie. 'Amanda's parents are stuck-up pigs and won't let us anywhere near.'

'Did you meet them?' Simon asked.

'No, they never came to the flat, but we knew how much Amanda detested them.'

'It's odd then that she would be so fond of her childhood toy,' Barbara said, but got no response from any of them.

Dan hovered behind them as they opened the front door.

'Who do you think killed her?' he asked.

'I wish we knew.'

'I wouldn't put it past one of those paparazzi bastards. They made her life hell, wouldn't leave her alone.'

'Maybe that was because she was forever tipping them off, telling them where she was going and who she was shagging,' Jeannie said dismissively.

'They were scaring the life out of her. She told me she was gonna take them to court and accuse them of harassment. She said she'd talked to a lawyer about it and she was gonna get compensation.'

'She wouldn't do that and you know it. She needed them to boost her career and she was such a liar. As if!' Jeannie shook her head and gave Simon a smile.

'If there is anything else, anything you recall that might be of interest, will you call me on this number?' Simon passed out his card.

'Did she leave a will?' Felicity asked.

Dan glanced at her, and she flushed.

'I just thought it might have something for us in it,' she mumbled.

'I'm sure if there is, you will be contacted. You'll also be contacted by an officer as we will need to process your fingerprints for elimination purposes.'

'Did you have a key to her mews place?' Simon asked them, glad for the fresh air by the open door.

Dan shook his head. 'No, like we didn't see her that much as soon as she bought it, and she wouldn't have wanted us there. She was beginning to really hit the big time.'

Felicity started to cry and Dan put his arm around her skinny shoulders. Jeannie seemed to be trying to keep her distance from the other two; she gave a sweet smile when Simon thanked them all for being so helpful.

As they returned to their car, Barbara reflected how sad the three kids were, in their basement full of broken dreams. It was odd to think that Amanda, earning huge sums of money, had kept on living there in such squalor.

'It wasn't that bad. Christ, you should have seen my place when I was a student.' Simon bleeped open his Saab.

But as they drove off, Barbara could still hear Jeannie's voice, see her leaning forward and gesturing with her finger and thumb to demonstrate how close she had come to stardom. Barbara doubted it would ever happen for her now, even with her so-called rival Amanda Delany no longer alive.

Colin O'Dell's film unit was on the outskirts of Dublin, working out of a massive disused brick factory. He had the largest Winnebago trailer, with his name on a cardboard notice pinned to the side. Anna knocked and Colin swung open the door, cigarette dangling from his lips. He was very handsome, with blond hair styled in a crew cut. He was also much shorter than Anna had thought he would be. Gesturing for her to sit on one of the comfortable, thickly cushioned sofas built around the luxurious main sitting room, he then offered her a drink.

'I'd like some water,' she replied.

'Right. Still or sparkling?' he asked in a soft Irish accent. Although she asked for still, he unscrewed a cap of sparkling, handing it to her. He then almost jumped onto the sofa opposite and put his feet up on the coffee-table between them.

'I'm not wanted for a couple of scenes so we have some time, but if they need me I'll have to spring into action, and oh ...!' He touched his face, which was covered in bruises and scratchmarks. 'Make-up ... I've just been beaten up by another prisoner, so don't think for a second it's real.'

'It's very authentic,' Anna said, taking out her note-book.

'You should see the set, it's fucking brilliant. Even the cell doors have the right weight to them. A few of the guys were getting really agitated when they were locked in.' He laughed mischievously. 'I think some of the extras have done time!'

He had a lovely warm smile; his blue eyes twinkled.

He had such an easy manner to him that Anna immediately felt relaxed.

'You must know why I'm here,' she said.

He took his feet off the table and bent forward, resting
his elbows on his knees.

'Christ! Yes, of course I do. If there's anything I can
think of that'll be of help, I'm ready . . . I loved her, you
know. She was crackers, but she was a sweetheart and a
good actress, but that face . . . I used to look at her when
she was sleeping. Sometimes it took my breath away.
Every feature was perfect, you know?'

'When was the last time you saw her?'

'Got to be maybe four weeks. I've been here for three
and I saw her briefly at the Silver Star, a club in the West
End. Maybe a tad before that, say five weeks ago.'

As Anna went through the usual jargon about needing to know his whereabouts at the time of Amanda's
murder, he gave a wide-armed gesture to his trailer.

'I was here. We were doing some night filming, so I
slept in the bed in there rather than schlep back to my
hotel. To be honest, I'd had a few beers with some of the
crew, so they sort of poured me into bed.'

Anna smiled. He put his feet onto the coffee-table
again.

'I couldn't believe it when I read about it, really
knocked me for six.'

'Did you ever hear her talk of anyone who had a
grudge against her or was following her, anyone making
threats?'

He shook his head. 'No. I mean, she was such a
little doll – who would want to harm her? We'd split
up. I suppose you know we were an item. Well, according to the press, we were about to get married, which

was bullshit. We had a real sexy romp, but that was it.'

'You paid a visit to her when she was in the Drury Clinic?'

He looked surprised. 'I did, yes. We've all been in there at one time or another but, yes, I went in to see her. She was a real party animal and with the booze and the coke she was just exhausted. She still looked terrific and we had a good laugh; she even asked if I'd brought in some charlie.'

'Did you accompany Scott Myers?'

'To rehab? No, I bloody didn't. He was after me like a demented dog. She left him for me – well, I think they had a sort of similar scene going on, but silly sod took it further and left his wife and kids. Amanda told me she had never wanted it to get that serious.'

'Were you aware that she had had an abortion?'

'No, that's the first I've heard of it.'

'Could the child have been yours?'

'Christ, no. I'd ask old Scott, considering the number of kids he's fathered. No way was it mine, and besides I'm a good Catholic and against abortion.'

'Did she ever mention to you that she was pregnant?'

'No. She was a bit naughty, you know, and even if she had told me, which she didn't, I would have asked for a DNA test.'

Anna continued to ask if, when he went to the Drury, he had had any indication how sick she was, physically and mentally. He hadn't. As far as he knew, she was probably there for a detox.

'She was anorexic,' Anna pointed out.

'I'm not surprised. She was skinny, but then so are most of the young starlets and models. I knew she had fake tits, you could tell.' He smiled. Anna was getting irritated by his total lack of feeling for the dead Amanda.

'What was done to her?' he asked suddenly.

'She was attacked and died from multiple stab wounds.'

'Jesus, she didn't deserve that!'

'You said you were Catholic – do you wear a crucifix?'

O'Dell raised a hand to his neck and then gestured as if it was a stupid question.

When Anna showed him the little gold crucifix, he didn't recall ever seeing Amanda wearing it. He did remember the stuffed rabbit and recalled her carrying it around with her, and even bringing it to his flat when she stayed over.

'It was a horrible, bald, smelly little thing with floppy ears. She used to keep her stash of skunk in it. Liked a joint, did Amanda.' For the first time, he seemed genuinely moved. 'She told me it had always been with her since she was a child and that she couldn't sleep without it.' Then he grinned. 'I think it was the skunk she couldn't sleep without, she was so often out of her head.'

'It's missing.'

He leaned forward. 'What?'

'The rabbit is missing from her home.'

There seemed nothing to add and he glanced at his watch.

'Did you have a front-door key to her house?'

He stood up. Answered, 'No. What do you think, I went there and nicked her rabbit?'

'Mr O'Dell, if my queries amuse you it is not my intention. I am investigating Miss Delany's murder, and it's a very serious crime.'

O'Dell cocked his head to one side and gave a grimace, as if to apologise for his joke.

'I only ever went there once. She showed me around – she was very proud of it and, to be honest, I was surprised. You know, I was taken aback that she'd got it together. It was a very nice place, classy and worth a bit.' He dug his hands into the pockets of his jeans.

'She was no one's fool, our Amanda. I mean, she appeared to be doped up and needy, but at the same time she was pretty astute. She gave her agent a right runaround, went for the big money, not that she'd spend it; she was quite a tightwad. I don't ever remember her paying for a single meal and she liked to eat out at the best places.'

Anna gave a brittle smile. 'Not that she'd eat much.'

'She'd tuck in and chuck it all up later, but she had hollow legs and she could drink me under the table.' O'Dell ruffled his hair, then put his hands back into his pockets. 'You asked me if she was scared of someone or anything. Well, I think she was terrified of being alone, or . . . more frightened of sleeping. That sounds crazy, but she would take speed or anything to keep going and not go to bed.'

'Did you ever meet anyone from the flat she shared?'

He had never been there, he told her, never really wanted to from what Scott had told him – how her flatmates were real losers and dope heads.

'Why do you think she kept on living there even though she had money?'

'Like I said, she was a tightwad and, to be honest, she bedhopped and was always moving in with whoever took her fancy.'

'How long did she live with you?'

O'Dell walked to the door and looked out, before turning back.

'Maybe six months off and on, because we both had to work on location. Like I said before, it was an easy sex thing we had, never serious.'

'Did she leave you for Rupert Mitchell?'

'You've certainly been reading up on me or reading the tabloids,' O'Dell said, and the easy smile was gone. 'I introduced her to him. We were clubbing and he was there with his wife. We had a few drinks and then left. But at some point during the night, she must have got his number because he called me to ask if it was OK for him to see her, as they might be working together. I said, "Be my guest . . ."'

'Didn't that make you angry?'

He clearly didn't like the question; for a fleeting moment he was unable to hide the look of anger on his face.

'What I didn't like was having the fucking press all over me like a rash. It didn't make much difference to me that she was screwing him, because soon after I went to France for a shoot and met Daniella Duprès, a French actress . . .'

Anna put her notebook away and stood up. She thanked him for his time and he swung open the trailer door.

'Can you find your way back, only I should get over to make-up and tidy up my bruises?'

'I'm sure I can manage, and when it is convenient we'll need to take your fingerprints for elimination purposes.'

'OK.'

By the time Anna was on her way back to Dublin airport, Colin O'Dell was sitting in the make-up chair with a robe around his shoulders. The make-up artist checked one side of his face and added a touch of foundation, but she didn't try to touch up the other side as it was still painful. They had joked about how lucky he was that the scenes being shot required him to have bruises after a fist-fight with one of the actors playing a prisoner. O'Dell explained that he'd had too much to drink and had fallen on the steps up to his trailer. There was also a deep scratch around his neck, but his collar hid most of it so they didn't bother to cover it with make-up.

When he was through, he remained sitting in the chair chatting up the girl assigned to him. He'd already dated one of them and had quite a reputation round the set. He made no mention of being interviewed by the police, but word had already got out that a detective had been in his trailer questioning him about Amanda Delany.

'Was she Irish?' the make-up artist asked.

'Who?'

'The girl that was murdered. Wasn't her surname Delany?'

'Yeah, but she wasn't Irish. Can you just add a bit more mascara?'

'I can't do much more, it'll look like make-up,' she said, unscrewing the mascara tube.

'I'll be the judge of that,' O'Dell snapped. Then: 'She was crazy enough to be,' he added softly.

Chapter Six

On the return flight to London, Anna sat thumbing through her notebook. The last interview would be with Rupert Mitchell, who had agreed to see her at his home in Kingston at six-thirty that evening. Two movie stars down and she had not reckoned either actor to be a suspect, nor had she found them nearly as attractive as the girls at the station made out. She was not impressed by them and was glad that she had never become involved with men like that. They had used Amanda as nothing but a sex object and she could detect no real feelings in either man for her.

Anna became preoccupied with trying to piece together Amanda Delany's last few weeks alive. From all the interviews she and Simon had completed, from the film-unit crew to the actors, she still had no indication of a motive and did not believe they had, as yet, a suspect. Were they focusing on the wrong place? Was there some extraneous element they had not uncovered? The fact that they had no hard evidence to implicate anyone was disconcerting. Again she thought about the two movie star ex-boyfriends and leafed through her notebook, checking her jottings and remarks. The parents were, in many ways, as lacking in genuine grief as Colin O'Dell and Scott Myers. Although the latter's marital situation was in turmoil, with jealousy and anger mixed with betrayal, she did not think it was enough for someone like Fiona to have committed a murder. The more Anna thought about how abused their victim had been, the more she couldn't help thinking about her own situation.

Anna had felt betrayed by James Langton, yet she had loved him and he still had a strong hold over her emotions. Working with him on their last case had proved very difficult. Perhaps though, he had been right to challenge her over her affair with Damien as being unprofessional, even though she didn't like to think so. She had been foolish with her almost-relationship with Pete Jenkins; yet her personal life in comparison to Amanda's seemed very unadventurous. Anna closed her eyes, leaning back in her seat. Langton had been controlling, though never abusive, but because he could not or would not give her the commitment she wanted, it had ended. He was now happily ensconced, she believed, in a relationship with his ex-wife, and he had a stepdaughter Kitty and a young baby son Tommy.

Anna remembered how she had felt when she went into his office and had seen his family photographs on his desk. Was she the one at fault? Did she still hanker to be with him again? She sighed. Whenever she thought of him, she had mixed feelings of anger and sadness. With him being such a high-ranking officer now, she told herself, there was no possible way they could get back together. She also doubted that he had any interest in ever being with her again, even more so after the way he had lectured her about Damien. Yet part of her was really thinking that perhaps he had been the love of her life, and she would never feel that way about anyone again. Unlike Fiona, she had no real bitterness towards him – well, not now anyway. She felt, she came to realise, a deep sadness because Langton was someone special, he was also someone that she admired, and then it all twisted. She had been the one to instigate the break, she had been the one to acknowledge they couldn't live together; and now, after all this time, she wondered if it was because he would never commit to her and deep down she had always known it.

As Anna walked through customs at Heathrow to collect her car, it felt as if she had been on automatic pilot. It was later than she had expected and she knew that she would have to get a move on if she was to be able to get to Kingston to meet with Rupert Mitchell at the time arranged. She called the incident room to check in with Barbara to see if there had been any major developments. Barbara recapped the meeting with Amanda's flatmates; according to Simon, she said, none could be suspected of Amanda's murder and none had a motive; in fact, far from it.

'Why is that?' Anna asked.

'They're junkies and she used to pay their rent and buy their groceries – so why kill her?'

'Thanks, Barbara. Anything else I should know about?'

'Oh yeah, Simon has been checking into the victim's finances. The mews house is valued at over three million, and there's a heavy wad in her bank account at Coutts. She's worth over four million.'

'*What?*'

'Yeah. Joan and I wish we were in the film business! And she was only twenty-four years old. I've got a mortgage round my neck and two credit-card debts.

Apparently there's more due as her agent was talking to Simon, but we don't have the numbers yet.'

'What about a will?'

'Nothing specific yet. Simon's checking it out, and her life insurance policy.'

Anna thanked her and cut off the call. It appeared that Simon, for all her irritation with him, was keeping himself busy, but it was yet another inconclusive result, apart from the fact that their victim was worth millions. Anna wondered if Amanda's wealth could be a motive, but without knowledge of a will or who the beneficiaries were, it was yet another loose end. She was still waiting for Andrea Lesser to return her call.

Rupert Mitchell was much more the movie-actor type that Anna was expecting. He was tall, over six feet, slim, his hair a dark chestnut and worn long enough for it to be scraped back into a ponytail. He was exceptionally handsome. His dark eyes were heavy-lidded and he had a slight hooked nose which seemed to accentuate his eyes and thick lips. He glided into the elegant sitting room where Anna was waiting, lifting his hand in an apologetic gesture, and saying, 'I'm sorry. I expected you earlier and we have dinner guests at eight.'

'This shouldn't take long.' Anna felt shy. Unlike Myers and O'Dell, Mitchell had more weight to him and an aura about him that was unnerving.

'Do you want a drink?' he asked, sitting down in a leather chair. It was obvious that he had no intention of fetching her one.

'No, thank you. I'll keep this as short as possible if you have guests. It's just a preliminary query.'

'About Amanda Delany, obviously,' he said quietly.

'Yes. I need to know when you last saw her and what you were doing around the time she was murdered.'

Anna listened as he told her he was at home with his wife and had not seen Amanda socially for weeks prior to her death, although they were filming together.

'Did you ever sense that she was frightened or threatened by anyone?'

'No, I didn't.'

Anna found it difficult to question him. His eyes bore into her with an unbelievably steady gaze. She took out the photograph of the crucifix and asked if he had ever seen Amanda wearing it. Mitchell studied it for a while and then shook his head.

'Do you ever recall seeing a fluffy toy rabbit?'

'Seeing it where?' he said abruptly.

Anna explained that Amanda used to sleep with it and he gave a nonchalant shrug of his shoulders.

'I don't remember ever seeing it.'

'Did you ever go to her mews house?'

'No. I knew she had moved into a new place, but I didn't visit.'

'Did you ever go to the flat where she previously lived?'

'No.'

There was a pause and he gestured to the door.

'My wife is here if you wish to ask her about that evening?'

Anna explained that, before she spoke to his wife, she wanted to know more about his relationship with Amanda.

'My relationship?'

'Yes.'

He shifted his weight on the chair and then got up to

open a drinks cabinet. He poured himself a whisky, a large one.

'I wouldn't actually describe it as a relationship – an act of madness, perhaps – but for a while I did see her on an intimate basis.'

He returned to the chair and carefully placed the glass down on a side table, adding, 'Embarrassing, yes!'

He began to pick up the glass and then put it down, moving it like a chesspiece.

'My wife and I had been having a difficult time, very strained. We had not discussed the possibility of a divorce, far from it, but . . .'

He picked up his glass and drained it.

'She is desperate to start a family and we have been through IVF treatment but sadly she didn't fall pregnant. Anyway, it caused some grief as you can imagine and, to be honest, I found it very difficult. I should have been more supportive, but instead I was the exact opposite.'

Anna listened as Mitchell described meeting Amanda. They had exchanged phone numbers at a nightclub. He had begun the affair after taking her out to dinner, even though he knew it was foolish. It was a wretched few weeks as the press got to know about it and he was hounded at home. He left his wife and rented a flat on Baker Street. Amanda had moved in with him for a while and then, when he realised his stupidity, he returned to his wife. Amanda had already bought her new house and was waiting for it to be refurbished. He thought she had gone back to live with her friends, but they did not see each other again until they started filming *Gaslight* together.

'It's incongruous, if that's the right word, but I play the husband in the film who attempts to frighten her to death and bring on her madness. By this time, Amanda was very cool with me, but that helped with our scenes together.' He finished his second whisky, then pointedly looked at the clock on the mantelpiece.

'Were you aware that Amanda had been pregnant?'

Mitchell looked up, unable to hide his surprise. 'Pregnant?'

'Yes, she had an abortion.'

'Good God no, I didn't know. Well, she never mentioned it to me. When was this?'

Anna explained that the termination probably took place before Amanda went into the Drury Clinic, so it would have been some time before she started filming *Gaslight*. He seemed relieved.

'Well, that lets me off the paternity suit. Sorry, that was crass. I didn't see or start seeing her until about six weeks before we started shooting the movie and it was all over before filming began.'

He fetched a refill and stood with his back to Anna, as he replaced the bottle in the cabinet.

'You didn't have a key to her mews house?'

'Certainly not. As I said, it was rather cool between us and she did her best to ignore me, so there is no way she would have given me her front-door key.'

Hearing a light knock on the door, Mitchell quickly rose to his feet thinking it was his wife, but it was their maid.

'Madam says that the guests will be here shortly and she needs you to open the wines.'

Anna stood up and asked if she could speak with Mrs Mitchell for a moment.

'Is that necessary?'

'Yes. I'll be very diplomatic, but I do need her to

verify that you were at home on the night of the murder.'

'He was.' Mrs Mitchell walked into the room. She was tall and blonde with her hair swept up into a chignon and was wearing a chic black cocktail dress, with high stilettos.

She shook Anna's hand. 'I'm Helen. If you could just let my husband open some wine to breathe, he can rejoin you.'

'That won't be necessary,' Anna said, and thanked him for his time.

Helen took his seat, crossing her slender legs.

'This is all rather wretched, isn't it?' she said softly when Mitchell had left the room.

'Yes. So your husband was with you the night Miss Delany was murdered?'

'We were here together. I am certain of it because he was very tired as they were night filming and he had had a difficult time with her. I had a meal prepared for him on a tray and he ate, had a few glasses of wine and came to bed. It was very late, around five in the morning. His driver brought him home at about four, I think.'

Anna jotted down the times in her notebook, then asked: 'Did you ever meet Miss Delany?'

'No.'

'It was rather public knowledge that she and your husband were seeing each other . . .'

Helen leaned forward. 'It was an awful time, quite dreadful because the press were outside and calling all the time. To be frank, I felt that Amanda had probably tipped them off. They seemed to know whenever Rupert came home and were hovering outside.'

'He moved out, didn't he?'

'Yes, he took a flat on Baker Street, but all his clothes and belongings were still here. In fact, he only packed a suitcase.' She fingered a diamond solitaire earring, twisting it.

'It must have been very distressing for you.'

'It was.'

'You never met Miss Delany at the film unit?'

'No.'

'Did you ever go to her mews house?'

Helen sighed, shaking her head. 'This is rather silly, isn't it? I have said I never met Miss Delany and so therefore I would never have been to her mews house. Let me add that I had no desire to meet or even have a conversation with her. She made my life hell when I really needed to be calm and the stress almost gave me a nervous breakdown.'

'I'm sorry to ask you these questions, but I am trying to find out as much as I can about Amanda Delany's background,' Anna explained.

'I'm afraid I can't help you at all. I did not know her, I never met her, and all I do know about her is what I have read in the newspapers.'

'Thank you for your time.' Anna stood up, but Helen remained seated.

'This is very difficult. My husband is starring in her last movie and he will obviously be subjected to a lot of press enquiries. We've arranged to go and stay on my father's yacht in the South of France. I hope we will be allowed to go, I really need to rest.'

'I don't see any reason why you shouldn't be allowed to go, but we will need Mr Mitchell to give us his finger-prints, so before you go, I'll get an officer to contact you and arrange a time.'

Helen stood up. She seemed to tower above Anna.

'Why do you want his fingerprints?' she asked.

'Just for elimination purposes.'

'From her house?'

'Yes.'

'But he never went there so it's a waste of time.'

Anna picked up her briefcase.

'Nevertheless, due to his previous relationship with Miss Delany, we will require his prints.'

Anna stepped back as Helen swept past her to open the door. Mitchell was in the hall.

'You have to give your fingerprints,' his wife told him.

'Really? What on earth for?'

Anna was feeling tense.

'It's just, as I explained to your wife, for elimination purposes. Even though you claim you had never been to her mews house, we are also testing personal items . . .'

'I told you that I hadn't.' His voice was sharp.

'I'm sorry, but an officer will make an appointment,' Anna said as firmly as she could, then headed for the front door. 'Just one more thing. Did Amanda ever mention to you that she was writing a book?'

Mitchell shook his head, muttering, 'That's preposterous. What kind of book?'

'Perhaps an autobiography?'

'She was only bloody twenty-four years old, for God's sake. What on earth would *she* be writing a book about?'

Anna gave him a frosty smile. 'Perhaps naming the father of the child she aborted!'

He stepped away from her as if he had been slapped, but had the good manners to hurry and open the front door. Anna left, sure that Rupert Mitchell had been lying and *had* been a visitor to the mews. But she would have to prove it.

She was about to drive away when she saw a Silver Cloud Rolls-Royce draw up and park in the Mitchells' driveway. An elderly couple made their way to the front door as Anna jotted down the numberplate. She was certain they were Helen Mitchell's parents, but she had to be sure, for no other reason than wanting to confirm that Helen Mitchell came from a very wealthy family. Perhaps that was what drew her husband home.

Anna didn't get into the station until well after eight that evening, and again, only the night staff were working. She was just packing up to go home when her mobile rang. It was Andrea Lesser.

'Thank you for getting back to me,' Anna said sweetly, even though Miss Lesser had certainly taken her time in doing so.

'I talked to Detective Dunn earlier today.' Miss Lesser could not recall Amanda ever wearing a gold crucifix and was unable to identify it. She did remember the stuffed rabbit, but again was unable to add very much, apart from the fact that she knew it was something Amanda was almost obsessive about.

'Thank you. There is something else. I wanted to ask you if Amanda had been offered a publishing deal.'

'I'm sorry?'

'Was she writing a book?'

'A book?'

'Yes.'

'Er, I'm not really taking this in. Are you asking me if Amanda was going to publish something?'

'Yes, maybe an autobiography, something like that.'

There was a pause and Miss Lesser gave a long sigh.

'You know,' she said, 'we had so many offers of work for Amanda, but I don't recall her mentioning any kind of publishing proposal. I am sure she wouldn't have been able to write one herself, but then nowadays these young actresses get ghost writers. But really I doubt it.'

'We have found some chapters on her laptop,' Anna lied.

'I don't understand. Where did you say you got these chapters from?'

Anna said that they had removed a laptop from Amanda's study and had opened files that appeared to show the start of a book.

Miss Lesser paused. 'Perhaps I should have made a few things clear. We had not been getting along. Basically, I was becoming very tired of Amanda's unprofessionalism and also of having to do so much for her, things that are not really an agent's job. By this, I mean handling the refurbishing of her mews house.'

'Yes?'

'Well, we had words. My main worry was the bad publicity she was generating by all her sexual exploits; it wasn't exactly geared to helping her career.'

'I would have thought the publicity would have been very useful,' Anna responded.

'Then you would be wrong. In case you are not aware, there is not only a morality clause in every film contract but also a requirement to go through a stiff medical test. With the news coverage of her drug-taking and affairs, it wasn't looking good for Amanda, especially with regard to work offers from the United States. Which is why, if you recall, I told you we had been having words about her permissive lifestyle and she had assured me she was behaving herself. The director on her last film really put pressure on me to assure him that Amanda wouldn't misbehave . . .'

'So you weren't aware of any kind of offer for her to write a book.'

'I've already told you, I was not privy to this information.'

'Would there be anyone else I should talk to?'

Again there was a long pause from Miss Lesser. Eventually she told Anna that it was a possibility that Amanda Delany was about to switch agents.

'She was going to leave your agency?'

'Let's say she threatened to do so. We never had a legal conversation about it, but she could have been approached by another agency.'

'Was she contracted to your agency?'

'Well, not on paper, more of a verbal contract. We don't contract our artists, it's not worth it. Basically, if they are not happy with our representation, they can leave.'

'Was Amanda going to leave your agency?' Anna asked.

'We had discussed it, but then I heard nothing more so I very much doubt she intended to do anything as drastic. You see we had managed her career from her first movie break.'

Anna was late getting home yet again, having arranged to meet Andrea Lesser at her office the next morning. She was determined to finish going through the files from Amanda's laptop. She went back to her first file and scrolled through the pages until she came to the heading *Chapter One*, followed by what looked like a block of writing over two pages. It seemed that there had been something written or deleted before the first paragraph:

. . . so many different schools and because my father was stationed in Germany for a while I was sent to boarding school. It was in Cardiff, a small private school with two dormitories, the beds close together. I hated it from the moment I arrived. The nuns were very strict and I had never been away from my mother before. I cried myself to sleep and had to hide beneath the bedcovers so as not to be heard. There was a prefect called Natalie who was supposed to take me under her wing, being a new girl. She was very beautiful. I think she may have been smoking dope because she had a strange musty smell to her clothes and hair.

Anna continued reading about how the school was run and Amanda's growing relationship with Natalie. Amanda seemed to have been below average in her lessons and was constantly sent to receive extra tuition from the senior girls, especially Natalie, who helped her with her spelling and arithmetic. Then Anna came across a paragraph which seemed to have no connection to the last.

He used to play polo and was always making me learn riding, and the smell of the stables made me sick. Everyone was always so nasty because I wouldn't muck out and help brush the ponies.

Anna flipped over a few more disconnected pages that contained similar jottings about events in her childhood. Then on one page one line was repeated over and over.

I hate him. I hate him. I hate him. I hate him.

It wasn't until midway through the file that there was a heading at the top of the page – *AUDITIONS* – with details about her entrance audition for RADA. Amanda described how nervous she had been as she had only done elocution lessons at school.

The day the envelope came through the letterbox was so important because I knew if I had been accepted into RADA he would have to believe that I was serious about wanting to be an actress. My father was for the first time in my life encouraging and took me and Mother out to lunch at the Ritz. He ordered champagne and I was allowed to celebrate as they both loved to go to the theatre.

Anna continued to read about how Amanda had been taken shopping by her mother and bought outfits for her to wear as she began her RADA training. There were pages of remarks about being left alone in London as her parents had returned to Germany, and jumbled stories about the other students and her tutors, and how she had been cast in various plays.

Anna doubted if any of the material would have been of interest to a publisher. It was not well-written and some of it was repetitive. She was yawning, no longer paying that much attention as she scrolled down page after page. There were a few more chapter headings, but the content was mostly about rehearsals and hoping to be cast as Juliet in *Romeo and Juliet*. There was a lengthy section about another student called Belinda who was a nymphomaniac, according to Amanda; she had had sex with every male student in her group *and* two of the tutors. She went on to describe her own first sexual experience with a student and how she had made a point of choosing the most experienced boy in her group.

Belinda said I had to lose my virginity. I didn't tell her that it had been taken a long time ago, I just went along with playing the naive and innocent. He ejaculated all over my stomach, it was horrible and messy and he was so full of himself. I couldn't wait for him to go but he stayed the night, all night, and tried to do it again in the morning. I wouldn't let him and he got really nasty, calling me a prickteaser.

In brackets there was a question: should she insert his real name, as he was now very well-known. Perhaps this was proof that Amanda had been approached to write her memoirs, otherwise why put in the query? As Anna continued wading through more childish descriptions of her sexual conquests, there were dots and dashes instead of names. Then there was a section about moving in with one of the students, and a longer, angry section about having a meeting with her father.

He went crazy about my spending too much money and said that he would cut off my allowance. He was furious that I'd left the two guard dogs he'd put to watch me and made me promise to use my credit card for rent and food only. Of course I did a lot of crying and he said that he and Mother would come to the finals at the Vanbrugh Theatre. I didn't tell him that I'd not been given a decent part ... I didn't tell him that I was not going back for the next term anyway. I'd had enough and if he'd known, he'd have dragged me home to Germany. As soon as he'd left, me and Belinda went to Harrods and did a bit of shoplifting, then we used my chequebook to buy loads of gear. Next thing, Mother turns up in a terrible state as he'd found out I'd quit, the bastard had checked up on me at the Academy and he was going apeshit. She said he was withdrawing my allowance and wanted my credit card back and I told her that they were both well out of touch if they thought I'd been able to live on the pittance he'd organised. Of course she didn't believe me, didn't believe that I had to take money off guys for sex in order to pay my way.

Anna sighed, unsure if what she was reading was true or not, though it had certainly got more interesting. Amanda went on to describe how hard it was finding work as an actress. With little experience and no agent, she had been doing the rounds of open auditions and failing to get any work, bar a couple of days as an extra. However, the girl she shared a flat with, an actress called Jeannie Bale, was getting a lot of work and also had a good agent. Jeannie was thrilled about the possibility of starring in a movie about a young waitress who fell in love with a rock star. Amanda described how she had gone into her flatmate's room and found the script, read it and seen the address of where they were still holding auditions. By this time Jeannie had been asked to do a film test for the role. Amanda had cheeked her way into the auditions and the director had been blown away by her and suggested she be tested for the same role as Jeannie. She never told Jeannie; instead she had called a top theatrical agent, Andrea Lesser, asking if they could meet as she had been asked to do a film test for *Rock Baby*.

Anna sat up, intrigued by Amanda's deviousness.

I'd got the part, and I couldn't really take it in. I was to star in a movie and Miss Lesser agreed to represent me. I was over the moon and as it turned out, it was the break every actress dreams of and it proved to be the kick-start of my career. It was a huge success for a small independent film and . . .

Anna was eager to turn the page and discover how her flatmate had taken the news of her so-called friend robbing her of the role she had coveted. Disappointingly, the next page virtually repeated everything she had just read and then came another poem.

They are doing in my head
I can't sleep in my bed
I just want to make it end
want to stop the persecution
the ever-present hounding why
won't they LEAVE ME ALONE!
They are doing in my brain
I think I am going insane
and feel them watching me
chasing me and . . . there is
no one helping me but drugs.

Anna closed the file. Surely no publisher would want such drivel! She must ask Simon if he'd got any feedback from Jeannie Bale; could she be a possible suspect? It was imperative the team got a thorough line of dates regarding Amanda's time at the Drury, her abortion, her various love affairs and also her career, because she now knew that her first big break had been on the movie *Rock Baby*. They still had no motive, no strong suspect, and the case would soon start growing very cold.

Chapter Seven

Anna had forgotten to switch on her alarm and she woke up late, with a headache and no time for breakfast. She couldn't find any aspirin so took two of the Sudafed tablets she kept in her bathroom cabinet for when she had a cold. Driving to the station, she felt light-headed and realised that she had eaten nothing substantial for days.

The team were already gathered and Mathews had been taking a briefing. He acknowledged Anna as she hurried to join everyone, still wearing her coat.

'We'll be doing a press conference this morning. Telling the media what progress we've made is going to be difficult because right now we have nothing to give them. I've asked the press office to get us some time on one of the crime shows, as I think we should ask the public about her missing cuddly toy . . .'

Simon stood up and gestured to the board. He felt that maybe they should hold that back. It was, after all, the most significant thing missing. Mathews was dismissive: they needed all the help they could get. Then his mobile rang and he suggested they carry on the briefing without him.

'Probably a golfing date,' Simon muttered. 'Anyone

have anything to add to the void?' He looked around and Anna moved forward.

'I think we need a list of the exact dates Amanda had the affairs with the actors. We've got a pretty good idea from the newspapers, but we must get organised. This also applies to her career, her finances and . . .'

She elaborated on how important it was that they had a clear picture of their victim's life. She asked Joan to double-check that the files she had contained all the material that had been taken off the laptop. Nothing she had read, she explained, really provided anything useful: there were mostly poems and what looked like sections about her childhood and student days at RADA. Anna still made no mention of her thoughts on a publishing deal; by now she had doubts.

A while later, Simon joined her in her office and flipped open the file on her desk.

'I read some of it, it's rubbish. I couldn't keep on read-ing the rest. Did you find anything in it?' he asked Anna.

'Not really. There was only one odd thing. When she was writing about having a scene with one of the students at drama school, she didn't write down his name, but put in brackets something about whether she should include the names of whoever she'd been having sex with because they could be famous by now.'

'What do you mean?'

'I wondered if she was writing an autobiography and someone didn't like the idea. It could be a motive.'

'Bit of a long shot.'

'That's as maybe, but I did have a conversation with Andrea Lesser last night and she inferred that Amanda was toying with the idea of switching agents, but nothing was confirmed.'

'You think that could be a motive?'

'I don't know, but if we had a sense of exactly how much of a valued client she was, it might be. They wouldn't want to lose her.'

'Yeah, but surely not enough to fucking kill her. Either way that's the client gone.'

'Yes, I know that,' Anna snapped. Simon was annoying her. 'By the way . . .'

When she asked him about Jeannie Bale, he confirmed that he believed all the flatmates had alibis for the time of the murder. He doubted if any one of them would kill off the golden goose, as their victim more than likely kept them living there rent-free.

'Jeannie Bale said she was this close,' he held up his finger and thumb, 'to getting a part in the movie that made Amanda a star. The lead role should have been hers, but it seems our victim pipped her to the post.'

'Was she upset about it?'

'Too damned right, I'd say so. It was a long time ago, mind you, and if she'd really wanted to kill her she'd have done it when it went down, not wait all these years.'

Anna rubbed her head; it was really throbbing by now.

'Well, I didn't get much from any of the ex-boyfriends,' she said. 'They all had alibis, and denied having anything to do with the baby or the abortion. On the contrary, they almost treated it as a joke.'

'We should dig into that,' Simon said as he moved towards the door.

'I'm going to visit Andrea Lesser and question her further.' Anna picked up her bag, ready to go up to the canteen.

'There was something one of her flatmates said, but I need to check it out.' Simon swung her office door back and forth with his foot. 'The junkie, Dan Hutchins . . .'

Before he could say any more, Mathews appeared.

'We got anything from the CCTV footage at the mews?'

'No, sir.'

'Christ, if they agree to us doing the TV show, we've got bugger all to put out.'

'They can use footage of her movies to fill in the time slot,' Simon grinned.

'You must be joking. Getting permission to show any clips is gonna be a runaround and could cost an arm and a leg.' Mathews glanced at Anna and then back to Simon. 'Which one of you can I put forward to do the TV interview?'

Simon put his hands up. 'Not me, please. Anna will be much better.' He was out of the office fast as Mathews looked at Anna.

'You'll do it?'

'Maybe we should wait.'

'For what? We need all the help we can get, so as soon as I hear we've got a slot I'll let you know.'

'Yes, sir.'

Her stomach churned. She had only ever done one live television interview and she had been so nervous she could hardly string two words together. It wouldn't be easy either, as they truly had so little; the network would want a lot more. Even doing a reconstruction would be of no interest, as all they knew was that Amanda Delany had been driven home from the film unit and then discovered dead in bed later that day. No one had come forward with any sighting of her leaving the mews after she was dropped off or returning to it.

★

By the time Anna had downed two cups of awful canteen coffee and eaten some toast and honey, Simon had left the station. She had still not mentioned to anyone that she wanted to talk to Dilys Summers who had worked at the Drury, but she did inform the office manager out of courtesy that she was going to talk to Andrea Lesser.

Joan was busy piecing together details of Amanda's film career from newspapers and press releases, and running checks with the Internet Movie Database. Anna asked her to check too when Amanda had entered the Drury and when she left, when she purchased the mews house and the date she had moved in.

'We also have to find out if she kept a diary, so see if you can get any information on that. We've not had any luck so far.'

'Yes, Ma'am.'

Barbara was working on the details of Amanda's finances and had already asked Andrea Lesser to supply them with details of how much she had been paid.

'She was rather prickly and said it was none of our business.'

'I'll have a talk to her this morning,' Anna replied.

'Do we know about a funeral?' Barbara went on. 'Should I contact the coroner to see when the body is being released to the family?'

'Yes, do that. Also, see if the forensic team have come up with anything more for us.'

'Yes, Ma'am.'

The pair watched Anna return to her office and pick up her coat and briefcase.

'She's barking up the wrong tree there with that one.' Barbara pointed at Jeannie Bale's name up on the board.

'I felt sorry for her. She almost got the movie that made Amanda's career.'

'It must be really tough, you know, trying to get work as an actress. There's a lot of them out there and in some ways it all boils down to luck.' Joan was settling back into her job.

'How much work do you think she had done on her face?' Barbara continued, looking at the row of glamorous photographs of Amanda Delany.

'I've no idea, but she was only young, so I doubt if she'd had much. Now I've got to crack on, matey.'

Joan sighed as she looked at the pictures of their victim from the casebook file. The girl really did have the most perfect features, yet there was such a fragile quality to her beauty. The lab photographs of her skeleton-thin torso, taken at the murder site and after the autopsy, were in horrendous contrast. The autopsy photographs showed the multiple stab wounds to her chest and throat. The breast implants were lopsided, one of them having been slashed by the knife; her tiny frame was pitiful. Her long legs had no muscle tone, her knees were knobbly and her feet had bunions from wearing too high and too tight shoes.

Joan shut the file. It was hard to believe that the pictures were of a girl of only twenty-four years of age, and even harder to believe that she had been a movie star and the envy of thousands of teenagers.

Anna parked her Mini in a large car park in Poland Street and made her way to Andrea Lesser's agency. To her annoyance, the agent had left for an emergency appointment. She was due to return in the early afternoon.

A plump dark-haired girl appeared and introduced herself as Amy, Andrea Lesser's secretary.

'I'm sorry Andrea's not here.' Amy was apologetic. 'She was expecting you but we had a big problem over at the BBC, as they've switched schedules and a client of ours is filming elsewhere. Can I make another appointment?'

'When do you expect her back?'

'She has a meeting here at one, but she should be free around two.'

'I'll come back this afternoon, but before I go, could I ask you something? Do you have any details regarding a possible publishing deal with Amanda Delany?'

Amy shrugged and shook her head. 'No, sorry.'

Anna persisted. 'Do you know if she was considering leaving the agency?'

'No, and I would doubt it because Andrea took great care of her as she was such an important client. I know Amanda had been approached. They always are . . .'

'I'm sorry?'

'When you are as famous as Amanda Delany and with a big earning capacity, there's always another agent sniffing around.'

'Do you have any names of agents who might have tried to poach Amanda?'

The young girl hesitated.

'Let me get you a copy of *Spotlight*. That's where all the agents are listed.' She disappeared through a frosted-glass partition behind the reception desk and came back with the book of contacts. 'Here, you can take this away as it's last year's.'

'Thank you very much. Please inform Miss Lesser that

I will be back here at two. If it's inconvenient, she has my mobile number.'

Anna was loath to move her car as she'd paid for three expensive hours of parking, so she put in a call to Dilys Summers to see if it was convenient for her to meet earlier than arranged. Miss Summers agreed so Anna took a taxi to Paddington.

Dilys Summers lived in a highrise council estate not far from the Ladbroke Grove flyover. It was neat and clean, just as Anna remembered it. The woman had a pot of tea and biscuits ready and waiting.

'This is not to do with your relationship with Lord Halesbury,' Anna said immediately, to put her at ease. 'Do you mind me calling you Dilys?'

'Not at all. It's good to see you again. Please sit down and help yourself to tea.'

'Thank you.'

'You want to ask me about working at the Drury?'

'Specifically about Amanda Delany. You were working there when she was admitted?'

'Yes, I was. I left shortly afterwards to work for His Lordship, as I didn't really enjoy my time there.' Dilys paused. 'I don't need to go into what happened afterwards, as you know more than anyone about that.'

She looked across at Anna and said rather shakily, 'I miss him dreadfully, but I've found part-time work at a local clinic for the elderly, so at least I'm working and keeping my mind off what might have been.'

Anna sipped her tea and ate two custard creams before taking out her notebook.

'What can you tell me about Amanda Delany?' she asked.

'Well, I can tell you as much as I knew or was privy to whilst I was working there. It's a very well-run clinic with high-profile clients and we do have to sign a confidentiality contract.'

'I'm sure you do, but Miss Delany is dead.'

'All those headlines in the papers, it's shocking. She was such a beautiful girl, troubled but still so gorgeous and very sweet.'

Anna nodded, toying with the idea of taking another biscuit, then decided against it.

'Take me through when you first met her.'

'Amanda wasn't assigned to me; she was obviously in a private room. We all knew who it was in there as there had been a lot of paparazzi outside. I think someone eventually called the police to move them on.'

'I was on night duty, so she had maybe been resident for just twenty-four hours, I know it wasn't long. Anyway, the buzzer was in the staff bay, which just had a small desk and chair; the private rooms were along a corridor. It was late, about one-fifteen in the morning . . .' The other nurse on duty was tending to another patient, so Dilys had gone to see Amanda. She was looking like a child, sitting up in bed in a frilly nightdress and clutching a soft toy. When Anna asked if it was a rabbit, Dilys couldn't recall.

'Her hair was dishevelled and her face was pale, with deep dark circles around her eyes. I knew she had refused to eat any supper and I asked her what the problem was.'

Amanda had said she was hungry and wanted chicken noodle soup. Dilys made her a cup of tea. She noticed how dreadfully thin Amanda was, how shaky her skinny arms were, sticking out from the negligée. Dilys also noticed her badly bitten fingernails as she lifted the cup to her lips with both hands.

147

'You know, it was hard for me to believe that the child was a film star. She looked sickly and was so nervous, saying she couldn't sleep.'

The following night, Dilys had brought in two packets of chicken noodle soup.

'She was so thankful, saying that she couldn't eat anything. From her charts I saw that she had been given special meals, but there were notes beside them saying that she had refused them.'

So for the next couple of nights Dilys had taken in soup on a tray and added thin slices of toast. She also noticed that the nurse assigned to her care had administered sleeping tablets.

'"They don't work", Amanda said to me.'

When it came to Dilys's last night on duty, she told Amanda that she had brought in packets of soup for the other staff to continue to make up for her.

'She was so grateful and asked me to sit beside her. I sat with her for quite a while and she held onto my hand. I watched her doze off and I eased my hand away. Then, just as I was walking out, she started to scream.'

'Was she still asleep?'

'Yes, that was what was odd. She screamed so loudly. It was a horrible wretched scream, like one long howl, but she was definitely asleep. I remained at the door, and just as I was about to leave, it happened again. This time though, Amanda had sat up and looked terrified. I talked to her and after a while she calmed down, but I wasn't sure if she was awake or asleep, or if she was even hearing herself. She eventually lay back and hugged her soft toy to her chest, so I left. The next morning when my shift was over, I stopped in to see her.'

When Dilys had told her that she had screamed in her sleep, Amanda said nothing.

'"You must have been having a bad dream,"' I said to her, and she looked at me with those beautiful wide eyes. "You gave me quite a scare."'

'"It never goes away," she told me. "That's why I hate to go to sleep, because that's what I used to do when I was a child, pretend it wasn't happening, and I'd bite down on my blanket, but I wanted to scream then. Now it sometimes wakes me, but I didn't realise everybody could hear. I thought it was still inside me . . ."'

'Did she ever explain to you what happened to her as a child?' Anna queried.

'No, it's not really my job to ask about those kinds of things, they have psychiatrists for that. I just felt very sorry for her, but I did mention it to one or other of the nurses and they said they'd heard her a few times. It was really a horrible sound, as if someone was in terrible pain.'

Dilys had no contact with Amanda for over two weeks as she was transferred to a different section. It was only when she went back onto night duty that she saw her again.

'She was like a different girl, very bright and her skin had cleared up. She had acne when I'd first seen her and now she looked very fresh and you could sort of understand why she was an actress. One of the other staff told me they'd weaned her off drugs and that was why she was looking so much better – and she'd also been eating.'

Anna accepted a second cup of tea. 'Did you ever hear of any visitors?' she asked.

'Yes, I did. A few days later, I heard that Amanda had had a visitor that afternoon – a very famous actor.'

149

'Do you recall his name?'

'He was Irish.'

'Was it Colin O'Dell?'

Dilys nodded hesitantly. She did remember another famous actor being mentioned – and this time she was sure of his name: Scott Myers. After he left, Amanda had been very troubled.

Dilys paused and started to stack the cups and saucers onto a tray.

'I shouldn't really be repeating this, you know,' she said guiltily.

'You've said nothing that could create any kind of a problem for you,' Anna reassured her.

'It was after that actor O'Dell came in that she went a bit crazy – very difficult to handle. She was rude to all the staff, and I have to say, I have never heard language like it before or since. She could swear like a trooper. They had to drag her back to her room as she had wanted to make phone calls; she was shouting that she wanted her mobile phone. One of the nurses asked me if I could go and talk to her, you know, seeing as how I'd got along with her.'

But Amanda had been very rude to Dilys too, and insisted that she was being held at the clinic against her will. When Dilys had offered her noodle soup, she had screamed at her to leave her alone.

'I'd taken in a bowl of the soup and she threw it at the wall. I told her that she should be ashamed of herself. I had to get a bucket and mop to clean it up and she sat on the bed, cross-legged, looking like a little devil, and then she started laughing as if it was all one big joke.'

'It must have been very unpleasant for you,' Anna prompted.

'Yes, it was. She kept on asking me if I knew who she was and I said to her that it didn't matter who she was. I think these visitors had brought her in some champagne and God knows what else, but she behaved as if she was in a hotel and throwing a party, uncontrollable. Then I heard she had left, not that they could do anything to stop her going, she was there of her own free will and paying for it . . .'

'By "these visitors" – do you mean Colin O'Dell and Scott Myers?'

'I suppose so. Remember, I never actually saw who came to see her, but I know there was a third actor because one of the nurses had got his autograph. I'd never heard of him but she said he was famous.'

'Rupert Mitchell?'

Dilys was unsure.

'The paparazzi were outside like hornets, they'd be there for hours on end. I don't think it was just for Amanda Delany – we had a few other celebrities there as well, but when she left us they apparently went crazy and chased her car down the road.'

'Do you know if her parents ever visited?'

Dilys took a moment to think. Amanda's father might have been with her when she was admitted, but she didn't know for sure.

Anna left Dilys Summers and caught a taxi back into Soho. She went into Marks & Spencer on Oxford Street and did a big grocery shop, carrying the goods back to her car, by which time she hoped Andrea Lesser had returned to the agency. However, it was another fifteen minutes before Amy said her boss could see her.

Anna was taken aback by the size of the ultra–modern

office, its windows overlooking Wardour Street. Andrea Lesser had numerous signed pictures of her clients on the walls but they were dominated by a photograph of Amanda Delany, wearing a white wig with a diamond tiara and a low-cut gown and large diamond necklace. The film title was in big bold red letters: *The Heiress*.

Andrea Lesser lifted her hand towards Anna as she entered.

'Sit down, please. Sorry if I kept you waiting, but I'm afraid I can't give you too long as I have another meeting.'

'I just need to get a few things straightened out,' Anna said quickly. 'Basically, I need a timeframe from when Miss Delany first starred in *Rock Baby*, and her subsequent films.'

'What on earth for?'

'I am still attempting to get a complete picture of Miss Delany's work and of the people she had worked with. It's what we call "full victim profile".'

'Really?' Andrea Lesser opened a drawer and sifted through several files before she opened one and took out a neatly typed sheet of paper. 'This is her CV. We would send this to whoever wanted to know her experience; you'll see we've attached names of her co-stars, directors and producers. There is also a website that you can access. This is used by companies, as well as her CV, to check up on whether or not, in Amanda's case, she was fit and well. If necessary they could contact people direct to get a more personal background.'

'Is this usual?'

'I'm sorry?'

'Do you do this with every actor you represent?'

'Yes, when the casting directors like to know what

152

work the actors have already done and if there is anything coming out that could clash with their project, it's
quite usual . . . we update it all the time. But we do not
include any figures. That is always negotiable, especially
the more popular an artist is.'

'I would like to have details of Miss Delany's salary.'

'No, that is private. I'm sure you can gain access to
her bank accounts, but we would not agree to giving
you access to her fees from here. The fee for her last film
I can tell you though, was over three million.'

'Good heavens!'

'Miss Delany was really one of the biggest up-and-
coming British stars, with plenty of work on offer here
and in the States.'

Anna asked if Amanda's career had been jeopardised
by the bad press about her drug-taking.

'Not really. We were able to say she had a clean slate
after her stay at the Drury.'

'But that was a while back.'

'I'm well aware of that, but since then Amanda, to
my knowledge, was free of drugs. Sometimes she drank
too much champagne, but she was really trying to get
herself in shape for a meeting we were setting up in
LA.'

'That would be after *Gaslight* was completed?'

'Exactly. The tragedy is, I've seen some of the rushes
of that film and she's exceptionally good.'

When Anna asked Andrea Lesser to explain how she
had come to represent Amanda, she got a terse reply.
All she would admit to was that one of the secretaries in
the office had taken a phone call from a young actress,
without representation, who had been offered a film test
for the new independent film *Rock Baby*.

'It's quite rare that this happens, but I liked the look of her and the rest is history.'

'She got the part?'

'She got the part.'

'Did you know that her flatmate was also up for the same role?'

'No. Look, I'm finding this rather tedious and I don't quite understand what on earth this has to do with the present day. It was all a very long time ago.'

'We're looking into every possible motive for her death.'

'I don't see how something that happened years ago could now surface as a motive!'

'Did you know that Amanda had once been raped?'

Andrea Lesser pushed her chair back. 'No.'

'Were you aware how sick, both mentally and physically, Miss Delany was?'

'Absolutely not. I don't know where you got this information from, but for her to start shooting *Gaslight* we had to agree to a full medical test. If Amanda had not been given a clean slate, they wouldn't have insured her for the role.'

'Could you give me the name of the doctor who did that test?'

The woman stood up, saying, 'You can obtain it from the production company; now, I really feel I have given you more than enough of my time.'

Anna wasn't shifting an inch. She remained seated.

'I'd just like you to read something taken from a file we removed from Miss Delany's laptop.'

She passed a sheet of paper over to Andrea Lesser, who sat down and picked up her reading glasses. She scanned the page slowly, then eventually looked up.

'What is it I am supposed to find? This all reads rather like a teenager's tacky memoir.'

'That may be so, but if you look at the paragraph that I've highlighted – the one asking if she should use someone's real name . . .'

'What about it?'

'Did you know she was writing her memoirs, tacky as they may be? It seems to me that she is asking someone to give her the legal go-ahead to put a name into that paragraph.'

'It wasn't me,' Andrea Lesser replied. 'I had no notion she was writing anything. In fact, I couldn't be more surprised.' She passed the page back to Anna, then carefully removed her reading glasses, putting them back into their case.

'You know, Detective Travis, you did bring this up on the telephone and I assured you then that I had never discussed this with Amanda, so I could not be privy to whether or not she had a publishing deal. All I can tell you is that I would be very surprised.'

'And you're as certain that she did not intend leaving you as her agent?'

'Why on earth are we going over this again! I represented that poor girl since her first film. Any tension between us was only temporary – just one of those things.'

'I suspect it would be very worrying if she had left you. Three million for her last film and probably substantially more for her next – that must be a very lucrative percentage for your agency.'

'It is, although we have many more, far better paid stars, both here and in America.'

Andrea Lesser stood up again and this time Anna really

had no option but to stand as well, collecting her brief-case and notebook. She thanked the agent for agreeing to give her the time and left.

Anna was about to drive out of the car park when Simon called her.

'Why didn't you tell me you were going to interview Miss Lesser?' he said. 'I've just tried to speak to her and her assistant told me you'd just been in.'

Anna explained that she would fill him in on her return to the station. She then asked him to contact the producer of *Gaslight* for the name of the doctor who had given Amanda Delany a medical test.

'Christ, what do you want to know about that for?'

'Four years ago she was sick as a dog, being weaned off hard drugs, anorexic and, according to the psychiatrist from the Drury, in no fit state to work. She'd had an abortion and—'

Simon interrupted her. 'For fuck's sake, Anna, you just said that was four years ago. I had my appendix out about then and I'm fitter than ever. This is wasting time.'

'Fine, leave it with me then,' she snapped.

'No, no, I'll bloody contact him, but you know, we have to get something to crack this case open or we are looking at it, as Mathews loves to say, flatlining.'

'That is, Simon, exactly what I am trying to find – a motive – be it four or more years ago; something from then could have triggered off the murder.'

Anna shut off her mobile and closed her eyes. She was certain now that the scream Amanda said had woken her had been her own. Something in Amanda's past, possibly when she was a child – had she been abused by her father? – had forced her to bite on a blanket and scream from inside, a silent scream that in her nightmares became vocal.

As Anna nosed her Mini into Poland Street, and then turned right into Great Marlborough Street, she saw Andrea Lesser hurrying past. She was almost able to keep up with the woman as the pavements and roads were so congested.

Anna watched her pushing past people as she crossed over Carnaby Street and stopped at the entrance to Liberty. There, by the flowerseller, she was joined by a man, smartly dressed, like a City banker, in a dark navy overcoat and suit. Anna saw him take Andrea Lesser by the elbow; she looked as if she was crying. Anna was able to take one clear shot of them both with her mobile phone as the couple entered the store. She then had no option but to carry on driving towards the traffic-lights and across Regent Street.

Anna didn't know why that encounter interested her so much. Was this the meeting Andrea Lesser had mentioned? Had something that Anna had inadvertently dropped into their conversation upset her? She might not have recognised the gentleman with Miss Lesser, but she had a strong suspicion that something was being covered up.

Chapter Eight

Anna knew something was wrong when she returned to the station. The incident room was quiet apart from the telephones ringing incessantly. Everyone was working without the usual banter and chit chat. As she went into her office, she could see across the corridor Simon talking on his phone; DCI Mathews's door was closed and the blinds were down.

Anna began to type up the report on her meeting with Andrea Lesser. Once again she decided that the information from Dilys Summers was not enough to warrant adding to the report. She was about to call Barbara in to check through the contacts book Andrea Lesser's assistant had given her, then she hesitated, unsure as to how exactly she would go about finding out if another agent had approached Amanda Delany. There were hundreds of theatrical and film agents, but which of those listed would have the clout to even be considered by their victim to handle her career?

She placed a call into *Spotlight*, the theatrical information company, and asked if someone could give her details of who the top agents were. She was told that the fastest way to get that information would be to go online, as *Spotlight* now had an internet service, but she would be charged to use it. Anna was becoming impatient.

'What if I were to list some famous actors – could you tell me who represents them, to save time?'

When the girl at the other end asked who she wished to know about, Anna was stuck. Never having been interested in either the theatre or film, she couldn't really think of any names that would apply, apart from the three actors she had interviewed. She cut off the call. It had taken fifteen minutes to get no result and during that time she had seen a trolley with coffee and teapots, and plates of sandwiches, being wheeled into the incident room. Then came a request over the Tannoy for all personnel to gather in the incident room immediately. Anna watched Simon hurry out of his office, adjusting his tie.

The incident room was filling up with civilian staff and uniformed officers, as well as detectives.

'Do you want to sit in the front?' Joan asked, and Anna answered her with another question.

'What's going on?'

Before Joan could reply, Mathews's office door opened and he stood aside. DCS James Langton walked out ahead of him. Anna flushed as she sat down; she'd known he would be making an appearance at some point, but wished she'd had advance warning. She gave him a covert glance as he walked to the front. He was tanned and he looked fit and more handsome than she had ever seen him look before. He was, as always, exceptionally well-dressed in an immaculate dark pin-striped suit, white shirt and dark navy, Met Police Murder Squad tie. There was a steely strength to him as he gave a slow, studied glance around the gathered officers. The room fell silent as everyone sat waiting expectantly.

'For those of you who don't know me, I am Detective Chief Superintendent James Langton. I have worked with a few of you previously.' He gave a brief expressionless nod to Anna, Barbara and Joan, then turned towards the incident board.

'We have confirmation that your victim is to be buried next Tuesday. We will require a show of the top level, and I want some plainclothes there as well, as I strongly believe that our killer will be present.'

He suggested they carry cameras as unobtrusively as possible, and had already arranged two CCTV cameras to cover all the mourners entering and exiting the church. No doubt the paparazzi would be there in full force. 'One of the *Crime Night* specials has agreed to feature the case,' he went on, 'and hopefully that will be beneficial. I say hopefully, as to date we have virtually nothing. It appears to me that the investigation is slipshod and without much incentive or imagination. This is a front-page case, the victim a film actress, and yet there has been little or no forthcoming evidence. We need to have a focused direction and clear lines of enquiry.'

They sat, poker-faced, especially DCI Mathews who was over to one side. Langton continued in a quiet, controlled voice. They had no murder weapon and, more importantly, no viable suspect.

'Right now, I want to go over with each member of the team exactly where they are in the enquiry. I want to start with those of you who have been assigned to check on CCTV footage. A CCTV camera must have been in operation in the vicinity of the victim's mews. This is a smart luxury mews, with only one entrance and exit, via the archway leading into the courtyard. You have properties side by side to the value of three or four million, with even more expensive properties backing onto both sides of the mews.'

Anna kept her eyes down. It was unusual to criticise an investigation in front of the entire team; in this case, it publicly demeaned DCI Mathews. But then James Langton was never one to play by the rules. It was only a matter of time before he tore a strip off her and Simon.

The two officers who had been checking on the CCTV cameras were satisfied that they had been diligent. They had photographs of the mews entrance and there were clearly no cameras. They had made enquiries in and around the road beyond the mews and had been given only one camera position. They had checked the footage for the time of the murder, but had gleaned little apart from a list of the vehicles passing before and after the time of Amanda's death. All the vehicle owners had been traced and none appeared to have any connection to the dead girl. Not one had driven into the mews and all of them, after being questioned, had a good reason for being in the location. Anna was watching Langton closely. She knew that hooded look of old; he appeared to be paying attention, often nodding in agreement, a notebook open in front of him. He glanced up when the officers finished their explanation.

'What is the number of the victim's house?'

'Fourteen, sir.'

'What are the numbers of the houses at the dead end of the courtyard?'

There was a blank glance between the officers.

'OK, what is the number of the house that your victim's garden backs onto?'

'I'm not sure, sir,' said one.

Langton nodded. He then described how a mews property would once have been part of the large house it backed onto, that at one time, all the houses in the mews would have been stables or garage facilities. Anna was wondering where he was going with this, when Langton gestured for Joan to bring him a large drawing board with a black marker pen. He drew a cul-de-sac, with eight houses on either side, and two houses at the end, blocking it off. The dwellings on the left were numbered 1 to 8, and on the right, 11 to 18, with numbers 9 and 10 knocked into one big property at the closed end of the mews. He then wrote the word MEWS at the top in thick letters. Each small mews house was connected, apart from number 16, which was detached.

Langton pointed to numbers nine and ten. 'This double property at the end of the mews is valued at six million pounds, credit crunch or not.' He loosened his tie. 'Did anyone interview the occupants?'

'No, sir. We were told that the owners were away on holiday in Antigua.'

'Really?'

'Yes, sir, and—'

Langton held up his hand.

'You also,' he interrupted, 'received the same response, "nobody at home", from the house that backs onto your victim's property – correct?'

'Yes, sir, but their neighbour said they would be back at the end of this week. They didn't have any security cameras.'

'Bollocks, fucking rubbish! Are you trying to tell me that substantial properties like these do not have any kind of surveillance cameras? What kind of crap statement is that!'

'We did make enquiries.'

'Did you – either one of you – find out if there was a housekeeper in residence? Or if someone was checking the properties for the owners? Did you make that a priority? Didn't you think to check whether or not the premises have a police registered response alarm? Think about it, think about the value of those houses. If the owners had any sense of security, they would have the police connection – which would mean they would have two nominated key-holders and must assign one if they are away. If you had checked this out, you might get access to the premises via the key-holder, to seize CCTV footage if there is any.'

'We were intending to return when the owners came back.'

The young officer was red-faced. Langton picked up the black marker and drew the number 14 on Amanda's house, then he took a red pen and made a huge cross and kept going over and over it until it almost obscured the entire block of number fourteen.

'You have a young girl stabbed to death here and you are fucking waiting until these owners return home? Haven't you heard of a telephone? Because I am telling you now that numbers nine and ten do, in fact, have very high-tech surveillance cameras. They have four in all; two are focused on the entrance of the mews, and a further two are actually on the rear sides of the property. They wanted to make sure they were bloody well-covered back and front, one of the reasons being . . .'

Again, he picked up the black marker pen and then drew over the small narrow path.

'There is a gate from the property behind number sixteen; it's been there since the houses were built in 1856. The people living in the main house also own the mews house and use it for their domestics to live in – very luxurious it may sound, but they are exceptionally wealthy people. This gate opens at the rear of their garden – it's well-hidden with bushes – and the path runs from their back garden along to the back garden of their mews courtyard.'

He gave a cold glance around the incident room.

'But it doesn't stop there. It narrows and continues right out into the mews courtyard. This means it's possible that someone used it that night and didn't enter the main mews courtyard but climbed over the walls to get into the victim's garden. If the gate is hidden by bushes it should be very easy to ascertain if there has been any recent disturbance.'

He sighed and shrugged his shoulders. 'Check it out.'

Simon gestured to Langton.

'There was no sign of a break-in either to the rear or the front of our victim's house,' he said.

Langton glared at him.

'From memory I read that on the previous night, your victim was woken by a scream. Did she go and check her rear patio garden? Maybe if she did, she left the French windows open, didn't lock them behind her, so that's a possible entry. Have we any further details on this scream she heard? Any reports made about an attack or burglary?'

'No, sir. All the doors and windows were checked when the body was discovered. We're going on the assumption that Miss Delany knew her killer, who may have had a key to her front door. During the refurbishing there would have been a lot of people with access to her house.'

'Really? Have you questioned all the builders and decorators then?'

'Not as yet, we're still tracing them all, but the designer has given us the details of everyone he worked with. He also had a key, which he returned to Miss Delany's agent.'

'Who made the keys?'

'Pardon?'

Langton said impatiently, 'When the victim moved in, I presume she had new locks fitted. Do we know how many keys were cut?'

'No, we have no details of that.'

'Check it out. Next!' He turned to the board again, pointing. 'No weapon. All we know is that it was a six- or seven-inch knife, double-bladed, non-serrated edges with some kind of a hilt, correct?'

He turned back to the room.

'I want a fingertip search, better late than never, of that entire area of number sixteen. That's the path, the gate, the garden.'

No one dared mention that there had been a very thorough search; it was starting to feel very uncomfortable in the incident room.

'Motive,' Langton snapped, and then looked at everyone. 'Well? Anyone come up with anything tangible?'

There was an awkward silence as Langton started to pace up and down. A number of officers brought up the details regarding Amanda's pregnancy and the abortion and he shook his head.

'How many bloody years ago was that, for chrissakes? It doesn't work for me, and I tell you what else doesn't –

the possibility that one of her former flatmates, knocked out of playing in a movie *eight* years ago, was still envious enough to want to commit a murder. None of this is to my mind relevant. It has to be something that belongs in the present – a crazed fan is a possibility – something happening right now that flips someone into a fury that results in . . . how many stab wounds?'

Anna made a note: to date they had not checked any of Amanda's fanmail.

'Listen up. The fact that we have a sick, anorexic girl, the fact that she was snorting cocaine and smoking crack cocaine are not motives – character knowledge, yes – but more important is how many of the famous movie stars she was fucking would also have a motive. Why? They'd already been trashed in the papers. This is a murder enquiry, it's not a burglary that went wrong. Somebody wanted that girl dead, and somebody had to have a reason. Now we can look at some variations on that . . .'

Langton pulled up a chair and sat down, then counted on his fingers.

'One, who else was she screwing? Somebody new, not the guys you've already questioned and eliminated. Two, drug dealers. Get onto who she scored from and find out if she owed a dealer or was about to—'

Simon interrupted him. 'She usually scored from her flatmate, ex-heroin addict Dan Hutchins, and it was never that much.'

'Pull him in and scare the pants off him.'

Langton ticked another finger.

'Money. Turns out she's got quite a nice stash of cash. Who benefits? Check them out, the beneficiaries . . .'

Anna hesitated, waiting for the right moment to speak

up as Langton continued, his manner becoming more and more aggressive.

'I don't like the parents. Dig more on them. I know you'd been enjoying yourselves visiting the movie set, hobnobbing with the extras and the actors, but look into the finances. What happens with the movie backers, now she is dead? She was a little golden goose for a lot of people. That could maybe be a motive, or . . .'

Langton took a deep breath. 'We've got a random killer, a crazy fan maybe, but as you've not unearthed anything about a maniac stalker, I'm not sure that is the route to go down. Last but not least, we have two items of interest.

'The stuffed toy! Why is it missing? Could be a simple explanation or we might get something from the TV interviews. Maybe she did leave the mews that morning, maybe she did go to see someone, and maybe that person returned home with her and killed her. Also interesting is the crucifix and chain we found. Was it torn from her neck or from the killer's . . . and where is the rest of the chain?'

He stood up and put his hands on his hips. 'So come on, anyone have any ideas?'

Anna stood up and he gave a lopsided smile.

'Detective Travis.'

She coughed and her cheeks were flushed.

'I haven't checked it all out, and most of it I came by today, so it does need confirmation.'

'Well, spill it out, for chrissakes.'

'It's possible that Amanda was about to change agents. I'm unsure what this actually gives us and it's not that much of a motive. Either way now she's dead, it's maybe not going to benefit her present agent or whoever else she might have been going to be represented by, but it does muddy the waters.'

'Is that it?'

'We took her laptop from the house.'

The team were swivelling around in their chairs to look at her as Anna nervously explained that after having read the contents from a file, she thought it was possible that Amanda Delany was writing her memoirs.

Langton pointed at her. 'That's a motive. Little crack-head about to spill the beans. Get it verified, and another thing . . .' He paused and rubbed his head. 'Money. We need to get access to her accounts and her accountant, so bring him in. Do we know who it is?'

They had not even gone down that route yet.

'Right, now we move on two possible motives. If Amanda was leaving her agent it might throw up a little bit of skulduggery on her finances, and if, as Detective Travis thinks is possible, she was writing a memoir, this could also be a motive if someone didn't want her spilling out something that would be damaging. But,' he shook his finger, 'constantly keep in your minds: people could get angry and afraid, if this little screwball was about to publish something derogatory about them, but to plan a murder and knife her is a long way off from either of the emotions I just mentioned. Hatred kills, and fear can only be measured by how important a person they are. If we were to discover she had been screwing the Prime Minister or one of his cronies, for example . . .' Langton laughed humourlessly.

'You hire someone to kill, and this could be a contract murder. An even stronger possibility is that the murder could have been staged to make it appear different from the real reason she was killed.'

It was another half-hour before Langton wound up the meeting. He had gone through all the evidence to date in detail but also underlined that, to him, the most important items were information brought to them by Anna Travis.

They finished off the refreshments as Langton made a point of talking to each and every one of them. Anna had returned to her office to patch up her report quickly on the publishing possibility. She looked up to see him laughing with Barbara and Joan; the latter was obviously very enamoured. She saw him enter Simon's office and have a lengthy conversation with him. Then he headed in her direction. She was typing furiously, sensing he was about to walk in, and when he did so she looked up, acting surprised.

'OK, this is what I have suggested to Mathews. I want Dunn out and I am bringing in Barolli and Lewis.'

Anna was taken aback.

'I need him on something else,' Langton said by way of explanation. He drew up the only extra chair and leaned his elbows on her desk. 'If they come on board, don't keep any information you get. Pass it out, understand me?'

'Yes, of course.'

'It's imperative, Anna, that you learn this. I mean, how long have you known about this book?'

'I don't know. It was just reading some of the material from Amanda's laptop last night.'

'And the agent thing?'

'I'd only just got back from a meeting with Andrea Lesser when you arrived.'

'Really?'

'Yes.'

'I know you too well, Anna,' he said softly.

'Maybe you do, but I didn't think it was ready for the team to take on board until I was sure.'

He stared hard at her and she refused to look away. He suddenly stood up.

'OK, you should really move on it now.'

'Yes. I was going to ask DCI Mathews if we could get onto this *Spotlight* website to check out theatrical agents. Reason I haven't done it already is because it costs.'

Langton paused at her door, cocking his head to one side.

'Do it. You should be running rings around this crowd. I know how hard you worked on that trial with Lord Whatsit.'

'Lord Halesbury.'

'Yeah, you had a good result, proving me right. You've got quite a career ahead of you, and I know you get along with Lewis and Barolli. They're both good detectives; I miss working alongside them.' He paused and smiled. 'And you.'

'Thank you.'

'I mean it.'

'Thanks again.'

'How's life treating you?'

'Fine. You look well.'

'Yeah, I took a long break, feel rested. I needed it.'

She hesitated. 'How's the family?'

He gave a soft laugh. 'We're doing fine. My son has grown a lot, and my step-daughter . . .'

'Kitty?'

'Yeah, only now she likes to be called Catherine. She's grown into a lovely girl.'

171

'Good.'

He looked at Anna before giving her that smile of his that always touched a chord inside her.

'I'll be around until I think we've got this case under wraps, so I'll no doubt see you again.'

She smiled and could think of nothing else to say to him as he walked out. She watched him sitting with Simon and then she saw him go into Mathews's office. It was another fifteen minutes before he came out and looked over to her window, giving her a small salute as he left the station.

Anna sighed. As always he'd taken everyone by storm, his energy and drive stronger than ever. She decided to leave for the night. She didn't bother saying goodnight to anyone in her eagerness to get home.

In the car park, Barbara was walking out with Joan. She looked over to Anna.

'I miss him, don't you?'

Anna nodded. She missed him more than anyone would ever realise. Seeing him again, watching him at work had, as always, made her admire him. Yet at the same time she felt that he was calmer now, less angry. She had known him before, known and loved him, was still in love with him and try as she could, it was harder than ever to disassociate herself from those feelings.

She sat for a while in her Mini, thinking, remembering, and not until she started the engine did she really force herself to concentrate on driving, refusing to allow any more thoughts of Langton to invade her mind. It *was* like an invasion; his dominance over her that she had really felt was a thing of the past. He was still very much a part of her, only now it was so distant it was easier. If he was going to be on the Delany case, she knew it was vital that she keep any latent feelings well below the surface.

It was not until she was getting ready for bed that Anna remembered the photograph she had taken of Andrea Lesser and the man she had met outside Liberty. She clicked onto the picture; it was a good clear shot of him and she made a mental note to mention it first thing in the morning. With Langton watching her, she knew that from now on she had better inform the team of every piece of information she came by.

Chapter Nine

'I suppose you know.'

Anna acted surprised when Simon appeared at her office door at 8.15 the next morning, Saturday.

'I'm off the case, going onto another investigation in Hampstead. At least it's not looking as if I've got shafted, unlike poor old Mathews.'

'What?'

'Oh come on, don't tell me you don't know about him either. He's been given a research and policy desk job until his retirement, poor sod. He got well pissed last night. Langton really rode roughshod over him.'

'I had no idea.'

Simon gave a mirthless laugh. 'No? How did Langton know I was knocking off that little actress from the movie set, if it didn't come from you?'

'I beg your pardon!'

'"I didn't know",' he mimicked.

'Simon, I didn't.'

'Well, he bloody knew about it, so somebody ratted on me, and I guessed it could only be you. Anyway, I suppose you're so well in with him you might have let it slip.'

'What do you mean by that?' Anna said angrily.

'What do you take us all for? Everyone knows that

you and he were shacked up for a time together, so it's unlikely he's gonna kick *you* off this investigation.'

'Whatever my past relationship with DCS Langton, that is not only none of your business or anyone else's, but it was over a long time ago. I resent you suggesting that there's any favouritism being shown towards me.'

'Yeah, I hear you. Well, good luck. Truth be known is, I wouldn't want that control freak looking over my shoulder, so I'm gone and good riddance.'

'Who's taking over from Mathews?' Anna asked Joan, who nodded over to Mathews's office. The door was closed and blinds were down.

'It's Mike Lewis. He's a DCI now.'

'I didn't know he'd been promoted.'

'Well, he has. Also Barolli's on board, so it's gonna be like old times.'

Anna gave a brittle smile and returned to her office. Langton always moved fast and fifteen minutes later, she knew just how fast he had moved this time when Mike Lewis came into her office.

'Congratulations,' she said, meaning it. She had always liked Mike.

'Yeah, well, let's say I needed the break. I've got three kids now.'

'Three?'

'Yeah, we had twins the last time and they're a handful. Never mind financially, it's the sleep deprivation. That was a joke! They're great kids. What about you? Married yet?'

'No, no, still single.'

He checked the time. He was waiting on Tony Barolli to arrive before he started the briefing.

'We had a pretty strong one last night from Langton,' Anna told him.

'Yeah, I know. Between you and me and the gatepost, he's had me sort of sniffing around on this for a while. Anyway, good to see you again. Let's hope we can crack this one together.'

'I'm sure we will.'

'See you in a bit then. Oh, I've been told you're up for promotion. A word of advice: do your homework. It's like going back to school exams, only with a lot more at stake.'

'Did Mathews tell you?'

Mike shrugged and grinned. 'He must have.'

Anna had copies of the photo of Andrea Lesser and her companion that she had taken on her mobile ready to hand out. She was using the time before the briefing to connect with the *Spotlight* website. She sought Joan's advice.

'Joan, would you know who's famous or maybe up-and-coming in showbiz? I need to know the names of the major theatrical agencies – you know, the ones that already have famous people on their books.'

Joan was helpful. 'Scott Myers is with the same agent as Amanda Delany was, and O'Dell and Mitchell are with Independent and William Morris. They've also got counterpart agents in the US, so I'd say if you wanted the main ones, they must be up at the top.'

'Call both of them, will you, and arrange for me to see someone there. It's not urgent, but make it soon, and also check out a few others – specifically ones that are up-and-coming and after new talent.'

★

Mike Lewis eventually called the team together and introduced himself. Anna noticed he was quite nervous and wondered when he had been promoted. She doubted if it had been that long ago.

'Right, let's see how much progress we've made in piecing together our victim's career. The film industry in the UK is tight-knit, so that should help us find out if she's worked with any of the same people in other films. She may have been murdered by someone she knew, someone she might have had sexual contact with or someone who had a grudge against her.'

Barolli stepped forwards, saying, 'All we have been able to mark up are the actual films she starred in. We'll need to go to production offices or wherever to get the lists of the cast, crew members, et cetera. Her agent Andrea Lesser has given us videos and DVDs of the pro- ductions, which everyone should look through . . . These have just arrived.'

This amount of information could not have been assessed overnight, Anna knew; it meant that Langton had been preparing to take over the case almost since they started.

'We know that Amanda left RADA aged sixteen in 2001,' Barolli continued. 'She got her big break shortly afterwards, starring in a film called *Rock Baby*. She won awards and went straight on to film *Gabriella*, then she worked virtually on back-to-back films. In 2003 there was *Jail Girls* and *Marian's Heart*; neither of these were blockbusters, they were small independents. Then we have a gap from 2003 to 2004 when she starred in *Little Liars*, which was a bigger budget and her salary would have jumped up . . .'

Anna interrupted, standing up. 'Is the gap in the filming the time she was pregnant?'

Barolli shrugged; it would have been possible.

'So we should check back to see if she was seeing anyone from that film?'

'Correct. Her co-star was Scott Myers.'

'But, timewise, as we know O'Dell visited her in the Drury, she must have known him before making that film *The Mansion* with him, later,' Anna said.

'Let's just get the timeframe sorted first before we determine who knew her when, eh?' Barolli said impatiently.

Joan turned to Anna. 'I saw that one,' she confided, 'but I can't remember much about it. It was a horror film, wasn't it?'

Barolli glared at Joan, before continuing, 'OK, after she shot *Little Liars* we have her in a really big budget film called *The Last Soldier*, followed by *The Heiress*, and hard on its heels comes a remake of *Lady Hamilton* and then *The Mansion*. Lastly, she was starring with Rupert Mitchell in *Gaslight*, which brings us up to date.'

He stepped back from the board and faced the team.

'What we get now is a clear picture of how and when she met the three actors we have questioned. I want cast and crew listed from all these movies. Let's see who else worked with her on more than one film.'

'I know the make-up girl had worked with her before and I think one of the unit drivers did too,' Anna said.

'Right, now you see what I'm after. We also need to verify exactly when she had the termination, and whether it did occur between the two films, *Marian's Heart* and *Little Liars*.'

179

'Was *Marian's Heart* about Maid Marian and Robin Hood?' Joan asked and Barolli turned on her.

'I don't bloody know, Joan, I've not seen any of them.'

'Just that I saw that as well, and I'm sure Rupert Mitchell was in it. Mind you, I could be wrong.'

'Then you, Joan – and you, Barbara, start the cross-reference going and get onto the companies for their production staff, cast and crew lists.'

Anna sat frowning, returning to her notebook and back to the board.

'Are you saying that she was older or younger than the age we have down for her? Because I didn't think you could get into RADA unless you were eighteen, but if we go by this and she was twenty-four when she died, then she must have only been fifteen when she went to RADA.'

'Check with her parents. Her real age has to be on the death certificate.'

Barolli clapped his hands as everyone started to get up, thinking the meeting was over.

'Hold it there. I'm not through yet.' He looked towards Anna. 'You're digging into the possibility that she was about to switch agents, correct?'

'Yes.'

'Mike thinks we should concentrate first on whether she had some kind of publishing deal, so I'll leave that with you too. We also want to bring in her accountant to discuss her finances. Mike is handling that.' He crossed to stand beside Anna. 'According to Mike, Andrea Lesser has been really helpful, but you have misgivings about her?'

'Not exactly. I just don't think she has been as helpful to me. Also, she seemed very agitated when she was seen with this man, just shortly after I had my meeting with her yesterday.' She showed Barolli the photograph of the two of them together.

'We should take a close look round at the funeral and see if he shows up,' Barolli told everyone.

'Or ask her directly.' Anna was feeling snappy.

'Not cool. You don't want to antagonise her and get her paranoid that you've been following her around.'

'It wasn't that at all! I just happened to catch her with the guy.'

'Nah. Just let it hang loose for a while.'

Barolli and Lewis had certainly picked up a lot of Langton's traits. Anna would have to have a quiet word with Barolli, ask him to show her more respect, especially in front of the team, so as to not undermine her. She didn't like the way he had spoken to her.

'Joan!'

The DC arrived expectantly at Anna's office door.

'Which publishing companies might be most likely to offer someone like Amanda a book deal? I know you're an avid reader.'

An hour or so later, Joan returned with a list of publishers, together with the advances the big media stars had been paid, according to the press.

'Good God, two million. But she's just a model!' Anna exclaimed.

Joan chuckled. 'Goes to show what breast implants can do for you. All of those books were on the bestseller lists, and the topless porno star has had another book commissioned.'

'Thank you for this, Joan. It's after five now so maybe I'll leave it until Monday, but if you could arrange appointments with . . .'

'Already onto it,' Joan interrupted, and looked at her watch. 'I've got a family commitment tomorrow, and they haven't stopped weekend leave, so I'd like to get going as soon as I can.'

'Thank you. I really appreciate this. I'll take a couple of the DVDs of Amanda's films home with me.'

Anna too wanted to make a quick getaway. She was looking forward to a Sunday off, not that she had, like Joan, any family commitments. She just needed to get some space between herself and the station.

From the first moment Amanda appeared on the screen, the hairs on Anna's neck stood up. She sat propped on pillows in bed at home, watching as Amanda walked through what was supposed to be Sherwood Forest, silky chestnut hair down to her waist, wearing a gown of soft pale cream wool, caught at the waist by a coiled belt. Her beauty was translucent, her slender neck and shoulders like porcelain. Anna leaned forwards, watching the scene in *Marian's Heart* where Marian meets Robin Hood for the first time – and the pair fall in love. It was very Mills & Boon, and yet Amanda's performance lifted it onto a higher level; she was so watchable that whenever she was not on screen it became tiresome. Anna found it almost impossible to block out this ethereal creature and remember the stick-thin, bruised body at the mortuary.

Having had a good night's sleep, helped by a sleeping tablet, Anna was determined to use her one day off to get herself more organised. She knew she had been lacking her usual energy and was annoyed with herself for asking Joan to do work checking out publishers and theatrical agents that if she'd been on form she'd have done herself. She had to start making more of an impression; come Monday she would be more confident, especially as Langton was now overseeing the case. Simon's transfer, although she had not really got along with him, had unnerved her. As always, her loss of her confidence was because of Langton, and she grew more determined to prove her position within the team.

After breakfast Anna sat reading the Sunday newspapers. In every one there were articles about Amanda Delany, photographs and gossip columns rehashing her past indiscretions, and interviews from so-called close friends who were heartbroken by the tragic murder. One paper bore the headline POLICE NO NEARER TO ARREST FOR MOVIE STAR'S BRUTAL MURDER and there were other snide comments. She came across a lengthy interview with Julian Pike, the director of *Gaslight*. Expressing his shock and sadness, he described Amanda as a consummate actress of massive talent that was proven by her brilliant performance in his film. While he hoped the police would eventually discover the killer, he could think of no one who had held a grudge against Amanda; she was a true inspiration for young girls, and he hoped *Gaslight* would garner her many posthumous awards.

By late afternoon, Anna was feeling at a loose end. It was just after six when she drove to the station to collect more DVDs of Amanda's films to take home to watch that evening. She was surprised to see so many cars in the car park; with it being Sunday, there would surely be only part of the team working.

When Anna walked into the incident room, she found it a hive of activity. No one really paid her any attention as they stood grouped around the incident board listening to Mike Lewis. Catching Joan's eye, Anna gestured for her to join her in her office.

'How come everyone's in today?' she wanted to know.

Joan raised her eyes to the ceiling. 'Sunday leave was cancelled.'

'Nobody told me.'

'It was on the board. I had to cancel my family lunch. I'd got all the food in as well.'

'Did it come from Mike Lewis?'

'Yeah. Barbara had a hissy fit as she was supposed to take her kids to a football match.'

'Did something come up?'

'No, I think that's why we're all here. They were wondering where you were, but it's a bit late now as we're packing it in at six-thirty.'

'Really . . . Would you ask Barolli if he has a minute as I'd like to see him and I'd also like the DVDs of *The Mansion* and *The Heiress*. I've brought back the two I watched.'

Anna was tightlipped as she passed over the boxes. Joan glanced at them.

'Sort of unexpected, wasn't it – you know, that she was such a good actress. But then considering what they were paying her . . .'

'Do we have the figures?'

'Yes, Mike Lewis had Miss Lesser here this morning. Not a happy woman, but she brought in copies of contracts so we've been—'

Just then, Barbara passed the open office door, saying, 'I'm going home. We're calling it quits for tonight.' Anna then heard her mutter under her breath, 'All right for some,' with a glance towards her.

Anna was infuriated. Joan left, and she folded her arms

waiting for Barolli, her foot tapping with annoyance.

'Where were you this morning?' he said, the moment he walked in.

'I was at home, and if I had been aware that weekend leave had been cancelled, I would have been here.'

'We called you.'

'I might have been at the laundry.'

'Well, it was on the board.'

Anna stood up. 'I don't give a shit!' she said angrily. 'It would have been manners if you had spoken to me about it. I also resent the way you're behaving towards me. Twice you've been less than respectful. Perhaps you forget that I'm a rank above you, and as such I want to be made aware of any team reports.'

'Excuse me for living,' Barolli retorted sarcastically.

'No, I don't excuse you, Tony. Now be kind enough to give me details of what has been taking place today.'

'I was just going home.'

'I'll be in the incident room in five minutes.'

She stared hard at him and he hovered.

'Listen, I'm sorry if I've appeared disrespectful to you in any way – there was never any intention of that. But you know, coming in on the case this late, we've had a lot of catching up to do, and with Langton on our shoulders, I've been run ragged.'

'Five minutes.'

Anna took a couple of deep breaths. She was shaking as he left her office; she had never dressed down an officer before. Joan returned with the DVDs, buttoning up her coat.

'See you in the morning,' she said, eager to be gone.

'Whose idea was it to bring in Andrea Lesser?' Anna asked Barolli when she joined him in the incident room.

'Langton's, and she didn't like it. We didn't bring her in here, but had a meeting with her in one of the interview rooms. He's also arranged for the accountant to be brought in first thing tomorrow morning as he wants to know how much dosh Amanda had earned.'

'Was Langton here?'

'Yes, left just before lunch.'

'I see. Well, I'd like an update.'

Barolli sighed. She could tell he was annoyed but she held her ground. He fetched a file and sat on the edge of one of the desks.

'Lesser was very unpleasant to start off with, bleating on about how it was all highly confidential and she didn't understand why we were interested as she couldn't see that there was any connection between what her client had earned and her murder.'

He laughed.

'You should have seen old Langton working her over. Eventually she was helpful and we were all taken aback at how much her little star was worth. But what surfaced was that there is no way Lesser or anyone from any theatrical agency would have wanted anything to do with Amanda's death. There were so many offers on the table, and a Hollywood studio after her that Lesser said could lift Amanda Delany's fees into around twelve million a film. It's a lot of money and, to be honest, I can't see it.'

'Can't see what?'

'How that anorexic little tart was worth it.'

'Have you watched any of her films?'

'Not had the time,' he said pointedly.

'Maybe you should. She was very talented.'

Barolli shrugged and passed the file to Anna.

'It's all there. It's confidential, of course, but Joan reckons a lot of it was in the press anyway, so that could also open up a motive.'

'How come?'

'You get some dickhead reading about how much the victim was worth and that's an incentive for Christ knows what.'

'Blackmail?'

'Possibly.'

'What about fraud?' Anna said. 'We'll need to see the accountant to make sure there haven't been any underhand dealings.'

'By whom?'

Anna sighed. She was determined to make the over-confident Barolli take a step down.

'Possibly her agent. There was quite a scandal a few years ago about a theatrical agent not paying their client their full wages. Sometimes the movie stars get to earn so much they don't know what they are due. This is why I've been attempting to track down the possibility of a publishing deal. The fact that Amanda was going to spill some beans may have given someone a motive.'

'How far have you got with it?'

'I haven't. There are a lot of publishing houses that might have been interested, and as Miss Lesser has denied any knowledge of anyone offering Amanda a deal, and we have no one else to confirm it, I'll just have to wade through all the companies known to offer lucrative book contracts to models and actors.'

'Right.' Barolli was now rather subdued.

'Thank you for this. I'll see you in the morning.' Anna patted the file and strode away towards her office.

★

Anna was eager to leave the station but, still angry at not having known about the cancellation of their weekend leave, she wanted to be seen to be working. Mike Lewis came out of his office, ready to go home. He looked tired out, but came and tapped on her door then entered.

'Sorry there was a hiccup over the team meeting up today,' he told her. 'We're under a lot of pressure to get a result. You saw the Sunday papers?'

'Yes. No one seems to think we are doing anything positive, but the reality is we don't have a suspect.'

'Tell me about it. The Guv is getting very edgy and we really need to pull out all the stops this coming week. You know we had her agent in?'

'Yes, I was told.'

He yawned. 'I gotta get home and give the wife a break. She's had the kids by herself all day as it's the au pair's day off.'

'See you tomorrow,' Anna said as he walked out.

Amanda had been paid one and half million pounds to star in *Lady Hamilton*, and from looking at her film contracts Anna knew her asking price had risen as fast as her stardom. What was odd was that her fee on *Gaslight* was lower at £500,000. Added in were back-end deals and a percentage which Anna couldn't quite understand. Amanda's accountant would no doubt explain it all the following morning, so she put the file aside and concentrated on watching *The Mansion*, which also starred Colin O'Dell and Scott Myers. In the film, a group of young people club together to buy a rundown old mansion. They are qualified as plumbers, carpenters, electricians or builders and have bought the mansion in the hope that they will not only make homes for themselves, but sell off one of the larger wings to cover their costs. It started with a slow build-up of various 'accidents', then began to twist into horror as terrifying things happened to all the couples, resulting in the breakdown of their friendships and ending in murder.

Anna was struck yet again by Amanda Delany's talent as an actress. Her role demanded that she play not only the girlfriend of the electrician Colin O'Dell, but she was also the ghost that haunted the mansion. Scott Myers played the part of a carpenter who fell in love with Amanda. There were a few explicit love scenes in which he was unable to determine if he had been making love to the ghost or the living girl. Anna found it at first quite enthralling but its need to shock the audience became preposterous. The ghost had vampire qualities, and the only way to kill her was by hammering a stake into her heart. The last scene when Amanda appeared in a blood-stained nightdress was only rendered plausible by her quiet and tragic performance.

Anna was about to switch the TV off, when she decided to play the last scene again. She froze it and peered closely at the screen. Amanda was wearing a small gold cross on a gold chain, very similar to the one they had discovered caught in her sheets. Next, Anna slowed down the lists of credits, making notes. One important name that cropped up was the costume designer Joanna Villiers who also did the costumes for *Gaslight*. Anna intended to check out the cross with her first thing in the morning. She was determined to gain more respect from the team, and especially from Mike Lewis and Barolli.

Chapter Ten

Anna was parking her car the next morning when Barolli passed her, heading for a waiting patrol car. He hurried over to her.

'We got some developments this morning and a possible OD with one of Amanda's flatmates.'

Anna gasped. 'Who?'

'The kid, Dan Hutchins. I'm on my way over there now.'

'Is that the main development?'

He paused, and looked back.

'No, it's from Joan.'

Anna dumped her things in her office and went immediately to the incident room. Barbara turned to greet her.

'Dan Hutchins was found dead this morning – OD, we think. And Joan's come up trumps; she's in with Mike now.'

'Like what?'

Barbara moved closer. 'You know she's a bit of a film buff. Well, she reckons that Amanda was wearing the gold crucifix in one of the films she was watching.'

'*The Mansion*,' Anna said flatly.

'Right. Mike's looking at it now and then they'll get onto the costume designer. Joan's certain it was identical to the one found at the victim's house.'

Anna nodded. The rug had been pulled from under her feet. She was sure Joan was correct, but she would have liked to be the one who brought it to the team's attention.

She turned her own attention to arranging a visit to the first publishing house on Joan's list. The commissioning editor, Noel Kenrick, was expected into work at ten that morning.

'I'll see him then,' she told his assistant over the phone, as she introduced herself.

With time to kill she left the station and made her way over to Pimlico and the office of Kenrick & Carter. It was a large, white, Art Deco building with glass-fronted reception doors emblazoned with their logo. Knowing she was very early Anna sat, wishing she had not escaped the incident room so quickly. She put in a call to Barolli on his mobile, but it was switched off. It was still only 9.15 a.m. so, frustrated, she called the second name on Joan's list of publishers and arranged an appointment at 11.30 a.m. at their office near to Waterloo Bridge.

At the flat in Maida Vale, Barolli was questioning Felicity Turner and a distraught Jeannie Bale. All they could tell him was that they had been out at a party and Dan had been with them. He had left early and they had not returned to the shared flat until 3 a.m. When they knocked on his bedroom door to see if he wanted some coffee, they found him on the floor, having some kind of seizure. They called an ambulance but he was dead before it arrived. Barolli reckoned that the young man had simply overdosed. The girls suspected that he might have scored heroin at the party and returned home to inject himself. Neither knew of anyone at the party dealing drugs, but since the murder of Amanda, Dan had been very depressed, they said, and had hardly left their flat.

Back at the station, Mike Lewis was questioning Joanna Villiers about the gold crucifix. She agreed that the cross in the evidence bag was identical, but whether or not it was the one used in the film, she couldn't be 100 per cent sure. Asked if the hire company would have retained it, she said that it had been part of the costume department and they had actually bought two, just in case one was damaged during the scene when the stake was driven through the vampire's heart.

'So what happened to the crucifixes after the filming?'

Jo Villiers was able to give them the name of the jeweller where she had bought them. She knew Amanda had taken one, but the other . . . She shrugged her shoulders, explaining that often at the end of filming, actors could buy their costumes at a 70 per cent reduction of the original cost. As it had been a costume drama and most of the costumes had been hired or made specifically for the actors, none of them were sold. However, she did have a note in the cost report she had brought with her that neither cross was returned.

'But they were gold,' Mike observed.

'I know. You have no idea how much stuff actors nick. Like I said, I knew Amanda had taken one. She sort of hinted that she'd like to keep it and I let it go, but the other one just went walkabout; and that's something that happens all the time like you wouldn't believe. Maybe she took both of them.'

'How much were they worth?'

'Oh, not that much. Maybe forty, fifty pounds, and to be honest, every film unit usually lets its stars walk off with stuff. If it keeps them happy, they don't care. I've had actors nick their entire costumes and not pay for them.'

'But you were shown a picture of the cross by Detective Travis.'

'I just didn't recognise it. The film was made quite some time ago, and it wasn't until you showed me the section again that I remembered the crucifixes being worn. I'm really sorry, but I've worked on so many movies since then.'

'Do you know if Colin O'Dell took the second cross?'

'I have no idea. It was in a leather case on the set, so it could have been taken by anyone really – from the props department or the electricians, even extras. You have to keep your eyes open.'

'So you never reported it missing?'

No, Joanna said. It had been a difficult sequence to film and it had taken two days. The special effects, like the fake breasts used for the stake to be hammered into the vampire's heart, had cost a fortune. The blood bags beneath used to spurt blood had taken a considerable time to set up and she had to have four changes of identical costume for Amanda. It was a disappointing result for Mike, since God knows how many other people would have to be questioned about the crucifix.

Before she left, Joanna gave Mike the names of the people she recalled who had also been attached to both films, notably the unit drivers Harry James and his brother Tony, who she thought had worked on both sets. Mike wasted no time in earmarking a team to bring them both in to be questioned.

By now, Barolli was back from the Maida Vale flat. Rereading the interviews of Jeannie Bale and Felicity Turner, he felt there was no connection to their investigation. Mike suggested another session with the girls when the distress of their flatmate's death had eased. Next time, he wanted them brought into the station.

He looked around and gestured at Anna's empty office, asking, 'Where's Travis?'

'She's off talking to publishers, trying to find out if Amanda had any publishing deal,' Barolli replied.

There was an undercurrent of irritation about this between them, as it was now after midday, but neither said anything in front of the team.

Anna had interviewed two commissioning editors from two top publishing companies. Their response had been almost identical, dismissing any possible deal ever offered to Amanda Delany as bordering on the ridiculous. They were adamant that they didn't, unlike some companies, pay exorbitant advances to starlets, strippers or game-show winners; they were very much literary publishers.

They both advised her to meet with Golden Arrow publishers. Although a small company, it had made substantial profits from three celebrity books published in the past year. Their offices, in comparison to the previous two publishers, were scruffy and occupied the second floor in a rundown four-storey building on Ladbroke Grove. Anna had been given the name of Josh Lyons, commissioning editor and part-owner of Golden Arrow, and he had agreed to see her straight away.

Josh Lyons's office was dominated by a massive desk

and a bookcase containing rows of paperbacks, a large plasma TV and walls decorated with posters of their recently published books – *Sex Slave*, *My Drug Horror*, *Days as Page Three*, *Life After Game Show*. Mr Lyons himself was nowhere to be seen. Anna sat in an uncomfortable red plastic chair placed in front of the desk and looked over the lurid book titles. Then Lyons, a small, well-preserved, sun-tanned medallion-weaving type, swept in and beamed at Anna.

'Sorry, I was in a meeting.' Heavy cologne permeated the office.

Anna introduced herself, certain it was going to be a waste of her time. Lyons sat behind his desk in an over-large leather chair, listening as she explained that she was investigating the murder of Amanda Delany.

'God, that was terrible, beyond belief. I mean, she was so special, a real talent. I wouldn't say I knew her well, but what a shock, she was lovely.'

'So you had met her?'

'Yeah, I'd met her – course I had.'

'How do you mean?'

They had first met at a nightclub, he explained, and met up again shortly afterwards.

'She came here?'

'No, we had lunch at Le Caprice. I've got the exact date somewhere.' He opened a drawer and took out a desk diary.

'Could you tell me why she contacted you?'

He thumbed through his diary, preoccupied.

'It was four months ago. We'd exchanged numbers 'cos I said I would like to talk to her.'

'Can I ask you what it was about?'

'Yeah, sure. I offered her a book deal. You know, she

was a real star and in the press every two minutes and I just reckoned she'd be up for it.' He jabbed at a page of his diary. 'Here you go! It was exactly four months ago that we met to discuss writing her memoir. I'd even got a good ghostwriter to work with her. Believe you me, she would have needed a lot of help.'

'Did she submit material to you?'

'She did. What I said to her was that we'd need some indication that she'd be able to come up with the goods – know what I mean? Not in those exact words, of course.' He laughed.

'So, would you mind telling me how far you got with—' Anna started, but Lyons interrupted.

'We were about to draw up a contract and ...' He shook his head. 'Can you imagine what it would be worth to us now? Jesus, sorry, that sounds so money-grabbing, but you know what I mean.'

'How far had the negotiations gone?'

Lyons rocked in his chair. 'We had a very expensive lunch.'

'Who was she with when you first met her at the nightclub?'

As far as he could remember, she was with a number of people, but he didn't recognise any of them. He had simply approached her and given her his card, asking if she had ever considered writing her autobiography. At first she didn't seem interested, but when he said he had published many Number One bestsellers, she was more intrigued.

'She didn't mince her words, but came straight out and asked how much she would get. I told her that we had paid a considerable amount for these.' He gestured to his framed posters on the wall. 'I obviously couldn't start talking money there and then and I told her so, but she was quite insistent. I eventually said that depending on ghostwriters or whatever was required from us, she could be looking at starting at around half a million.'

'And her reaction?'

'She agreed to meet me and, in fact, called the next afternoon and we arranged to have lunch.'

'Could you take me through what happened at lunch?'

'Sure. She was delightful and very enthusiastic and also, which surprised me, eager to write it herself.'

'Did you discuss money again?'

'She'd checked out what a number of other show-business people had been advanced and she said that she would want over a million. I was a bit flabbergasted, but the reality is that this is the kind of money we've been paying for this lot.' Again, he gestured to his posters.

'Did she not want her agent to be present?'

'Absolutely not – though that would be the usual route. If they didn't use their theatrical agent, they usually got a literary agent to handle the negotiations, but Amanda seemed to be intent on dealing with it all herself, and I have to say she seemed pretty well clued-up.'

'How did it progress from there?'

Lyons spread his hands wide.

'I suggested to her that before we finalised any negotiations we have another meeting, allowing both of us to think about the project.'

'Did you ask her to show you chapters or any samples of her writing?'

'Yes, I did. She didn't want to come into the office here in case any press were to see her. She wanted our discussions kept very secret, so that no one knew what she was up to.'

'But she met you at Le Caprice. That's a very popular restaurant, isn't it?'

'Yes, but she came by car and it dropped her directly at the front – and unless someone inside the restaurant recognised her, I doubt if anyone would have known what we were meeting about. I also left before her.'

'Did you see her drive herself?'

'No, she had a driver.'

'The next meeting?'

Lyons looked in his diary. 'I went to a flat belonging to some friends of hers, nasty little dump in Maida Vale.'

'Did you meet anyone there other than Amanda?'

'No, she was alone.'

Anna waited for him to continue.

'She showed me some pages she had printed off from her laptop. She refused to allow me to leave with them, but insisted I read them there and then. It was a bit ridiculous as they were pages of poems and not exactly what I was after. I explained to her that the whole point of writing her memoirs was really to focus more on her childhood, her lovers, her career as an actress; I wasn't that interested in her poetry! Frankly, I doubted if anyone else would be either.'

He described how she took the pages back, tore them up in front of him and then asked him exactly what kind of thing he wanted her to write.

'Her relationships with various actors, I said, would need to be part of the book. Maybe a few brief chapters about her childhood, but basically we would have to have as much scandal as possible to sell the book, and obviously the more explicit, the easier it would be for us to promote it. If we were to pay her a big advance, I would need some indication from her as to how far she would be prepared to go, and I would also require photographs and so on.'

Anna jotted down a few notes and asked if Amanda had done as he had asked.

'No. She called me twice to ask about the legal side – you know, how far should she go in naming names, and I explained to her that she should not worry too much about that as our legal team would obviously look into anything that could have repercussions.'

By then Lyons was certain that they would need a ghostwriter to help her, but was waiting for the right opportunity to tell her so. In the meantime, he simply encouraged her to start thinking about what the content of the book would eventually be.

'I reckoned by the next call or meeting she would either come up with the goods and then we would be able to negotiate her advance, but ...' He shook his head. 'She was dead, a great shock to me and to some of my staff.'

'So they knew she was possibly writing her memoirs?'

'Not everyone, but my editor-in-chief knew and we had approached a writer. But nothing was confirmed and I'd given strict instructions that we had to keep the author's name under wraps.'

'Why do you think Miss Delany didn't want her agent to know about your proposition?'

'I have no idea. She inferred that if the deal was leaked to the press she would deny any dealings with this company. I understood; we've often kept authors' identities top secret and used other names on their manuscripts so as to keep everything confidential.'

'Did you agree on an advance?'

He nodded.

'Could you tell me what it was?'

'I can, but it was still negotiable. We hadn't exchanged any contracts and, as I've said, for such a young woman, she was extraordinarily confident and knowledgeable. She wanted one and half million, half to be paid when we signed the contract and half on publication.'

'Did you agree to this amount?'

'In theory, I suppose I did – but I told her that it would be dependent on how far she would be prepared to go to spill the beans about her life.' He halted. 'I'll always remember what she said. You know, she was extraordinarily pretty, with the clearest blue eyes. She was very skinny, of course, and she just picked at her food.'

Lyons looked away for a moment, sighing.

'She was wearing a skimpy T-shirt, a denim mini-skirt – none of it looked as if it had been washed or ironed – and these big furry boots that made her legs look skeleton-thin. There was no jewellery, nothing that indicated she was already not only famous, but wealthy. They say the camera never lies, don't they? I think what she had was a perfect photogenic face . . .'

Anna waited while he stared at some point on the wall behind her head.

'What was it she said to you, Mr Lyons?' she prompted.

'She said that she would "dish the dirt on all the bastards who had felt they were too good for her, that she'd name names and make sure they all paid for what they had done to her" . . .'

Anna was being ushered out of Josh Lyons's office when she remembered to ask him if he knew whether Amanda had kept a diary. He didn't hesitate. At their last lunch she had brought a thick book with her. It looked very well-thumbed, with a small lock, and was pinkish-coloured if somewhat grubby. When at some point he'd asked if she would be able to remember things from her past, she had patted it. Giggling, she said that she never forgot anything. This was a five-year diary and she wrote in it every night. She had had it beside her when he visited her flat.

Anna thanked Lyons for being so helpful and smiled when he suggested that if ever she wanted to write about her own life, she should contact him.

'Just a joke,' he said pleasantly, as the lift door opened.

Chapter Eleven

Justin Smalls was a blond-haired man in his early thirties, wearing a snazzy suit with the cuffs turned back to reveal a green satin lining, pleasant but with a snobbish air about him. Before introducing himself as one of the agents with International Theatrical Agents, ITA, he asked Anna if she was there to discuss the parking arrangements; they had been having some difficulty with their landlord. Anna quickly showed him her ID. He sat down promptly, but at some distance from her.

'Wow, that sounds rather ominous,' he commented when she outlined the reason she was there and asked him if he had met Amanda Delany.

'You see,' she went on, 'I really want to know if anyone from ITA had approached her to represent her.'

Smalls shook his head. He himself had never approached Miss Delany, nor, he believed, had any of his fellow agents. He suggested that perhaps Anna had been given incorrect information.

'Andrea Lesser had represented Amanda since the start of her career,' he pointed out. 'I really doubt Miss Delany would have considered leaving her, as Andrea is extremely well-respected.'

Anna stood up, ready to leave.

'Have you been told otherwise?' he asked.

'We are just making enquiries, so thank you for your time.' She felt uneasy. He seemed to look down at her as being hardly worth wasting his time on.

But if she felt that Justin Smalls had been dismissive of her, it was even worse at Payne & Hudson, a much smaller agency with offices in a rundown mews off Wardour Street.

'Amanda Delany,' Jennifer Hudson, the owner, barked in an upper-crust tone, tossing her hair and making her looped earrings swing. 'I don't say that I wouldn't have jumped at the chance, but she was very firmly with Andrea Lesser and I would never have tried to poach her. I've had enough run-ins to last me, and if I *had* tried to represent Amanda, Andrea would really have gone for the jugular.'

'Do you know of anyone who might have been interested?'

Jennifer Hudson took off the large green glasses perched on her nose and squinted at Anna.

'Any agent worth their salt would have wanted her. She had tremendous potential and was to my mind a far better actress than she was ever given credit for. That said, she was also trouble, with her penchant for seducing her leading men, plus her known drug problems, but, one has to be honest in this sad day and age, it doesn't seem to really harm their careers; on the contrary. But she might have done some damage as far as working in the US was concerned, as they are really very much against employing anyone from here with a history of drug abuse. Mind you, there are strings that can be pulled and I am sure that Andrea Lesser knew everyone who could work the system.'

'So there was never any rumour that she was contemplating changing agents?'

'Not to my knowledge – and word would certainly spread. It's a very small industry so not a lot goes past me or anyone I know.'

Anna stood up, then as an afterthought, she took out a photograph.

'Could I ask if you recognise this man?' She passed over the photograph that she had taken outside Liberty.

'I don't know him, but I do know who he is. He works in the City, and I believe handles some actors' investments. I think, but please don't quote me on this, he was hit very hard in the recent banking nightmare. Fortunately, none of my clients lost money – but I know a number of people who went down a bundle.'

'His name?' Anna prompted.

'Andrew Smith-Barker.'

'Do you have a contact number or an address?'

Jennifer Hudson peered over her thick-rimmed glasses and shook her head.

'Sorry, no. Andrea Lesser would, of course. I've seen her with him at a few social functions.'

Headed back to the car park, Anna put in a call to the incident room and asked Barbara to track down Andrew Smith-Barker. She was stuck in a traffic jam in Regents Street on her way back to the station when her mobile rang.

'Hi, Anna, it's Pete.'

She put him onto speaker.

'It's not much, but something's been bothering me and it might mean going back to the pathologist to double-check.'

'I'm all ears,' Anna said, inching forwards. Whichever way she looked, the traffic was solid.

'When I was at Amanda Delany's place – and I got the call-out early – Scene of Crime Officers were already working and she had been certified as dead, but the body was still *in situ* until I'd completed my scene examination.'

'Yes?' Anna was impatient to hear what he had to say.

'Well, I recall the bedroom was small, the whole place was not very spacious, and with so many people coming and going . . .'

'Yes? Come on, Pete, don't keep me in suspense any longer. What is it?'

'It was quite a cold day for summer and had been a chilly night, as I recall. Lots of people have been putting the heating on, haven't they, and Amanda obviously did too. Judy, my assistant, remembered one of the officers saying they had been sweating, as the central heating system had been turned up very high when they arrived. So someone, and I don't know who, had turned it off. As it was, it was still very stuffy and we had to open a window to get some air into the place. I think the Crime Scene Manager at the time of the examination gave the wrong temperature.'

'Sorry, I don't understand where you're going with this.' Anna eased the car another few feet forward.

'Time of death. If the heating had been on full blast when she was killed, this would have advanced decomposition; rigor mortis had already come and gone. It would mean, Anna, that the timeframe for her murder was possibly a few hours earlier than has been estimated. I've had a chat to the pathologist and he agrees.'

'OK, I'll look into it, but I know the central-heating timer and thermostat would have been checked.'

'Yeah, yeah, I'm sure. Anyways, apart from that, I'm sorry to say we've come up with nothing that I think can help your case. We're still enhancing and examining the fingerprints from the house, but as I told you, it was remarkably devoid of prints as she had only just moved in. I've sent what matches we have from the voluntary prints taken and brought to us. None, by the way, matched any criminal ones on our database, but we're still checking.'

'Thank you.'

'You free for dinner at all?'

'Not for a while, Pete. We're working round the clock on this one, but as soon as I do have some free time, I'll call you.'

'OK, nice talking to you.'

No sooner had Anna cut off the call from Pete than her mobile rang again. This time it was Barbara. She had traced the Knightsbridge address and phone number of Andrew Smith-Barker, and Anna decided she would make an unscheduled call on him.

'Good morning.'

Anna, sitting waiting in the reception area of Andrew Smith-Barker's offices, stood up.

'Please come into my office. It's Detective Travis, correct?'

'Yes.' She picked up her briefcase and followed him, surprised that he appeared to be so handsome, more so than when she had first seen him through her car window with Andrea Lesser. He was tall, at least six feet three, and was wearing an immaculately tailored suit. His thick hair was cut short and flecked with grey, and he had dark brown eyes in an angular face with a slight hooked nose. She could smell Cuban cigars and subtle cologne, like magnolia flowers.

Andrew Smith-Barker's office was spacious and elegantly furnished, dominated by a carved oak desk. The walls were lined with files and books and a couple of oil paintings. Nothing was out of place, not a loose paper to be seen.

Smith-Barker gestured for Anna to sit in a comfortable leather chair opposite himself as he went behind his desk. He had, she noticed, manicured hands with short-cut nails and a heavy gold ring on the little finger of his left hand.

'How can I be of help? My assistant tells me you want to ask me some questions.'

She cleared her throat. 'I'm making enquiries into the death of Amanda Delany,' she said, showing him her ID. 'Was she a client?'

He stared at her and then leaned back. 'How is this connected to her death?'

'We are looking into all Miss Delany's affairs, both business and private, to build up a background that might assist our investigation. I believe you know her agent, Miss Andrea Lesser?'

'Yes, I do.'

'So, Mr Smith-Barker, could you tell me if you handled any investments for Miss Delany? I believe that is what your company does.'

'I am an investment consultant; I work here in my offices and in the City for part of the week.'

'Was Miss Delany a client?' Anna asked again.

'Whether or not she was, I don't think I am prepared

to divulge any details regarding my business transactions with Miss Delany'. He gave a slow intake of breath. 'I can't see how my connection to Miss Lesser or Miss Delany can give you any assistance in your enquiry.'

'That, sir, is for me to decide.'

'Really? Any business transaction my company deals with is private and confidential and I have to have written permission from Miss Delany's beneficiaries, or Miss Delany's executor, to discuss her affairs. I'll obviously be contacted by an administrator if there is no will and, as I am sure you are aware, they will be appointed by the court to enable them to deal with a deceased person's estate.'

'So you do admit that you handled Miss Delany's investments?'

'I admit that I have in the past dealt with some investments for Miss Delany, but to give you access to them would require, as I have said, permission – and you would need a court order to view the accounts.'

'Did Miss Delany lose any money?'

'I'm afraid I will not discuss my business dealings with you.'

Anna couldn't budge him; she had rarely come across someone so intransigent and with such a confident manner.

'Did you have an interaction with Miss Delany on a personal level?'

'My relationship with Miss Delany was purely business. I did not socialise with her, if that is what you are asking.'

'Did you ever visit her mews house?'

'No, I did not.'

At this point, Smith–Barker stood up as if to indicate

that the meeting was over, and Anna had no option but to leave. As a parting shot she said, very quietly, that perhaps she would return with a warrant for him to surrender the records of his financial dealings with Miss Delany. He gave a slight shrug of his shoulders; if that was necessary, so be it.

'Do you know who Miss Delany's beneficiaries are?' Anna asked him.

'No, I do not. I am waiting for confirmation from her solicitors.'

'Does that mean you are holding some of her money?'

'I suggest you return with a warrant, then you will no doubt be privy to all my records and documents concerning Amanda Delany's accounts.'

Anna was irritated. She hadn't handled the interview well and she knew it. That said, she was unsure what else she could have done under the circumstances. She would put it to the team that they get a search warrant to force the obdurate Mr Smith-Barker into giving further details, since the gut feeling she had had on first seeing this man with Andrea Lesser had returned – and it told her that something wasn't right, or even legal.

By the time Anna arrived at the station, Mike Lewis was starting a briefing. He gave her a cool glance and looked pointedly at his watch. Anna took a seat at the back of the incident room to listen to all the updated information.

The interim post-mortem report on Amanda's old flatmate, Dan Hutchins, concluded that his death was indeed caused by an overdose of heroin. He had very high levels of alcohol in his urine, as well as 153 grams of morphine in every litre of blood, consistent with heroin overdose. He was also severely underweight. The hypodermic needle and tinfoil wrap of heroin discovered beside the body had only his fingerprints on them.

Mike went on to report that a second and extensive fingertip search of the small lane between the mews properties where Amanda Delany had lived and the surrounding gardens had yielded nothing that could be connected to their case. The home-owners from the end double mews property had been contacted and would be producing their security footage for the team to review. None of the residents of the mews who had been questioned again had any new information. Mike then gestured to the incident board and to the photograph of the gold crucifix.

'We now know that there were, in fact, two of these crucifixes used on the film, *The Mansion*. The costume designer has verified that the one discovered in Amanda's house was one of them. She believes Amanda had taken it, but we are still trying to locate the second cross.'

Then it was Barbara's turn. The work she and Joan had been doing in cross-referencing employees on Amanda Delany's films was still ongoing; checking out the crews and stars from the various production offices was taking considerable and painstaking time. However, they had a list of numerous members of the crew from *Gaslight* who had worked with Amanda on earlier films, including unit drivers, make-up and wardrobe personnel and two props men. Anna paid close attention to the list of names and was so intent on writing them down that she only suddenly became aware that the room was silent and all eyes were on her.

'Detective Inspector Travis, you've been gone all day. Want to fill us in?' Mike Lewis was asking.

'Yes, yes, I do.' She went to the front and stood beside the incident board.

'The people who worked with Amanda and who I've already interviewed need to be questioned again,' she began. 'We really need to underline as fast as possible anyone listed as being involved in the murder. I'm sorry, Barbara, but I want us to go further back, to her earlier filmwork. The dates when she was pregnant fall between two of them, and it could be that she became pregnant by someone she was working with.'

Anna paused as she opened her notebook.

'That it?' Mike grunted.

'No, not by a long shot. Today, I got confirmation that Golden Arrow Publishers were commissioning Amanda Delany to write her autobiography.'

Anna raised a quiet gasp when she disclosed how much the deal would have been worth. She had barely let that information settle before she raised her meeting with Andrew Smith-Barker.

'It is imperative that we get access to Andrea Lesser's accounts. If we need a search warrant court order, we should use it to determine whether this so-called City Investor has lost our victim's money or even been involved in some kind of fraud. He was far too defensive, and I smell a rat. If this proves to be correct, then it is yet another motive.'

'Did he strike you as the kind of man who would go to such lengths?' Mike asked.

'No, he didn't. But we need to know his circumstances, and whether he is desperate. If he really is, then he could have hired someone to commit the murder. It's been done before.'

'Come on. There were too many knife-wounds for a contract killing.'

Anna turned on Barolli. 'Unless it was made to look like a frenzied attack committed out of anger. We've all certainly been going down that route! And if you would just let me finish!'

As Barolli sat back down again, he gave a raised eyebrow to Barbara, who sniggered.

'A frenzied attack by someone with a front-door key because there were no signs of a break-in,' he muttered under his breath.

'Andrew Smith-Barker is a close friend of Andrea Lesser,' Anna retorted. 'She could have given him the key – all right? *All right?*'

'Yes, it's possible.' He lifted his hands up in a gesture of defeat.

'Thank you. And I'm not through yet.'

Tension was building in the room.

'I could be on the wrong track with the investment scenario,' Anna admitted, 'but I'm simply running everything by you that I've been working on today. Next, I believe that Amanda Delany kept a diary, and not for jotting down her pick-up times for film schedules, as we found those on the wall calendar in her kitchen. This is a five-year diary – a pink one with a lock. She told the publisher that she wrote in it every day; she even showed it to him.'

Finally Anna had Mike Lewis's attention.

'So three things are missing: a soft toy, the other gold chain and crucifix and, most importantly, Amanda's diary. We get a search warrant to look over the flat in Maida Vale that she shared . . . which is where she was interviewed by the publisher. If it isn't hidden there, it could mean the killer took it.'

Anna gestured to Joan to get her some water from the cooler and turned over the next page in her notebook.

'I'm not a qualified profiler, but I have done some of their courses. What I think is being thrown up here is that whoever killed Amanda took the diary – which would mean they knew about the book deal. According to the publisher, Amanda was insistent on keeping it very quiet; she even refused to discuss it with her agent, so whoever knew about it had to be someone close to her. Secondly, why take a cuddly toy? It could mean that the killer wanted some kind of a token, a keepsake that he or she knew Amanda cared about. Again, it would mean that they knew her well, which excludes hiring some hitman to kill her.'

Joan handed her a beaker of water and she took a few sips before she continued.

'Lastly, I spoke to Pete Jenkins this afternoon. He thinks it's possible that we have the time of death wrong. The heating was turned on very high when the officers first entered the house, but apparently it was turned off as the room was stuffy and they were all feeling pretty uncomfortable. If the heating had been turned up high, it would mean decomposition had set in faster and that we could be out by a few hours. She could have died later than we thought. We'll need to verify this with the pathologist. Last but not least, we need this meeting with her accountant and we also really have to find out who are her beneficiaries.'

Anna turned to Mike Lewis. 'That's it.'

Mike nodded, then stood up and clapped his hands for attention.

'OK, everyone, let's get moving on Travis's information and remember, tomorrow is the funeral. Details on the board with a list of who will be required to be present.'

Anna made her way to her office and then froze. DCS Langton was sitting behind her desk, swivelling from side to side.

'Very impressive, Travis. You've been a busy girl.'

'Yes.' She placed her briefcase onto her desk.

'Tell me about this investment banker chap.'

'You think she does it on purpose?'

'What?'

Barbara and Joan were packing up for the day.

'You know, comes on with the X factor all the time and makes everyone else look like dimwits.'

'Joan!'

'Well, did you see the blokes' faces?' Barbara smirked. 'Especially Barolli's — he was so tight-jawed it looked locked!'

They both gave a furtive look at Anna's office window and could see she was in deep conversation with Langton.

'Have you heard about them?'

'Everyone has, Barbara. But you know Langton, he's got a terrible reputation. He goes through the ranks like a dose of salts, or he used to. Now he's got two children and the ex-wife back living with him. Went back to her after he finished with Travis.'

'Wasn't it because he was almost killed in that case by the bloke and his machete?'

'I don't know, I wasn't on that. This is only the second time I've worked with him.' Joan suddenly dug Barbara in the ribs. 'Shush, he's coming.'

'Evening, sir,' Barbara said brightly.

Langton gave both women a charming smile as he crossed to the incident board and stood quietly, out of their earshot, staring at it. He turned as Mike joined him.

'I didn't know you were here,' Mike said, surprised.

'No, I didn't think you did. There are some good developments and you should thank Travis for that.' Langton drew out a chair and sat down.

'Has there been a thorough search of this flat your victim used?' he went on.

'Not yet.'

Langton chuckled, repeating under his breath, 'Not yet.' Then he turned and glared at Mike. '*Get your fucking finger out!* I want a result on this case and right now it's been meandering around like a lost cow! I've had the Deputy Assistant Commissioner onto me. You any idea how many cases I'm overseeing? And this one is getting more press than all the others put together.'

'Jimmy, I'm really covering everything you suggested and more, but we go up one blind alley after another.'

'From what you're saying, it's the blind leading the blind.'

'No, I'm not saying that and, as you said, Travis has made some interesting connections.'

'Interesting? She's bloody giving you motives.'

'I know that.'

Langton stood up, almost kicking his chair aside. 'Then get to grips with them and start taking the reins. I'm disappointed, Mike.' He paused. 'You know she's up for promotion?'

'Yes, I had heard.'

'You got yours — now prove I was right to back you.'

'Yes, sir.'

Langton was about to walk out but stopped, saying, 'I want Travis to do the television crime show and it would be good if you had something tangible to give them. Goodnight.'

Mike remained seated, feeling depressed and annoyed that he had been made to look so useless.

'Did you know he was here?' Mike asked Anna when she emerged from her office. He was still sitting in the incident room.

'No, I didn't.'

'He was in your office.'

'He must have gone in when I was in here.' She paused and moved closer. 'Are you all right?'

'I'm just great. Are you deliberately setting out to make me look like a prick in front of him?'

'I told you I'd no idea he was in my office.'

'Really? You hear him ripping into me?'

'Did you hear him doing the same to me?'

'What?'

Anna put down her briefcase and sat in the chair Langton had used.

'I think we'd better straighten things out between us.'

'What's there to straighten out?'

She sighed. 'I didn't give any feedback on anything as the day progressed because, to be honest, Mike, I wasn't sure where it was all leading. Langton said that I should have reported back my interview with the publishing company straight away, but I was returning to the station when Joan called me about the two meetings she'd fixed with the theatrical agents. As I was already in the West End, I decided to do them. I didn't get anything from either of them as to whether or not Amanda was

217

changing agents, but I did get Andrew Smith-Barker identified so I went straight to interview him, as he was only in Knightsbridge.'

'Why are you telling me this? You already outlined it at the briefing.'

'I know I did, but I wanted to explain why it might have looked like I hadn't kept you in the loop, so to speak, and so I apologise.'

Mike stood up and stretched.

'Langton said I was out of line, so that's why I'm apologising to you,' she said quietly.

'Accepted.'

'Thank you.' What Anna did not add was that Langton had also warned her that if he was to discover any further evidence that she hadn't shared with the team, she would be in trouble.

'You're doing the television interview, Anna,' Mike said suddenly. 'It's lined up to be after the funeral. Joan'll give you details. It's at the BBC.'

'Oh God no, I hate being in front of the camera.'

'Boss wants it.' Mike looked at her. 'Are you still seeing him?' he asked after a moment.

'No, I am not. I hadn't seen him for months until this case. I sort of resent you even asking. Even if I was, it would be none of your business.'

'Still bruised, are we?'

Anna straightened up and kept her temper.

'I never was — all right? Now, if you'll excuse me, I'm going home.'

Chapter Twelve

Anna was in the shower the following morning when she remembered something. Amanda had used a driver when she first met with Josh Lyons from Golden Arrow. It might not be important but, on the other hand, whoever drove her to the lunch at Le Caprice might also have been privy to who she was meeting. And that would mean that there was someone else who knew her intentions to write her story.

The team were instructed to make their own way to the funeral, to make sure they integrated with the mourners. They were to keep their eyes and ears open. Anna set out early. The funeral was taking place at midday in the centre of Covent Garden at St Paul's church, known as 'the Actor's Church' due to the number of famous thespians buried in its small churchyard. A red carpet had been laid down from the entrance of the chapel to the gates. A choir was singing 'Ave Maria' as the mourners entered. In pride of place was a six-foot-tall photograph of Amanda, wearing what looked like a bridal gown and on her head a rosebud crown. One could not fail to be taken by her stunning beauty, the sweet vacant smile on her lips. As the congregation entered and took their places, four ushers wearing tailcoats handed out the service sheets, each adorned with another picture of Amanda.

The first six pews were reserved while the back pews were for fans and visitors wanting to be part of the service. As the church began to fill, there was a hubbub of voices and the constant flashing of cameras as the press lined up outside along the red carpet. Anna had seen Mike Lewis, Barolli and two other officers, but she didn't recognise anyone else. She was startled when Langton moved along the pew to squeeze in beside her. She inched up as far as she could to enable him to sit in comfort. He opened the thick manila Order of Service and read through it. Then he looked, as did everyone gathered, at the photograph of Amanda at the front of the church.

'So beautiful,' he murmured softly.

A Mercedes with dark tinted windows drew up outside the church gates. Colin O'Dell, wearing a denim jacket, jeans and a T-shirt with a silk scarf wrapped around his neck, hurried from the car, his French girlfriend rushing to catch him up as he kept his head down to pass the waiting photographers. He was quickly followed by Andrea Lesser and Andrew Smith-Barker, who held her elbow tightly as they made their way inside. Next came Scott Myers in a tailored dark suit and dark glasses, accompanied by his wife Fiona.

The photographers surged forwards, but were held back by the ushers who were on hand to guide in the latecomers. Then came Rupert Mitchell, and Felicity and Jeannie from Amanda's flat. Anna recognised them from photos at the Yard. Unlike the star turns, Jeannie was keen to pose for photographers, but now there was a crush of mourners standing shoulder-to-shoulder in the small entrance.

The sound of a light bell began to ring as the coffin arrived and was carried towards the altar. It was unusual, like a woven wicker basket, the top laden with white lilies; it seemed so tiny and light. The bell continued to ring as the Archdeacon in full robes moved down the centre aisle to step onto the raised rostrum beside the choir. He looked surprisingly young, with a ruddy complexion, and as he spoke his voice rang round the church.

When he asked the congregation to stand to sing the first hymn, Anna caught her first glimpse of Amanda's parents in the front pew. Her mother was wearing a wide-brimmed black straw hat and black suit. Her father, in a charcoal-grey suit, held onto her arm, his face drawn.

Anna, sitting so close to Langton, found his nearness uncomfortable, and as they stood to sing side-by-side, she wished the service would end as quickly as possible. None of it felt real; the body in the wicker-basket coffin had been murdered – and yet the entire service was more fitting for a wedding. There were prayers and eulogies from various actors and then it was Jeannie Bale's turn. Dressed in a low-cut cream chiffon dress, her arms bare, she walked up to the front.

'I am going to read for Amanda her favourite poem. It is by Meredith Kinmont.' Jeannie's voice wavered as she paused and opened a typed sheet of paper, as if she were auditioning.

Langton leaned close to Anna. 'How long is this going on for?'

She gave him a stern glance and he sighed.

I am the green grass
I am the blonde hair caught between your fingers
I am the light in your eyes when you look at me
I am the light gone out of your eyes when you look away
Don't look away
I like you
See, I am smiling
Don't go away
Stay
You want to stay, don't you?
Take off your shoes
You love me, don't you?
I can tell
You've always loved me, haven't you?
You can't help it
I am the secret you daren't whisper
I am the green grass.

During the reading, Anna took a covert look around. Both Amanda's parents bowed their heads. Colin O'Dell hung his head low, as if trying to hide his face from view. Scott Myers was openly crying, and Andrea Lesser held a tissue to her eyes. Right at the back was one of the unit drivers Simon had interviewed. She watched closely as he stood poker-faced, but with tears trickling down his cheeks.

Jeannie finished reading in her soft sweet voice and it was as if she expected applause but none came, just silence and the odd sound of muffled weeping. The Archdeacon came to stand in front of the coffin.

'Amanda Mary Delany,' he said, and turned to the large photograph and raised his hand. 'We must celebrate her short life and feel compassion for her family and friends gathered here today. She was a star, a rare beauty cut down in the prime of her life. As success and stardom made Amanda known to many, loved by many and admired by all who knew her, we must also pray that she rests in peace. To have been taken from us, so brutally, is cause for us all to feel untold sorrow and anguish that we should lose such a treasured young woman.'

On cue, Colin O'Dell moved from his pew to stand on the rostrum. He seemed nervous, mumbling his words and barely looking up. Afterwards he returned to his seat and knelt in prayer, holding his face in his hands.

'That was a good performance,' Langton whispered to Anna as he stood to sing the next hymn. He had a terrible voice, offkey and too loud; it made Anna cringe. Then it was the turn of Scott Myers. He was more eloquent than Colin O'Dell as he read a short poem by Rossetti, before returning to sit beside his frozen-faced wife. Another hymn and then Andrea Lesser walked from her seat with what looked like a thick wad of notes. Anna glanced sideways at Langton, who took a discreet look at his watch. It was by now incredibly hot and uncomfortable and people were fanning themselves with their service sheets. Andrea Lesser held a tissue in her hand, as she put on some reading glasses.

'Amanda was asked by a journalist, when doing some promotional work for her last film, if she would describe her own funeral. Little did any of us who loved her so dearly, know that in so short a time her life would be taken. Amanda described the unusual wicker casket and with the help of her friends we have endeavoured to make this sad day the one she would have wanted. The hymns, the flowers and the church lit by hundreds of candles, even the poems read by her friends, were

Amanda's choice. I thank you everyone for coming and hope she rests in peace . . .' She had to stop and swallow back the tears.

'I'm so sorry, but Amanda was like a daughter to me. Having represented her since her career began, we spent so much time together and as her career became successful we formed a strong bond of trust. She will be forever in my mind and now I would like you to listen to Amanda reading a poem she recorded. I think it will make us all understand how much of a loss she is. Thank you.'

There was a pause before Amanda's voice was heard from speakers positioned directly behind her photograph.

'My name is Amanda Delany' – her voice was low, with a slight gravel tone – 'and this is one of my favourite poems by Meredith Kinmont, one I have loved since I was a child. If ever I had to say goodbye to this world, this is how I would like to be remembered . . . going with a smile.'

There was another pause and then her voice seemed to lift, clearer, sweeter, as if she were about to break into laughter; it was very moving.

'Not many people see the funny side of things these days.
Most people only laugh when everyone else does
so as not to feel left out
In fact, not many people laugh much at all
these days, except at rather sad things
Not many people, for instance, would have the slightest idea
how funny
how madly
utterly
absurdly

> *absolutely*
> *outrageously*
> *hysterically funny it is*
> *for me to be here*
> *with you'*

It was brilliant sunshine outside, after the service, and the press were still there in force. Amanda's parents stood side by side, thanking the mourners for coming, Andrea Lesser beside them, wiping her eyes. As people exited from the church, there was an overall feeling of relief and the babble of voices rose, mixed with loud laughter. The press had a field day; flashlights were popping more in tune with a movie première than a funeral.

Langton held Anna by her elbow and leaned down to whisper to her: now was the time to 'mingle'. Already Mike Lewis could be seen close to the altar, looking at all the floral displays, noting down the names on the cards beside them. Barolli was outside, moving unobtrusively from group to group as people waited for their cars. Then Anna realised her mobile phone wasn't in her pocket. She remembered turning it off just as Langton had joined her in the pew; it must have fallen from her pocket when she knelt to pray.

It was eerie inside the now-empty church; only a cleric remained, extinguishing the candles with a long silver snuffer. Anna hurried towards the pew she had occupied and then bent down low, looking for the phone beneath the bench. There it was, kicked further back under the pew. As she reached for it, she heard voices.

'Come on – we're waiting, we're by the gates. Where's the car? If it's close, we'll walk to it as the fucking press are all over us.'

'Sorry, I was going to leave the back way but the door's locked.'

Anna recognised the first voice. It was Colin O'Dell's, but she couldn't see who he was talking to, since that person was hidden behind Amanda's photograph.

'I'm parked on a meter by Covent Garden tube station; it'll take me two minutes,' the stranger's voice said.

'I'll come with you,' O'Dell said as he moved closer to where Anna crouched, hidden.

'You getting a quick snort in, are you?' the other man asked.

'Leave it out.' O'Dell moved even closer, then turned to see the cleric still snuffing out the candles. He lowered his voice. 'You scored for me?'

Anna watched as he disappeared from view for a few moments behind the photograph. Then he reappeared, pocketing a small white envelope as one of the unit drivers from *Gaslight* came into view. He was putting money into a wallet.

'Come on – let's get going,' Anna heard O'Dell say. 'Sooner I'm out of this the better.'

'You going for the drinks at the Ivy Club?'

'No way, I've had enough crap to last me for today.'

The two men walked along the aisle and out of the church before Anna stood up. She followed after a moment, not wanting them to see her, and by the time she made it outside, there were few people left and none of the team from the station. So the actors employed the unit driver for private use, did they? She couldn't help wondering if this was the same driver who had taken Amanda to Le Caprice to meet Josh Lyons.

Just as Anna reached the church gate, a Bentley drove

past. Andrew Smith-Barker was in the driving seat, Andrea Lesser next to him. Neither saw her. Anna recognised Jeannie Bale up ahead, walking with Felicity Turner and heading towards Garrick Street. She hurried to catch up with them.

'Hi, I saw you in the church,' she said rather breathlessly.

Felicity gave Anna a blank-eyed stare, while Jeannie smiled politely at her.

'I thought you read the poem beautifully,' Anna continued.

'Oh, thank you, but I wish I'd known that there'd be a recording of Amanda reading one too.'

'It didn't matter; your poem was very moving.'

When Jeannie then asked if she was going to the post-funeral drinks at the Ivy Club, a few minutes away in West Street, Anna jumped at the chance.

At the bar, on arrival, they each took a glass of champagne. Jeannie nudged Felicity, warning her to behave herself, and then smiled at Anna.

'Are you with an agency?' she asked.

Anna shook her head, but Jeannie was so busy looking around the crowded bar she didn't even ask who Anna was. By this time she was obviously eager to mingle and soon moved off. As Felicity had gone to the loo, Anna followed Jeannie's lead and started looking for someone she could have a conversation with, but as the champagne flowed, she was ignored. She recognised some faces from the film unit, amongst them the director Julian Pike, and Emma Field, the stand-in, looking very attractive and laughing with Scott Myers. As Anna spotted them, Fiona Myers, who had obviously had too much to drink, barged in between them.

'My God, I can't leave you alone for a minute,' she said aggressively. 'Who's this little tart?'

Anna circled around them, not wishing to be seen, and moved deeper into the room towards the exit onto the roof garden. Several guests were outside smoking. Carol and Cynthia, the make-up girls from the film, were standing to one side talking to Mike Reynolds, the line producer on *Gaslight*. He was just turning away from the women when he saw Anna.

'Hi, there,' he said jovially, then: 'Help me out. I know you, don't I?'

'Anna Travis, Detective Travis. We met on the set last week.'

'Ah, right, sorry. Were you at the funeral?'

'Yes, I was. Look, can I ask you something?'

He nodded. His eyes never met hers, but constantly flicked around the room.

'The unit drivers — are they also hired by the artists privately?'

'Yes, I'd think they would be. They can do with the extra cash. Not a lot of movies up and rolling at the moment — the British film industry is in a real slack period.' He smiled across the room to Emma Field and then excused himself without waiting for a reply, leaving Anna standing alone again. She watched Reynolds make a play for the very attractive Miss Field, then turned as a soft voice from behind her said her name.

'Detective Travis.'

She looked up at Andrew Smith-Barker.

'Can I get you a refill?' he asked.

'Er no, I'm fine, thank you.'

'I'm sure you are. Here, let me take your glass.' He reached out and took her half-full glass, giving her a cold arrogant smile as he moved off. She knew she had better make a quick exit as he was heading towards Andrea Lesser. Anna skirted around the crowd and felt her elbow tugged.

'I want to go and I can't find Jeannie. She's somewhere schmoozing and I've not got any money on me.' Felicity had obviously had more champagne. Her face was flushed, her vacant eyes were even more glazed.

'Do you want a lift?' Anna offered. 'I can give you one as I'm on my way out.'

'Yes, you are.' It was Andrea Lesser, her face tight with anger. 'I don't know how you dare intrude. This is a private party for close friends and associates of Amanda. I'd like you to leave immediately.'

Anna was about to apologise, but to her astonishment Felicity pushed Miss Lesser.

'Why don't you go fuck yourself?'

'I beg your pardon?'

'Stuck-up bitch, I know all about you. Amanda couldn't stand the sight of you, nor half the creeps who are here. It's all a fucking sham.'

Andrea Lesser seemed to teeter backwards slightly as Andrew Smith–Barker appeared and took hold of Felicity's arm.

'It's time you left, young lady.'

'Gerroff me, I know all about you as well.' Felicity was so unsteady on her feet that she clung onto Anna.

'This is a private party and you either leave quietly or I will get the staff to remove you.'

'*Fuck off.*'

Smith–Barker got a hard shove in his chest as Felicity released her hold of Anna and fell forwards. He caught her and gripped her tightly, drawing her away. The rest of the room was picking up on the fracas and now Jeannie pushed her way towards them.

'What are you doing?' she asked.

Andrea Lesser turned on her, saying angrily, 'Please, all of you leave. This is neither the time nor the place for anything unpleasant.' She glared at Anna. 'You will accompany these two girls out of here. This is an invitation-only event.'

Now Jeannie got her own temper up and faced Miss Lesser.

'You get me to read a poem, but don't want me here. Terrific. I knew Amanda better than any of this fucking crowd, so you had to invite me, whether you liked it or not, but you don't want anyone to know just how much Amanda hated you. She knew what you were doing, she told me, so why don't you stop this fucking charade, and *you* fuck off.'

Two members of the staff quickly stepped between them and took Felicity and Jeannie by the arm and led them out. Red in the face, Miss Lesser pointed her finger at Anna.

'I am going to report you to your superiors. How dare you sneak your way in here?'

'I'm sorry. I'll leave now.'

'I should damned well hope so.'

Shame-faced with everyone staring, Anna followed the two girls out of the club. Two paparazzi photographers were snapping away and Jeannie was shouting out her name to them, making sure they spelled it right. With a few flash bulbs still going off behind them, Anna waved away the doorman's offer of a taxi. He held onto her arm.

'Please take your hands off me!' she said, annoyed.

Anxious to get away, she walked a few paces down the street, noticing a number of Mercedes parked with their drivers sitting inside, one of whom she recognised. It was the man who had been with Colin O'Dell in the church.

She tapped on his window and he lowered it.

'No way, I'm waiting for someone.'

Anna flipped open her ID and he said immediately, 'Sorry, no offence. Didn't know it was you.'

'Can we have a quick chat?'

'Here?'

'Why not? It won't take a moment.'

Anna got into the passenger seat and closed the car door. The driver pressed himself as far away from her as possible. The engine was on; he had been watching a movie so he turned it off.

'You were at the film unit, right?' he asked.

'Correct. And you're one of the James brothers.'

'Yeah. I'm Tony, the handsome one.' But he didn't crack a smile as he said it.

'Do you also do private chauffeur work, Tony?'

'Yeah, when it suits I do.'

'Did you drive Amanda Delany?'

'On occasions, yeah, but me older brother Harry was her driver on *Gaslight*. Sometimes I stood in for him.'

'Did she employ you when you weren't working for a film company?'

'A few times, if work was a bit thin on the ground.'

'You're driving Colin O'Dell today, aren't you?'

'Well, I was. He went back to his hotel and I took over from another guy who got a gig out at Heathrow, so I'm here for Scott Myers and his wife now.'

'But you were at the funeral.'

'Yeah, out of respect.'

231

'You seemed very distraught.'

He clenched his fists. 'What is this? I knew Amanda – she was a little darlin' – and seeing that basket for a coffin, it . . . it didn't seem right to me. Got me all upset to know that she was inside it.'

'Can you tell me about the times you drove Amanda Delany?'

He sighed. 'Not much *to* tell. It wasn't that often, but if she had a première or a big do, she'd call one of us.'

'Do you remember driving her to a lunch at Le Caprice restaurant?'

'No. That said, I don't remember all the jobs. How recent was it?'

'Maybe four months ago?'

'Nah, not me. I was in Turkey on a shoot.'

'Did your brother also drive Miss Delany on a personal basis?'

'Sometimes.'

'Do you retain a logbook for private events?'

'Yeah, some of the time. All depends if it's on account or cash.'

There was a flurry of activity outside the club and the flash bulbs were popping.

'You gotta get out, here's my ride.'

'Do you have a card, Tony?'

He shoved one into Anna's hand as he got out, signalling to Scott Myers and his wife. Anna was caught between Fiona and Scott as the photographers chased them down the road. The Myers were quick to get into the car, and by the time Anna was passing the club's entrance, the Mercedes had driven away. Scott stared at her from the passenger window as the car went by.

★

Anna was in a fury; she got back to her parking spot to find that her Mini had been clamped. She couldn't believe it as she was no more than ten minutes over the allocated parking time. When she called to get the clamp unlocked, she was told it would be at least an hour before they could be in her area. She paced up and down the pavement, waiting. She tried to put in a call to the station, but there was no signal. Whether or not her phone had been damaged when it fell onto the stone floor at the church, she couldn't tell. She dared not leave the car to find a call box in case the clampers returned to release the car and she wasn't there.

The team made their way back from the funeral in dribs, and drabs, and it was at least three hours before Mike Lewis held a briefing to discuss what, if anything, they had found out. Anna's absence was noticed; Barolli suggested she might have taken the afternoon off to do some shopping in Covent Garden. No one had anything of real interest to report. The consensus was that attending the funeral had been a waste of time. Then Langton appeared.

'Where is Travis?'

'Not sure, Guv. We left her at the church, expected her back with everyone else.'

Langton pursed his lips and nodded to Mike; they left the incident room and went into his office.

It wasn't until seven that evening, having hit the rush-hour traffic, that Anna made it back to the station. She was about to take off her coat when Mike Lewis walked in and slapped the *Evening Standard* down on her desk. A large photograph of Scott Myers and Colin

O'Dell dominated the front page, alongside a picture of Amanda's unusual coffin. The headline read: STARS BID GOODBYE TO AMANDA DELANY.

'Heavens, they work fast, don't they?' Anna said, looking at it.

Mike gestured for her to open the paper.

On page three, under the headline CAT FIGHT AT MURDER VICTIM'S FUNERAL, was a picture of Anna caught between the doorman and Jeannie and Felicity. The way it had been photographed or doctored made it look as if she was about to punch the doorman. She gasped and sat back in her chair.

'My God, I don't believe it!'

'You'd better. Langton is going apeshit. The only good thing is they don't have you identified.'

'Is he here?'

'He was, and got pissed off waiting. We've called your home and your mobile. What in Christ's name were you doing?'

Anna sighed.

'I went to the drinks party after the funeral,' she said.

'Were you drunk or something?'

'No, I wasn't. I can't speak for either of the other two girls, but I was sober and . . . Listen, let me try and explain everything.'

'All I want to know is if you got something for us?'

'Well, not exactly.'

'Right. In that case, save the excuses for tomorrow morning. Goodnight.'

Lewis slammed her door, hard, leaving Anna staring at the newspaper. After a while, she went into the incident room and saw that someone had cut out the picture from the *Standard* and pinned it up. There was a red ring around her face. Angrily she tore it down.

Chapter Thirteen

The doorbell rang, making Anna jump. It was almost eleven. She had opened a bottle of wine and was sitting in her kitchen working on her laptop, reflecting on what she had witnessed that afternoon and listing everything she thought was relevant. Jeannie Bale and Felicity Turner must be questioned again and a warrant issued to search their premises. She wanted Tony James checked out to see if he had any criminal record, his brother Harry too, and . . . Anna stared at the screen. She had not come up with any fresh details, rather underlined the old. Yet she was still certain something was being covered up between Andrea Lesser and Andrew Smith-Barker.

Anna hurried to the front door and looked through the spy-hole. Langton was standing there, his face in profile. She unlocked the Yale and opened the door.

'How did you get up to my floor?' she asked.

'Car-park doors were open so I walked in. You might have refused to let me come up.'

She gestured for him to go into the lounge, but instead he walked into her kitchen.

'I'm starving. What have you got to eat?'

'Bacon sandwich?'

'Lovely, and a cup of tea.' He picked up the bottle of wine and looked at the label.

'Do you want a glass?'

'Nope, tea's fine.' He sat down at her laptop, reading where she had left off.

Anna behaved as if she wasn't in any way surprised by his visit, but her heart was thudding in her chest. She made the tea, put bacon under the grill while Langton remained seated, pressing her laptop commands and reading her notes.

'Some of that is private,' she said quietly.

He swivelled round to face her.

'What am I going to do with you, Anna Travis?'

She said nothing as she carried on preparing his sandwich. He poured some wine into her glass and sipped. Then grimaced.

'Not chilled enough,' he muttered.

'Are you here because of the *Evening Standard*?'

'Quite possibly. So far they haven't put out your name or your connection to the Met, or the fact that you are investigating the murder of Amanda Delany, so no harm done. However, someone might recognise you if you do the TV interview so I'm pulling you out and putting Mike Lewis on it.'

'Fine.'

'No, it isn't fine, Anna. I need to know what the fuck you are playing at! Do you want to get chucked out on your ear because, if so, you are going the right way about it!'

'I can explain.'

'I certainly hope you can because I've had that Miss Lesser onto me. She's made a formal complaint to the Commissioner and he's ferreting around and not liking the fact that we've got bugger-all so far. And it doesn't help seeing one of his officers pissed and having a cat fight outside the Ivy Club.'

'I was not pissed,' she snapped.

'Looked like it, and you were gone all afternoon.'

Anna banged the grill to turn the bacon over and filled the teapot.

'Having asked you to make it a priority to keep the team informed of your movements, you totally disregard me. No one could contact you.'

'I dropped my phone in the church. It must have got damaged because I couldn't make any calls.' She fetched a mug and jug of milk and put them on the counter.

'So when was that? Directly after the service?'

'Yes. I went back in to look for it.' She poured him a cup of tea and took him through the events of the afternoon.

'You already interviewed the unit drivers, didn't you?' Langton asked when she told him about her conversation with Tony James.

'Simon did. They didn't give us any reason to be suspicious, but I saw Tony James in the church passing what could have been drugs to Colin O'Dell.'

'That's making you suspicious now?'

She sighed. She was getting increasingly rattled by him.

'It's possible that the James brothers knew more about Amanda than we at first thought, if she also used them as private chauffeurs. They may have known about the book she was going to write, and if it was going to be a big exposé of her lovers, then—'

'You think that Tony was having an affair with her?'

'No, but it's possible that if he had that information, he might have told someone or tipped them off.'

'I don't buy it,' Langton said, wiping the crusts of toast around his plate.

'Don't buy what?'

'That some movie star who screwed her would go to such lengths – murder – so as not to be written about in her cheap little book.'

'It wasn't cheap. She was going to be paid over a million pounds for it.'

'I was referring to the contents, sweetheart.'

Anna chewed her lips, feeling stressed out by his presence. She wasn't going to let him know though, so she continued.

'Another motive would be if her agent, Andrea Lesser, and this investment guy, Andrew Smith-Barker, had been embezzling her money. They could have hired someone to do it. I told you what Jeannie and her druggie friend said to them at the Ivy Club.'

'Nah. Still don't buy it.' Langton stared into the mug, holding it cupped in his hands. 'Why take her cuddly little rabbit?'

'What?'

'You brought it up, Anna. Why *did* whoever killed her take that old rag toy she slept with?'

'Isn't it more important to know who took her diary?'

'Maybe it would make sense to take that, if you were concerned about her writing something that could be damaging to your career or your business, or even if she was going to accuse you of some kind of fraud. But why take the rabbit?'

He held out the mug for a refill.

'I've been thinking about something you said,' he went on, 'that it could have been taken as a keepsake, sick as that might sound. In psycho-babble it often means that the murderer wants to keep something close to them, like a token or a trophy. But this isn't a serial killer.'

Amanda kept her drugs hidden inside the toy, Anna reminded him.

Langton laughed softly. 'You don't stab someone, give them multiple wounds hard enough to leave bruises, the imprint of the shaft on the skin – you don't do that for a few measly grams of coke.'

He suddenly slapped the table with the flat of his hand. 'This was not a professional hit! This was someone with a lot of hate, a lot of anger – and I am damned sure it was done by someone she knew and knew well.'

'I don't think any of the actors we interviewed hated her that much. You know they've all had their prints taken to see if they match with those from her mews.'

'You got some whisky?'

She opened a cupboard and handed him a half-bottle of Johnnie Walker. He reached for a glass.

'I've never met anyone who bought a half-bottle of Scotch,' he grumbled.

'It takes all kinds,' she said under her breath.

Langton sipped his drink. He didn't seem inclined to leave or move from the kitchen to a more comfortable place to sit, but stayed perched on the stool.

'OK, go back to what I said about the stab wounds, and think what you brought up about Amanda knowing the killer. It had to have been someone who cared, you said, to spread her hair out over the pillow, someone who didn't want to touch her face, not an actor, no way an actor.'

Anna started to wash up the dishes, anything to keep her hands occupied as she had a real inclination to punch him.

'Keys,' he said softly.

She watched as he lifted the glass a fraction and then put it back onto the table, making a circle.

'The front-door keys. We know the interior designer had one, we know Andrea Lesser had one and that the designer gave his back when he'd finished the job. Amanda had one obviously. According to Lewis, they checked with the locksmith and there were *four* keys cut, so that leaves us with one key unaccounted for. She could have easily had others cut, but I doubt it. It's possible one of the people working on her place got one cut but again, I doubt it. This was her first home, her own place and I don't think, the more I get to know of Amanda Delany, that she would have handed them out.'

'She hated to sleep alone,' Anna observed. 'In fact, she was afraid to go to sleep. She used speed, coke and uppers to keep herself awake.'

She pulled up a stool to sit beside him. Langton wasn't listening. She knew him too well; he could easily tune out when he was concentrating on something. After a moment of silence, she continued.

'No sign of a break-in, the killer let himself in, but there's nothing on CCTV. The driver brought her back from the film set, watched her go in before he drove away. He returned later that day, couldn't rouse her, called her mobile, called her landline ... are you listening to me?'

Langton nodded. By now Anna had fetched a glass and was pouring herself a Scotch. The bottle was just over half-full and he took it from her to top up his own drink, screwing the cap back on very slowly.

'Then Andrea Lesser turns up with a key to open the

front door and she finds the body. If tests prove that Amanda had been dead a much shorter time than we were told at first, it would mean she was actually killed later that morning,' Anna said.

'Keys . . .' he repeated. Langton started to pace; even in the cramped, small kitchen he still managed two or three paces back and forth.

'Keys – it's the keys,' he repeated. 'Take a look in your handbag.'

Anna frowned. 'I don't understand.'

Langton took a set of keys out of his pocket – car keys, house keys, office keys and another for his pedal-bike lock. He hooked them onto his forefinger, twirling it slightly, then dangled his keyring in front of Anna.

'My keyring is an old medal from the First World War and belonged to my great-grandfather.'

He pulled the stool out to sit beside her again. The key discovered in Amanda's handbag, he recalled, was on a single ring, nothing else attached. She might have needed keys for her laptop, desk drawer, jewellery case and quite possibly the door keys from her old flat that she was still paying rent on. He counted on his fingers the number of keys that she would have needed. Anna sipped her Scotch, listening.

'New home . . . in my humble opinion, the girl would have had something special as a key ring. This was the first place that she owned.'

'What exactly does this add to the enquiry, apart from there might be a set of keys missing?' Anna asked.

Langton drained his glass and crossed to pour the rest of the bottle into it. He gave one of his rare smiles.

'We never saw anyone entering, nobody saw anyone around the mews, you said yourself she hated to go to sleep, she was scared of her nightmares. What if the killer was already inside the house?'

'It's possible,' Anna conceded. 'It would tie in with her knowing the killer, and that the previous night she had a nightmare and woke up screaming.'

Langton ruffled her hair. She had always hated it when he did that, as it made the red curls stand up on end. She flattened it down with her hand as he picked up his coat.

'I talked to a nurse who'd cared for her at the Drury Clinic,' she blurted out. 'She said that Amanda often screamed herself awake. So I don't think the scream she claimed she heard was connected to her murder.'

He stared at her. 'You talked to a nurse?'

Anna explained Dilys Summers's connection with the previous case she had worked on, how the same woman had looked after Amanda Delany at the clinic.

He nodded, then took a match and bit it, using it as a toothpick. 'Go on.'

'As I said, apparently Amanda often screamed herself awake and would get very distraught. Dilys Summers also mentioned that Amanda had visitors at the Drury – Colin O'Dell and Scott Myers, and someone else who she didn't know as she wasn't on duty, but it could have been Rupert Mitchell.'

'Really. And was this information passed on to the team?'

'Not exactly.'

'Not exactly. Jesus Christ! I want to know precisely what our victim was doing weeks before the murder.'

'She was *filming*, practically non-stop – very long hours. We know that as we have her schedule, we have her mobile phone and we've been checking all her contacts and calls made shortly before her murder.'

'He was inside the mews waiting for her,' Langton said softly.

'What?'

'I think her killer was already inside the mews cottage waiting for her to come home.'

Anna gave a wide-handed gesture. 'Whoever it was, are you saying he had house keys?'

'That is *exactly* what I am saying'. Langton shrugged into his coat. 'He would have time to maybe find that five-year diary, read it and get into a rage, angry enough to kill her.'

Langton walked towards the door and then stopped.

'No, no, that's not right because whoever it was came ready to kill. He had the knife, the weapon, on him.'

He flicked his coat collar up. 'Food for thought.'

Anna followed him as he headed into the hall.

'Can I ask you something?' she said.

He turned and cocked his head to one side. 'Yes.'

'Why did you come here tonight?'

'As I said, food for thought and, well, I missed . . .'

She thought he was going to reach out to her, tell her he missed her, but he didn't. He opened the front door.

'I miss these kinds of nights – you know, thrashing ideas around. This case is starting to really get to me. We have to establish who the lady was seeing, if they weren't connected to the film unit as we suspected. I'd wager it was someone she had been close to for some time.'

He tapped the door with his foot, then reached forwards, cupping her face between his hands.

'Brings back memories. Thanks for the sandwich. G'night.' Then he kissed her cheek with no more feeling than if he'd been a family friend, never a lover.

All of a sudden, Anna was riled. She resented the fact

that he felt he could drop by at eleven o'clock at night, not only drop in without notice, but get her to make him a bacon sandwich, a pot of tea, then polish off her Scotch. As the door was about to close, she dived towards it and pulled it wide open.

Startled, Langton turned. 'Remembered something else you've forgotten to disclose, have you?' he said sarkily.

'No. I'd just like you to know that if you intend making these late-night calls a habit, I'd appreciate you calling me first. Goodnight.'

And then she shut the door.

Unsettled and confused by Langton's sudden appearance, Anna didn't feel like going to bed; she knew she would not sleep. Instead, she used an old technique her father had taught her when he was in the force; she had watched him do it as a child. He would make up cards of suspects and, laying them out, would place them in order of suspicion. Anna wrote down the names of Lesser, Smith-Barker and the three male actors, then added both girls from the funeral, along with Amanda's parents, plus the drivers Harry and his younger brother Tony James. She laid them out in front of her as if she was playing Solo. Which one of them would have a strong enough motive to instigate the murder? Was the motive money? Fraud?

She stared at the names and knew that, without any incriminating evidence, neither Lesser nor Smith-Barker could be in first position so she placed them to one side. Next, the three actors: would any of them really have much to lose if there were extracts about their affairs with Amanda? They were media fodder already; Anna doubted there could be anything that would incite them to kill.

Amanda's parents were next. As much as she had sensed their near-indifference to their daughter's death, they surely had no motive strong enough to kill her because they were past caring for her wellbeing. She put the cards with their names to one side.

Felicity Turner had surprised her with her anger. She had been stoned at the party that afternoon and had had too much to drink, but Anna sensed there was more to learn from her. She placed the card bearing Felicity's name in the centre of the table and put Jeannie Bale's beneath it. Again, Anna had been taken aback by what the girl had said; her anger and hints that she knew a lot more put her under suspicion. She then picked up the unit drivers' names and placed their cards alongside the two girls'. A moment later, she moved Tony James's card in front of Felicity's, along with his brother's.

She printed the word MOTIVE on a card and sat staring at it. On another she wrote ABORTION and on a third card, KEYS, placing this one beside ABORTION. She was getting tired; it was after three in the morning. Looking over her cut-out jigsaw of names, Anna knew she was going round in circles. Literally, as by moving one card after another around on the table, she had unwittingly formed a sort of circle. She yawned; she knew she hadn't really gained anything from the exercise. She rested her chin on her hand, leaning her elbows on the table. If the killer, as Langton suspected, was well-known and sufficiently trusted to be given the dead girl's house keys, then someone, one of the listed, had to know his identity.

Anna rubbed her eyes and frowned. She recalled that

the young, very pretty girl – their victim's stand-in, Emma Field – had described Amanda as constantly using her mobile; she was always sending text messages. Anna was certain that the mobile Emma had handed to her had shown no sent or received text messages. Amanda must have had a second mobile phone or used a BlackBerry for texts and e-mails. *Where was it?*

She picked up another blank card and wrote on it MONEY and put it into the circle beside Andrew Smith-Barker's name. Then she used her forefinger to slide his card outside the circle. Crossing to turn the lights out, she hesitated and went back to the table. Frustrated, she swept all the cards to the floor and went to bed.

The following morning, by the time Anna arrived at the station, Mike Lewis had brought in Amanda Delany's accountant, a woman called Ronnie Hodgson. She was wearing a smart tailored suit with a cream silk collarless blouse beneath it, and high pointed stilettos that made her even taller than Mike. She placed a large leather briefcase onto the table before she sat down.

'I do apologise for not being able to meet with you before now, but I hope I'll be able to assist you and will endeavour to do so to the best of my ability. That said, I have to safeguard the fact that, although my client is now sadly deceased, there are certain problems of invasion of privacy that might arise.'

'Your client, Ms Hodgson, was murdered and I really doubt there'll be any issue of invasion of privacy,' Mike pointed out. 'We need you to outline Miss Delany's financial situation and help on a few queries pertaining to our investigation.'

Ronnie Hodgson had dark brown eyes and shoulder-length glossy hair, swept up to give her an attractive, surprisingly youthful look. Anna estimated her age to be late thirties. She wore no jewellery and no wedding ring. She clicked open her briefcase and took out several files and a shiny, black leather-covered notebook.

'Are you privy to Miss Delany's will?' Anna asked.

'Yes, I am.'

'We need to know who her beneficiaries are.'

Miss Hodgson nodded and opened her notebook. She scribbled something in it with a slim silver pen before removing Amanda Delany's Last Will and Testament from a file.

'I suggested that she use the solicitors Marchbank and Crawley, as they do a considerable amount of work for certain clients of mine. Amanda, I have to say, was in the habit of adding and removing certain bequests, but I had no reason to discuss any alterations with her over the past three months.'

'We'll also require details of Miss Delany's finances,' Anna explained, 'her different accounts, any payments and direct debits over the past six months. As you must be aware, you were served with a court order to hand over all the documents we require.'

Ronnie Hodgson nodded, saying, 'I think you'll find that all her accounts are in excellent order. Amanda was up to date with both income tax and VAT payments.' She passed two copies in neat bound plastic covers across the table.

'Does this include her investments?' Anna queried.

Miss Hodgson hesitated and withdrew another file. 'I think you should approach her investment banker about those.'

'That would be Andrew Smith-Barker?'

'Yes, that is correct.'

Mike Lewis flicked through the file in front of him and then glanced at Anna.

'These are accounts up to the previous year.'

'Yes, obviously this year's accounts haven't yet been completed.'

'But they are the ones we're most interested in,' he said quietly.

'I'm afraid they haven't been processed yet. We do work a year in advance, but you can't expect me to have any records to present to you yet, as under the circumstances we are having to deal without Miss Delany's up-to-date receipts and bank statements.'

'Do you have Power of Attorney?'

'No, I don't. That would be her agent, Andrea Lesser. I believe it was arranged during the purchase and refurbishing of Miss Delany's mews house.'

'Did you oversee the payments on the house, to the builders and so forth?' Mike asked.

'Yes, of course, as I was Miss Delany's accountant.'

Both Anna and Mike remained silent as they read through the files, and although neither expressed their astonishment at how much money their victim had earned, they could see heavy payments going out to the various companies working on the mews. Miss Hodgson passed over single pages of various mortgage contracts, savings accounts, dollar accounts, pensions, life insurance and policy insurance coverage; it all seemed very well-organised.

'The investments via Mr Smith-Barker?' Anna queried.

'I am not privy to his details. Obviously with the appalling situation in the City, I believe Miss Delany lost a considerable amount.'

'But surely you had to have handled the payments to him?'

'No, they were made directly by Amanda, and I am sure Mr Smith-Barker will give you the details of the most recent investments.'

Anna closed her file, resting her hands on top of it.

'Could you just explain the transaction for me, so that I clearly understand? If your client was contracted to do a film and the fees were arranged by Miss Lesser, wouldn't the cheques or manner of payment come to you first and then be passed to the investment company?'

Miss Hodgson nodded.

'That would be the usual method, but as Andrea Lesser had Power of Attorney, I believe certain investments were made directly via her agency to the investment bankers.'

'Surely you would have to keep a record of these transactions?'

'Yes, that's right, for tax and VAT payments.'

'So can you give us some indication of just how many investments were being made on Miss Delany's behalf?'

Miss Hodgson hesitated.

'This is rather difficult,' she said, looking down. 'As I explained, I don't have this year's accounts so I am not exactly aware of the details you want.'

Anna took a deep breath and leaned forwards.

'How much did she lose?'

Her composure coming apart and her hands nervously fingering her neat files, Miss Hodgson said she was not prepared to discuss that aspect of her late client's business.

'That is why you are here,' Mike said firmly.

She took out a white handkerchief from her handbag and dabbed at her upper lip. Anna could see they might not get any more from her if they continued to put the pressure on, so she glanced at Mike to slow down. She changed tack.

'We are very interested in whether or not Miss Delany owned a BlackBerry.'

'Yes, that was how I kept in touch with her. We had a lot of delay in getting her landline connected at the new house, so it was always the best way to contact her. Copies of the bills for the BlackBerry are in the file.'

'When was the last time you saw Miss Delany?'

'It would have been about a month before she died.'

'How did she appear to you?'

Ms Hodgson shrugged. It had been a very brief meeting, no more than fifteen minutes. Amanda had needed a few signatures on her tax forms and she had brought in her receipts for the VAT assessment.

'Explain to us how money paid to Miss Delany reaches you,' Anna asked.

'Amanda would have banked it and I'd work from her bank statements. I then did her accounts and she paid me for the work done.'

'Who paid her?'

'The film company would send their payments to her agent; she would take her percentage and then forward a cheque to Amanda.'

'So Miss Lesser would first put the cheque through the agency's account?'

'Yes.'

When Anna asked how much Amanda was being paid by the film company making *Gaslight*, Ronnie Hodgson said she wasn't sure. It would seem that she had not been paid, Anna pointed out, as according to the files they were looking at, there was no recent large deposit.

'That's correct. More than likely, Miss Lesser will be dealing with any payments due.'

Anna glanced at Mike as he read one page after another.

'We require this year's accounts up until her death,' he reiterated as he closed the file.

Anna noticed that Miss Hodgson was nervously pulling at the sleeves of her blouse.

'I haven't yet started my assessments for this year.'

'How long will it take?'

'I have to have a meeting with Miss Lesser as I am unsure what payments are due. Then there will be death duties and . . .' She was twisting her handkerchief round her fingers and sighed deeply. 'I feel terrible about discussing this, as she's a personal friend, and I was certain she would have an explanation.'

'Who are we talking about?' Anna asked.

'Andrea Lesser. I haven't been entirely truthful because I really don't want to cause any trouble until I know more details, and I trust her completely. We've worked together for many years, since Amanda became famous, and she was very good to bring Amanda to me as a client. I hate to cast aspersions because I don't have all the facts.'

She closed her eyes.

'When Amanda came to see me that last time, it was quite late and she hadn't got an appointment. I wasn't expecting her – in fact, I was just about to leave my office.'

'When was this?' Mike asked. Anna wanted to dig him in the ribs. She knew Miss Hodgson was about to deliver the goods and he was wrong to interrupt her.

'I already told you, it would have been about four weeks ago.'

253

Amanda, she went on, had turned up and appeared to have been drinking. She was very agitated and full of anger which at first she directed towards Ronnie Hodgson. There was a lot of money missing, she said as she calmed down. Because she had been so busy filming, she had not been paying attention to personal business.

'She claimed that there was a substantial amount of money owed her. I tried to follow what she was saying, but she was so angry it was hard to understand. She had found out from Scott Myers that he had been paid for the movie they had been in together and she had also asked another actor . . .' Miss Hodgson then described how Amanda had insisted she call Andrea Lesser and ask her where her money was. She was becoming hysterical again.

'Anyway, when I did call there was no reply, just an answerphone as it was after seven in the evening. Amanda wouldn't leave my office and wanted me to go through all her accounts, which I refused to do. I said I would speak to her agent the following morning as I was sure there must be a logical explanation.'

Although Amanda was a valued client, they occasionally had words as she was often late sending in her receipts and statements, and they would sometimes arrive in a plastic grocery bag. Amanda was by no means incapable of sorting her own finances out – on the contrary, but she was also erratic and on a number of occasions had insisted she had sent things when she hadn't.

'So knowing this, and seeing her behaving in a very strange way, too much to drink or maybe it was drugs, and knowing Andrea Lesser as I do, I was certain that what Amanda was insinuating was wrong.'

'Which was what exactly?' Anna asked.

'Theft, fraud. She kept on telling me it was millions, but when I called Andrea the next morning, she was shocked. She said there had been some monies invested for Amanda by a very reputable investment banking firm and that more than likely she had forgotten their agreement.'

Mike sighed. 'So what happened next?'

'Well, nothing. She didn't call me again, so I was certain that all her accusations were unfounded.'

'Were they?' asked Anna. 'If you didn't see any contracts regarding payments to your client, you wouldn't really know if any monies were embezzled, would you?'

There was a pause and then Miss Hodgson shook her head, but she wouldn't look at Anna.

'You have to understand that there are always delays in payments and collecting clients' residuals, often from repeat adverts or television work. It can take months to track them down. I want to make it very clear that I do not believe Miss Lesser would have ever contemplated doing anything illegal.'

'But Miss Delany implied to you that was the case?' Mike was becoming bored by Miss Hodgson's evasive manner.

'She did make accusations but, as I said, she was drunk or drugged and quite abusive. And Andrea Lesser assured me that Amanda knew about the investments Andrew Smith-Barker had made on her behalf.'

'Ah, and this was when Miss Lesser denied any such—' Mike was interrupted.

'Of course she did.'

Anna closed the files in front of her. 'Can I see the copy of Miss Delany's will?'

Miss Hodgson passed it over and began putting the files back into her briefcase.

'And who is handling her estate?'

'Andrea Lesser.'

'We will require this year's accounts to be brought in, whether or not they have been completed,' Mike added.

Miss Hodgson said she would have them sent to the station the following morning.

It was another half-hour before the interview was terminated. Left alone in the interview room, Anna checked over all the documents as Mike saw Miss Hodgson out.

'What do you make of her?' he asked Anna when he returned.

'I think she's lying through her teeth.'

The will, dated over a year ago, made interesting reading. Andrea Lesser featured, as did Amanda's parents, her former flatmates and numerous charities, the latter taking the bulk of her fortune. The amounts to each named party were in the region of ten and twenty thousand pounds and the biggest slice went to Battersea Dogs' Home. Amanda appeared to have no cousins or distant relatives and no changes to her will had been listed.

The possibility of fraud and the fact that Amanda had accused Andrea Lesser of underhand dealings with her money, but not confronted her as far as Ronnie Hodgson knew, had to be a strong motive for murder. Under suspicion were obviously Miss Lesser and Andrew Smith-Barker. Mike Lewis decided to save time by obtaining a magistrate's search warrant for both Miss Lesser's agency and Andrew Smith-Barker's company. Officers experienced in fraud would need to go through the mountain of documents that would no doubt be seized. Anna asked if Mike would also get a search warrant for Amanda's old flat. He was in his office with Barolli, co-ordinating the searches, and seemed frazzled.

'You won't believe this, but Mr Delany is refusing to allow us to use any personal photographs and is getting a lawyer to try and stop the television interview going ahead.'

'He can't do that, can he?' Anna asked.

'He can. We can override his request, but he's refusing to give any assistance and insists that if we go ahead without his consent, he'll call a press conference saying that we've been less than professional and accusing us of invading his privacy.'

'But his daughter was murdered, for God's sake!' Anna said angrily.

'Right. You'd think he'd want everything done to nail her killer, but he's just kicking up about incompetent policework and poor investigation techniques. This is all we need, with the Deputy Assistant Commissioner putting pressure on us through Langton.'

'So are you going ahead with the crime special?'

'I need permission from Langton.'

Anna asked whether, in the meantime, she could re-question both Felicity Turner and Jeannie Bale.

'Let's push this fraud thing forward first,' was Mike's response, 'and hold back on them because the last thing we need is for those two press-crazy girls to start acting up.'

'But Mike, I think they know a lot more. If you won't allow me a search warrant, at least let me talk to them.

You're going to have your hands full with the other searches going ahead this morning.'

Before Mike could answer, Joan appeared. Mr Delany, she announced, was in reception with a lawyer.

'Shit! Thanks, Joan, put them into an interview room. I'll talk to him.'

'I'll do it if you like,' Anna offered.

Mike rubbed his head, making his hair stand up on end. Then Barbara put her head round the door. The producer of their TV slot was on the phone and Langton on hold waiting.

'Christ! OK, OK, Anna. You and Barolli take Mr Delany, and as soon as I've sorted these calls I'll join you.'

Anna and Barolli headed down the corridor towards the interview rooms.

'I thought you were going to do the TV interview,' Barolli said.

'I was, then Langton put Mike onto it.'

They paused outside the interview room and looked through the glass window to see a stony-faced Mr Delany sitting alongside a small dapper man.

'Let's do it,' Barolli said as they entered.

Mr Delany's manner was even more aloof than when Anna had first met with him.

'I do not want any further publicity surrounding the death of my daughter,' he insisted. 'I am fully aware that the television company wants to interview some of her . . . for want of a better word *boyfriends* . . . and I refuse to have her private life broadcast yet again. It was bad enough for my wife and me when she was alive. If you are dependent on trash media television shows to assist in your enquiries, that is tantamount to admitting your total failure in this case.'

Anna kept her voice low and persuasive as she said, 'Mr Delany, we have found in the past that these programmes, contrary to what you are suggesting, have proved invaluable.'

'When, tell me, did you have a victim as well-known as my daughter?'

'Not recently, but by asking the public for their assistance, we have in the past gained vital information.'

'What do you need exactly?'

Barolli leaned forward.

'Missing from your daughter's mews house is a soft rabbit toy and a diary. We also found a gold cross and chain caught in her mattress, which might have been worn by the killer.'

'Then why haven't you discovered who took the missing things?'

'We are endeavouring to do so, but to show these items on a live television broadcast might well bring us the evidence we need.'

'Apparently you believe that my daughter knew her killer, is that correct?'

'We are considering that possibility.'

'Well, if that is true, why do you need the public to be made aware of these missing items?'

'The killer may have taken them with him and someone might have seen them,' Barolli continued. He was having difficulty controlling his temper.

'Rubbish. I refuse to allow my daughter to be vilified and for a publicity-crazed public to gloat over her murder. Instead of wasting time you should, in my opinion, be investigating all her known associates without delay.'

'That is exactly what we are doing,' Barolli snapped.

'Without result! Then may I suggest you continue to do so. To date, the press have been reissuing ghastly material concerning my daughter's promiscuity. It is abhorrent to me and to my wife. If you believe that one or other of these liaisons resulted in her death, then *do* something about it rather than continuing to . . .' He turned to Anna and pointed a bony finger towards her. 'I recognise you, madam, as having the audacity to infiltrate a private gathering and then putting on a disgusting show for the press with two other, equally unsavoury women.'

'I resent your rudeness, Mr Delany,' Anna said icily.

'You may well, but it is nevertheless the truth. Even in death my daughter was made out to be nothing better than a whore and I am now, with legal advice, refusing to allow—'

At that moment, Mike Lewis walked in. They had withdrawn the television interview, he stated.

'Thank you,' Mr Delany said.

Mike turned and walked out. Barolli followed, while Anna waited for Mr Delany and his lawyer to leave.

'Did you care for your daughter, Mr Delany?' she asked suddenly.

'I beg your pardon?'

'I have interviewed many grieving parents whose loved ones have been murdered, and I have never come across anyone as lacking in any emotion as you, and I include your wife.'

Mr Delany's mouth dropped open, shocked.

'We are doing everything possible to track down her killer, and to be honest, our officers show genuine care for Amanda and want nothing more than to succeed in arresting the perpetrator.'

He lifted his hand.

'*Don't point at me, Mr Delany!* If your daughter's personal life disgusts you, then perhaps when she was alive you should have done more to protect her and tried to understand why she seemed hellbent on destroying herself. We appear to be the only people who do care enough.'

'You . . .' he spat out, and although he didn't point his finger at her this time, it felt to Anna as if he was pushing her in the chest.

'You have no knowledge about what we have been forced to endure. And you have no right whatsoever to insinuate that as parents, my wife and I were lacking in affection for our daughter!'

'Then why have you refused to assist us?'

'Refused to assist! You are professional detectives, that is what you are paid to do – investigate – not harass and give grieving parents more heartbreak than they are already suffering.'

Mr Delany turned and walked out, followed hard on his heels by his lawyer, who paused in the doorway and glared at Anna.

'You should be ashamed of yourself, Detective Travis.'

Mike and Barolli had already set the wheels in motion for the searches. By the time Anna had gained control and calmed down, they had left the station. She sat in her office, knowing she had overstepped her position with Mr Delany. The comparison between her own father, and this cold, vicious man, were like chalk and cheese. She had been adored and encouraged and admired; rightly or wrongly, it seemed to Anna that their victim had been cut off from any such loving support. She wondered if there was a different reason for Mr Delany's stance, something stronger than Amanda's promiscuity and her desire to feature on the front pages of the newspapers.

Fetching a coffee, Anna shut her office door and cleared the surface of her desk to lay out all the press clippings that had been accrued. Many of them were not in chronological order, so she began to sift and mix and match . . .

Andrea Lesser burst into tears when Mike Lewis showed her the search warrant. They required only the files and recent contracts relating to her client, Amanda Delany, he said. When she claimed that she had sent over files days ago to the station via Ronnie Hodgson, he thanked her and pointed out that they now required the updated ones.

Barolli was standing by a shredding machine in Andrew Smith–Barker's office. It had, he noticed, been recently in use as there were bags of shredded material beside it. It was also obvious that the company was closing; the offices were nearly empty and pictures were being taken down from the walls in the reception area. When Mr Smith–Barker was shown the search warrant, he claimed he had very little documentation regarding the investments made by his company for Amanda Delany. He may have spent hours shredding hard copies, but it would all still be on his computer files. Even if he had attempted to delete them, they would still be able to find them, Barolli knew. The man stared, white with anger, as his computers were seized.

Chapter Fourteen

At last Anna had all the cuttings in order and placed in long lines along her desk. Ten months, she calculated, had elapsed between Amanda's stint at the Drury Clinic and beginning filming again. She must have been pregnant and had an abortion at some point during this time. Both Colin O'Dell and Scott Myers denied they were responsible for her pregnancy, but they both admitted visiting her at the clinic. Then she became a patient of Dr Eamon Suchet, by which time she was anorexic, self-harming and, according to him, very fragile. Yet, shortly afterwards, Amanda returned to a highly lucrative film career.

Next, Anna checked through Amanda's passport, working backwards. There were stamps for two trips to Los Angeles, another to New York in the past two years. She came across a receipt from a jeweller in the South of France and a boarding-pass stub for a flight there three months earlier, tucked in the back of the passport. One of those trips coincided with the time Anna reckoned Amanda had been pregnant. Mr Delany had admitted that he knew about it; it was his wife who had booked his daughter into the Drury. Had Amanda gone to her parents for help? She did have considerable earnings by then, but nowhere near what she was bringing in more recently. Around this time, someone had arranged an abortion for her, and from what Anna knew it had been a terrible, botched job that had left the girl very ill and unable to have children. It was vital, Anna knew now, that she re-question Jeannie and Felicity who shared her flat throughout those years.

Neither Mike Lewis nor Barolli had returned to the station, so Anna decided to visit Jeannie and Felicity without a search warrant. She asked Barbara to put on her duty status that she had come up with some important queries she needed ironing out. She also asked if they had the address of the hotel in London where Mr and Mrs Delany were staying. Barbara had a contact number; it was a small hotel in Dover Court.

'Hadn't I told her to back off those two girls? Call her and get her back here immediately! We need her help to sort through these boxes.' Mike Lewis, who had returned laden with documents taken from Andrea Lesser's office, was furious when told what Anna was up to.

Barolli made the call. Anna's phone was switched off so he left a curt message telling her to get back to the station as quickly as she could.

Anna was sitting with Mrs Delany in their hotel suite when Barolli tried to call. She was thankful that Mark Delany was not there too; in fact, Mrs Delany herself seemed relieved.

'We're returning to France in the morning so he's just finishing up some business here.'

Anna went straight to the point, asking if Mrs Delany

could confirm the dates of her daughter's abortion. The woman immediately became very agitated.

'Mrs Delany, I'm trying to piece together who Amanda knew and who could be a possible suspect. I need to find out who arranged for the abortion.'

'I can't see what this has to do with finding out who killed her. It was so long ago and we've tried hard to forget it all, put it behind us, my husband especially.'

'We seriously believe that your daughter knew her assailant and may have even passed him her house keys to let himself into her house. It would have been someone she trusted, someone who may perhaps have been . . '

'We never met any of them.'

'I'm sorry?'

'The men she was seeing. We read about them, of course, but we never met them. I doubt if her father would have wanted to, he was so distraught with her behaviour. She was using drugs and drinking and courting the awful publicity that made our lives miserable. They kept on calling us, you know, the press, asking if she was getting married and . . . He had paid so much money for her to go into the Drury Clinic, but when she left there, sometimes we had no idea where she was. And that dreadful place she lived in with those girls, she was such a thankless . . .' Her voice petered out as if she was ashamed of describing her dead daughter as 'thankless'.

'She was very young,' Anna said quietly.

Mrs Delany patted her hair and folded her hands in her lap.

'You know, she was such a beautiful child. I mean, people would come up to us in the street. She was like a little angel and I think we spoiled her dreadfully,

especially my husband, which made it all the more difficult for him to come to terms with what Amanda
became. She could have had anyone, anyone, she was
that gorgeous; instead, she threw herself at the wrong
men and disgusted him.'

'Who was the father of her unborn child?'

Mrs Delany turned away, murmuring, 'One of God
knows how many.'

'So you have no idea?'

'No, and she said she didn't know either.'

Anna opened her notebook. 'She came to the South
of France twice in the same year, about the time she was
pregnant . . .'

Mrs Delany stood up and went across the room.

'Would you like some water?' she asked.

'No, thank you.' Anna waited, watching as Mrs
Delany poured herself a glass then moved back to sit
further away from Anna.

'Did she discuss her pregnancy with you?'

'No. It wasn't showing.'

'So when did you find out?'

'I can't really remember.'

'What about the second time she came to see you?
Did she mention the pregnancy to you?'

'No. We didn't know anything until we got a call
from one of the girls in her flat to say she was very ill.
My husband went to see her and she was rushed into
hospital with internal bleeding.'

'Did you accompany him?'

'No, I didn't. I have two dogs and I couldn't leave
them.'

'So your husband found out about the abortion, got
her to hospital and then booked her into the Drury?'

'Yes, well, I made the call. I suggested she go there so I called from France.'

'Did you go to see her whilst she was there?'

'No, I had my dogs.'

Anna stared at Mrs Delany, with her manicured nails, her perfect hair and make-up. She was a very beautiful woman and it was obvious where Amanda got her looks from.

'After that, did you visit Amanda at all?'

'No, we travel a lot. As I have said, she was out of control and seemed set on embarrassing us.'

'There was never any leak to the press about an abortion, was there?'

'No, at least not to our knowledge. We only heard from her when she needed money.'

'But she was earning a lot from her acting.'

'It didn't take off straight away, and I think she wasted a lot of her money. For all the pain she had caused us, my husband still made sure she was financially taken care of – that was, until she didn't need it.'

'I think she caused herself a lot of pain, Mrs Delany.'

This prompted an odd reaction. Smoothing her pencil-slim skirt with the flat of her hand, Mrs Delany then touched her hair and looked away from Anna to the window.

'The pain was all mine,' she whispered. She tilted her head with a strange smile, murmuring, *'I am the secret you daren't whisper, I am the green grass.'*

Anna remembered it was a line from the poem read by Jeannie Bale at Amanda's funeral. She was certain that Mrs Delany was a consummate actress; again, perhaps her daughter had inherited this talent from her as well as her beauty. She might not gain anything further from

Mrs Delany, yet she was certain there was a lot more. When she had first met her, she sensed that the woman was afraid of her husband. Now she was alone with her, she didn't think that was true – but then who was manipulating whom? And why? Anna could feel it there like a buried seam, but she doubted she would be able to crack the outward veneer and she decided to leave.

'Thank you so much for giving me your time.'

'My pleasure. If there is anything else, you know where we are, but not for too long.'

'Of course, you have the dogs.'

Mrs Delany's eyes welled up. 'No, sadly I don't. They both died a couple of years ago.'

'I'm sorry.' Anna picked up her briefcase and was surprised when Mrs Delany rested her hand on her arm. She wore a large emerald and diamond ring and a diamond-encrusted wedding ring.

'Tell me, how long will it go on for? If you don't find who killed Amanda, how long will you continue the investigation?'

'As long as it takes.'

'But you don't have any results, do you?'

'No, sadly we don't as yet.'

'It's just that the sooner it is over, the sooner we don't have to be constantly pressured . . . Cold cases? Don't unsolved cases become cold cases?'

Anna wanted the soft hand moved away from her. It made her skin crawl.

'We won't give up on your daughter, Mrs Delany.' She would have liked to have added, 'unlike her parents', but held her tongue. Just as she reached the door to leave, she posed one final question.

'Amanda's toy rabbit – where did it come from?'

'She had a pet one when she was tiny and it died. She found it all stiff in its hutch and was inconsolable.' Mrs Delany's unlined brow managed a slight frown. 'She went away to school and I think my husband bought it for her, you know – one that would always be with her and couldn't die.'

'Unlike Amanda,' Anna said under her breath as she walked out.

Mike Lewis had done a considerable amount of work before Ronnie Hodgson arrived to help him go through the documents he had taken from Andrea Lesser's office. Using a calculator, he showed her how much money had been contracted for films and promotion, and the dates when it had been received by Andrea Lesser; clearly it had not been forwarded to Amanda's bank account.

Miss Hodgson was stunned. She had never been consulted about this money. Had she been, she would have been extremely concerned that she had not made provision for where it should have been banked in high- or low-interest accounts. She was astonished at the amounts that were showing in dollars; with the pound now much lower than when these monies had been paid, she would have automatically insisted the dollars be paid straight into an American account. She finally admitted that she had, at no time, been aware of these contracts and very large deposits, over four million pounds' worth. This figure was close to the sum of the investments made by Smith–Barker on behalf of Miss Delany – investments into pension plans and companies that had all been wiped out in the stock market crash.

★

269

Langton listened to both Mike and Barolli as they took him through the paper trail. They had, without a doubt, a motive for the murder of Amanda Delany. Their job was to tie in how the two, Andrea Lesser and Andrew Smith-Barker, could have arranged her death. Andrea Lesser had keys to the mews house, she could have easily hired someone to do the job, but now the team would have to prove it.

'Bring them in and grill the pants off the pair of them,' Langton ordered. 'Leave no stone unturned. It's difficult to prove fraud without a lot more evidence, which will be hard to come by with the victim dead.' He encouraged them to delve deep into both suspects' backgrounds, dig up anything they could to connect them to the actual killing and prove they had instigated fraud. They had only Miss Hodgson's verbal statement that Amanda had become suspicious.

'Suspicions but no real proof, if Miss Lesser is saying that Amanda knew of the transactions.'

'Ronnie Hodgson's still here, Guv. She's with the Fraud guys sifting through all the contracts.'

'OK, let me have a word with her.'

Ronnie Hodgson was nervous when Langton approached the interview room, but he quickly charmed her. He pulled out a chair for her while he perched on the edge of the table.

'This must be very distressing for you,' he began.

'Yes, yes, it is. We believe that four million pounds was due to my client.'

'Is it usual that an agent invests on behalf of a client?'

'It has been done, but always with the client's agreement. Film work often pays such a lot of money, it is necessary to be ready to deal with it, so to speak.'

'Deal with it, like investments?'

'Yes, pension plans and suchlike.'

'In the past, you received a cheque, did you not, with the agent's commission taken off?'

'Yes, but sometimes it was sent directly to my client's bank account and they would simply send me an invoice of expenses and percentages taken from the original payment.'

'Did you get any invoices regarding the four million pounds?'

'No, I did not.'

'Were you aware that these large sums were to be paid into your client's account?'

'No. I knew Amanda had accepted film work, but I had no indication how much she was being paid.'

'So you were dependant on Miss Lesser to contact you and send you the invoices.'

'Yes, that is correct.'

'Have you at any time in the past been worried about late payments?'

'No, never, but as I said, I was not always aware of which contracts Amanda had signed or what negotiations had been made on her behalf.'

'I see.'

'I have brought in all my files.'

'We really appreciate your assistance, but tell me – what do *you* think has taken place?'

Ronnie Hodgson licked her lips. 'I can't really say, just that it is unusual.'

'Unusual? I'd say it was a bit more than that, wouldn't

you? Four million invested over a lengthy period of time and your client seemingly unaware of the transactions. But she was becoming very suspicious, wasn't she?'

'Yes.'

'So what did *she* think was happening?'

'She thought it was being stolen.'

'Stolen?'

'Yes.'

'But you didn't?'

'When I asked Andrea Lesser about it, she assured me that there was nothing untoward taking place and that a few contracts were late being sent out so that monies were delayed being paid.'

'She lied.'

'Yes, I believe so now.'

'Why do you think she lied to you?'

'Because, according to the contracts, I've seen that the money *was* paid in full to her agency and on time – and should have been forwarded immediately into Amanda's bank account.'

'So she put the money elsewhere?'

'It appears so. She must have passed it on to Andrew Smith-Barker, an investment banker, who I know to be a personal friend of hers.'

Langton moved from the table with a smile.

'Thank you so much. I would appreciate it if you kept this information private and confidential until we have made further investigations.'

'Oh yes, yes, I will,' she assured him.

'I am sure you will, as I believe you to be a very honest woman and I would hate any of this to be detrimental to your business, which could well happen. But I will endeavour to give you every protection . . . We

272

don't want the tar-brush syndrome, do we? You could, Miss Hodgson, be seen as very much a part of this theft of your client's money.'

Langton ushered her out to continue her work with the Fraud Squad. He took Mike aside.

'She's a good witness. Lesser and Smith-Barker must be brought in as soon as possible. I'd say they've been shredding anything that might implicate them in swindling our victim out of her earnings.'

He tapped Mike on the shoulder.

'Don't go easy on them. We need a result because if they didn't kill Amanda, somebody else did. Push the agent woman, sounds like she's besotted with the banker . . . OK?'

Mike watched Langton stroll down the corridor before he turned back into the interview room. When he entered, Ronnie Hodgson was crying. He wondered what Langton had said to her; she was more eager to help than she had been before.

Anna waited for Felicity to come into the scruffy lounge. She had opened the door of the Maida Vale flat in her dressing-gown and gone to get dressed. It was almost three in the afternoon. The room had been cleaned up since Dan Hutchins had died. The smell of stale tobacco and wine remained, but at least there were no dirty food cartons left littered around. Anna was pleased that Felicity was alone, although she was expecting Jeannie back from an audition, some play on the fringe.

'You want a cup of tea?' Felicity asked as she returned in jeans and a T-shirt, but barefoot.

'No, thank you.'

She disappeared and returned with a cracked mug and a slice of white bread covered in thick jam. She sat on a dirty cushion, jam smeared across her pallid cheeks.

'Are you an actress?' Anna asked.

'Not really. I was at RADA but on the stage-management side.'

'Can I ask you about Amanda? She used to live here, didn't she?'

'Yeah, off and on, between blokes. She kind of used this as a base and we got all her mail here. Well, we never knew who she was dossing down with and she'd just turn up and collect it.'

Felicity slurped her tea and waved her hand around the room.

'We're gonna do it all up when we get the money from her will.'

'Do you know how much Amanda left you?'

'Yeah, well, we called her agent and asked about it and she was pretty rude and told us that she'd send us a cheque as she was the ex . . .' Felicity stared into space, trying to recall what had been said to her. Then she went on, 'We want to rent out poor Dan's room. We've not done nothing as he was paid up until the end of this month.'

She took a bite of her bread and then tossed the rest into an overflowing wastebin. It hit the side and dropped onto the floor.

'I miss him,' she said.

'You must miss Amanda too.'

'Yeah, but not as much, as she hadn't really been around that often. You know, she was a bit out of our league and it was hard for Jeannie as she was always so jealous. Not for me really as I'm not an actress. I just do the odd stage-management gig, but mostly I'm on the dole and . . .'

There was a pause as Felicity slurped her mug of tea, then took out a packet of Silk Cut cigarettes and turned on the electric fire to light her cigarette from the only bar that was working. She blew out smoke and stared at Anna.

'What do you want?'

'Just to talk really, find out a few things.'

'Executor, that's the word I was lookin' for. Miss Lesser is the executor of Amanda's will, so she will be paying us but I'm not sure how much. Do you know how long it will take?'

'No. I think solicitors and death duties have to be sorted before any beneficiary is paid.'

'Oh.'

'You knew Amanda for a long time, didn't you?'

'Yes.'

Anna hesitated, not wanting to push too hard until she felt Felicity was at ease with her. But just as she was about to say something, the girl moved across the floor to sit closer to her, picking up an old shell to use as an ashtray.

'Dan loved her, you know, he'd do anything for her and she was always kind to him, but he was just . . . depressed a lot. He could never see anything in his future because he reckoned everyone lived and then they died and there was not much point in bothering with what happened in between.'

'I find that very sad.'

'Yeah, but when you think about it, that's what happened to him. He lived a bit then he died, but you know, I never understood where he got the dough from to buy the gear that killed him. I mean, he was always broke and it was him that started Amanda wondering what was going on with her money.'

Anna leaned forward as Felicity stubbed out her cigarette.

'When she could, she got him jobs as an extra on her films, and he got friendly with a couple of actors.'

She took out another cigarette and went across to the electric fire again to light it.

'What do you mean about her money?'

Felicity sat hunched up beside the fire.

'He'd been at some internet café and met up with an actor he'd worked with on her film, *The Mansion*. Did you see it?'

'Yes, I did.'

'Well, they got chatting and then he showed Dan his new car. He said he'd got paid more than he expected. It was a secondhand Mini, but in good nick, a convertible. Anyway, Amanda came round a few days later maybe and he said to her about the Mini and that she should get herself a car, but she said she didn't have a licence and preferred usin' a driver. Then she said that it was odd about the other actor buyin' a car because she hadn't been paid a cent for the film yet, and she was quite pissed off about it. Anyway, she called from here and spoke to Andrea Lesser.'

There was a pause as Felicity puffed away on her cigarette.

'What happened when she called her?'

'Not a lot, but she said she was gonna check up and see where her money was. I didn't hear what she said as the phone is in the hall, then she left.'

Anna waited, hoping there was more to it.

'We all talked about it, you know after she'd left, and then . . .' She started to giggle.

'Then what?'

'He shouldn't have done it, but we were all a bit stoned and he called that stuck-up Miss Lesser, who wouldn't take on Jeannie when she was doin' a play at the Tricycle Theatre. She sent a letter asking her to come and see her in the play, but when she heard nothin' back, she called her and she didn't even come to the fucking phone.'

'Go on. Dan called Andrea Lesser?'

'Yeah. He said he needed to speak to her urgent, right – that he was an agent.' She curled up, still giggling.

Anna was getting impatient.

'He said that he was checking up about Miss Delany's cash. She kept on asking him who he was . . . then cut him off. It was ever so funny.'

'I bet it was.' Anna sneaked a look at her watch, and Felicity sat with her eyes closed.

'You said all Amanda's mail came to this address?'

'Yeah, fanmail. She used to pay Dan for answering some of them, but it was so boring and they would come in sackfuls. In the end he didn't bother.'

'Did Amanda take it with her?'

'What?'

'The fanmail.'

'Oh no, she was bored shitless with all the weirdoes and crappy people. She was supposed to send back signed autographed photographs, but she couldn't be bothered, 'cos I mean they hardly ever give a stamped addressed envelope.'

'Do you still have any of the letters?'

'Yeah, we got bags of them, used them when it got cold to light the fire, but it always smoked something awful, to be honest. You're sittin' on some as that sofa's springs are broken.'

Anna stood up and removed one of the hideous orange foam-filled pads. Beneath them were black bin-liners tied with string. She opened one and found it full of letters and cards.

'Would you mind if I took these with me?'

Felicity shrugged. Anna stacked the bags side by side and then replaced the foam cushion which sank down almost to the floor.

Before Anna could ask Felicity anything further, the front door slammed shut and Jeannie barged into the room, carrying a big leather bag.

'I didn't get it, I fucking didn't get it.'

Jeannie was wearing cowboy boots and a long full black skirt with a top with mutton-chop sleeves. Her dyed blonde hair was caught up with two big bow slides at each side of her head. When she saw Anna, she apologised.

'I didn't know we had company. I've just come from an audition for this Victorian play on at the Bush. The bastards didn't even ask me to fucking read.' She delved into the bag and brought out a litre bottle of cider. 'I'm gonna get smashed tonight. I've not worked for friggin' months and this was *my part!*'

Jeannie was so upset and angry she didn't appear to make any connection as to who Anna was and it wasn't until she had lit a cigarette and drunk half a tumbler of cider that she seemed to realise.

'What are you here for?'

Before Anna could reply, Felicity told her that she had needed to ask them some questions about Amanda. She pointed to the binliners saying that Anna wanted to take them away.

'I'm sick to death of her,' Jeannie complained. 'You don't know what it's like to be so close to stardom and lose out; you don't know what it does to your head.'

'Did you know she'd been pregnant?'

Anna caught the look between the two girls.

'You did know, didn't you? Tell me about it.'

Jeannie shrugged. 'Don't suppose it matters now she's dead.'

'Who was the father?' Anna asked

'She had an abortion,' Felicity said. They had sworn never to talk about it, but Jeannie muttered that it didn't matter now.

'We were short of money so Amanda went to France to see her parents, you know they're loaded, and she'd spent all the money she'd got from the film. It wasn't that much, right, and we owed rent on this place and . . .'

The girls fell silent and Anna waited, but neither said a word.

'Did something happen in France?' she prompted.

'She got raped, we never really got to the bottom of it all, but it was someone her father knew and she came back in a right state, and then a few weeks later she found out she was pregnant.'

'She went back to France to try and get it all sorted out,' Felicity interjected, 'but her dad had gone ballistic and refused to believe her that any of his polo-playing friends would have touched his daughter.'

'He was a right bastard,' Jeannie said. Amanda had

279

returned to London, she confirmed, by now four months' pregnant, with a film in the offing and her agent pressing her to begin work.

'So she had an abortion,' Anna said softly.

'Yeah, and that far gone it wasn't easy for her to find someone who would do it. Some guy she had worked with on the movie helped her out, gave her a name.'

'Do you know who that was?'

They both shook their heads. All they knew was, he had been on the movie with her and he drove her to the place wherever it was and then she had returned and gone to bed.

'It was terrible 'cos she started screaming and then there was all this blood and we was in an awful state as we didn't know what to do. In the end we called an ambulance and then we called her parents and they came to London.'

'She nearly died,' Jeannie said softly.

'She was never really the same after she came out of hospital, was she?' Felicity looked at Jeannie, then leaned towards her and whispered.

'We don't know that,' Jeannie said.

'Know what?' Anna asked.

'Well, if you ask me,' Felicity said, 'something was goin' on with her father. She was scared of him and she hated him, but she once said to me that things had happened to her, even when she was a kid.'

'She never admitted anything,' Jeannie added. 'We just suspected stuff and they did a botched job on her, left something in her stomach that had festered or poisoned her, and she had to have a hysterectomy.'

'Did her parents come here?'

Jeannie shook her head. They had arranged a private

clinic and then had taken her into the Drury a few months later, but they had never come to the flat.

Anna was trying to assess all their information and inference that the rape could have involved Amanda's own father. She also had to get the dates straight. However, neither could really recall the exact timeframe; they had all been pretty drugged up at the time.

'This driver you say Amanda used to take her for the operation . . .'

'Never met him, he'd just draw up outside – nice Merc. I think he was one of the unit drivers off the movie,' Jeannie said.

'Did you ever actually see his face?'

They shook their heads. All they could add was that Amanda seemed to depend on him a great deal.

When Anna mentioned a possible publishing deal, they looked blank. Nor did they remember her meeting Josh Lyons at the flat.

'It must have been at a time when neither of you were at home. Josh Lyons remembers coming to this flat and seeing Amanda's diary. A big thick five-year one with a pink cover.'

'Well, if we weren't here, we wouldn't have met him,' Felicity retorted. 'She never said nothin' to me about writin' anything and I never saw her with a diary like that. Her BlackBerry, yeah, she was always texting and gettin' messages and, to be honest, I can't imagine what she could write about as she couldn't remember what day it was, most of the time. Was he going to pay her a lot of money for it?'

'A lot,' nodded Anna.

'Like how much?'

But Anna quickly changed the subject.

'You're now in Amanda's room, aren't you?' She looked at Jeannie, whose expression became defensive.

'Yeah, but I didn't, like, dive in there the moment she was dead. I mean, she said it was OK, 'cos she had that new mews house and wouldn't be living with us.'

'Did she leave anything in there?'

'Well, a lot of clothes and make-up, shoes – we wear the same size and that was all. She would buy all these clothes and never wear them. Some have still got the price-tags on them.' Jeannie hesitated, then agreed to let Anna look over her room.

Something bothered Anna. It was the two girls' lack of interest in the proposed book; she couldn't make out if they were lying or not. She followed Jeannie down the dark hallway. There was a strong smell of mildew, mixed with incense and stale cigarettes.

'This was Dan's room.' Jeannie punched a closed door open, pointing to the floor. 'That's where we found him.'

The room was dark, curtains drawn across a barred window. There was a small crumpled single bed with dirty sheets, and strewn around were old sneakers, magazines and books. Three full black binliners were stacked by the wall.

'That's his stuff but nobody wants it, so we'll take it to the Salvation Army.'

'What about family?'

'He's only got an aunt and she's really old. Dunno if he got anyone else that would want them. His older brother is taking care of his funeral, but he said he didn't want nothin'.'

Anna stared into the dank, dark room with its overflowing ashtrays and empty beer cans. It seemed strange that they would have packed up his clothes and yet not bothered to clean anything else.

'We'll rent it out soon. When we get our money we'll get the place painted but it's ever so damp and we got no central heating.'

Jeannie's bedroom was larger than Dan's, almost twice the size. On the bed, against the pillows, lay a row of dolls with big china faces and wearing lace dresses.

'They're all mine, I collect them.'

'Amanda had a little toy rabbit, didn't she?'

'Yeah, but she always took it with her.'

Clothes lay in piles all over the room, and the dressing-table was stacked with make-up, mirrors and perfumes, hairpieces and wigs; hooked over the handles of the drawers were rows of pearls and chains.

'You never saw this five-year diary?' Anna asked again.

Jeannie shook her head, picking up a sweater and opening a drawer to stuff it in.

'You didn't think it was strange that she asked to use the flat when you were out?'

'Nope, she often asked us to disappear for an afternoon when she brought one or other of her boyfriends here for a shag. We didn't argue about it; she was often paying the rent, after all.'

'And you're sure she never mentioned anything about publishing a book?'

Jeannie walked out, not answering. By now loud music was coming from the lounge. Anna just wanted to get out of this room with its overpowering smell of sweet lilacs. She followed Jeannie into the hall.

'Thank you for your time, Jeannie. I really appreciate it.'

'That's OK. Did you see the photograph of us in the paper?'

Anna nodded.

'We had a lot of press outside, you know, trying to ask us about Amanda, but we never let them in and they kept on taking photographs of us. I wouldn't mind getting some of them – costs a lot to keep my portfolio up to date.'

'I'm sorry you didn't get the part this afternoon.'

'Yeah, well, they pay a pittance, and I'll get more from modelling.'

Jeannie stood watching Anna as she headed up the basement steps, lugging the binliners filled with fan mail. She hadn't offered to help her carry them out. She shut the door and threw a bolt across it, hurrying back into the lounge.

'You stupid cow, what you light up for? She was a fucking policewoman.'

Felicity giggled and said she'd forgotten. Then she rolled off the cushion, delving beneath it.

'I've got it. I thought she might have even seen it on the fucking bookshelf.'

She held up the pink diary. Jeannie snatched it from her.

'How much you think it's worth? She said it was a lot, didn't she?'

Felicity shrugged, watching as Jeannie flicked through the pages. 'You remember the name of that publishing firm?'

Jeannie nodded, still intent on the diary. Then she kissed it.

'Golden Arrow . . . but we gotta wait a while, let all

the fuss die down, and then we go to . . . shit, what was that bloke's name?'

She knew it was pointless asking Felicity who was now spreadeagled over the cushions, puffing on the joint. Jeannie didn't feel guilty; on the contrary, the resentment she had felt all those years about losing the film part to Amanda had always been close to the surface. She didn't even bother really reading the diary's scrawled hand-written pages; all she cared about was whether it was worth money – money she felt was owed to her. She had always believed that if she hadn't mentioned the film role she was up for, Amanda would never have auditioned for it. The fact that she was neither as beautiful nor as talented never came into the equation. She, Jeannie Bale, had been robbed of stardom.

She nudged Felicity with her foot.

'Don't mention this to anybody, you understand me? We gotta wait for the right time to sell it.'

'OK.'

'I know how to handle the business side and we'll split the profits, but you gotta keep your mouth shut.'

'OK.'

Jeannie went into her bedroom. She opened the diary and sifted through the last few pages until she found the name of Josh Lyons. She would keep it from Felicity. She knelt beside her bed, about to hide the diary underneath the mattress, then changed her mind and instead took one of her china-faced dolls and, lifting her lace dress, pushed the diary inside and pulled down the doll's vest. It was bulky, but the frilly dress covered it, and when she set it back alongside the other dolls, she was certain no one would ever suspect anything was hidden there.

★

285

Felicity had actually been in the flat on the afternoon Amanda had arranged the meeting with Josh Lyons. She had intended to be out as Amanda had asked, but she had got so stoned the night before that she had crashed out in her bedroom and slept through most of the afternoon. She had only woken when she heard voices. Then she heard the front door slam shut and Amanda go into the kitchen, but she didn't dare move. Only when it was quiet had she peeked out to see Amanda in her bedroom opposite on her hands and knees, lifting the corner of the carpet by her wardrobe. It seemed an age before Amanda left the flat, and not until the front door closed, did Felicity emerge from her bedroom. She went into Amanda's room, straight to the same spot where she had seen her kneeling, thinking that maybe she had been hiding cash. Instead she found a five-year diary; it still had the small leather flap and the lock intact. She didn't dare open it, but put it back under the carpet.

That was the last time Amanda was in the flat; now the diary was hidden away again and was likely to make them a lot of money one day.

Chapter Fifteen

Anna slapped the steering-wheel with the flat of her hand; she was in big trouble and she knew it. She had switched on her mobile phone to check her messages. All of them were from the station, asking her to call in as soon as she could. As she drove away from the flat in Maida Vale, she was put through to Mike Lewis who tore a strip off her. While she had been 'gallivanting around doing her own investigation', Andrea Lesser and Andrew Smith-Barker had been brought in for questioning, and they had the result they wanted. Langton was even asking if Anna was now part-time. Mike ended the call by warning her that her disappearing acts could have severe consequences.

Joan gave her more details about the twosome.

'Fraud. They've been robbing our victim and we've got the evidence. It's pretty conclusive and the Guv thinks it's a big motive for them to . . .' There was a gasp, then Joan whispered that she had to go. A briefing was about to start.

'Just do one thing for me, Joan. Run the name Anthony James through the Police National Computer. He's a unit driver, could be—'

'I've got to go.' The phone went dead.

Anna felt her whole body tense. She was barely concentrating and before she knew it, she had gone into the back of the van in front, which had braked suddenly.

'Oh shit!'

Shaken, she got out of her car. The right headlight was smashed and her bumper badly dented. The van appeared to have no damage, but both she and the driver had to pull over to exchange insurance details. Seeing the steam coming out of her grill, she knew it was going to take some time for her to get to the station.

It was an hour before the AA came to tow her car away and Anna had to take a taxi the rest of the way to the station. As the cab drew up, she saw Andrea Lesser being taken from a patrol car escorted by two uniformed officers, Barolli walking alongside her. Anna waited, making sure they were some way ahead of her before she followed, dragging the plastic binliners of letters from Amanda's flat with her. As she sneaked into her office, she could see Barolli across the incident room talking to Mike Lewis; she felt like a naughty schoolgirl who had been playing truant. Mike moved off, not even glancing towards her. Barolli gathered up a set of files, then looked over at her office.

'Been on a sabbatical, have we?'

She ignored him.

'You had better do some catching up. We've built up a really strong stack of evidence against both—'

'Yes, I know, you've brought in Andrea Lesser and Andrew Smith-Barker.'

'He's not here yet and she's waiting for her brief. In the meantime, I suggest you get tooled up in case you're wanted in the interviews.'

'Thank you.'

'If it's not a rude question, where've you been all day?'

'Mind your own fucking business,' Anna snapped.

'Don't worry, sweetheart, I can mind mine. Reality is, whilst you were doing your own thing, we've cracked the case.' He tapped the file with a finger. 'There's your motive.'

'Really?'

'I'd put money on it, they hired someone to—' He turned as Barbara appeared at the door to say that Andrew Smith-Barker was being brought into the reception.

Barolli grinned, gave a pat to Barbara's bottom as she walked out, then turned to Anna.

'It's the two of them.'

He waltzed off, full of himself, as Anna opened the file. Barbara returned with a beaker of coffee.

'You look as if you needed this.'

'Thank you.'

'If he taps my bum one more time I'm going to swipe his nasty little paw from here to that wall.'

Anna smiled and sipped the coffee. She did really need it and hadn't eaten all day.

'You all right?' Barbara asked. 'Only you had a prang in your car, right?'

'Yes, nothing serious, entirely my fault and no one got hurt except my little Mini.'

'Ah, never mind, eh? Good news they got a big development in the Amanda Delany case. The Boss man is coming in to congratulate the boys.'

'Langton?'

'Yes. I gotta go. See you in a minute.'

'Is Joan free?'

'No, she went off for an early dinner-break. Mike wants us here until late tonight.'

Anna remained in her office reading up on the files. Her head was throbbing and she took two aspirin. She could barely concentrate on the mass of conflicting information and accounting lists, and her headache grew worse. She took her coat, rolled it into a ball and lay down behind her desk, closing her eyes.

Andrea Lesser had been waiting in the interview room for half an hour. She sat like a coiled spring with her legs entwined around each other. Her solicitor was held up in rush-hour traffic. It was just after six o'clock. Seated in the interview room next door was Andrew Smith-Barker. As yet no charges had been brought against him, but he was in deep conversation with his solicitor, Barnaby Treesom, who was making copious notes. Unlike his client, Treesom seemed uncomfortable and constantly shifted his weight as if he was restricted in the chair provided. He was wearing a tracksuit as he had been about to play squash when he was summoned; his client however looked immaculate, adjusting his shirt-cuffs with heavy gold cufflinks.

'Let me run this by you, Andrew,' said Treesom, 'so you know exactly how serious this is. You have been arrested on suspicion of fraud and murder, right?'

Andrew nodded.

'Now I've been given disclosure and the officers have verbal and documentary evidence that you were stealing from Amanda Delany. It is alleged that she had found out and to stop her revealing the theft, you either killed or conspired with others to have her killed.'

Andrew Smith-Barker lost none of his composure. In fact, he was smiling.

'It's farcical and totally untrue. There was no fraud, and there is no way I had anything whatsoever to do with her death.'

Barnaby Treesom didn't doubt his client for a moment. He checked his watch, and said he hoped the interview wouldn't take long.

'Maybe I'll get back to my squash game,' he joked.

By the time Andrea Lesser's solicitor arrived it was almost seven o'clock. Anna woke with a start as someone rapped hard on her office door. She had only just got to her feet when Mike Lewis appeared.

'I want you in with Andrea Lesser.'

She tried to straighten her skirt and hoped he hadn't caught her asleep.

'Mike, can I explain about this afternoon?'

'No, you'll have plenty of time later. It could be a long night.'

'Have you charged them?'

'Not yet . . . Interview Room One.' He walked off.

Anna combed her hair and drank the cold remains of her coffee. The sleep had worked; her headache had gone. She had another swift glance over the file, then went to Joan to ask her a favour.

'There's some binliners in my office – Amanda Delany's fanmail. Could you have a quick look over them, see if there's anything useful?'

Joan rolled her eyes. 'Will do . . . how many?'

Anna grinned and held up three fingers.

★

Barolli and Barbara sat in front of Andrew Smith-Barker and his solicitor. Barolli sat stiffly in his chair; without doubt, he explained to Barnaby Treesom, Amanda Delany's investments had been obtained by illegal means.

'What exactly do you mean by "illegal means"? Why has my client been brought here to explain business transactions between him and Miss Andrea Lesser that to his knowledge were made with Miss Delany's approval?'

'Miss Delany was found brutally murdered,' Barolli said. 'Her death coincides with discrepancies in her financial interaction with Mr Andrew Smith-Barker – which makes your client a viable suspect. We need to know his whereabouts around the time Miss Delany was killed.'

'Let me get this straight.' Treesom cleared his throat. 'You are now not only questioning my client regarding financial transactions between himself and Miss Lesser on behalf of Amanda Delany, but you are also attempting to determine if he had any connection to her death.'

'That's it,' Barolli said. 'He has given a detailed alibi for the time of the murder, but we will be checking his past phone calls. Although he may not have been in the vicinity of Miss Delany's home when she was murdered, the discovery of the fraud may have proved so detrimental to his business that he hired someone to—'

'This is preposterous,' Smith-Barker said angrily. 'I acted at all times with the full cooperation of Miss Lesser and her client, Miss Delany.'

It was clear what Andrew Smith-Barker was doing: extricating himself and placing the entire fraud on Andrea Lesser's shoulders.

Barolli, unruffled, took a moment before he continued.

'We need to know from your client, Mr Treesom, when and where he invested the monies. If no documents can be produced . . .'

Smith–Barker lifted his hand, interrupting him again.

'My solicitor has all the documents to this effect,' he said.

Barnaby Treesom put a file on the table and leaned back in his chair. He was fully aware that it would take considerable time to trace movements of monies and be even more time-consuming to disprove anything his client had submitted.

Langton sat with a coffee and a sandwich in the small room adjoining the interview sections, watching the interview with Smith–Barker on a screen. His foot tapped constantly as he listened. He knew they had jumped the gun. They should not have brought this pompous man in until they had further evidence of his possible connection to the murder. He admitted there was a motive and a strong one, but he felt the team had not done enough digging into Smith–Barker's private life, nor had they assessed his home and office phone calls. Then again, would a man like Smith–Barker make any compromising calls from his office? Langton didn't think so. He was certain they were looking at a sophisticated conman.

Langton then turned his attention to the interview coming up on screen two. He saw Anna and Mike Lewis take their seats. Mike was explaining to Andrea Lesser that she had not been charged with anything; she was there to answer questions regarding the financial arrangements she had instigated on Miss Delany's behalf.

Andrea Lesser was agitated and constantly twisted a strand of hair between her fingers.

'You do not have to say anything,' Mike continued, 'but it may harm your defence if you do not mention now anything which you later rely on in court. Anything you do say may be given in evidence.'

Andrea Lesser was silent.

Mike then outlined the number of fees from film contracts which had been paid into her agency. They had no record of this money being transferred to Miss Delany's account; this had been verified by her accountant. Could she explain this? Unlike Smith-Barker, Andrea Lesser answered without referring to her solicitor.

'Yes. I had a verbal agreement with Miss Delany that, as the amount was considerable, it should be invested without delay. She agreed and I contacted a reputable investment company for her. She knew exactly what I intended doing and, as I've just said, was in full agreement.'

'This investment you arranged, could you give us the company you chose to use?'

'Yes, it was with a Mr Andrew Smith-Barker who had handled a number of my client's investments on many previous occasions.'

'What is your relationship with this gentleman?'

'Purely business.'

'So you had no personal or social interaction with him prior to this transaction for Miss Delany?'

'No. I was acting on behalf of my client's investments.'

'So you transferred, directly to this company, considerable funds from Miss Delany's film work?' Mike asked.

'Yes, I did.'

'At what point did you make Miss Delany aware that,

contrary to the money invested bearing dividends, it was in fact losing?'

'It wasn't just Miss Delany's loss, but many others after the appalling crash in many City banks; it was totally out of my control.'

'Can you give us written confirmation that Miss Delany approved this transfer of her earnings to Smith-Barker's investment company?'

'It was a verbal agreement, and as I had Power of Attorney for Miss Delany, it wasn't necessary for me to have any written permission. At the time I was also overseeing the purchase and refurbishment of her mews house.'

'So you're saying that she was privy to the entire transaction that you say you instigated on her behalf?'

'Yes, she was.'

'At what point did you inform Miss Delany that she had lost a very considerable amount of money?'

Andrea Lesser turned away, becoming tearful.

'Amanda was dead before I could broach the subject with her.'

'So you're saying she was unaware of the loss?'

'She was busy working on a film and I felt that it wouldn't be the right time to give her bad news. However, seeing we were in this deep recession I felt sure she must have been aware that there could have been problems.'

There was a pause as Mike sifted through his file. Anna remained silent, watching Andrea Lesser's impressive performance.

'How do you think she would have reacted to this loss of earnings?' Mike continued.

Andrea Lesser gave a slight shrug of her shoulders.

'Well, it was not as if she was financially insecure. Her future was looking very promising with numerous scripts being offered to her. She'd have been upset, but accepted that I had only acted in her best interests. It wasn't as if this was a situation unique to her. The recession was affecting everyone.'

'Would you say that Miss Delany's death was very opportune?'

'I don't understand.'

'You never had to tell her you had lost millions of her hard-earned money, did you?' Mike insisted.

'I don't understand.'

'Miss Delany's murder meant that you did not have to inform her that you had misappropriated her funds. That must have been quite a relief.'

'I don't like what you are implying; I did not find any relief. On the contrary. Amanda was not only someone I cared deeply about, but as a client she was a highly valued actress with a big future ahead of her. As I have said, we had numerous offers of work and a possible Hollywood deal . . .'

'So do you believe that if Miss Delany had been alive, had been aware of your transactions, she would have remained with you as a client?'

'Yes, I do. I had managed her career from the first film she made. She trusted me.'

'Trusted you?' Mike repeated.

'Yes. I would have hoped to be able to reinvest further monies and recoup some of her losses.'

'Without her permission?'

'She knew exactly what my intentions were and had verbally agreed to allow me to handle the investment.'

At this moment, her solicitor leaned forward and

tapped the table with the tip of his pen. He spoke quietly but with a condescending air, wafting his pen around to demonstrate his points.

'We seem to be going around in circles. Miss Lesser has explained in detail how the investments came about and that Miss Delany was fully aware of her endeavours to secure what she hoped would be a viable financial future. We all know what has occurred with the present global débâcle and Miss Lesser cannot be held responsible for that. Your inference that there has been some kind of fraud is strongly refuted, and any involvement with the death of Miss Delany cannot be proved, unless of course you have some documentary evidence to the contrary or with which to substantiate your unfounded allegations. If you have any further questions for my client I would be grateful if you would present them now or allow my client to leave immediately.'

During his speech Anna saw Barolli signalling through the window of the door of the interview room. She got up quietly and left to talk to him. She was away for less than a few moments and she returned, just as Miss Lesser's solicitor was asking for his client to be released. He confidently closed his notebook and lifted his brief-case onto the table to pack away his papers. Anna sat down and wrote a note to Mike, passing it to him. He read it and then folded it, running his finger along the crease of the paper.

'Could you explain to me how Miss Delany's payments came into the agency?' he asked.

Andrea Lesser sighed and glanced at her solicitor, who gave her a small nod to continue.

'I've explained this before. The agency would invoice the company she was working for; the company would

297

then send the cheques to us. We would bank them, take off our commission and I would forward the monies to Miss Delany's account and send her our invoice with details of any payments we had taken as our percentage.'

'Thank you.'

Mike sat for a moment and Anna glanced at him. She then leaned forward to whisper to him and he nodded.

'Let's return to your relationship with Andrew Smith-Barker.'

'Really, there was no relationship bar a business one. As I said, we had done business together in the past.'

'Are you aware that he is being questioned this evening?'

'No.'

'Mr Smith-Barker also maintains that you had a business arrangement, but he claims that he was unaware of the fact that Miss Delany had not been informed about nor had approved the money you passed to him for investments.'

'This is outrageous. I have told you repeatedly that I had a verbal agreement with Amanda and there was no need for me to acquire any written approval.'

'So you passed over Miss Delany's money to . . .'

'Yes, I forwarded a cheque to his company,' she snapped.

'You say that you also had other clients' investments with Mr Smith-Barker?'

'Yes.'

'Then surely you must have been aware that his company was in dire financial straits.'

She leaned forward angrily. 'I was never made aware that he was in any kind of financial trouble! On the contrary, he assured me that his company was in good shape.'

'Do you reside at twenty-two, Atherton Gardens?'

'Yes,' she sighed, irritated.

'Are you aware that Mr Smith-Barker's house and offices have been repossessed?'

She shook her head and glanced at her solicitor.

'During the period his house was being repossessed, he was, I believe, staying with you at your flat. Is that correct?'

Andrea Lesser gasped and leaned back in her chair.

'So this "business relationship" did extend to you having him as a house guest. We have witness statements from your porter and two other residents that—'

'Yes, I admit he did stay with me for a while. I was just helping him until he regained . . . his property.'

'But this would have been *before* Miss Delany's investments?'

'Possibly. I don't recall the exact dates.'

'Do you expect us to believe that you have someone staying with you, in your flat, and at no time discuss their reason for being there? Unless you have lied and the relationship was sexual and he was lying to you about his financial situation.'

Andrea Lesser was taking short sharp breaths, constantly looking at her solicitor.

Langton yawned as he sat back in his chair, hoping one or other of them would push the agent further. He knew that his team were on shaky ground even if Lesser and Smith-Barker had been going at it like rabbits. They could not prove that she did *not* have the verbal agreement of their victim, nor could they prove that there had been anything underhand. The team suspected that Amanda Delany had been murdered because she had uncovered the fraud, but they had no proof.

Langton personally did not believe that either of their suspects would have gone to such lengths as murder as a way out of their predicament. Andrea Lesser could have continued taking money from Amanda; her client was drunk and drugged up often enough not to know what was happening, and might well have been too dumb not to have noticed until they had turned things around. Fraud was always a lengthy and difficult crime to prove; it could take months if not years to solve.

Now Anna was talking for the first time. Langton leaned forward. She had opened her file and was speaking in a low soft voice, Mike beside her, sitting back in his chair, looking exhausted.

'Miss Lesser, I believe you have been lying to us,' Anna began. 'I know through my enquiries that, contrary to what you have stated – that Miss Delany had agreed verbally that you make investments on her behalf – she was completely unaware, and when she *did* find out, she was very angry. Shortly before her death, one of her flatmates met another actor from the film *The Mansion* who, having been paid in full, had purchased a new car. Miss Delany became aware only when told . . .'

'That is not true,' Andrea Lesser interrupted. 'Actors often get paid at different times, especially ones taking the lion's share of the finances.'

Anna ignored her and continued.

'Miss Delany's friend called your office to accuse you of stealing from your client. This was just before her brutal murder and you refused to listen. You cut off the caller.'

'I do not recall anyone contacting me, nor did I receive any harsh words from Amanda.'

'I never mentioned the word "harsh", Miss Lesser, but now you have mentioned it, did you not get threatened by your client that unless she received full payment of what was owed her from *The Mansion*, she was going to leave your agency?'

'No, that is not true.'

'You were also aware that Miss Delany had been offered a substantial amount of money from a publishing company to write her memoirs. In these memoirs, she was more than likely to write about the fact that she felt she had been robbed by the one person she trusted. You, Miss Lesser.'

'I was not aware of any book deal.'

'It's strange then, isn't it, that just as Miss Delany discovers she has money missing and is offered a publishing deal, she is found murdered.'

'I don't understand what you are insinuating.'

'I am not insinuating, Miss Lesser, I am elaborating on a very strong motive to get rid of your client. Not only would your professional career be in shreds, but you could be arrested for embezzlement.'

'No, no . . . I swear I didn't know!'

Anna upped the temperature by raising her voice.

'Miss Lesser, you have been lying to us! You have insisted that you had only a business relationship with Mr Smith-Barker, yet he was living with you in your flat. You knew *exactly* what state his finances were in, and yet you kept on feeding him more and more money to try and get his company solvent.'

'That is not true.'

'*Yes, it is*. And now we have a statement from Andrew

Smith-Barker denying that he had ever been told that the monies you handed over to him were *stolen*, for want of a better word, from your client Miss Delany, and that had he known, he would not have invested or continued his friendship with you, as his business is built on respect, not theft!'

Miss Lesser bit her lip, trying not to cry.

'The motive is stronger, isn't it? Miss Lesser, did you also lie to Mr Smith-Barker? Were you so enamoured of him that you couldn't stop yourself? He denies ever having any kind of feelings for you. You were infatuated with him but he never encouraged or wanted that attention. I believe that you were in such a horrendous situation that you had no option but to get rid of Amanda Delany.'

The floodgates opened as Andrea Lesser broke down weeping. She seemed very distressed by the revelation that Smith-Barker denied any knowledge of what she was doing, and that he had no feelings for her. In that way, he had really put the boot in.

Mike glanced at Anna and then took over.

'Miss Lesser, we will now charge you on suspicion of fraud against Amanda Delany and . . .'

Andrea Lesser got up. The chair fell behind her and she was sobbing.

'No, no, that is not true!'

Langton watched the woman breaking down as she denied that she had anything to do with Amanda's murder. They had no proof that she had instigated the killing or that she had hired someone to do it. He watched as the interrogation continued and the distraught woman veered from fury at her lover to confessing that she had, without Amanda Delany's permission, embezzled two and a half million pounds, which she said Smith-Barker had persuaded her that he could turn around. She was in love with him, she sobbed; he had used her emotions to make her do something that she now regretted. She knew her career was finished.

Her statement implicated Smith-Barker as being wholly aware of what she was doing, and claimed that he had, in fact, instigated it. With no evidence as yet to implicate either in the murder, they were both charged with fraud and held in the cells in the station overnight before being taken to the magistrate's court the following morning. Langton had refused to let either leave the station in case they left the country before charges were formally brought. It was a good result, if not the one they all wanted, but they had at last made a major step forward in their case.

Anna left the interview room and went to her office. Her headache had returned with a vengeance and she was feeling queasy. She still had to meet Mike to tell him about her afternoon enquiries, but felt so ill that she decided to write him a note and take a taxi home. As she began writing, she dropped her pen and, bending down to retrieve it, she was violently sick. Barbara, suspecting whiplash after the prang in her car, called an ambulance and accompanied Anna to the nearest Out Patients hospital.

It was a long wait, the pain so excruciating that Anna wanted to weep, desiring nothing more than to go home to bed. Only after she had been X-rayed and prescribed painkillers did Barbara put her in a taxi, wearing a plastic collar round her sore neck. It was indeed a case of whiplash and the doctor suggested she take a couple of days to rest.

It felt so calm and peaceful to be in her own bed with its crisp, newly-laundered sheets, the fresh smell so unlike the hideous basement flat she'd been in all after-noon. Anna had a shower, put the plastic collar back around her neck and took two painkillers. Then she fell into a deep, exhausted sleep.

Langton gave Mike and Barolli a long grilling. Offering congratulations on the development, he went on to say that he did not believe they had their murderer in custody. He hoped Anna would be back at work as soon as possible, was his parting shot to Mike. Yet again, she had proved her ability in the interrogation.

Mike snapped at Barolli when Langton was gone.

'She fucking did it again. Where the fuck did she get all that, about phone calls to that Lesser bitch? I am getting sick and tired of being made to look like a fuck-ing prat. She's constantly working this case on her own.'

'Tell me about it,' Barolli complained.

Mike jabbed the air with his finger.

'I tell you, I'm gonna put this in a report. Langton thinks the sun shines out of her arse, well, she's gonna trip herself up and I'm gonna be right behind her, giving a push.'

Chapter Sixteen

The next morning, Anna felt terrible. The pain in her neck had shifted further down her back and every limb in her body ached. She felt dizzy just getting out of bed. With the neckbrace in place and a hot water bottle strapped to her back, she cooked some eggs and bacon and made a coffee. She knew she should call into the station at eight; it was still not seven. She was anxious about the lecture she knew she would be in for from Mike Lewis when she went back to work. At no time did she even contemplate how she had steered the interrogation of Andrea Lesser to get her to admit the fraud. In fact, she didn't really have a clear memory of anything she had said.

Back in bed she dozed off for a while, then on waking burst into tears. She couldn't stop crying; whether or not it was the aftermath of the past evening, she felt utterly at a loss. Before she had a chance to call the station, Barbara rang to say she mustn't even think about coming into work. Anna had no sooner put the phone back when it rang again. It was Langton. She felt a twinge of pain as she sat up. He asked how she was, praised her efforts on the previous evening and gave her the number of a good chiropractor. She thanked him, on the brink of tears again.

'You all right?'

'Yes.'

'Well, call this guy, he's special – and get back to work when you feel you can. You can have seven days' uncertified sickness before you need a doctor's note.'

'I will.' Anna wrote down the number on the pad on her bedside table.

'If you need anything, just call the station.'

'Thank you.'

He hung up and she rested back, closing her eyes. She must have fallen asleep because it was after midday when she woke. She eased herself out of bed, feeling less achy. After lunch she took two more painkillers, beginning to feel more like herself.

She called the station to ask Joan about the unit driver Tony James. Joan confirmed that she had run the check and there was no police record. 'Barolli was also mentioning him,' she told Anna.

'Really? What did he say?'

'He wanted to know why you were asking about him, I think.'

Anna was fazed, wondering how Barolli had got onto the unit driver. She had her suspicions.

'My brother had his neck in a brace for weeks. Didn't do any good; in the end he threw it away,' Joan chattered on.

'Well, I'm still wearing mine.'

'What you need is a good massage.'

'I'll think about it. Thanks, Joan.'

'That's OK. We're trying to get the smell of sick out of your office. You know you threw up all over your carpet.'

'I'm sorry.'

'Just call if you need anything. Bye now.'

Anna lay staring into space, then leaned over to look at the number of Dr Berry, the chiropractor Langton had suggested. She phoned and got through to Berry's receptionist, who asked who had made the recommendation. When Anna gave Langton's name, there was a soft laugh.

'Is it urgent?' the woman asked.

'Sort of. I think I have whiplash.'

She booked Anna in for a late session at 6 p.m.; the address was a private clinic on Marylebone High Street. That done, Anna went into the lounge to go through the thick files piled up at the table. In one was a list of the film crew she and Simon had interviewed. Beside each name and job description was a tick. Anna looked down the list. The actors she was familiar with as they had both interviewed them, so she paid more attention to the rest of the crew whom Simon had questioned. There were over fifty names, ranging from executive producers and script editors to floor-runners and gaffers. None of them, according to Simon's notes, could be linked to Amanda Delany's murder.

On the last page was a list of drivers: the extras van driver, the costume and make-up drivers and the grip truck driver. Lastly, underlined by Simon, were four unit drivers, their names and addresses listed. Two were the brothers they had met on set: Harry James, the unit driver allocated to Amanda Delany, and his younger brother Tony who, Simon had noted, covered for his brother when required. The third was a guy called Bruce Mason. What surprised Anna was the name of the fourth and last standby driver: Lester James. In brackets Simon had written *(another brother)*. Anna had not heard his name mentioned before; she had no idea if he was connected to any of the other films.

She checked Lester James's address and phone number, and eased herself onto her feet to use the telephone. First she rang Bruce Mason, who answered almost immediately.

She hadn't quite worked out what she was going to ask him.

'Mr Mason?'

'Speaking.'

'I hope you don't mind me calling, but I am part of the police team investigating the death of Amanda Delany and I wondered if I could ask you a few questions?'

'I've got a POB right now. Gimme your number and I'll call you back.'

'Thank you.' She replaced the receiver, wondering if POB meant passenger on board. Either way she'd wait. She called Joan.

'I need a favour. Run three names through the Police National Computer for me, would you? And, Joan, just keep it quiet for the time being, eh?'

'Whatever.'

Anna, having been given a 'no previous record' for Anthony James, supplied the names of Harry and Lester James, and Bruce Mason, and then hung up.

It was over two hours before Anna heard back from Bruce Mason. In the interim she had arranged for her car to be fixed and called her insurance company to learn that the van driver had contacted them: apparently on closer inspection, he *had* found damage to his exhaust and rear bumper. The damage to her own car was going to cost, at a low estimate, two thousand pounds – plus she would lose her No Claim bonus.

When her mobile phone rang, she snatched it up. 'Yes?'

'Bruce Mason. You called earlier.'

'Ah yes, I did. I wanted to clarify exactly what a unit driver's job is.'

'It's a bit bloody obvious, isn't it?'

'Pardon?' Anna was taken aback by his rudeness.

'A unit driver is hired by the film company to chauffeur their actors around. Is this some kind of joke?'

'No, it isn't, Mr Mason. We can have this discussion now or, if you would prefer, you could come into the station to assist our enquiries.'

'Tell me who you are again,' he said.

'Detective Inspector Anna Travis of the Metropolitan Police.'

'You having me on?'

Anna sighed with impatience.

'I'd like to see who I'm talking to; this sounds a bit unethical to me,' Mason continued.

Anna arranged to meet him at 5 p.m. in a café close to the chiropractor's surgery on Marylebone High Street.

Sitting outside the café, the plastic collar round her neck, Anna realised that she had no idea what Bruce Mason looked like. Then she saw a Mercedes park up just outside the café, and the driver got out, and looked around. She signalled to him.

'You the Detective?' Mason asked, as he joined her.

'Yes.'

He fed the parking meter, sat down opposite and smiled. 'What's with the collar?'

'Whiplash.'

'Oh yeah? High-speed chase in a patrol car, was it?'

When Anna showed him her ID, he loosened his coat and seemed to accept her as bona fide.

Mason was heavy set, broad-shouldered, with thinning hair, good-looking in a rugged sort of way. He was also smartly dressed; beneath his coat he wore a suit and tie. His fingers were thick and stubby and he sported a heavy gold wedding ring.

Anna chose her words carefully to make him feel at ease, to draw him out. Mason explained that the unit drivers belonged to a company and were hired out by the film units to be on call for whichever actor they had been assigned to.

'We pick them up, take them to locations or the film set, and drive them home when they've wrapped for the day.'

'So is all your work through the company?'

'Not always. When it's quiet we do some private clients — bodyguards, you name it. I did Madonna last year, was part of her entourage. It's about supply and demand. If the stars get to like you they'll use you as personal chauffeurs. When the film industry is quiet, which it has been of late, we get what work we can.'

'Tell me about the James brothers.'

'The James brothers?' Mason gave a shrug of his wide shoulders.

They were quite a formidable team, he said, often taking the cream of jobs. The eldest brother Harry had money in the company, so it was always first come first served for them. They were a team you didn't want to mess with, but they always saw to it that he did all right. Although he was on the drivers' unit, he didn't get to drive the top stars – the brothers always took them. If one or other of the brothers couldn't make it, they would bring in someone like himself.

'Amanda Delany was a top star. Did you drive her?'

'No, the brothers always handled her and did work for her when she was not attached to a film.'

'Which one of them drove her most frequently?'

He shrugged, unable to say. He insisted that they were a highly professional team, who knew their place. Anna asked if he could tell her some stories about Amanda. At first Mason hesitated, then gave a few instances of occasions she had had to be carried out of certain clubs, how the drivers often had to go to various hotels to collect her for filming. She was a naughty girl and had even had sex in the back of the cars.

'But you never drove her?'

'No, like I said, the brothers were around her, very protective of her, especially the youngest, Lester. He'd known her for years ever since she did her first movie so she trusted him, and there were times when he had to fight off the paparazzi. But he could handle himself.'

'What do you mean, handle himself?'

'Lester was a British karate champion. Nobody messed with the kid, but he was quite a handful and I often heard his brothers havin' a bit of a fit over what he'd got himself into.' Bruce held up his own big hand. 'With someone who had as high a ranking as Lester, his hands were classified as lethal weapons, at least in the States.'

'And you know for sure that Lester drove Amanda Delany?'

'Yeah, often.'

'What about on *Gaslight*?'

Mason shook his head. As far as he knew, Lester wasn't on that movie, just Tony and Harry. He himself had been brought in for a couple of days towards the end of the shoot.

'After Miss Delany's death?'

'Yeah, that's right. It was a bit of a downer, you know. Everyone felt that maybe they should have closed the film, but that's money.'

Anna checked the time. It was almost six, time for her appointment, so she would have to leave. As she walked Mason to his car, she asked if he knew if Lester could have worked on *Gaslight* without him knowing. It was possible, Mason responded; the director was a wanker and often didn't keep to the schedule, which was always a nightmare for the drivers.

'Why you so interested in Lester?' he concluded.

'We've interviewed everyone but him who worked on the film.'

When she thanked him, he gave her a card. If she ever needed a driver, someone with experience as a bodyguard, he said, she should call on him.

As soon as Mason saw Anna leave, he called Tony James. He'd had a weird interview with a detective from the Met, he told him, a woman attached to the murder investigation of Amanda Delany. In no way had he said anything derogatory about the brothers, he reassured Tony; he just wanted him to know that a policewoman was sniffing around.

'Was it Anna Travis?' Anthony asked.

'Yeah. Detective Anna Travis.'

*

Anna headed into an old building on Marylebone High Street that had once housed exclusive apartments. The clinic was in the basement.

'You must be Anna.' A pretty, dark-haired girl was at the reception desk. 'Dr Berry's actually ready to see you, but could you first fill in this form, please?'

Anna had almost completed it when the door to one of the surgery rooms was flung open. She glanced up to see an attractive and youngish man with wild curly hair wearing a white medical coat. He clapped his hands, turning to Anna.

'Anna? Yes? Come on through.' Dr Berry turned to his receptionist and said she could close up for the night. With a hand on the small of her back, he guided Anna into his surgery. It was a large, all-white room with a massage bed in one corner. There were arrays of candles, and lists of the therapy choices in frames on the wall: hot stone massage, therapy massage, Indian head and shoulder massage, Thai foot massage and manual lymphatic drainage.

'I'm Gordon,' he said. 'First, let me take this contraption off you. I hate them and they often do more damage than good.' He undid the collar and tossed it onto a low chair. 'Now, tell me exactly what happened.'

He had long slender fingers, with straight-cut nails, and had to bend slightly towards her as he was so tall. He gently felt the side of her neck and then up to her skull, putting a little pressure around the nape of her neck. He lit two perfumed candles and turned on a stereo unit; the music was sweet and low, and sounded like water and flutes. Next, he took out some small bottles of oils from a glass-fronted cabinet and uncorked them.

'Take off your coat and let me see what you have on underneath.'

Anna was wearing a T-shirt and jeans. He asked her to remove her trainers and shirt and lie on the massage bed, face down.

Anna felt uneasy; she remembered hearing Berry tell the receptionist that she could leave.

'It's just my neck,' she said, and he turned and smiled at her.

'You have a problem about being here with me?'

'Not really.'

'It's up to you. But I'll be using oils and don't want to mess up your clothes. Also, I want to massage your shoulders and down your back. You'll find towels behind the screen.'

He still had the smile on his face and, blushing, Anna went quickly behind the screen to undress.

While she was thus occupied, Gordon Berry laid fresh towels along the massage table.

'I don't think you have any damage other than muscle strain,' he said. 'Nothing seems to be out of line, on the contrary. Often these minor types of injuries cause dis-comfort – it's Nature's way of saying ouch, but I think the stress of what happened has made you stiffen and we can remedy that easily.'

Anna wrapped a soft white towel around herself and came from behind the screen. He had his back to her and was testing the heat of the stones he was going to use on her.

'Have you ever had hot stone massage?'

'No.'

'It's James Langton's favourite, and I have to say we've seen a lot of progress with his leg injury. Often, having knee surgery makes you limp and it throws the back out of line. Although James had some serious internal injuries, we're making great moves forward. I know he finds the sessions very relaxing.'

He turned to her. 'Is he a close friend of yours?'

'No, he's my boss actually.'

'Ah well. Up you get, face down and rest your head in the ring here.'

It felt strange staring down at the floor. The piped music was very faint and she closed her eyes.

'You're a detective?'

'Yes,' she murmured.

He moved the towel away, and inched down her jeans to feel the base of her spine.

'You're very tense around the shoulders, so just relax and I'll get started.'

The oil smelled slightly of liniment and he was quickly onto the area that was painful. He explained that he would be placing the stones down her back; if they were too hot, she just had to tell him. It was extraordinary how good the heat felt. Now he was using the perfumed oils and applying more pressure, massaging her back and sides.

'He's quite a character, isn't he?'

'Yes, he is.'

'I actually met him through his wife, who's been a regular client for many years. It took quite a lot of persuading for him to come to me, but now he's here twice a week and I think he's found it very beneficial. That was some injury. We've also been working on the scars on his chest.'

Anna said nothing, surprised that Gordon had referred to Langton's wife. She wasn't sure if he had remarried, further proof of how little she really knew about Langton in the passing months since they had parted. She put the thought out of her head and began to relax.

'Ah, that's better. Now you are giving up to me,' Gordon said softly.

'I have been a bit stressed out, actually.'

'I suppose it's part of your profession. Are you working on any specific case?'

Without going into details, Anna told him about the constant pressure the team was under to produce a result in big cases, how much time it took for them to eliminate suspects, how she was always in trouble for going it alone and not sharing her findings with the team.

'Well, in every business there are rules and sometimes it's hard to adhere to them, especially if you are onto something you feel is going to be productive.'

'Yes, it just sort of takes over your life. You go to bed thinking about who did what, trying to remember everything, and then when you suddenly find a link, it gets exciting. I don't seem able to share things until I have dug deeper, re-questioned, tracked down information – and so I'm constantly in hot water.'

'I bet old James can be a hard taskmaster.'

'That's very true.' Anna closed her eyes as Gordon moved behind her to gently massage her scalp and face. It felt wonderful and she sighed.

'Maybe you're not a team player.'

'Mmmm . . .'

'What, besides work, do you enjoy doing?'

'Not a lot. In fact, I don't really seem to find the time to do anything.'

'You should – it's always good to be able to stand aside

for a time. You should make it a priority to have what I call private time.'

'Do you?'

'Yes, I play polo. I ride out at Ham Gate in Richmond and play for their team. I don't own a horse, not got the finances for that, but every weekend I ride or play squash, try and catch a show in town. You like the theatre?'

'I haven't been since . . .' She couldn't recall the last time she had been to see a West End show.

'Movies?'

She closed her eyes and told him how many films she had been watching recently connected to her investigation.

'Ah, but that's still work. So what case are you on?'

Anna hesitated and then described the case. By now he had laid a warm facecloth over her forehead and more hot stones around her shoulders. He placed one in each hand.

'Shush now, just relax, and when you feel ready you should slowly sit up. I'll be back in a moment.'

Anna lay in a blissful state, her breathing shallow and calm. When he returned, he removed the facecloth and gently brushed her hair from her face with his hands.

'Feeling better?'

She smiled up at him and nodded. He took the stones from her hands and she sat up slowly, feeling a little dizzy but incredibly relaxed. She laughed.

'Good, that's a nice sound,' he said, watching as she swung her legs down from the bed, one arm holding the towel in place around her chest.

'Right, go and get dressed and I'll be in reception.'

★

'You have a car?' Gordon asked as he stood behind the small reception counter closing up his appointment book.

'Yes, but it's still in the garage,' Anna replied, handing him a cheque.

'Whereabouts are you going?'

'Tower Bridge.'

'Let me give you a lift. I live further up the river in an old warehouse conversion.' He fetched his jacket and turned off the lights, waiting at the door.

'Are you sure?'

'I wouldn't have offered if I wasn't. Don't forget your neck brace, but I wouldn't advise you wear it.'

'Thank you. A lift would be great.' She held the neck brace over her arm and followed him out.

'Are you married?' he asked casually as he drove through the West End.

'No.'

'Just to your job?'

'I suppose so.' She wanted to ask him the same question, but felt awkward. When they arrived at her block of flats, he asked if it was also a warehouse conversion. It was just a matter of course to ask him up to see her top-floor flat.

'This is really great,' he said, as she opened the doors onto the small balcony.

They went into the lounge. Seeing her jumble of files and printed cards, laid out over the floor and on the table, she apologised.

'Hey, you don't have to worry, but I can see you bring your work home with you.'

She opened a bottle of wine and fetched glasses from

the kitchen. When she returned, he was looking over the cards.

'What are these names?' he asked.

'Suspects.'

'In the Amanda Delany case?'

'Yes.'

As they sat on the sofa and ate cheese and crackers, Anna couldn't remember a time when she had, with an almost total stranger, not only discussed a case she was working on, but talked about her suspicions.

'It's a hard one to piece together, as we have a slew of suspects who had some kind of axe to grind against the victim, from ex-lovers to agents and even parents.'

Gordon was an attentive listener. He asked sensible questions and Anna enjoyed talking to him and hearing his views. She described how Amanda's body had been found, what items were missing from her house, how every time they made a strong move forward they took two steps back. How the team strongly believed that both her agent and the investment banker had a motive, but that she herself felt that neither would be capable of murder. She didn't even consider how unethical it was, divulging so much confidential material to a near-stranger.

'Unless they hired someone,' Gordon suggested.

'Even that's hard to believe. I think her agent was driven by her emotional tie to the investment banker.'

'Well, a woman in love is capable of Christ only knows what. Obsession can drive someone to do the unthinkable.'

'But to hire a hitman? Come on, I don't think so. Also would a hitman rape her?'

Gordon picked up a photograph of Amanda.

'She was very beautiful, very famous – and if you think about the rumour that someone had sexual intercourse with Marilyn Monroe in the mortuary, maybe the killer couldn't resist.'

Anna frowned.

'Men have sexual obsessions,' he continued, 'and if you take away the hitman, then that will leave you with a man who was obsessed by her, someone whom she may have hurt, betrayed or made to look foolish, and that could result in a fury that made him stab her with such ferocity. You say he left marks of the hilt of the knife?'

Anna sipped her wine, listening, aware that she had also come to this conclusion.

Gordon looked through the file of photographs showing the victim *in situ*.

'He never touched her face.'

Anna drained her glass, knowing she had gone too far.

'I'd better put those away. Everything we've discussed is highly confidential, so please don't mention any of it to James Langton.'

Gordon looked surprised. 'As if I would.'

'I shouldn't have shown you any of this or even discussed the case. It's very unprofessional of me.'

'Well, it's quite unprofessional of me to do this.' He reached over and drew her close and kissed her. She was so surprised she didn't resist, nor when he kissed her again.

'How's your neck?' he asked softly.

She moved closer to rest in his arms. 'No pain.'

He was silent for a few moments and then looked down at her as she lay against his shoulder.

'I could leave and we make a date for tomorrow, or I can stay and still see you again.'

'I think . . .' she murmured.

He tilted her chin gently and rubbed her cheek with his thumb.

'I'd better go.'

'No, stay, or at least have another glass of wine.'

'Ah no, better not, Detective Travis. Drink driving and all that.'

He got up and reached for his jacket, while she remained on the sofa, wondering how she could persuade him to stay. He put his empty wine glass in the middle of her printed cards.

'Have you got a hunch as to which one is the killer?'

Anna joined him at the table and he slipped an arm around her.

'I don't know. I keep moving them around.'

'Maybe it isn't any of them. Then what do you do?'

She sighed. 'Go back to square one. Start all over again, and if that doesn't work, then we have a cold case.'

Gordon stared at her cards and then hugged her gently.

'I would think whoever it is will not be cold, but burning up, not with the fact that he got away with it, but with the knowledge of what he had done. Paid her back, then taken her precious little toy rabbit as a keepsake of when she slept with him and held it in her arms.'

Anna turned to him. 'How did you know that?'

'Everyone's a detective,' he said, smiling.

She stepped back, staring at him.

'No, the toy rabbit. I never mentioned it to you. How did you know that it's missing?'

'It's in the file.'

'Which file?'

Gordon sighed and lifted his hands up in a submissive gesture.

'All right, I'll come clean.'

'You better had,' she said sharply.

'Eh, come on, don't speak to me like that. If you must know, it was James who told me, at our last session. He was asking me . . .'

'He talked to you about the case?'

'Not that much of it, just a few bits and pieces.'

'Why didn't you tell me?'

'Maybe because of exactly what you said to me, that it was confidential. It only came about because he had his son with him and the lad had this teddy bear that he carries everywhere and James said how the kid creates when it goes missing.'

'His son came to one of the sessions with you?'

'Yeah, I also work with children, cranial massage. He's quite a handful.'

'Tommy?'

'Yeah. We started talking about the reasons kids retain something like a comfort blanket.'

Anna was nonplussed. She was angry, and at the same time couldn't really believe what she was hearing. Gordon put his jacket down and poured another glass of wine.

'We discussed the case, not in detail as I just said, but he asked me why I thought your victim's toy had been taken. I suggested that your killer may have had a perverse reason for taking it because he knew how much it meant to her.'

'You should have mentioned this to me.' Anna reached for the bottle of wine.

'Why? Like I said, it was confidential on the one hand

and on the other, I suppose I wanted to impress you.'

'Impress me?'

He put his glass down unfinished. 'I'd better go.'

But Anna was keen now to know exactly what else Langton had said. 'Did he discuss me at all?' She couldn't help it.

It was Gordon's turn to look phased. He shook his head.

'Did he call you to say he'd given me your number?'

'Yes, and he said that you were a kind of special person and would I look after you.'

'Kind of special?'

He frowned, as if annoyed at her persistence.

'Did he say anything else about me?'

'No. Just that you were in a bit of trouble and had hurt your neck and if I could see you he'd be grateful.'

Anna sat down on the sofa; she drank the entire remains of the wine in her glass.

'We had an affair, we lived together. It's over now, but I have trouble getting rid of the . . . leftover feelings.'

Gordon sat down a few feet away from her.

'He never mentioned that to me, Anna, nor has he ever discussed you in any previous sessions. When he came to me he was in a very bad way. His leg injury was excruciating and the chest wound hadn't healed well. He was in a really low state, mentally and physically. He was very concerned that he would have to retire and I could see that he had created more problems for himself by attempting to over-exercise, prove himself fit . . . This is, as you've got to realise, just as private and confidential as your telling me about the murder enquiry.'

She said nothing.

'I really like him, admire him – he's a very strong

individual and with a powerful magnetism, but he's also . . . I got him to cut down his smoking as that was killing him. And I want you to know, truthfully, that he did not discuss anything about you or any previous liaisons you had together, cross my heart.'

He turned, smiling as he crossed his heart with his right hand and reached for her with his left.

He kissed her hand. 'All right?'

She nodded and kept her hand in his.

'What did you mean by leftover feelings?'

Anna didn't want to get into it and tried to withdraw her hand but he held it firm.

'I wasn't just in love with him, I was enamoured of him. He is a brilliant detective, innovative and ruthless and obsessive, all those things rolled into one. He made me feel extraordinary, but he also made me feel incompetent and inexperienced, which I was. He was very difficult to be with when he was injured, a nightmare patient.'

Her eyes welled up with tears.

'I just couldn't deal with having so little of him. He had so many other commitments – women, children – and I knew I had to end it before he made me feel totally inadequate.'

'So these leftover feelings are what? Regrets?'

She bit her lip, trying to understand herself what she had said.

'I feel so much for him, but it's like I'm a schoolgirl whenever he's around. Part of me doesn't believe that I lived with him, that he ever appeared to care for me. I think he cared for me as much as he cares for anyone; he told me once that he could only give me so much, and I wanted and needed more. It's hard for me to be working

with him now. I can't ever say anything too personal
and a few of the team know that we were together, so I
think it makes him very cautious not to show me any
favours.'

Tears trickled down her cheeks. Having never had
anyone close with whom she could discuss her feelings
for Langton, it was incongruous that she was opening up
to an almost total stranger.

'I have such a lack of self-esteem and I think I try to
cover it up. What's the word to describe someone who is
always trying to please? Because that's what it feels like I
am doing, trying to please him because I keep thinking
that it was me who was at fault, my fault it never worked.
But then it was me who broke it off, not him . . .'

'That sounds to me like a lot of leftover feelings.'
Gordon touched her shoulder, patting it lightly.

'He doesn't respect me.'

'Do you respect him?'

'Of course I do. He's always had my respect; it's just
I hate feeling so inadequate around him.'

'Do you want him back?'

'No. No, I don't.'

Gordon smiled, said he felt the lady did protest too
much.

'It's as if I was fresh out of training school.' She stood
up and wiped her cheeks with the back of her hand. 'I'm
a bloody good detective. I've got results in one case after
another, and my old boss put me up for promotion. Then
in walks Langton, kicks him out, kicks half the team out,
brings in his old buddies and he even . . .' She drained
Gordon's glass. 'He even took me off a television crime
show because he felt I wasn't capable, as if I was a naughty
ten-year-old girl. He said it was because I might be

recognised but . . . I wasn't drunk; I wasn't in a cat fight . . .'

'Wow, you just lost me there.'

'I never knew Amanda, I'd never even seen one of her films, so I have had to immerse myself into who she was, and the more I find out, the more wretched I think she was . . . It's as if she was surrounded by people feeding off her, and all the time she was crying out for help.'

Unable to stop the tears, Anna broke into sobs. Gordon held her in his arms.

'I don't know what's the matter with me,' Anna wept. 'I've never done this before.'

He stroked her hair.

'You know what they say about magical hands; I've just released a lot of bad things you've stored up. Next time you come to see me, I'll give you manual lymphatic drainage. It stimulates your lymph system, boosting the body's immune system and I've been told that some of my patients float out of my clinic.'

She laughed and stood on tiptoe to kiss him. She loved his smell, partly because of his perfumed oils and aftershave like fresh lemons. She loved the feel of him; he was slender yet muscular without an ounce of fat on his six-foot frame.

'You know, I think with a few sessions I'll get that son of a bitch out of my system.'

He looked into her bright, brilliant blue eyes, and eased her away from him.

'When you have done that, call me. I'm not going to get into any healing process, Anna, I deal with that all day.'

She was afraid he was going to walk away from her and she grabbed his hand.

'Listen to me. I have never, I swear, *never* told anyone how I feel about James Langton, and it's over; you've made it even more over.'

'No, it's not.'

'Yes, it is.'

'You sure?' Gordon cupped her chin to kiss her. He then whispered, 'Do you have something to eat? I'm starving.'

She sprang away, heading to the kitchen, saying, 'How about a toasted bacon sandwich?' She suddenly remembered that was exactly what Langton had ordered her to make for him.

'I'm a vegetarian.'

She offered toasted cheese, lettuce and tomatoes, and a chilled bottle of Pinot Grigio. Gordon slowly took off his jacket for the third time.

Chapter Seventeen

Anna slept beside Gordon with no thought of Amanda Delany, no thought of Langton, no anxiety and, crooked in the security of his arms after they had made love, no bad dreams. All her pent-up emotions had been released.

Gordon was not so relaxed. He lay wide awake for hours, wondering if he had just been very foolish. When he looked down at Anna's sleeping face, so innocent, he wished that he had not been so easily drawn in. He'd had a number of these types of nights and had always extricated himself quickly, partly out of professional concern, but also partly to protect himself; his last love affair had left him badly hurt. What he would never admit to Anna was that he had, when Langton had talked about her, become enthralled. He remembered Langton's words.

'She's a total mystery to me, Gordon. She's childlike one moment and then the next she's a strong and forceful woman and I've never been able to deal with her strengths. She frightens the life out of me because I am constantly and inexplicably drawn to her. She rests inside my soul and inside my brain.'

Langton's opening up to him about his feelings for Anna had moved the young man deeply.

'I can't give her what she wants,' James observed morosely.

Gordon, as he massaged his back, asked what it was he felt she wanted.

After a long pause, Langton had said, 'Unconditional love. I don't have that much to give and I don't know of any man who would have it either. Reason being that everyone – I mean every man of my age – has old baggage clinging to him and she has none. That's what makes her so rare.'

Lying now with Anna in his arms, Gordon wasn't sure if he could deal with that rare quality of hers, maybe because she had been so honest with him about her feelings towards Langton. He doubted he could reciprocate. He wished, too, that he had been more cautious, certain that, if Langton was to discover he'd slept with Anna, he'd not only lose someone he now valued as a friend, but a client who had entrusted him with details of his private life.

'It's me. Open up.'

Anna hurtled back into the bedroom as Gordon stepped out of the shower. They had woken early the next morning and made love and would have gone on, but for the insistent ringing of the doorbell.

'It's Langton. For God's sake, get dressed.'

Gordon fumbled with his clothes. This was the last thing he wanted. It seemed they had only seconds before the doorbell rang again.

'I came to see how you were,' Langton said when Anna finally opened the door, and presented her with a modest bunch of flowers. Then he stared past her as Gordon appeared down the hall.

'Morning, James,' Gordon said coolly. 'Anna left this in my surgery last night,' he swung her collar brace, 'so I dropped it back this morning. You know my feelings about these things though.'

Langton nodded as Gordon handed Anna the brace, then held out his hand to shake hers.

'Thanks for the coffee. I'm sorry I got here so early.' He turned, smiling, to Langton. 'Off to play squash. I'll no doubt see you at the surgery later in the week.'

'You want a coffee?' Anna asked Langton when Gordon had gone.

'No, I just came by to see how you were. Recovered, it seems.'

'I was worried during the night about not wearing the brace, as the hospital had said I should keep it on. But then I didn't have my car and I couldn't face using public transport to go all the way back to Dr Berry's surgery, so I gave him a call.'

Langton nodded and walked past her into the lounge. She had a moment of panic wondering if she'd left the wine glasses out. Then she remembered they'd opened another bottle in the kitchen and taken the glasses with them. She glanced into the kitchen and, seeing the debris of their evening snack left on the breakfast counter, she closed the door.

'You've been working,' he said, staring at her printed cards and then looking to the sofa with all her files stacked across it.

'Yes, well, I couldn't sleep.'

He cocked his head to one side. 'So how did you find young Gordon?'

'You gave me the address.'

'I know that. I meant, did he make you feel he'd done some good?'

'Oh yes, fantastic, which is why I foolishly skipped off without the brace. I felt light-headed.'

Langton checked his watch. 'You going to come into the station today?'

'I was planning to, but wasn't sure.'

'You look all right to me.' He stared at her and she flushed. 'I always liked it when you'd just woken up – no make-up, cheeks flushed. Not running a temperature, are you?'

She shook her head.

'We've got a result coming in. The poor bastards who've been glued to the TV watching hours of CCTV footage are positive about some vehicle, and at long last we've retrieved the security footage from the mews. Apparently it's not much good though, as the cameras were directed towards the front of the house rather than the mews yard.'

'I'll get dressed and come in.'

He nodded and swung the door back and forth with the toe of his foot.

'Want me to wait?'

'No, no, I'll take a shower and get a taxi in.'

When Langton left, shutting the door behind him, Anna remained standing, unable to move. Eventually she returned to her bedroom and the unmade bed and flopped down, hugging a pillow close to her. She had lied to Langton and now she knew just how good a liar Gordon was; she had no idea whether Langton suspected they had spent the night together. She punched the pillow angrily. Even if he did, she thought, so what?

He had nothing to do with her private life, yet he still came round first thing in the morning as if he had a right. This was the second time he had just appeared on her doorstep, albeit this time with a bunch of cheap flowers. She would have to talk to him.

Holding her head under the jets of warm water in the shower, Anna remembered him saying how much he had liked the way she looked first thing in the morning. By the time she had dressed and dried her hair, she realised that Langton was not prepared to let her go. His cool attitude towards her belied the fact that he still cared, more perhaps than he wanted to admit. Instead of anger, Anna found this gave her more confidence. She felt sure that she could handle it and use it to her benefit. She felt even more buoyant when, collecting her mail, she came across a letter approving her application for promotion. The date for her first interview was in two weeks' time.

Andrea Lesser and Andrew Smith–Barker had been charged and released on bail to await trial for fraud. Their passports had been relinquished and warnings given that neither should attempt to leave the country. There was still a possibility that they might have hired someone to kill Amanda. Both suspects' mobile phone and landline call lists were being checked to see if they threw up anything suspicious.

Arriving back at the station, Anna joined the gathering in the incident room and listened as Barolli gave details of the new CCTV developments. Officers had been sifting through hours of black and white footage taken from the streets in and around the mews. They also had the security film from the mews house.

'We've not got anything too exciting, but we can con-
firm that on the night before her murder the unit driver
Tony James did, as he stated, drop Amanda Delany home.
She was subsequently collected the following afternoon.
We also have footage of a second driver driving her home
on the night of her murder . . .'

Barolli gave a signal for the large TV to be turned on.

'It's very grainy and we can't make out the numberplate but here, you can see, is a black Mercedes dropping
her off at four-fifteen a.m. There you can see Amanda
walking from the car.'

Everyone leaned forward, unable to see the top half of
Amanda's torso, merely her legs and a section of her skirt.
They also saw the driver – again, only his legs were in
view – walk round from his side of the Mercedes and wait
slightly behind her as she entered the house and closed
the door. The same driver returned to the Mercedes. The
car made a three-point turn in the mews yard, before the
tail-lights disappeared.

'OK, here he comes again. We've got better shots as
it's now afternoon.'

'Do we know which driver this is?' Anna asked.

'Yes, this is Harry James,' Barolli snapped at her,
irritated. 'We have his written statement. Now we see
him returning at five-twenty p.m. to collect Miss Delany.'

They watched the driver walk to the front door, wait,
then crouch down to look through the letterbox. This
was the only time they got a reasonable full shot, but his
face was unclear as it was turned away from the security
camera. He then returned to the car and got inside. After
fifteen minutes, he started up the car and did the same
three-point turn as the Mercedes had done the night
before, and drove out of the mews.

'OK, we got a numberplate. It coincides with the vehicle driven by Mr Harry James.'

Next they watched the same car returning, another vehicle hidden behind it, the taxi used by Andrea Lesser. They saw her hurrying to the front door; again they had no full shot, just her legs in high-heeled shoes. They saw her entering the house. Once the body had been discovered, police cars and various other vehicles all listed by their licence plates, pulled into the mews.

Eventually Barolli turned the film off. As the tapes of CCTV footage from the surrounding streets were set up, Anna asked how far back they had been working. 'We can't go back any further than a week before the murder as the tapes had been reused,' Barolli said. 'Now watch closely. There are four vehicles which we've been unable to trace, partly due to their numberplates being obscured. First up is a black Lexus. We've seen this vehicle on two occasions.'

Anna raised her hand: she recalled that Scott Myers drove a black Lexus. 'We're aware of that, Anna,' was Barolli's terse response.

Then there were two shots of a black Mercedes with tinted windows, similar to the ones used by the unit drivers. Lastly, a Rolls-Royce was seen driving into the road away from the mews, its licence plate obscured by parked traffic.

Anna couldn't help wondering out loud if the Rolls-Royce could be the same one she had seen being parked outside Rupert Mitchell's house in Kingston. She asked if any of the fingerprints from Amanda's house being matched at forensic had been linked to Rupert Mitchell, Scott Myers and lastly Colin O'Dell.

There had been a match with Colin O'Dell, Barolli

confirmed, also Scott Myers . . . but none with Rupert Mitchell. O'Dell and Myers, who had denied ever going to Amanda's mews, would be brought in and re-questioned.

Barolli looked around the room.

'We still haven't traced Amanda's complete set of keys. We know that four front-door keys were cut and two are missing. Did Amanda give her set to someone, and was that someone inside her mews on the night she returned home?'

That still left one key missing.

When Mike Lewis asked if anyone had anything new to add to the case, Anna debated with herself. She was loath to discuss her theories in front of the entire team because they were still just theories, without any strong evidence that linked to the murder.

'I wouldn't mind just running a few things by you later,' she murmured.

'Fine. I want to run a few things by you too, so in my office, say, in ten minutes?'

Joan had, as Anna had requested, run all three James brothers through the database. Harry James had no police record, nor had the middle brother Tony, but the youngest brother Lester had had a number of small-time convictions. None of them were serious: when he was sixteen he had been on probation for handling stolen property, and he had been arrested twice for drunken assault, but served only community service. His last brush-in with the law had been more serious but took place over seven years ago. Lester had been arrested for attacking a man in a bar, was given a six-month suspended sentence and fined two thousand pounds. The

Judge had warned him that if he was ever brought before a court again, he would serve a lengthy prison sentence.

Joan had worked hard, tracking as much as possible on young Lester James. Up on the screen she had a photograph of him winning a karate championship at Crystal Palace; he was a 7th Dan Shotokan expert and she had found a display of his ability using karate weapons.

'Shit, was this shown to any of the team?' Anna asked.

'Not yet. I've only just finished the Google job I've done on him. Do you want me to print out the material?'

'Yes, please. I want a full suspect intelligence file prepared on him. What has he got down as a profession?'

'Chauffeur and bodyguard, like his brothers.'

'You get anything of interest from the fanmail?'

'I've not had time to go through it all,' Joan admitted, 'just one bag so far, and it all seems legit. Young girls wanting Amanda's photograph and so on, but I'll keep checking.'

Armed with paperwork from Joan and a photograph of Lester showing him in a white karate Gi and with a crewcut hairstyle, Anna headed for Mike's office. Lester James was handsome in a rough way, six feet two, with the same piercing blue eyes as his brothers. He was twenty-seven, unmarried, and lived in Esher.

Anna had only just sat down in Mike's office when Langton walked in.

'Just having a word with Anna,' Mike said rather unnecessarily.

'Mind if I sit in?'

'No.'

Langton pulled up a chair to sit a few feet from Anna in front of Mike's desk. She opened her file.

'I wanted to run some stuff by Mike that I've been checking out. Some of it I think could be relevant, but some I'm not sure about.'

'We'll be the ones to decide,' Langton said, crossing his legs. He seemed irritable.

'Right.'

Anna described her meeting with Mrs Delany and her impression that, as parents, she and her husband appeared to be lacking in any genuine emotion. Then she described how she had worked out, from talking to the two girls Jeannie Bale and Felicity Turner, the date and timeline of the victim's pregnancy.

'I honestly can't see how an abortion four or five years ago has any connection to the murder,' Langton interjected.

Anna didn't look up from her file.

'Amanda took two return flights to France, three months apart. On the second visit she was pregnant. When she returned to London, she had an abortion that resulted in her very nearly losing her life. As it was, she was given a hysterectomy, which for a girl her age had to be physically and emotionally very stressful.'

Mike breathed heavily through his nose, as if to telegraph his impatience. Langton pinched at the crease in his trousers.

'Go on. I'm assuming there's a reason for this back-tracking.'

Anna continued. She had no proof, but she felt there was a strong possibility that their victim could have been molested by a family member. She believed it could have begun when Amanda was very young, which would be one of the reasons why she was so attached to the toy rabbit. She may have gone to her parents for money and they refused her, perhaps even refusing to believe she was pregnant, or in total denial that it could have been by someone known to them.

'For chrissakes, Anna, what has this to do with her murder?' Langton leaned forward, tapping the desk.

'I'm just getting to it,' she snapped back. 'Her parents, or her father alone, did come to London and did put his daughter into the Drury Clinic. Her mother stayed in France. Again, to my mind, that is suspicious, heartless.

'If Amanda was sexually abused by a family member,' she went on, 'maybe even her father, and her parents heard that she was writing her memoirs, it would be a very strong motive to try and stop publication.'

Langton stood up and paced the room, rubbing at his knee. 'I don't buy it. They may not have liked it, but murder their own daughter? No.'

Someone close to Amanda had to have arranged the abortion, Anna insisted. Someone she trusted. She had not told her flatmates about the operation; all they knew was that she was collected afterwards by a 'driver' and then brought back home. Later that night, they had had to call an ambulance as Amanda was bleeding all over the place. They also phoned her parents.

'Missing from her mews house, we believe, are a set of keys, her toy rabbit and part of a gold crucifix chain and, most important of all, as it could be crucial evidence, her five-year diary.'

Langton stood up and leaned against the wall, his eyes half-closed. Mike had now straightened in his desk chair, no longer swivelling as if he was bored.

Anna changed tack. She talked about the post mortem, the description of the knife wounds, the fact that the hilt of the knife had left an imprint on Amanda's body. She took out a sheet of black and white photographs of various karate knives, all different shapes and sizes, and laid it on Mike's desk. She showed them a combat knife, a typical weapon used by bodyguards. The knife wounds had been deep and methodical, inflicted by someone with great strength stabbing in a downward motion, angry rather than frenzied, taking care not to leave a mark on her face.

Langton sat down again and rested his chin on his hand, listening.

'Right now, I do not have a shred of evidence,' Anna admitted. 'All I do know is that there was a book offer for over a million pounds, there was a diary Amanda kept up to date and there was her cuddly toy. These items were removed by someone who knew a lot about Amanda, but who also cared about her, was perhaps in love with her, and she had either humiliated or abused them and this was a revenge murder.'

Langton gave her a sidelong glance, as she showed them the picture of Lester James.

'Both this man's brothers worked as unit drivers on *Gaslight*, but sometimes, though I have no concrete evidence that this occurred, when they were busy they would bring another driver on board to cover for them. This is when both Harry and Tony used their own brother Lester, who had driven Amanda, not only on her first movie, but on two subsequent films. This man knew her, this man would have access to her private life.'

'Anyone interviewed him?' Langton asked.

'It's the first I've bloody heard about him,' Mike said angrily.

'We have to move very carefully,' Langton observed. 'If Lester James is the killer, he must believe he has got

340

away with it. He could be a very dangerous man and as yet, we do not have a single piece of evidence against him.' He looked at Anna. 'Correct?'

'Yes, sir. We need to try and discover if he was in the mews house; he'll have his fingerprints on record. We have to prove that he was in the house and he killed her.'

Mike was very quiet, hating that Anna had divulged all this in front of his boss. Langton gave nothing away, merely suggesting that Anna return to her office and type up her report. As she reached the door, he asked if there was anything else she might have left out. There was a note of sarcasm in his voice.

'There is one thing,' she said. 'The pink diary was last seen at her flat by the publisher of Golden Arrow, whose name is Josh Lyons. Days ago, I suggested that we get a warrant issued to search the flat, just in case Amanda left it hidden there.'

Anna walked out, closing the door quietly behind her. As she made her way along the corridor, she couldn't help smiling. She could so easily have said something like, 'Screw you, Mike, you refused to get me that search warrant,' but she knew Langton would be onto it fast.

Typing up her report was tedious and time-consuming work. When she got as far as the conversation between Felicity and Jeannie, something jolted inside Anna's brain. In the incident room she searched the board for details of Dan Hutchins's death, written up because of his connection to Amanda, and looked at the photographs of the boy's body. Felicity had said they had found him lying on the floor, a syringe beside him. The photos of the dead boy were as she described, his face partly turned away as he had vomited over himself, his sleeve rolled up

341

and the rubber tie used to pump up his veins still attached to his arm. Anna tried to remember exactly what the girls had said. Dan had been very distressed at Amanda's death, but they didn't know where he had got the money to buy the amount of heroin he needed to satisfy his addiction.

Anna read through the post-mortem report; the boy had taken a massive overdose, choking on his own vomit, lying on the floor of his bedroom.

Anna tapped on Mike's office door and he shouted for her to come in. Both he and Langton looked as if they had been in the middle of a heated exchange.

'Sorry to interrupt, there's something else. I can't be certain, but something doesn't add up . . .'

She laid down the photographs of Dan Hutchins's body. The autopsy report gave cause of death as an accidental heroin overdose with no other suspicious circumstances, yet the deceased also had a very high alcohol content. Dan was a drug addict and had been on a methadone programme for more than six months. Before that, he had been on heroin, thus highly experienced in the use of hypodermic needles. This was confirmed by the report; a number of injection sites had been found on the body.

'What is your point, Anna?' Langton asked.

'If you look at the way the rubber tubing is knotted around his right upper arm, it indicates that he used his left hand to wrap it round and tighten it. Often addicts put one end in their mouths to adjust the band tighter, but the longer end is facing towards the camera, not as it should be towards the dead boy. It could be that someone helped him to inject or forced the needle into his arm.'

Langton and Mike Lewis remained silent as they passed the photographs back and forth, then put them onto the desk.

As Anna continued, Langton stared at her, a strange expression on his face.

'Both girls said that Dan had no money. They also said he was very distressed by Amanda's death. Where did he get the cash to pay for the heroin? Also, where did he get the heroin *from*? All they knew was that he left a party early and by the time they returned home two hours later, he was dead.'

Again there was silence. Anna shifted her weight from one foot to the other. 'Why did he inject himself on the floor – why not in his bed?' she persisted. 'I mean, if you were a junkie and had scored heroin, why lie on the floor?'

Both his trainers had been removed and he had only one sock on.

'As an experienced addict, he may have been preparing to inject himself between his toes, but wouldn't he still have been on his bed?'

Mike and Langton checked the photographs again and then looked at her, as if willing her to draw some conclusion.

'Dan Hutchins adored Amanda Delany – they had been students together. She trusted him. All I'm suggesting is that he possibly knew something, something that warranted his death. We are missing a set of keys. You, sir, brought up the possibility of her owning a larger set than the single key found at her mews. Maybe whoever had them, used them to enter Dan's flat and inject the boy with enough heroin to kill him.'

'Christ, Anna, this is all supposition.'

'I know, sir, but if Dan was killed to shut him up, what *did* he know? This also makes me deeply concerned about the two girls still living there.'

'You think they know something?'

'Possibly.'

'Like what?'

'I don't know,' Anna said.

'Terrific,' Mike muttered.

Anna excused herself and returned to her office to continue finishing her report. She had no idea if they believed her theory about Dan Hutchins's death. She didn't hear Langton give Mike the order to pick up Lester James for questioning and to get a search warrant for the girls' flat.

Anna completed her reports and submitted them to the office manager; the details would be chalked up on the incident room board. Barbara indicated that she wanted to have a word.

'This Lester James. We have an address, but he's not—'

Anna was furious. She felt that they were moving too fast and without sufficient evidence. She walked away before Barbara could finish and went to confront Mike Lewis. In no uncertain terms she said that she felt they were jumping the gun.

'Tell that to Langton – he's the one who wants Lester James brought in. I agree with you, but right now James is the prime suspect.'

'But you only have my suppositions. We don't have enough to make an arrest!'

'We're just bringing him in for questioning.'

'Why not put him under surveillance instead, while we do some more digging around?'

'Too late, the wheels are already in motion. I repeat, this is Langton putting on the pressure, not me. Added to that, you said yourself that you were concerned for the safety of those two girls. We can't take the risk if he is our killer, so we need to bring him in for questioning.'

'Who's bringing him in?'

'Paul Barolli and two from the team.'

'Fine. Well, at least get me in on the interview. I hope they keep a low profile because we don't have enough to hold him.'

'I am aware of that,' snapped Mike.

'Are they going in with a search warrant?'

'Yes.'

'Make sure they strip down his car.'

Anna walked out, seething, and returned to her office. She was still angry when Barbara came in with an update. Lester James was not at home and according to the woman who lived in the flat above his, he had not been there for a few weeks.

'Check with his brother, Harry James. See if Lester is working on a movie.'

'Right.'

Barbara closed the door and Anna sat, drumming her fingers on her desk. She sighed, then picked up her coat, making sure this time that the team were aware of where she was going and what she was doing.

Mrs Delany gave a resigned sigh as Anna apologised for not making an appointment; she needed only a few moments to ask her some questions. Their suitcases were packed and Mr Delany was due to return shortly. Mrs Delany was very tense.

'I don't know what else I can tell you. All I want to do

is to go home to France and try and pick up my life. This has been a dreadful time.'

'I'm sure it must be, to lose your daughter in such tragic circumstances. It can't have been easy to deal with.'

'No, it wasn't.'

'But you've had family troubles before this, haven't you?'

Mrs Delany fingered the pearl necklace she was wearing.

'I'm not sure I understand you. We have had nothing that I would describe as family troubles, quite the contrary.'

'Your daughter's pregnancy must have been very shocking.'

'Any mother would be distressed by her only daughter's misfortune, and believe you me, Amanda had not been an easy child.'

'Did you ever discover why that was?'

Mrs Delany tugged at the necklace, but made no reply.

'Did Amanda ever suggest to you that she was being abused? By that, I mean sexually abused – and quite possibly from an early age?'

Mrs Delany stood up, her face set in anger.

'I don't know how you dare make such a dreadful accusation. I categorically deny any such thing ever occurred in my family, and I am appalled that you, knowing I am still in mourning for my daughter, want to further my anguish! If you have got this from someone, then I want to know exactly who is spreading such a rumour.'

'It comes from someone Amanda knew for many years.'

'They are lying.'

'Did she ever tell you who the father of her child was?'

'No, she did not. All she wanted was money and in the past we had been more than generous. She didn't get a scholarship to RADA, so my husband had to pay for the tuition fees for her course, pay for her accommodation, give her an allowance. Amanda had run up considerable debts and we had to deal with them. We didn't believe her when she told us she was pregnant. We felt it was just another trick to get more money out of us.'

'But it wasn't, was it?'

'We know that now, of course. As soon as we knew how ill she was, due to the abortion, my husband came straight to London. He paid for the hospital, paid for her to go to the Drury Clinic, and in the end he decided that enough was enough.'

'By this time she was earning a lot of money herself as an actress,' Anna remarked.

'She never told us what she was earning. In fact, after the wretched business of the abortion, we barely saw her again.'

'How did that make you feel?'

'Feel? I don't understand?'

'Well, Amanda was very successful, a star.'

Mrs Delany gripped hold of her chair.

'She was a constant source of embarrassment. The media coverage of her sexual exploits made our life a misery. You know that. Why she did what she did, I will never understand. She was given everything a young girl could want, and to flaunt herself, drunk, and wearing these dreadful clothes . . .'

Anna turned. Mr Delany had entered the suite. He closed the door behind him with the heel of his shoe.

'Thank God you're here,' Mrs Delany gasped.

'I know why *I* am here, but I'd like to know why *you* are.' He stared coldly at Anna.

'She is asking about Amanda – someone has told her that she was sexually abused as a child. I just can't believe we are being subjected to this.'

'Nor can I.' Mr Delany removed his coat, folding it over the back of a chair. 'I'd like the name of this person so I can sue them. As if we haven't had enough heart-break. This is an invasion of our privacy and I would like you to leave.'

Anna stood up. He was a daunting man; his face was impassive, but his eyes were cold and bore into her. She noticed that his fists were clenched, the knuckles white as he fought to control himself.

'I'm sorry, but in our investigation we need to cover every possible avenue.'

'How could it have any bearing on your investigation? The fact is that it is a total lie.'

'It could also be a motive, sir.'

'Motive?' he snarled.

'Yes. You see, we know that Amanda was about to sign a publishing deal to write her memoirs.'

'She told us that,' Mrs Delany said. Her husband turned on her, gesturing with his hand for her to be silent.

'It was more than likely yet another of her lies. We dismissed it as nonsense. Who could write their memoirs at twenty-four? It's ridiculous!'

'It wasn't a lie, sir. I have met with the publisher.'

He shrugged.

'You see, if Amanda had been subjected to sexual

abuse as a child, she would probably have intended writing about it.'

'She wasn't.'

'But you must understand why I have to ask these questions. As I said, it is a possible motive.'

'What do you mean?' He stepped closer to Anna.

'I think you understand, sir. You and your wife would have featured very prominently in your daughter's—'

'Get out.' Delany gripped Anna by her arm and drew her towards the door. 'I have heard enough. I will make a complaint to your superiors so *out* – get the hell out of this suite!'

Anna jerked her arm free. She was almost knocked off her feet as he opened the door and pushed her out, slamming it behind her.

Anna returned to the patrol car, shaken but certain of a few more facts. In reality she doubted that Mr Delany had any part in the murder of his daughter, nor had his wife. She was sure, however, that there had been some kind of abuse inside the family, but it would be almost impossible to prove. Unless they found the diary and the diary contained any details of what Amanda had suffered.

Mrs Delany was retouching her make-up in the bathroom, her hands shaking as she heard her husband ordering a taxi to take them to St Pancras. They had decided to stay at The Grand in Paris before returning to their villa in the South of France.

She physically jumped when he opened the bathroom door.

'We've got about half an hour. Do you want coffee and sandwiches sent up?'

'No, nothing, thank you.' She stared at him from the mirror as he came towards her, gently rubbing her shoulders.

'Everything will be all right as soon as we get home.'

She nodded, her eyes brimming with tears. 'She loved that little rabbit, didn't she?'

He nodded. 'Why bring that up?'

'It's missing – they think the killer took it. I remember her cuddling it. She'd have been no more than six, never would go to sleep without it.'

'I know.'

Slowly she turned to face him, but then couldn't meet his eyes. He reached out and gripped her face in his hands.

'He's dead now, Carmen. We have to get on with our lives – we must put it all behind us.'

'It's just hard for me sometimes,' she whispered.

'I know, but you can't blame yourself.'

'Yes, I can,' she breathed.

He sighed, and turned to leave.

'We should have protected her,' his wife cried out. 'I should have, but I didn't honestly believe he would . . . How many times when we went on holiday did we leave her with him, how many times . . .?' She broke down in tears.

'Shush,' he said, walking out.

Mrs Delany looked back to the mirror. She had not come to London when Amanda was almost dying because she was attending her father's funeral. They had lived close by him for most of their married life. Christian de Wolf was a very wealthy, handsome widower, a wine importer with a string of polo ponies, and she, his only child, had been molested by him from an early age. When

she had admitted it to her husband, he had used a riding
crop on his father-in-law, until the latter begged forgive-
ness. He had never touched his daughter again, and
moved into a small lodge attached to the villa, having
arranged for a massive annual allowance to be settled on
his daughter.

Mrs Delany suspected her father was becoming overly
fond of his young granddaughter, but when she confronted him, he denied it and threatened to halt the
allowance they lived on and force them out of the villa.
She couldn't stop the tears now. Had her father made
Amanda terrified to tell anyone, just as he had done with
his own daughter? Terrified that she would be taken
away and given up for adoption? Was that why she had
kept the secret for so long?

Mr Delany couldn't go to her even when he heard her
crying in the hotel room. He couldn't face any more
problems, any more anguish. During one of her final
trips home, when Amanda had claimed that her grandfather had raped her, he refused to believe her, as did his
wife. When she returned to London, he confronted the
man he detested; de Wolf had sworn on his knees that
he had never touched their precious child. Two weeks
later he died from a heart-attack, leaving the rest of his
fortune to his only daughter. Mr Delany sat staring at
the matching Gucci suitcases stacked up by the door. He
had failed to protect Amanda; he knew it, but until now
had denied it.

He recalled taking the toy to her bedroom. She looked
like a princess, in her bedroom with its pink carpet and
pink drapes. He had put the rabbit in her arms and whispered that he loved her and would never let any harm

come to her. She had reached up to put her arms around his neck, asking if he would promise, and he had kissed her.

'I promise, Princess. This little rabbit will always look after you.'

'I'll call him Promise,' she had said.

He knew he had broken that promise, he had broken it for money, and he was ashamed. He had lived in total denial, watched helplessly as his Princess became a little monster, hellbent with her string of sexual conquests on making them ashamed of her.

Mrs Delany had regained her composure as she joined her husband, slipping her mink-lined cashmere coat around her shoulders.

'Did you have any success?' she asked him.

'No. There was no one in and I didn't want to stay around in case I was seen.'

'We have probably been over-reacting. Without Amanda, I'd say they couldn't publish anything anyway.'

'I'm sure you're right.'

'How much would you have been prepared to pay for it?'

Delany shrugged, knowing he would have paid a good price to get his hands on his daughter's diary. He looked at his elegant, beautiful wife, with her make-up and immaculate hair, and he reached for her hand.

'It's over, darling.'

'Not yet. Not until they find who killed her.'

He doubted that they ever would; it had already been too long. She threaded her fingers through his, her diamond rings glinting, her nails perfectly manicured. She had soft hands, delicate. She was a delicate creature and one he had protected, but he should have taken her away before she confronted her father. For him, having been overprotective of his beloved wife, his daughter had paid the price.

'Shall I call for the porter?' she asked.

'Yes, we should be on our way.'

'You have the passports and tickets?'

He patted his pocket and nodded. Soon they would be able to create yet another protective shell to hide the guilt that was inside them both. For his part, he reasoned that he would not have been able to provide for his wife on his own in the manner to which she was accustomed. She, for her part, had lived in luxury like a caged exotic bird, never making any decisions for herself and never being a good mother. She was too damaged; the threat her own father had whispered to her, that he could take everything from her and leave her with nothing, was a persistent nightmare. There had been a time when she had often woken up screaming, just like her daughter. But while she had been protected by her doting husband, Amanda had had only the warmth of a cuddly toy rabbit.

Chapter Eighteen

Lester James had been working on a TV series in Manchester when his brother Harry called to say that the police were sniffing around in connection with the Amanda Delany case. He drove straight to Manchester airport and boarded a flight to Amsterdam, and although he had told his brother that he was not in any kind of trouble, his disappearing act was highly suspicious. Tony was very edgy when he met up with Harry, asking if there could be any link between their youngest brother and the murder.

'No way, but you know, if he has any more trouble he'll get nicked and it'll be prison for him. Is he still dealing shit?'

'He swore he wasn't, but he gave me a wrap to pass over to that Colin O'Dell at the fucking funeral. He told me he wasn't doin' that any more – we've had enough problems with him in the past. So what do we do, apart from keeping him at arm's length for a while?'

Harry had always been a father figure to both his brothers; now he said he would see to it that Lester would be looked after. He left Tony sitting in a small café. He didn't believe his kid brother would have anything to do with the murder, but at the same time, he knew that Lester had been scoring and dealing drugs. Even when they had warned him to cut it out, he still beefed up his legitimate salary, mostly dealing in small amounts to the cast and crew of the films he was working on. It was those dealings that made both brothers wary of having the police question Lester.

Armed with a search warrant, Barolli and his team brought in two Scene of Crime Officers to search Lester James's flat in Esher. They found an array of sharp suits and shoes and multi-coloured shirts, and shaving equipment and bottles of cheap aftershave lined up in the bathroom cabinet. In the small box room were his karate medals and cups, and his Gi in pristine condition. The single bed was covered in a dark green candlewick bedspread; the blinds on the window were drawn. Barolli stared around the living room with its hideous couch and two matching easy chairs. There was a large plasma screen in the corner and numerous karate championship videos and DVDs piled next to it. Stacked on a bookshelf were boxes of vitamins and karate magazines. Caught between two pages was a torn piece of paper listing plane times to Amsterdam. In the fridge in the kitchen were butter and eggs, all well past their sell-by date, and open cartons of rice and noodles, along with four cans of Red Bull.

Barolli instructed the team to remove some of the DVDs and a couple of videos, but there was nothing else of interest, no passport, no money, nothing incriminating. That was, until they found a large polished wooden box containing a collection of karate knives.

The officers outside Jeannie and Felicity's flat also found no one at home. They knocked, rang the bell and, climbing into the back yard area, shone torches through the windows, front and back. After fifteen minutes they called the search off when Mike Lewis instructed them to put a surveillance team in place outside.

It was late afternoon when both teams returned to the station. Anna was only just back herself. 'We really need more evidence on Lester James,' she said to Barolli.

'Terrific. Right now the bastard could be anywhere.' He was eager to get the box of knives for forensic testing. 'Maybe someone tipped him off. If he's done a disappearing act, something or someone had to have given him a nudge that we were interested in him.'

Lester James was now listed as prime suspect and both his brothers had agreed to come in for questioning. Also earmarked for interview were Scott Myers and Colin O'Dell. As both were filming during the day, they were to be questioned on video early the following evening.

Left alone, Anna felt a hot flush coming on. She had reprimanded Barolli about a tip-off to Lester James, but she now had a pretty good idea where it had come from: Bruce Mason. She waited to calm down before she went back into the incident room to talk to Barolli.

'This Lester James,' she began, 'on his previous he'd had some connection to drug dealing. If he was a serious player then maybe he scored from Amsterdam, which would be why he's skipped over there. Maybe he knows people who'd give him a place to stay. The Amsterdam drug squad might have a contact. You found a note about plane times, right?'

'Forever on the ball, aren't we?'

'Someone has to be,' she said sarcastically. In her

handbag was Bruce Mason's card; back in her office she tapped it against her teeth. Her own car wouldn't be ready for collection for a couple more days. If she asked to use him as a driver, she'd be able to question him without him giving the James brothers a heads-up. She decided to wait, reckoning she'd be at the station for a very long time that evening.

Harry James, being interviewed by Anna and Barolli, complained that he had already given a statement: he and Tony were indeed the two drivers from the unit who handled Amanda's collection and pickups on *Gaslight*. He was her named driver but, on the night before her murder, his brother Tony had taken over. Harry denied that Lester was ever used during the days running up to the murder; he and his brother would be willing to co-operate and show the police the records.

'What was your brother Lester's relationship with Amanda Delany?' Barolli asked.

'Relationship?' Harry queried. 'He was just a unit driver, like us. There wasn't no relationship bar passenger and driver — it's more than our job's worth to ever get involved with clients. We pick them up and take them home, then do it all over again the next day.'

'Did Lester ever socialise with Miss Delany when she wasn't working?'

'Not that I know of. He's got a big mouth and if he did, he wouldn't have kept it quiet, so no way.'

'But didn't Amanda use him on a private basis?'

'You got me there. I wouldn't know. She did use a few of us guys, but whether one of them was Lester, I couldn't tell you.'

'Where is he?' Barolli wanted to know.

'Manchester. He's doing a TV stint. It isn't good money, but you have to take what you can get.'

'When was the last time you saw him?'

'Be more than a week ago. Came back for her funeral, we all showed our respects.'

'When did you last speak to him?'

'I just told you. At the funeral. I've not talked to him since.' Harry leaned across the table. 'What's this about? I mean, I've come here and I'm answering everything you want, but I dunno why, to be honest.'

'Helping enquiries, Mr James,' Barolli replied. 'We are still investigating the murder of Amanda Delany and we have to backtrack on some dates to give us a clearer overall picture.'

'Bloody 'ell, you're taking your time, but I dunno how I can help you. I've already given a statement and I can't add nothing more to it.'

It was Anna's turn.

'Your brother Lester's had a few run-ins with the police, hasn't he?'

'He's just a kid.'

'Assault twice. He was lucky not to get locked up.'

'I agree, but we got a job lined up for him and the Judge was a right straight bloke. He knew what problems Lester had.'

'Like what?'

'His fists. He's a karate champion. He goes out with his mates and there's always some Charlie wantin' to prove hisself.'

'When do you expect to see your brother again?'

'Like I said, he's in Manchester and I dunno when his stint up there is finished. Why are you so interested in Lester?'

'Just a formality. Does he own his Mercedes?'

'Yeah – well, me and Tony chipped in for it. It's secondhand but you got to have a good-looking motor for driving the actors around and he didn't have no money. He's been paying us off on a monthly basis. He's a good kid.'

'Did your brother deal in drugs?'

'What?'

Barolli glanced at Anna and then he took over.

'Let's just stop the bullshit, shall we, Harry? We know he supplemented his earnings—'

'Not with fucking drugs, pal, no way. Lester is an athlete, know what I mean? He would never touch that crap. He was a champion karate Seventh Dan and you don't get to be that high up without making your body a bloody temple. He went over to Japan to get his belt and he worked from when he was no more than twelve at major dojos. He gave years to accomplish his karate. Now if he was boxin' he'd be making money, but with karate it's more like a fucking charity.'

Harry seemed upset. Both Barolli and Anna remained deliberately silent, to see what more he'd come up with.

'When he was made champion, crowds at Crystal Palace were cheering him. He's got cups and awards filling his cupboards. We was there, me and Tony, and afterwards he says to me that he's British Champion – and you know what he got beside this cup? His tube fare. His fucking *tube fare*!'

Harry was sweating and he loosened his tie. 'Bloody disgrace,' he went on, choked. 'Anyways, that's when we said to him he was gonna have to earn a livin', right, so we got him his Merc and he came on board with us as a unit driver. He's worked hard to come up to scratch.

He knows the streets like the back of his hand now, he's a good kid and I'm telling you he done nothin' wrong.'

'Maybe he didn't use drugs himself, but did he score for other people?'

'No, course not. What – and lose his livelihood? There's no way he ever got into dealing.'

'But he was arrested and accused of selling drugs,' Barolli persisted.

'That case was dismissed, he was never charged. It was some bloke what left them in his car.'

'So you say he was out of work, broke, and you buy him a Mercedes. So what about you? Supplement your earnings, do you?'

'No, I fucking don't, and I resent you even thinking I would be that dumb. I value my job and it comes with a lot of aggravation sometimes and relies a lot on word of mouth, know what I mean?'

'Did your brother Lester carry a weapon?'

'You mean a shooter? He wouldn't need to carry a weapon, he had his fists.'

'What about a knife?' Barolli asked.

'No, no . . .'

'But didn't he give exhibitions using combat swords and knives?'

'He might have done, but I never saw him with any kind of a weapon.'

'But he did have a collection of martial arts weapons.'

'Did he?'

Barolli opened his notebook, flicking through the pages.

'In his flat we discovered a Cord-Grip Thrower Triple Set, Wing Chun Butterfly Knives, Kenpo Karate Knives and a Phoenix Knife.'

Harry sat back in his chair. He was sweating profusely and undid the top button of his shirt.

'I dunno nothing about them.'

Barolli closed his notebook and quietly explained how serious the findings were. Amanda Delany had been stabbed many times with what the pathologist and forensic teams described as possibly a karate knife. He related how the wounds were inflicted by a very strong person who thrust the murder weapon in up to the hilt. He then passed over a photograph of the injuries.

'Jesus God.' Harry took a deep breath. 'I come here in good faith, on my life. I am telling you my brother wouldn't have done that, not Lester, not to her.'

'Why are you so certain?'

The man squirmed in his chair.

'He thought a lot of her, admired her. This is making me feel ill. I reckon if you want to question me more, I should get a solicitor. I don't want to get Lester in trouble and I dunno if I'm saying stuff that could go against him.'

Mike Lewis and Barbara were getting the same responses from Tony. He categorically denied that his brother would have ever jeopardised his job by dealing drugs to supplement his income. Like Harry, Tony went into a lengthy description of his brother's prowess at karate. He described him as a gentle giant, a quiet and dedicated young man who had found himself broke and with no future in the world of karate. He and Harry had bought him his car and he had worked hard at becoming a unit driver, to get accepted by the company.

Tony also denied that there had been any kind of

relationship between Lester and Amanda, only a professional one.

'Listen to me. I could tell you stories that'd make your hair stand on end. Really famous movie stars, you'd not believe what they get up to, an' we gotta turn a blind eye. We become invisible to them. You've gotta learn to keep your mouth shut and not gossip about it. I've been offered big money by the paparazzi to give them the lowdown on some of my clients, but you can't. Do it once and word spreads, and the next minute you're unemployable. Hear no evil, speak no evil and bloody keep your eyes shut while you're at it . . .'

'On *Gaslight*, did you have any experiences of what you've just described?' Mike asked.

Tony shook his head. It was a busy shoot, he said, under a lot of pressure with money running short and overscheduling the day scene counts. The director had been running around like a headless chicken. It meant the actors were on set for long periods and then back at work early the following day.

'There wasn't much activity except the filming and, anyway, the two stars Rupert Mitchell and Amanda Delany didn't get along that well. Apart from him there wasn't that much excitement, no high testosterone levels. You only get the real crackerjacks going down when they use the sexy young male stars, then they have their work cut out for them.'

'How do you mean?'

Tony gave a wide-handed gesture. 'Well, if you got a lead actor and he's screwing the make-up girl or the costume designer or the stand-in, whatever, we gotta know where to pick them up from in the morning. I've had to scour nightclubs and pull out legless actors and get them onto the set in time, and it's not always the male stars; some of the ladies are just as bad. God forbid we ever complain, but you'd not believe what I've had to deal with – and Amanda, well, she was a naughty girl. I seen her hooverin' up stuff. She would be all sweet and like a kid, then get herself tanked up and be giving blow jobs in the back of the Merc. Couple of times I had her throwing up. She was a mess, you know. She'd take anything to get high.'

Mike and Barbara acted surprised, Barbara shaking her head, looking stunned.

'Oh yeah, I had her picking up total strangers from nightclubs. She was a nymphomaniac, if you ask me, and if she wasn't pulling in strangers, she'd be going through the cast like a dose of salts. The first movie I worked on with her was *The Mansion* and, my God, what a time I had.' He stopped, suddenly aware that he was talking too much.

Mike leaned forward. 'Anything you say in here is confidential. Now, out of interest, these actors . . .'

'She'd have gone through the whole of *Spotlight* if she'd stayed alive,' Tony sighed. 'Once she was in the car and she told me that she was bored. You know, there she was earning millions, and she was bored. She says to me that she was sick of actors and their egos, and this was the time she was supposed to be crazy in love with Scott Myers. I'll tell you something else for free: I used to hear her tipping off the press. Honest to God, she would call them up and tell them she was in such and such a club, then when it all comes out in the papers she's crying, saying how can they do that to her!'

'So did your brother drive her to some of these clubs?'

'Harry was her one on one, yeah.'

'No, I mean Lester.'

Tony thought about it. He might have driven her a couple of times, but he wasn't sure.

'Do you think it possible that Lester also became one of her conquests?'

'No chance. Listen, we keep it quiet what's going down, but everyone knew she was a right little trollop and there is no way he would have got himself involved with her, no way.'

'But it's possible?'

'No, me and Harry would have warned him off her.'

'But if he also did private work for her, you wouldn't have known, would you?'

There was a long pause, as if Tony knew he had revealed too much. It was at this point that Mike passed across the photographs of the victim, showing the deep knife wounds made by the weapon.

Tony glanced at them and shuddered. 'Poor little mare. Whatever I said about her, she didn't deserve that.'

There was another lengthy pause.

'You don't seriously think Lester had anything to do with it?'

'We're just following a line of enquiry.'

'Then you follow another one, pal,' Tony said angrily, 'because my brother had nothing to do with that.'

'Why has he gone to Amsterdam?'

Tony looked phased. 'Eh? I didn't know he had.'

'Do you know if he makes frequent trips to Amsterdam?' Tony shook his head. 'Perhaps he goes there so he can score drugs?' Mike continued. 'You've said that you know Miss Delany was taking drugs. Have you any idea where she got them?'

'No.'

'From your brother Lester maybe?'

'*No.*'

Tony had had enough. 'Listen, if you had any evidence, you wouldn't be grilling me. I am telling you that Lester's got nothin' to do with any of this, and you got nothin' on him apart from his collection of knives – and that is not evidence. It was his career before bein' a driver, and I'd say he got permission to have them for his displays. You're trying to get me to trap my brother and I am now saying to you, I'm out of here unless you got some trumped-up charge against *me*!'

After half an hour the James brothers were released. The teams compared notes and everyone was of the same opinion. Lester James remained their prime suspect. But he was a suspect with not a scrap of evidence against him, and so far forensic had been unable to identify any of the karate knives as the weapon used to kill Amanda. The team stepped up their contacts in Amsterdam to help them trace Lester James, and their drug unit was checking if they had any previous link to him through any of their known dealers. Both brothers had given a mobile phone number for Lester, but it was only used for work and not personal calls. When they tried it, it was switched off. They contacted the server only to find the phone had not been used for months.

Anna had not given any thought to Gordon Berry or, for that matter, to their night together. Tired out as she was by the time she got home, she was pleased to find he had left two messages on her answerphone saying he wanted to see her. She returned his calls straight away, feeling warm and girlish. They made a date for dinner the following evening. Anna liked sleeping in her unmade bed, curling her body around a pillow that still smelled of Gordon's aftershave.

There had been no sighting of either Jeannie Bale or Felicity Turner, so the next morning Barolli went to the flat in Maida Vale with the warrant to enter and search.

Anna put a call through to Rupert Mitchell's home. The maid answered: neither Mr nor Mrs Mitchell was at home. When Anna asked if she could help with the licence plate of the Rolls-Royce, she was surprised when the girl offered to go and check outside.

'Is it parked at the house?'

'Yes, Mam. It belongs to Mrs Mitchell's parents, but they're abroad. They often leave it here for Mrs Mitchell to use to collect them from the airport.'

It was indeed the same car seen passing on numerous occasions along the street running across Amanda Delany's mews. The reason there had been a delay in identifying the owner was that the licence plates were Maltese.

Next, Anna checked out the fingerprints which were still being brought in from the mews. Eight were unidentified, left by persons unknown, with no police record. They had the match with Colin O'Dell and Scott Myers who, as agreed, had come into the station to have their prints taken. They had also eliminated Miss Lesser's, the designer and three workmen, plus a plumber and an electrician.

'You've got eight outstanding?' Anna asked Joan.

'Yep. Apparently there was a gardener and a window cleaner, and I'm just tracking them down.'

'Do me a favour, Joan, tell the office manager I'm going to see if I can talk to the Mitchells about the Roller. Be back straight after.'

Then she swore; her car was still not ready for collection, and she had to wait for a patrol car to be freed up before she could leave the station. She had sensed a strange flatness all round; this was unlike any previous case she had worked on. There was urgency, but the painstaking enquiry was so desperately slow that it was having an effect on everyone.

Surveillance officers were standing by the basement railings of Jeannie Bale's and Felicity Turner's flat. Barolli headed down the steps, kicking aside the litter and old newspapers that had blown down there. He cupped his hands around his eyes to get a look through the window into the lounge. The grubby curtains were partly drawn and he couldn't see anything. The surveillance team had already checked round the back and talked to a woman in the flat on the ground floor. She hadn't seen the girls recently, but knew about the death of the young boy because of all the police and ambulances. They were waiting for the landlord to arrive with the key; that would save them breaking down the door.

Barolli checked his watch; it was still only just after nine. He looked into an old coal chute, dragging the door back to find it was filled with junk and broken furniture. It was filthy and he had no intention of getting any closer. He stared up at the dirty windows and back to street level. At one time these houses would have been occupied by one family, the basement used for the cooks and maids, and four floors up there would have been small rooms for the butlers and valets, the long-windowed, elegant rooms on the floors in between for the family.

'Times change, huh,' he said to one of the officers.

An Indian man peered over the railings; this was the landlord with the keys to the property. Mr Singh took considerable time sorting through the keys until he got the correct one, complaining all the time about the rubbish on the steps and the mess in the small basement courtyard.

'Two minutes with a broom,' he kept repeating, but judging by the overflowing wheelie bins, a lot more than a broom was required.

Eventually the door to the flat was opened and Barolli asked for Mr Singh to wait as they went inside; he would need to be a witness if they removed anything.

'Christ, it stinks in here,' Barolli muttered, stepping over ashtrays and Coke cans in the lounge. He went from room to room accompanied by the two surveillance officers. It looked almost as if a robbery had taken place, but it could as easily have been the way the place was left.

The pink bedroom was a mess. Clothes were left in piles on the floor, and two battered suitcases lay open on the floor, their handles broken. Wardrobe doors hung ajar, drawers were pulled out, shoes discarded by the wardrobe. The second bedroom was less untidy; this Barolli knew to be Dan Hutchins's room. The third bedroom, Felicity's, was also a tip; clothes had been stuffed into plastic bags and left in piles on the bed. The kitchen was disgusting and smelled of sour milk. Empty takeaway food cartons were stacked in an overflowing flip-top waste-bin. Dirty towels lay on the bathroom floor, the medicine cabinet was open, empty but for some talcum powder and a half-full perfume bottle. Make-up was caked around the washbasin and on the sides of the bath.

Barolli tutted to himself. He was searching for any clue that indicated something untoward had happened, but there were no pools of blood, no splattering, just a nasty mess everywhere.

The surveillance guys were digging around in the hope that they'd find some notes or letters, but were having no luck. Barolli returned to the pink bedroom which he knew to have been Amanda Delany's. Photo albums were stacked up and it looked as if papers had been burning in the old blocked-up fireplace. He looked through some of the albums; they belonged to Jeannie Bale and were full of photographs and flyers for fringe theatre productions.

Barolli called into the station to report his findings. He couldn't tell if anything had happened to the two girls; it appeared more likely they had upped and run.

'Place is a shit hole,' he told Mike Lewis. 'There are suitcases and belongings stuffed into plastic bags, but no sign of either occupant and, judging by the smell of stale milk, they've been gone a good few days.'

Mike instructed him to have a really thorough search and see if he could find any indication of where the girls could have gone. It was the last thing Barolli wanted; the awful mildew damp was seeping into his bones.

He sat on the unmade bed in Amanda's old room, stared around slowly, then looked down to his feet to see blonde hair sticking out from beneath the bed. When he pulled it out, the doll gave a plaintive cry of '*Mama Mama*'. Its china face was cracked. Barolli remained alone in the flat for another half an hour, rifling through drawers and cupboards. Two female officers joined him and they began a thorough search of the whole flat. They upended waste-bins, checked all the crunched-up paper, envelopes, anything with any handwriting or type, but there were no clues as to where the girls might have gone. With so many discarded clothes, make-up and hairbrushes left lying about, it was impossible to know if anything significant was missing.

Anna was led by the maid into the same small study where she had first met Rupert Mitchell. Helen Mitchell received her coldly. When Anna asked if her husband was at home, Helen said he was away filming; she suggested Anna make an appointment with his agent.

'It's not Rupert I want to see. I just need a few words with you, please.'

'Really? Well, I don't have long.'

'This shouldn't take long,' Anna responded.

Helen was immaculate in a smart coal-grey skirt and cashmere sweater, her blonde hair tied in a loose band, her chiselled face even more attractive than Anna had remembered.

'The Rolls-Royce in your driveway?'

'My father's.'

'He is in Malta, is that correct?'

'Yes.'

Anna took out the pictures of the CCTV coverage from Amanda's neighbourhood, asking if anyone apart from her father drove it.

'I use it to collect them from the airport. Daddy is always reluctant to leave it in a long-stay car park so it remains here in the drive. Not that that's the best place, but we use our garage for Rupert's car and Daddy's is actually too large to fit into it.'

'Who else drives it?'

371

'No one else. Rupert wouldn't be seen dead in it.'

Anna laid out on the desk the CCTV pictures, asking if Helen's father was in London on the dates printed at the bottom of each picture.

'I have no idea. It's possible.'

'Would you look at the dates?'

Helen got up from her seat and bent over the desk, peering at the three photographs.

'I don't know. Is this why you are here? I mean, has my father not paid a parking ticket or something?'

'No, I am still investigating the murder of Amanda Delany.'

'What on earth has this got to do with Daddy's car?'

'Was he in London?' Anna asked again.

'I can't remember.' She returned to her seat.

'It's important.'

'Then I suggest you ask him.' She rattled off her father's mobile phone number.

'You see, Mrs Mitchell, this car, your father's Rolls-Royce, was seen close to Amanda Delany's mews on three different occasions.'

Helen was suddenly tense, patting her hair and twisting her rings round her fingers.

'You have stated that you never went to Miss Delany's mews.'

'Yes.'

'So was it possible your father maybe visited her?'

'No, he didn't know her.'

'Have another look at the dates. Perhaps your father wasn't the driver?'

Helen chewed at her lips.

'Could it have been your husband?'

'No.'

372

'You seem very sure.'

'I am . . . because it was me.' Helen gave an open-handed gesture and said that she was visiting friends in Elizabeth Street, which was in the same area. But when Anna pressed for their names she caved in.

'It was me, all right? I admit it.'

'So on three occasions you drove to Miss Delany's mews?'

'I admit I was in the area and I admit that I did drive past her mews on two occasions, but I did not go into the mews. I just drove past.'

'And on the third?'

'I parked in the road and I walked into the mews.'

'And?'

Helen was trying to keep calm, giving short intakes of breath, and then she bowed her head.

'I went to see her because she kept calling here. If I answered, she'd put the phone down. Once she spoke to me in French, but I knew it was her.' She gave a soft deprecating laugh, saying that she was fluent in French herself, and when she continued the conversation, the phone went down.

'Why did you go to see her?'

'Partly because of the phone calls, and I knew a couple of times she had talked to Rupert here at the house. He kept on telling me not to worry about it, that he had asked her to stop ringing.'

One evening she had overheard a conversation Rupert had had in his study as the door was ajar. She heard him telling the caller that they should not ring the house and that he was getting tired of the persistent phone calls, they were upsetting his wife. This all came at the worst possible time, Helen explained, as she was having fertility treatment. The stress was making her very agitated, exactly what she didn't need to be happening.

'So you went to confront her?'

'Yes. I know it was foolish, but I'd overheard Rupert on the phone that time agreeing to meet her.'

'When was this?'

'A few weeks into filming. He seemed jumpy, even angry. When I asked him who had been on the phone, he told me that it was nothing for me to worry about, then he went out for a walk. I checked the last caller's number on the phone and rang it and she answered. When I told her to stop pestering my husband, she was very rude. She said something like there was no need for her to pester any man and that she simply wished to talk to him about something personal.'

'What happened when you went to see her?'

'It was awful. I rang the doorbell, but I wasn't even sure she would be at home. But I knew because of Rupert's schedule for the filming that she wasn't called that evening.'

Helen had waited on the doorstep for quite a while before Amanda opened the door.

'I'm not being bitchy but, facing her, it was really hard for me to believe that my husband could have ever had any interest in her. She looked dreadful. Her hair was unwashed and her face spotty and she had a cold sore on her lip. She was wearing a sort of cotton shift nightdress and she was skin and bone and had a cigarette hanging out of her mouth.'

After she let Helen into the house, Amanda had told her to sit in the lounge; she was finishing off a meeting with someone. Helen had sat waiting, hearing muffled voices and then the bedroom door had opened and she caught a glimpse of a man leaving. When Anna asked her to describe him, she was hazy; all she could remember was that he had been blond and tough-looking. Then Amanda returned to the lounge to get her wallet and when she left, she closed the door so Helen was unable to see or hear any further interaction.

'When she came back, she had a small plastic bag and something wrapped in tinfoil. She stuffed whatever it was into her bag and then laughed, saying it was for party time.'

Anna asked Helen to repeat the description of the man she had seen. She had not really had more than a glimpse; all she recalled was that he was very well-built and fair. She had never seen him before or since. At this point, she got up and poured herself a glass of tonic water from the drinks cabinet. Anna asked if she would agree to look at a video ID parade. Helen nodded. 'I really had only a glimpse of him,' she repeated, 'but yes, I would be prepared to try and identify him.'

Helen sipped the tonic, returning to the armchair.

'I'm certain she knew why I was there, and when I asked her to leave my husband alone, she just shrugged her shoulders and said she had no interest in him whatso-ever. She said she had only called to ask if he'd come over as she'd something to discuss with him. He wasn't the only person she'd invited. Scott Myers and Colin O'Dell were coming over as well.'

Anna had her notebook open. She knew the date of Helen's visit, but needed to know when it was that Amanda had intended to have all three actors to her house. Helen was unsure, but thought it would have been a few nights before she was murdered. She wished she had never humiliated herself to such an extent. She stayed no more than a few minutes longer with Amanda and couldn't wait to leave.

'It was hideous. I felt as if she was laughing at me. I asked if she would help me, woman to woman. I told her I was undergoing fertility treatment and wanted to save my marriage.'

Helen frowned as if trying to remember something. Anna remained silent.

'I'm just trying to recall exactly what she said, something like, "It would be to his benefit". What she meant by that, I don't know. She also asked if it was true that my father was a multi-millionaire.'

Amanda had walked her to the front door and then, as Helen left, she had made a strange, doll-like, side-to-side swing of her head, 'Tell him it's in the diary,' she had said.

Helen had no idea what Amanda meant by that, and she never discussed the meeting with her husband. The next thing she knew, Amanda had been murdered.

'So you don't know if Rupert kept the date?' Anna had underlined the word *diary* in her notebook.

'He couldn't have, because they were night filming and I have his schedule.'

Anna stood up.

'Does he need to know about this?' Helen asked nervously.

Anna assured her that she had no reason to repeat their conversation. At the front door she paused.

'This man, the one you saw at Amanda's – is there anything else you can think of that you remember about him?'

'I doubt it. I think he might have been giving her drugs, you know, in the tinfoil wrapper that I saw, and

376

Rupert said Amanda was often very stoned. What is it about men?' Helen frowned. 'What makes them want to be with someone like that scrawny, drugged-up creature, her lips with that awful cold sore? I don't understand it.'

Anna looked at the glossy, elegant, beautiful woman.

'I think it's something to do with being needy. I don't know.'

Helen watched Anna walk down the path and get into the patrol car before she closed the front door.

At the station Mike Lewis headed up the briefing. They were now able to eliminate the Rolls from the investigation. Anna reported the possible meeting between the three actors, O'Dell, Myers and Mitchell, and their victim shortly before her murder. Barolli was next up, stressing his concern for Jeannie Bale and Felicity Turner's whereabouts. They had decided to wait before going public about the girls' disappearance until they had contacted their next-of-kin. Felicity Turner's parents in South Wales said they had not seen their daughter for years; Jeannie Bale's mother was still being traced. Jeannie's agent had not spoken to her client for a few days but promised to contact the station if she was to call in, which she usually did on a regular basis. Next, Barolli gestured to the board and the listed landline phone numbers they had been checking.

'One phone number is of particular interest – the number for the London hotel where Mr and Mrs Delany were staying. We have contacted the hotel and they confirmed that the Delanys were still in residence when two calls were made from there. They supplied the number: it was for Jeannie and Felicity's flat in Maida

Vale. Mr Delany had also asked reception to cash a cheque for him, for five thousand pounds, on the same morning that the calls were made.'

Anna gave a soft whistle. Could the girls have gone to the South of France with the Delanys? She doubted it, but the calls between the girls and Mr Delany were highly suspicious. Mike Lewis was ahead of her.

'This diary, because it continues to be a missing item and one worth a lot of money to our victim, if she was going to use it as material for her memoir – and we have the guy from Golden Arrow verifying that he had seen it – it might be that she left it in the flat and our two girls found it. These two calls the Delanys made to the flat may be connected to the whereabouts of the diary.'

'If Delany was paying the girls the five grand,' Barolli interjected, 'that's a pittance compared to what it could be worth. So I'm not sure I go along with the five grand pay-off.'

When Mike asked Anna if she knew whether the girls were aware of the publisher, she admitted that they might be, as she had mentioned him when she was asking them if they had found the diary.

'Well, bloody get onto him and see if those little cows have contacted him.'

'Gordon, Anna Travis called to say she'll be working late this evening so can't make dinner, and not to bother returning her call as she'll speak to you in the morning.'

Gordon Berry had just finished his treatment with Langton and was walking out from his surgery with him.

Langton glanced at Gordon. 'Bit unethical, isn't it, Gordon? Or do you need to make sure she's wearing her neck brace?' He smiled.

Gordon slammed the door of his surgery as soon as Langton had gone and rang Anna on her mobile, but it went straight to voicemail. He called her flat and left a message asking her to get in touch.

When his receptionist tapped on his door to say his next patient was waiting, he grunted. Surprised, she asked if everything was all right. He glared at her.

'No, it isn't. You just landed me right in it!'

She looked confused. He waved her away as his mobile rang.

'It's Anna,' he heard. 'You called me. I can't really talk as I'm about to start an interview briefing.'

'OK. Look, I'm sorry. One, not to be seeing you this evening, but two, more important, Langton knows about us.'

'How? Did you tell him?'

'No, and I don't want to get into it, but just so as you know.'

'Shit. Well, so what. I'll try and call you later, OK?'

Anna turned off her phone and closed her eyes. Barolli passed her window and rapped on it; she was wanted. She could see, through the blinds, Langton looking over the incident board.

Chapter Nineteen

Anna was one of the last to join everyone in the incident room and she sat right at the back. While he was impressed that there had been some developments, Langton said, it was nowhere near what he had hoped they would accomplish. The murder of Amanda Delany might no longer be front-page news, but the press could easily get wind of the fact that two movie actors were being questioned that evening.

'You never know, the press-hungry stars could even tip off the paparazzi themselves. We want this evening to be above board and get them in and out as soon as possible, so be prepared. They are just helping enquiries, there are no charges against them. We'll use the time now to discuss any queries you want ironed out.'

Anna was grateful that Langton was ignoring her; she hadn't yet decided how she would deal with him knowing about her and Gordon. Not that it was any of his business, but she wanted to be prepared for how he might react. It was impossible to predict.

Colin O'Dell looked as if he had slept in his clothes; his jeans and jacket were crumpled and his T-shirt stained. Even his boots looked scuffed and worn. Despite his appearance he was very self-assured, smiling at Anna and Barolli who were to conduct the interview. When he introduced his solicitor, he joked that he was there just for support and to make sure he didn't make a complete ass of himself.

In total contrast, Scott Myers was wearing a smart collarless suit with a silk scarf wrapped around his neck. He was quiet and rather nervous as he was led down the corridor to the interview room where Langton and Mike Lewis were waiting. They made it clear to him that he was not under arrest but there of his own free will, and they expressed their thanks for his cooperation. He accepted a bottle of water, snaking his scarf free, and sat down opposite Langton. He agreed to answer any questions put to him, but was wondering if he should have brought a solicitor.

'We can provide you with one, but we are just hoping that you may be able to help us with a few enquiries.' Langton gave a smile. 'On the other hand, if you are concerned or if you lied when previously questioned and held back information that could have repercussions . . .'

'No, I haven't lied about anything.'

'Then there shouldn't be any problems. We just want to iron out the details regarding your relationship with Amanda Delany.'

'I explained it all to the detective who interviewed me. We were no longer seeing each other, I wasn't involved with her in any way.'

'Yes, we know all that, Mr Myers, but we wondered if there was anything you might have forgotten to tell DI Travis.'

'Believe you me, nothing about my relationship with

Amanda escapes my memory – it was a nightmare,' Scott said. 'I left my wife and my children. I must have been out of my mind.'

'I'm sure your marital situation at the time was very distressing.'

'That's putting it mildly. Right now we're having a battle over money, and Fiona won't let me see the kids. I have visitation rights, but when I get to the house, she's taken them out!'

Langton commiserated, letting Myers wind himself up. Mike joined in, saying he had young kids. He could only imagine what it must be like, not to be allowed to see them.

'It's the money too, but I really only want the best for us all. I'm not working right now, a movie I was scheduled to start has folded due to lack of finances and so I'm in a legal wrangle with those guys too.' He gave a charming smile. 'I'm sorry. You probably don't want to hear all this.'

'It's really a question of clearing up some dates,' Langton said, and looked at Mike as if to give him a cue to open the file.

'OK, let's have a look at this. You stated that you had not been to Miss Delany's mews house. Is that correct?'

'I can't remember exactly what I said, but I was asked about a specific time, the night of Amanda's death, and I was not there then.'

'We have a match on your fingerprints, Mr Myers, so you may not have been there on that specific night, but you were at some time inside the house.'

Myers nodded. Then he sighed and twisted the silk scarf around his hands.

'All right. I said what I said because I didn't want to

get involved. The truth of it is, I was there but only once. When I was told she had been murdered, it made me even more wary of admitting that I'd been there.'

'Why?'

'Well, I've had a bad deal from the press about my relationship with Amanda and the break-up of my marriage, and I just didn't want it all to start up again. If it got out that I'd been with her . . .'

'What do you mean by being with her?'

'It's obvious, isn't it? Yes, we'd broken up, yes, I wasn't seeing her and didn't *want* to see her, but she asked me to meet with her, she said it was important. When I told her I wasn't interested, she said it was nothing to do with us getting back together.'

'When exactly was this?'

'A couple of nights before she was murdered. I'm not sure of the date.'

'So you went to the house?'

'Yeah, she was filming, said it was a night shoot and she'd see me there as she wasn't sure what time she'd be finished.'

Langton left a lengthy pause before asking how Scott would have entered the house if Amanda wasn't there. Drawing the scarf more tightly round his hands, the actor looked away and swore under his breath before answering.

'She gave me a key.'

Langton showed no reaction, playing the waiting game again, and Myers continued.

'Look, I'm sorry. I lied, all right, but I don't want you getting any ideas that I had anything to do with her murder. It's freaking me out. She gave me her key when I met her.'

'So she didn't just call you for this one meeting?'

'No, I met her in a café, the reason being I didn't want to see her again, I didn't want anything more to do with her, but she insisted. She said that if I didn't meet her, she'd start calling Fiona and I didn't want that either, so we met up.'

'Why didn't she tell you at this café why she wanted the other meeting?'

'She wouldn't tell me what it was all about, just that she needed to talk to me and that it would be . . .' This time he gave it up. 'She had cocaine, or said she was scoring some, and that's why I agreed to go.'

Scott Myers was sweating and fidgeting restlessly as he swore blind that he was now in a programme and wasn't doing drugs any more. Since that night, he had not scored again as he was trying to get his life back on track.

'Did you usually score for yourself?'

'No, I got the gear through Amanda. It's the truth – I mean, I couldn't risk it.'

'How come she was able to get it?'

'She had a good source; she was always able to get whatever she wanted.' He suddenly straightened out and folded the scarf on the table. 'I wasn't going to get him in on this, but now I think I need to, because whatever I'm telling you is putting me in deeper shit.'

'Do you want a solicitor present?'

'No, I don't need one because, one, I can prove that when she was murdered I have witnesses and an alibi and, two, I admit I went to her mews house and I admit that I've lied about that.'

'Do you still have her front-door key?'

'No, I tossed it. This makes me sound like a right

asshole. I know I should have come clean about it before, but I wasn't there alone.'

'At the mews?'

'Yeah. I wasn't alone with her, there was someone else there as well. I just haven't told you because I didn't want to get him involved.'

They waited expectantly. Was this other person Lester James? When they saw Myers hesitate, Langton asked if the other person was Amanda's driver. Myers looked confused.

'No, it was Colin O'Dell. He was there that same night.'

Anna and Barolli had put Colin O'Dell through the same questions and grilled him about irregularities in his original statement. He was almost treating the interview as a joke, saying that he couldn't remember what he had said as he was hungover that first time. Anna found him to be increasingly irritating; it was Barolli who sorted him out. Although he was there of his own free will to answer questions, it was clear, Barolli warned him, that hungover or not, he had lied.

'You stated that you had never been to Miss Delany's mews house, but we now have evidence that puts you right there – your fingerprints, Mr O'Dell – so I suggest you straighten out and don't play any more games or we will be charging you with attempting to pervert the course of justice. When were you there, in the house?'

As O'Dell turned to confer with his solicitor, there was a rap on the door. Mike Lewis signalled for Anna to join him.

'I can help you with the date and night you were there,' Anna said when she returned a minute later.

'Scott Myers recalls that you were with him at the house two nights before Amanda Delany was murdered.'

'Christ, listen to me. I had nothing to do with that, all right? So I was there, but I can't remember much about the evening, just that Amanda had called me to say to come on over as she had something she wanted to talk about.'

Anna glanced at Barolli.

'I know what it was,' O'Dell continued. 'She was worried about her agent. She couldn't remember if either Scott or I were represented by Andrea Lesser and she wanted to know if we'd been paid our fees for working on *The Mansion*. She was a bit out of it because it was me, not Scott, who'd been in the movie, and I had been paid. She was going on about not getting her money and what should she do? Apparently she knew someone else off the film who had been paid and she was starting to get really paranoid about it.'

Barolli flipped over the file of notes. 'So what time was this meeting?'

'Be late. I got there after Scott and he let me in. She was on night shoots, so it was Christ knows what time when she got home, and . . .' He laughed and pulled a face. 'She'd left some goodies for us to while away the time.' He touched his nose and snorted.

'Take me through what happened when Amanda arrived home,' Barolli asked.

O'Dell shrugged. 'She was all uptight about the missing money. I had to catch a flight back to Dublin and she said I could use her driver – she'd told him to wait, I think.'

Anna felt tense. 'This driver,' she said. 'Can you describe him?'

387

'Big bloke, fair hair, don't think I saw his face. Well, he was just the driver, know what I mean? We talk to the backs of their heads. I was well away, but he got me to the airport in time, very ragged I was.'

'So you and Scott Myers just had a talk about money, and . . .'

'Well, one thing led to another.'

'Like what?'

He whispered to his solicitor and eventually admitted that all three had gone into her bedroom.

'I was totally knackered, but she was a right little nympho and fuelled up on crack cocaine and didn't want us to leave – hung onto me, she did.' He paused. Anna was fast, fitting the pieces together like a jigsaw.

'You were in *The Mansion*, correct?'

'Yes.'

'You also wore a gold crucifix, didn't you?'

He puffed out his cheeks and repeated that he'd forgotten about it, and only now remembered that Amanda had given it to him from the costume department.

'What happened to the cross?'

'She almost choked me with it that evening, snapped it, and said she wanted me to stay, but I had to get my flight back and so we left.'

'You left with Scott Myers?'

'Yeah, the driver dropped him off at a taxi rank and drove me to Heathrow.'

Anna left the interview room and went next door to ask Scott Myers if he could identify the driver who had not only brought Amanda home, but had driven him to a taxi rank and taken O'Dell to the airport. Myers admitted to being very stoned and had been sick just after he'd been dropped off. He could not identify the driver

as he had hardly spoken to him; all he recalled was that
the driver was maybe fair-haired with broad shoulders.
When Anna asked what the two of them had talked
about in the back of the Mercedes, all he could remember was Colin O'Dell saying it was the best orgasm he'd
ever had, even though Amanda had almost choked him
to death, and then they had discussed the sexual high of
part-strangulations before ejaculating.

It was almost 9 p.m. when Scott Myers and Colin
O'Dell were released without charge. Langton was insistent they track down Lester James. A press conference
was arranged for the following morning. Concerns
for Jeannie Bale and Felicity Turner were growing. They
would ask the press to assist them and release photographs of the two of them. They had managed to track
down an aunt of Jeannie Bale's, but the girls seemed to
have disappeared into thin air.

Anna left the station and headed on foot to the nearest
tube. She had not gone far when Langton drew up in his
car and gestured to her to get in. With a sinking heart,
she opened the door of the old brown Rover. She was
quiet, waiting for him to bring up Gordon but he didn't.
Instead he talked about running over the security tapes
from Amanda's mews to try to get the numberplate or
some identifying connection to their suspect.

'Problem is, with the security cameras being on a
timer and not turned on during the day, we didn't even
get the fact that Rupert Mitchell's wife visited. So it's
doubtful whether or not we'll get anything more.'

Anna agreed. Everything hinged on Lester James.

'I think he was supplementing his earnings,' she

observed, 'if not a user himself, and was supplying Amanda with crack cocaine. We know for certain that she was a user, if not an addict. He was probably the man Helen Mitchell saw at the house and could also be the driver who picked up both the actors . . .'

Langton interrupted her. 'I'm not quite following you.'

'How do you think Lester James would feel if he was in love with her? Maybe she'd even had sex with him. She didn't restrict her liaisons to movie actors, she often picked up men from clubs, total strangers. And here is this driver having to collect two actors who'd been having sex games with her, discussing their prowess and boasting that she'd not wanted them to leave.'

Langton said nothing. They still had no evidence against Lester James, and until it was confirmed that he had indeed driven the two actors that night, it was pure supposition.

'Unless it was one or other of the brothers,' Anna went on, 'but I somehow doubt it was. Tony and Harry are older and wiser, more-than-my-job's-worth types, but we can't rule them out.'

'Talk to them again and go over their itinerary for the film unit, who drove whom, and so on.'

As Anna nodded, she felt her mobile vibrate in her pocket. There was a text message from Josh Lyons's secretary apologising for not returning a call Anna had made to his office earlier, and two voice messages from Gordon. She put the phone back in her pocket as they approached her block of flats.

'You going to ask me in for a drink?' he asked nonchalantly.

'I wasn't going to. It's been a long day and it's almost ten.'

'Never bothered you before.'

'It doesn't bother me, it's just that I am tired. We'll probably have another long day tomorrow.'

'Well then, we'll discuss it now.'

She tensed up but made no reply.

'What's going on between you and Gordon?'

She glanced at him and then looked away.

'It's fuckin' unethical, unprofessional.'

'I am not his patient any more,' Anna pointed out. 'I only needed one session and my neck is fine, so I can't see that it's either unethical or unprofessional, nor can I see that it's any of your business.'

'It is. I suggested you go to him.'

'So I did, and I really appreciate it, but whether or not I am seeing him outside hours shouldn't be any concern of yours.'

'What if it is?'

She was starting to get angry. 'What do you mean?'

'Just that I advised you to go and see him for treatment and he ends up fucking you and I feel in some way responsible.'

'Are you joking? Responsible? I took your point about my last relationship with Damien Nolan as being unprofessional, and I agreed and I ended it, and I haven't seen him since. But this has nothing to do with work and I can't see that I am your responsibility in any way at all.'

'Because I care about you.'

'I appreciate that and I thank you, but you have a wife and children, and whatever I am doing with my life is none of your business whatsoever. I don't ask you about your private life, so what gives you the right to judge mine?'

She had her hand on the door handle about to get out.

'Because I talked to him about you.'

She froze, turning to face him.

'You talked about me? When you called him to ask if he could see me for my neck injury?'

'No, before.'

'I don't understand. What sort of things did you tell him about me?'

Langton leaned across, opening the glove compartment, searching for a cigarette.

'Personal stuff. Is there a pack of cigarettes in here?'

She peered into the glove compartment, his face close to hers as she looked inside.

'There you go, Marlboros. But you shouldn't be smoking.'

He ignored her and lit the cigarette, lowering the window on his side.

'Like a therapist. Well, in some ways, I dunno, but under his influence . . . I just found it therapeutic to talk.'

Anna sighed. 'So you told him about us?'

'Not so much about us, more the way I had felt.'

'Pity you never tried talking to me.' She regretted saying it as soon as the words were out of her mouth. 'I have to go in.'

'Fine. I just wanted you to know, that's all.'

She turned to face him. The cigarette was dangling out of the side of his mouth, and in the semi–darkness his face was even more handsome, but she realised that she wasn't eager to be this close.

'Goodnight.'

She was out of the car and slamming the door shut before he could say anything. She walked away and then retraced her steps, opening the car door and bending down to confront him.

'I don't want to play any games with you and I don't want you thinking you have a priority over my feelings. You had that for too long and I have to get on with my life. I don't want to know what you told Gordon about me and, to be honest, I don't care.'

'Goodnight, Anna,' Langton replied, starting the engine and tossing his cigarette out of the window.

By the time she had got into her flat, hurled her brief-case aside, Anna's temper was really up. Listening to her phone messages made her even angrier. The fact that Gordon seemed to have got himself into a tailspin over Langton knowing about their night together irritated her. It was not until she had showered and was in bed that she calmed down. An odd feeling swept over her. The control Langton had over her was no longer something she was afraid of, emotionally or physically. It was, she knew now, really and truly something of the past. Tonight she had been able to confront him on an equal level. In some ways she felt sorry for him because she realised that, as much as she was over him, he was perhaps not over her.

'Chalk one up for me!' she said to herself. Just as she snuggled down under the duvet, her landline rang. She was in two minds as to whether to answer it when the answerphone clicked on.

'It's Gordon, just trying to touch base. I'll call you tomorrow.'

She switched off her bedside lamp. She knew the buzz she had felt being with Gordon had gone as well. She didn't know how much a part in that Langton had played, but her affair with Gordon was over before it had really begun.

Chapter Twenty

Mike Lewis headed up the press conference, requesting help from the public in tracing Jeannie Bale and Felicity Turner in connection with the murder of Amanda Delany. The safety of the girls was their overriding concern. If anyone knew the whereabouts of Lester James, he added, they should come forward as the police were anxious to speak to him. This was the first indication that the murder team were making progress in their investigation, and as a result they got front-page coverage. It was picked up on morning television, where repeated clips from Amanda Delany's films were shown.

But there were still gaping holes in their enquiry because they had no concrete evidence against Lester James. The officers assigned to the tedious detail of checking through the CCTV footage from the night of the murder were instructed to repeat their scanning from start to finish, in the hope that they had missed something. The statements from Helen Mitchell, Colin O'Dell and Scott Myers were to be checked and rechecked.

Then news came through that the body of a young woman had been found washed up at Tower Bridge. It fitted the description of Felicity Turner. The label in her jacket bore the name of Amanda Delany and the police marine support unit had contacted the incident room immediately.

The body was lying on a gurney in the unit's mortuary, draped in a green tarpaulin; water was still seeping down onto the tiled floor. Judging by the bloating, it had been in the river for about two days.

'If it is her . . .' Anna said quietly.

Barolli finished her sentence for her: '. . . God help Jeannie Bale. We've still got no information regarding her whereabouts.'

He fell silent as Anna moved round to get a look at the girl's face as the pathologist drew back the tarpaulin. She took her time, pushing the wet stinking hair away from the corpse's face, which was a hideous greenish colour, the sunken eyes open wide.

'Yes, it's Felicity Turner.'

At first glance, the pathologist said, she appeared to have no physical injuries. They had cut away her clothes and stacked them on a table, ready to be bagged and sent to forensics. Anna checked the collar of the sodden jacket. Amanda Delany's name was written on a tag and below it, very blurred, was the name of a theatrical costumiers – *Angels* – and a phone number. Anna checked quickly with the costumiers and learned that Amanda Delany had purchased the jacket after the first film she had starred in, *Rock Baby*. Anna could only assume that this was one of the many garments Amanda had given to Felicity and Jeannie.

The body had been discovered by a trawler, partly covered in mud and slime, wedged into a mud bank. As it was low tide, the girl was visible, but they found no weights tying the body down; it was possible she had been on one of the ferries or tourist boats travelling up and down the Thames. It was unlikely that she jumped from Tower Bridge as it was well-lit and no one had reported seeing her in the area. All ferry- and pleasure-boat staff would have to be shown Felicity's photograph and questioned.

The Golden Arrow publishing company seemed to be on the move. Boxes filled the reception area, where Anna and Barolli were waiting to see Josh Lyons.

'That's him now.' The receptionist pointed to a Porsche which was drawing up outside.

Anna moved forward as Lyons came through the front door.

'Mr Lyons? I am Detective Travis.' He obviously recognised her. 'Hi. Right yes, sorry.' He turned to the receptionist. 'Is my office cleared yet?'

'Not yet.'

He gestured for them to follow him into his office which was stripped of books and posters. His high-backed leather chair and desk were still there, however.

'It's a bloody nightmare. No matter how well you organise it, something always goes wrong. We've been preparing for this move for months. I've got publishing dates and Christ knows how many authors wantin' a slice of me, banks making my life a fucking nightmare, but the lease is up here and the new premises have got plumbing problems. The water sprinklers came on and you can imagine what that means if you're unpacking books. Thank God most of them were still crated up.'

At last he calmed down, sitting behind his large desk.

Barolli asked tersely if they could have his undivided attention; they were here to question him regarding something that had a connection to a murder enquiry.

Josh Lyons loosened his tie.

'Amanda Delany?' he asked. 'Only I told your colleague here' – he nodded towards Anna – 'as much as I knew and I've not really got anything else to add.'

'Have you been contacted by anyone with regard to Amanda Delany's memoirs?'

Anna then showed him the picture of Jeannie Bale.

'We're interested to know if this girl has been to see you.'

'Listen, I've not had a spare minute for a week.'

'Look at the photograph, Mr Lyons.'

He glanced at the picture and shook his head. 'She hasn't been here.'

'It would have been in connection with Amanda Delany's diary.'

'I told you – I saw it, but I don't have it.'

'Would anyone else here have spoken to Jeannie Bale or met with her?'

'I doubt it, but let me ask one of my editors.' He shot out of his chair and opened his office door, bellowing for someone called Adrian.

'This is another bloody waste of time,' Barolli said, checking his watch.

A few minutes later, Josh Lyons returned with a young guy, unshaven with straggly long hair and round wire-rimmed glasses.

'This is Adrian Skidmore. He's had two calls from someone,' Lyons said. 'What did she say her name was?' He turned to Adrian.

'Jeannie.'

'Tell them what she wanted,' Lyons prompted.

Anna sat on the edge of the empty desk.

'This is very important, Mr Skidmore. Can you tell us exactly what Jeannie said to you?'

Adrian Skidmore gave a shrug of his skinny shoulders.

'She said that she'd got the diary, and that she wanted to speak to Josh, but I said he wasn't available. I wasn't certain what she was talking about, so I asked her to tell me what it was she wanted.'

'*And?*' Barolli was so tense he looked as if he was about to put his hands round the young man's neck. 'Mr Skidmore, what did this Jeannie say to you.'

'I just told you, she said she had the diary and she wanted to speak to Josh.'

'What about the second call?' Barolli snapped.

'That was the day after, so that'd be two days ago. Yeah, two days ago, she called again. Josh was out at lunch so I took the call.'

'What did she say?'

'She wanted to discuss selling the diary to Josh. She said she was an actress too and had known Miss Delany since drama school. She said something about once being up for the same part.' He scratched his head. 'To be honest, she sounded a bit crazy, going on about how she could tell us a lot of other things about Amanda Delany and that she wanted to make a deal.'

'She definitely said that she had Amanda Delany's diary?' Anna asked.

Adrian nodded and looked nervously at Lyons.

'I couldn't discuss any deal with her, so again I said she'd have to talk to Mr Lyons. She said that she'd call back and for me to make sure Josh knew she had the diary. I wrote Josh a note about it all.'

'I never saw it,' Lyons said.

Anna folded her arms. 'But would you have been

interested?' she demanded. 'Would the diary of a murdered movie star be something you would negotiate money for?'

'Hard to say,' Lyons replied. 'Depends on the contents, but then it could be a minefield of legal problems.'

'Didn't Amanda suggest to you though, that it contained a lot of explosive information regarding her sex life?'

'Yes, she did – but again, without reading it, I wouldn't know what we could or couldn't do with it. Even if this girl owns it, it would be questionable. Does she?'

Anna glanced at Barolli. To their knowledge, the diary would be the property of Miss Delany's estate. They needed to recover it urgently, as it might contain information that they could act on.

Barolli had picked up on Anna's quiet, authoritative manner. He took out his card, saying that if Jeannie Bale contacted Golden Arrow they should get in touch with the incident room immediately, and ask for either himself or DI Travis. If Jeannie put in an appearance, they should call the police and try to detain her until they got there.

'Did she leave a number for you to call?' Barolli asked Skidmore.

'No. I'm sorry, if I'd had any indication it was important I would have asked for it. But, like I said, she did sound a bit crazy.'

When they left the building they had the exact time of the calls; they had come in the day after Anna had interviewed the two girls. She realised that the diary had to have been in the flat that day and was angry that Mike

Lewis had not had a search warrant issued, as she had requested. So, wherever Jeannie Bale was, she must have the damned diary. They decided that, once Felicity was formally identified, they would go to press with news of her death, hoping it might jolt Jeannie into coming forward.

Josh Lyons was blazing and Adrian Skidmore was taking the brunt of his anger.

'We could have had that fucking diary in our hands and you let it go walkabout!'

'But I was never told anything about it,' Adrian responded. 'Would we have published it?'

'I don't know, but it has to have something in it if the cops are after it. If Jeannie Bale calls, make sure I know about it. I'll take charge of it personally.'

'Have they arrested anyone for Delany's murder?'

'I don't fucking know.'

Adrian could almost see the wheels turning in his boss's brain.

'If the police wanted the diary, they must think it contains information, maybe even named her killer. If we get our hands on that diary, it might get us out of the financial shit we're in.'

Lyons took a slug of brandy and gasped as it hit him on an empty stomach.

The post-mortem report for Felicity Turner came in late afternoon. She had drowned. Both lungs and stomach contained substantial amounts of water, and she also had a very high alcohol content, eight times over the limit. The toxicology department was running tests on her hair for possible cocaine residue. They found no other wounds apart from a bruise to her lower back; it was possible that she had fallen against some railings and then into the river.

Anna was depressed as she read the report – such a waste of a young life. They put out a press release; it would feature on the six o'clock news. Meanwhile, officers were still questioning the ferry- and pleasure-boat staff, but as yet no one could identify her as having been a passenger. Sitting alone in her office, the sound of the forever-persistent phones ringing, Anna felt the sadness like a weight around her shoulders. She jolted when Barbara tapped on the door and entered.

'Line two,' she said. 'We have Mr Delany for you!'

'You're kidding me?' She had been trying to get hold of him since the discovery of Felicity's body.

'Nope.'

Anna took a deep breath and picked up the phone. 'Mr Delany, this is Detective Anna Travis.'

'I received a message that you wanted to talk to me.'

'Yes, yes, I did. Could I ask you where you are speaking from?'

'Paris. My wife and I are here for a short stay, to try and get some semblance of peace.'

'I'll not keep you longer than necessary. We see from your phone records at the hotel that two calls were—'

'My phone records?' he said coldly, interrupting her.

'. . . were made to your daughter's old flat in Maida Vale,' Anna continued. 'Can you tell me what they were about?'

'This is unbelievable!'

Anna waited; all she could hear from the other end of the phone was heavy breathing. It went on for a while too long.

'Mr Delany, I don't know if you have seen the late-night papers, but Felicity Turner's body has been recovered from the Thames.'

'What?'

'You are aware too that Dan Hutchins is also dead. We now have great concern regarding the whereabouts of the actress Jeannie Bale.'

'I don't understand what on earth this has to do with me!'

'Your daughter's diary, we believe, is with Miss Bale. This could be of importance to our investigation, but we won't know until we have read what it contains . . . Mr Delany?'

She heard the heavy breathing again, but this time she didn't pause.

'If you know anything, Mr Delany, if these calls to their flat were about the diary, I am asking you to please be honest with me. It's possible this girl's life could be in danger.'

'I still don't understand.'

'It's very simple, Mr Delany. The diary may contain details about your daughter's killer. It is therefore of the utmost importance that we gain access to it.'

'I don't have it.'

Anna sighed. After their dealings with Josh Lyons she believed Delany, but she nevertheless wanted to be certain. Then he murmured something she didn't hear.

'What did you say?'

'Oh, you may as well know. I was called by this girl. She wanted to meet with me. She said she had my daughter's diary, but she wanted money.'

Delany had agreed to pay her five thousand pounds, he said. He cashed a cheque at the hotel and gave the money to Felicity Turner, who had arrived at the hotel. Jeannie Bale was at the flat and was to hand over the diary to him. He had taken a taxi there, but no one was in. He returned to the hotel to find that Jeannie Bale had called again. She wanted a lot more money and when he refused, she hung up. He went back to the flat, but it was still empty. By this time he was worried he would miss his Eurostar trip to Paris.

'This was when I was with your wife at your hotel?' Anna asked.

'Yes. I felt that it was a rather pointless exercise and decided against taking it any further.'

'So you've had no further contact from Jeannie Bale?'

'No. If she attempts to blackmail any more money out of me, I'll have her arrested.'

'Blackmail?'

The heavy rasping breathing returned.

'So you believe that the diary contains inflammatory material that involved you?'

'I suspect it contains more filth about my daughter's lifestyle. I simply wish for it to be destroyed so she cannot create any further heartbreak for my wife and me.'

'Was there anything in your past involving your daughter that would also, if it became known, cause distress for you both?'

The heavy breathing was replaced by a cold anger. He told her he had nothing else to add.

'If Miss Bale does contact you again, I would be grateful if you could let us know. As I said, we are concerned about her and we want to find out where she is.'

'I doubt she will try and contact me again, Detective Travis, but if she does, I will tell you.'

He ended the call. Anna held the receiver in her hand, hearing the dead tone and she slowly hung up.

It had been Anna's idea, to contact Jeannie Bale's theatrical agent and ask her to pull a fast one on Jeannie, tell her that she was up for a big part and that the producer wanted to meet her. She and Felicity must have done a runner, taking Delany's five thousand in cash. Two of the flatmates were dead. Jeannie could be the next.

It was almost 6 p.m. that evening when Anna met with Sylvia Brandon and her assistant Kevin. Their office was in Chiswick, one room cluttered with posters and files and hundreds of photographs stacked in bunches on the floor. Sylvia Brandon was a plump, blonde woman in her late fifties, wearing heavy make-up and a flowing black wool dress. Her assistant, Kevin, wore bright red trainers that almost matched the extraordinary colour of his gelled hair.

'We've been shocked about Amanda Delany and we know they used to live together, but we've not heard from Jeannie for a week or so.' Kevin had a Newcastle accent and a lisp while Sylvia's voice was deep, loud and theatrical.

'Do you have Jeannie's mobile phone number?' Anna asked. 'She calls in on a regular basis, doesn't she?'

Kevin opened a thick file and started to thumb through it. 'Yes, but she hasn't for a while as things have been very slow.'

He found the page on Jeannie Bale. 'She's also got a message service, but I don't know about these numbers. Sylvia, have a look, would you, darling?'

Sylvia put on a pair of glasses with bright green frames.

Anna was getting impatient. 'We really need to talk to her, but she's no longer living at her flat. I would also like any contact numbers for people that you think know her.'

She then plunged into suggesting her ploy to catch Jeannie's attention.

The couple obviously loved the intrigue and started discussing what work they could say had been offered.

'You know the fringe play she went up for, Kevin?' Sylvia took off her glasses. 'It was a very good part. What if we were to leave a message for her to say they wanted to see her again because the actress they had cast was no longer available?'

'That's a good idea. She was very disappointed when she lost out on that one.'

'Kevin, you start calling, dear, and see what happens.'

'You'll also have to give her a time and location,' Anna added.

Kevin started making the calls. The only number that connected was the landline at the Maida Vale flat and it went onto the the message service. Kevin covered the receiver with his hand and had a moment of panic; he couldn't remember the theatre or the director's name.

'Tricycle Theatre in Kilburn and . . .' On went the green-framed glasses as Sylvia ran her chipped nail-varnished finger down the pages. 'Kim Mantley or Montgomery, I can't read my own writing. Here, Kevin, you look and tell me what his name is.'

Anna wondered how the pair of them ever found their clients any work, they were so inept and their office was such a tip. Kevin eventually redialled and in a posh voice said that Jeannie should call in as soon as possible and explained the job situation.

'Was that all right?' he said to Anna when he finished.

It wasn't, as he had forgotten to give the time and urgency of the proposed job, but rather than let him make yet another call, Anna nodded. Doubtful that it would work, she gave Kevin her direct line and said that he should contact her any time, day or night, if he did get a return call from Jeannie.

'If she phones in, what do I say?'

Anna could see the pair of them thinking themselves into a Miss Marple story. She made it very simple: if they did get a response, they should give Jeannie a time to be at the theatre and make sure there was also enough time for the police to be waiting for the girl when she turned up.

Anna reported back to Barolli with a few names of people that Sylvia and Kevin thought Jeannie knew; they didn't consider anyone they had on their books as a close friend of hers. She made him laugh as she described the pair of them cooking up the false job offer. She gave him the list of Jeannie's old numbers, two mobiles, the flat landline and the message service.

'They left a message on the landline as well, just in case she returns to the flat.'

'She won't have much luck getting in, if she goes back there.' The landlord had changed the locks, but they nevertheless retained surveillance on the place in case she reappeared.

'I'm just collecting my car from the garage, then I'm going off home. See you in the morning,' Anna said.

'Yeah, I'm taking off soon.'

Anna was paying off the taxi outside the garage when her phone rang. It was Barolli.

'Fucking hell, he's only bloody walked in – been in reception for ten minutes.'

'Who – *who*?'

'Lester James. They're bringing him up now, so get your arse back here and fast!'

Chapter Twenty-One

'What do you make of him?' Anna asked Barolli when she got back to the station.

Barolli shrugged. Lester James had come in of his own free will, and was sitting in the interview room, talking to his solicitor.

'He appears very calm and keen to be interviewed, to clear up any queries. He's obviously spoken with both his brothers, which was why he felt that he should have representation. They must have told him why we're looking for him.'

Anna sat with Barolli, going over the files and statements. Langton felt the interview should be relaxed. Rather than put too much pressure on him, they needed to find out just how much a suspect Lester James was, so it was imperative they get his movements on the night of the murder. They needed witnesses, corroborating evidence and details, and not until they had heard his side of events were they to infer he was in the frame for the murder.

'But he is, isn't he?' Barolli said to Mike Lewis.

'He's all we've fucking got, but if his alibi works out we're back to square one, unless we can trip him up.'

'So who's in with him?' Anna asked.

'You and Barolli. Langton wants you to lead it.'

'Do we bring up Felicity Turner and Dan Hutchins in this first round?'

'He says to hold off on them. Right now, both are down to "accidental deaths" and he wants to keep a softly, softly approach. If you get anything now, we hold him for further questioning.'

'And if we don't?' Anna asked quietly.

'He walks.'

Anna asked if Lester had turned up in his own car. Barolli said that a Mercedes was parked in the car park.

'Can we open it up and search it?'

'Not yet we can't,' said Barolli. 'Unless it's unlocked or hasn't got permission to be parked in the station yard.'

'Maybe just ask him if we can,' Mike suggested.

Anna stood up. She doubted there would be any incriminating evidence at this stage as their suspect had had more than enough time to get it cleaned. She asked to have some strong coffee brought in and a sandwich.

'We're wasting time,' Mike Lewis snapped.

'Instructions are to keep it low profile, so let's offer him something to eat and coffee. I need some too. Right, let's get started.'

They headed towards the interview room.

Mike Lewis met Langton in the incident room and together they went into the viewing room to watch the interview on the monitor screen. Langton was uneasy about questioning their prime suspect without sufficient evidence to make any charges stick, but at the same time it was a major step forward. If Lester James was, as the team believed, their killer, Langton was certain both his brothers would have primed him and even concocted an

410

alibi for the night of the murder. He had been far from satisfied with the Accidental Death verdicts on the two flatmates. If, however, Lester could prove that he had been in Amsterdam, he could not have been involved in the death of Felicity Turner and they had no evidence that he could be implicated in Dan Hutchins's overdose. Now Langton would be able to watch him being interviewed and come to his own conclusion. Lester had already given his permission for his interrogation to be on video.

Langton sat forward as Anna and Barolli entered the incident room and he saw their suspect for the first time. Lester James sat well back in his chair, his broad shoulders almost touching the Legal Aid duty solicitor, who was a small dapper man. Beside him, Lester James looked as if he was twice his size. He wore a light grey suit with a black polo-neck sweater, and his big square hands were folded over each other, resting on the Formica tabletop. He was much better-looking than his brothers, with blond hair cut short in a crew cut, and wide-set bright blue eyes. There was a freshness to him. Like an athlete, he exuded fitness and, to Langton's mind, a calmness that surprised him.

Lester also surprised Anna. He smiled as she sat down, and seemed totally at ease.

She kicked off with a soft encouraging tone in her voice.

'You sometimes drove Miss Delany on a private basis, is that correct, Mr James?'

'Yes.'

'Could you just elaborate on that for us?'

Lester nodded and recounted numerous occasions

when he had driven Amanda to premières and nightclubs. He gave a fond laugh, saying that she was never ready, he always had to wait; she was a very bad timekeeper.

'So you would collect her from her flat in Maida Vale?'

'Yes.'

'Did you meet any of the other occupants?'

He said that he had met them and had once driven them with Amanda to a venue.

'They would be Felicity Turner, Dan Hutchins and Jeannie Bale?'

'That's right.'

Anna eased into asking if he also collected Amanda from her new house.

'Yes, after she moved in.'

'On one of these occasions when you drove Miss Delany, did you take her to the restaurant called Le Caprice for lunch?'

'Yeah, I believe I did. It's that place behind the Ritz, isn't it?'

Anna nodded. 'On this occasion, did she mention who she was dining with?'

He shrugged. 'No. I just waited outside until she came out.'

'When Miss Delany returned to your car, how did she appear to you?'

'I don't understand.'

'Was she in a good mood or a bad one?'

'Oh, I see. Well, she was very hyper, sort of excited, and she'd obviously had a few glasses of champagne.'

'So, being in such a good mood, did she tell you what the meeting had been about?'

'Not really.'

'Think about it, Mr James. She was, as you have said, very excited. Surely she must have told you the reason?'

'Er . . . she might have said something about a deal. I don't remember what it was exactly, it was some time ago.'

'Was it something to do with a publishing offer?'

He looked down at his big hands. 'It might have been.'

'So you were aware that Miss Delany was going to write a book? Her autobiography?'

Lester leaned towards his solicitor and they had a whispered conversation. After a moment he looked at Anna.

'She said something about it but, like I already said, she had been drinking so she sort of rambled on a bit.'

'Did she mention a diary to you?'

Lester shook his head. Anna had had enough. By his reaction, she knew that Lester had been told by Amanda at least about the publishing deal if not her diary and, not wanting to unnerve him, she switched the subject, asking how long he had known Amanda.

Lester said that he had met the young actress when she had starred in her first film and continued to see her on various other productions. He was not often part of the main team of unit drivers, but someone they brought in as an extra and, because his brothers were well-known, they often got the work. He wasn't one of the official drivers on *Gaslight*, however, as there were only a few stars and a small cast.

'Did you like Miss Delany?'

His face took on an odd expression. 'Yes, she was a really nice person, very kind.'

'Did she ever come onto you?'

His blue eyes met Anna's and held them.

'No,' he said neutrally. 'I was just her driver.'

'But she was very promiscuous, wasn't she?'

'She was her own person and she could do what she liked.'

Barolli took over. 'You want to tell us about the night just before she was killed? You were hired to drive Colin O'Dell and Scott Myers, right?'

Lester nodded and whispered to his solicitor again. The latter established that his client did drive the two people mentioned, but for their sake, under client privilege, he did not wish to discuss it.

Barolli went in more strongly. As they had already interviewed both men, all they wanted was confirmation from Mr James that he did collect them from the mews house.

'Yes, I picked them up. I dropped one at a taxi rank and the other at Heathrow.'

'Clients' so-called privilege doesn't mean squat, does it, so please tell us about that evening.'

Lester straightened his massive shoulders.

'They were both out of it, drugged up or drunk. I was worried they'd throw up in the back seat.'

It must have pissed him off, Barolli observed, having to listen to the two of them talk about their sexual antics with Amanda Delany.

Lester leaned forward and said clearly, 'I'm just a driver, pal. What they talked about was no business of mine. See, hear, speak no evil – that's the code.'

'But for you, hearing about it must have really upset you.'

Lester sat back in his chair, the picture of self-control.

'Like I just said, it was no business of mine what they got up to.'

Anna now went for it.

'Come on, Lester, it must have really got to you because I think you felt a lot more for Amanda than just being her driver. I think, in fact, that you were obsessed by her. I also think that hearing them talking about her that way must have made you pig-sick.'

'*No*. What you're trying to infer is bullshit.'

Barolli brought out the photographs of the karate weapons they had found in his flat and laid them out in front of Lester.

'We found these weapons in your flat, Mr James. What have you got to say about them?'

'You had no right to take them,' Lester said steadily. 'They're for exhibitions, and I'm not going to be victimised because I own them. I use them in karate shows and you can't make out anything against me for having them. I've even got videos of me using them at Crystal Palace.'

Anna moved the pictures around the table.

'Amanda Delany was murdered by a weapon that was very possibly one of these types. She was stabbed repeatedly.'

She produced a photograph of Amanda taken at the mortuary, showing the stab wounds slashed across her naked body.

'Somebody did this to her, Lester. Look at her. Whoever did this didn't want to hurt her face. Look at the photographs, Mr James . . .'

Lester turned away as his solicitor drew the photograph towards him and glanced at it. He tapped Lester's arm and yet again they had a whispered conversation.

415

'My client denies that he had anything to do with this tragic event. I suggest that if you have any evidence that implicates Mr James, you make it a priority right now or I am advising my client to leave. You should have allowed me to view any photographs in my pre-interview disclosure. If my client is not under arrest, I will as from now warn him not to answer any further questions.'

Anna said quietly that they were not yet ready to end the interview and she asked Mr James to continue answering their questions.

'I reckon I've answered all I need to. I'm not stupid and I know what you are trying to make me out to be, but you have got it wrong.'

'We may have, so if you could just clear up a few more loose ends . . .'

Lester having admitted meeting Amanda's flatmates, Anna asked again if he had known all three at some time or other. Lester became less anxious and agreed that he had met them several times, and had also been in their flat. Anna turned the pages in her file.

'So you were aware that Dan Hutchins was a heroin addict?'

Lester nodded.

'You were also, I suspect, aware that Amanda used cocaine and crack cocaine and speed, and often took amphetamines and Ecstasy.'

'I knew. So what?'

'As her driver, you must be able to give us the name of her supplier?'

'No.'

'Come on, we know you were scoring the drugs for her, Lester.'

His solicitor jumped up and again angrily accused them of not submitting disclosure of these allegations. Lester turned and gestured for him to sit down.

'It's all right. I never supplied nothing. It's a lie.'

'Is it?' Anna persisted. 'You supplemented your earnings by supplying drugs. You would do anything she wanted, wouldn't you?'

'No.'

'How many times did you go into her mews house?'

'I never went in, I was just her driver.'

'We have your fingerprints, Lester; we know you were inside her mews. Why are you lying?'

'Jesus Christ, I am being set up here because I never done the drugs for her and . . . maybe I went into the house once, like when she first moved in, but I was always just her driver.'

'Did you have a key?'

'What?'

'To her house. Did you have a key, Mr James?'

'No, like I keep on saying to you, I was just her driver. I picked her up and I dropped her back at her place. That was my job.'

Barolli glanced at Anna and she gave a small nod as he began picking up the photographs and replacing them into the file.

'Can I go home now?'

'Just a few more things, Mr James,' Anna said softly.

Lester hung his head down as if he was tired.

'Do you recall seeing a fluffy toy rabbit? It was Miss Delany's favourite thing and she always went to sleep with it.'

Lester sighed. He wouldn't have known what she slept with, he said, as he was just her driver.

'Didn't she take it with her at all? Are you saying you never saw this rabbit?'

'No, I never saw nothing that she went to bed with. All I know is, she was an insomniac and would do anything to stave off going to sleep.'

'So she talked about that, did she?'

'Yeah. She also said she was scared of the dark. What people don't know is that she was really very vulnerable and had a lot of pent-up anger, especially towards her parents.'

'Did she ever tell you why she was angry with them?'

'No.'

'But she told you she was scared of the dark?'

'Yeah.'

'Did you ever sleep with her?'

Again, Lester stared at Anna with an unflinching, cold look.

'I was her driver, nothing more.'

'Did you want more?'

'She paid me for driving her.'

In the viewing room, Langton drummed his fingers on the table with impatience. They were getting nowhere. He turned to Mike.

'He said he did competition displays for karate, the knife collection – mentioned a video. Did anyone bring it in?'

Mike shook his head.

'I want to see it, and I want access to his bank accounts,' Langton said.

'What do you think?' Mike Lewis asked quietly, gesturing at the monitor screen.

'I'd say his brothers primed him, and unless we get

something that'll shift him, we've not got enough to hold him. In some ways he bloody jumped the gun by coming in of his own free will. I'd say we're losing out with him.'

It felt like that to Anna and Barolli. They were now requesting that Lester bring in confirmation of his invoices for work driving on the film units, as well as his private hire. He became belligerent; a lot of his work was cash in hand and he didn't have complete records. Barolli warned him they could inform the Inland Revenue. When Anna asked Lester for more details of how often he had met Amanda's flatmates, he was adamant that he had only met them on a few occasions.

'What about Jeannie Bale?'

'What about her? I said I met them through Miss Delany, but I had nothing else to do with them.'

'When was the last time you saw Miss Bale?'

'I dunno. Weeks ago? Like I said, I only met them when I was driving for Miss Delany. I never saw them socially and, to be honest, I wouldn't want to. The kid was a junkie and the other two were hangers-on.'

'Are you aware that Dan Hutchins is dead?' Anna asked.

Lester nodded. He had read it in the papers.

'Felicity Turner is also dead. Did you know that?'

Again, he said that he had read about her in the newspaper.

'But you were in Amsterdam, weren't you?'

He paused for a fraction, then said that he read British newspapers over there, which is where he had seen the report.

'We will need, Mr James, confirmation of when you left Amsterdam and returned to London.'

'I bought me ticket and I dunno if I've got anything else to prove it. They don't stamp passports any more.'

'Where was your car while you were away?'

'I left it in a mate's garage.'

'We'll also need to know when you left your vehicle and when you collected it.'

Lester gave a name and address to his solicitor.

'Why did you go to Amsterdam?' Anna asked.

'I got friends there.'

'We'll need their names and addresses.'

His solicitor made a note.

'On what date did you return to London?'

He said that he had only just returned the previous day. As soon as he knew they wanted to speak to him, he had, as was obvious, come into the station.

'And you claim you never saw a diary – Miss Delany's diary? It had a pink cover.'

'No, I never saw it.'

'Take us through the time when you last drove Miss Delany to her flat in Maida Vale. She had an important meeting?'

Lester blinked as if trying to recall the day. Anna repeated the date and he eventually concurred that he had driven her to the flat and waited outside for about an hour and a half.

'Did you see anyone enter the flat while she was there?'

'Yeah, some bloke drove up in a Porsche and went in.'

'Can you describe him?'

Lester gave a pretty good description of Josh Lyons, but could not recall if, when he left, he carried anything with him apart from the briefcase he went in with.

'How did Miss Delany appear to you when she came out after the meeting?'

'She was just like always. I drove her home, but she didn't talk much as she was texting somebody on her BlackBerry.'

Anna passed a note to Barolli; they had numerous mentions of Amanda's BlackBerry but still had not found one. They had already attempted to trace which phone company she used in the hope that they might be able to retrieve her account, which would list all her numbers, but so far had had no luck. Suddenly, Lester tapped the table.

'I just remembered. She said to me that she'd lost it — the diary — maybe left it on the film set or in her trailer. Yeah, she asked me if I'd found it in the Merc — maybe she'd dropped it.'

At last there was just a glimmer of hope. They knew that Amanda had left her mobile phone on the film set because the extra had handed it into them.

'So she asked you if you had found it in your car?'

'Yeah.'

'When exactly was this?'

'Few days after that meeting you asked me about.'

'When she was filming *Gaslight*?'

'Yeah, she asked me about it then.'

'At the film unit.'

'Yeah.'

Barolli jumped in fast. 'But you told us that you weren't one of the drivers connected to that specific film unit, so why were you there?'

They got just a small glint of hesitancy from Lester, but then he spread his hands wide.

'I popped in for a free dinner to talk to me brothers.'

'When was this?'

Again, there was just a slither of nerves and he cracked his knuckles.

'Be the night before her murder, I reckon.'

'Did you go into her trailer?'

He nodded and added that he looked over her trailer for her, just in case she'd dropped the diary somewhere and it was hidden under cushions.

'Was she in there when you were doing this?'

'No, she was called onto the film set.'

'Leaving you alone in her trailer?'

'That's right.'

'But you were just her driver; did you usually go into her trailer?'

He shifted his weight on the chair.

'On the odd occasion. That time she was very agitated. She told me she'd had this nightmare the night before, heard a woman screaming. It had woken her up and she didn't know whether or not it was an animal, but it had frightened her.'

'This would be the night before she was murdered?'

He nodded. They waited but he kept silent. His solicitor looked at him and then back to Anna and Barolli.

'Can I just get this right, Lester?' Anna asked. 'You weren't working for the film unit, you went there for a free dinner, correct?'

'Yeah, I often do that.'

'On this particular night, Miss Delany told you about her nightmare, the scream, and you said she was very anxious, correct?'

'Yes, that's right.'

'What did you do about it?'

'Nothing, I didn't do nothing. She went back on the set and I left. Ask my brothers, they'll tell you I left.'

'And you never saw her again?'

'No.'

Anna tried again, sounding him out about his karate expertise and the fact that he often worked as a body-guard. She asked him if he had tried to calm Amanda down, perhaps offering to check out the mews house for her.

'No, I did not. Ask me brothers. I left and went home.'

Langton had also had a moment of excitement; perhaps they had found a chink. He suspected that the killer could have been inside her mews house; had Lester gone to check the place out? If he had, he would have had a key to let himself in. But the moment passed and Langton kicked back his chair as Anna and Barolli agreed to release Lester. They warned him that he might be needed for further questioning and that he was not to leave the country. In the meantime, they would check out his alibis and contact all the people whose names and addresses he had supplied both in England and Amsterdam.

It was a depressed foursome that met in Mike Lewis's office. It was now 11 p.m. Langton was in a foul mood, snapping out instructions for them to concentrate on gathering as much evidence as possible. His gut feeling was that, contrary to what Lester had said, he did go to Amanda's house; maybe to check it out for their victim, which would mean he had a front-door key. He also felt that the brothers were covering up the fact that they used him to drive Amanda, either on the night of her murder or on the previous night. He wanted them brought back in for questioning.

'He's told us a lot of bullshit in my opinion, and it's your job to break it down. Get another warrant issued; get his car stripped and get hold of that video he said he made doing his karate exhibitions. You want his bank statements and you want to put pressure on him from every angle.'

'He's hard to budge,' Barolli said, describing how Lester had made direct eye-contact at all the most relevant moments, never wavering.

Lester was a 7th Dan Karate master, Langton snapped back. Control was uppermost in their training, but he had seen him hesitate twice. He wanted him brought back, and to do that, they needed hard evidence. Langton walked into the incident room, beckoning for them to join him at the board.

'OK. One, get his alibi sorted. Stag-night party, talk to them. If they were all pissed out of their heads, they probably wouldn't know what time they came or went anywhere, never mind who's driving them. Two, find this bloody missing woman, Jeannie Bale. Step up the possibility that those two other flatmates were murdered. I want both their deaths treated as suspicious and linked to the enquiry. Three, Lester's dealing drugs, I'd put my own money on it. If needs be, get over to Amsterdam and talk to these people he says he stayed with, get onto the airline security, show them his picture, find out when he returned to the UK, check his mobile details again, check what calls he made from Amsterdam and when he was back here in the UK. Open up his bank accounts, find out what money he's been stashing and check out this missing BlackBerry of Amanda's. Go through her accounts and get her accountant back in.'

He looked at Anna and wagged his finger.

'I dunno about this agent your missing girl's supposed to call. I think it's crass that you've got them leaving messages for her with some bogus part. She's out there somewhere and with this fucking diary that she reckons is going to make her fortune. Maybe she isn't interested in doing any more acting. Keep on the publisher, he's got the money she's after. Go to press on her again, I want her found.'

'How important do you think this diary is?' Barolli asked.

Langton ruffled his hair until it stood up on end.

'Who knows? It could be full of shit or it could be putting our prime suspect right in it. If that's the case, it's crucial we find the stupid bitch. Lester James is a karate expert. I think he is very dangerous and some things he said just don't add up. He'll want to get his hands on this diary if it does contain details that would implicate him, unless . . .'

He paused, then turned to the board.

'I know the guys are getting red eye from scouring the CCTV footage, but they've got to go over and over it, and the security footage from the other property. The killer went into that mews, stabbed our victim and walked out. He's got to be caught somewhere and we could just be missing it.'

He held up his hand as if he was stopping traffic.

'I've already arranged surveillance on Lester James. They were on his butt the moment he left the station. We have to get a result soon. I'm not pointing the finger at any of you, but you need to step up the hunt because we've got little time to keep an investigation of this size

425

ongoing, understand me? And I don't want to run out of time.'

He said a brusque goodnight and walked out, leaving them all feeling very down.

'OK, get some shut-eye and we go at it again in the morning.'

Mike was next to leave. Anna looked at Barolli.

'Well, we tried our best.'

'Yeah, it just wasn't good enough. But I dunno if we could have pushed him further. The boss didn't want us to go in too hard, remember?'

Anna gave a nonchalant shrug.

'Next time, let's see how *he* would do it,' Barolli went on. 'He's all over this case like a rash, while we run around like headless chickens.'

'Well, I didn't like the way he implied that the agent scenario I've set up is a waste of time. At least I'm trying. Every other avenue has failed to produce her.'

'Unless she's dead too,' Barolli said quietly.

Chapter Twenty-Two

Seventh Dan or not, Lester James was far from co-operative when Barolli and two officers woke him up at seven o'clock the following morning. When they showed him the search warrant, he accused them of harassment. They had already searched his place, he shouted, and he was not going to allow them to enter. If he didn't move out of their way, Barolli warned him, they would have to arrest him, so, swearing under his breath, he kicked his front door open wider.

Barbara and Joan began checking the list of names and addresses that Lester had supplied. Mike Lewis was putting pressure on the officers assigned to the CCTV footage and they were becoming belligerent; they had been closeted with the tapes for days and still had nothing new to add. Mike also put out for another round of door-to-door enquiries in and around the mews. Amanda's accountant was bringing in all the details she had of her previous accounts, including telephone bills and mobile phone accounts. Harry and Tony James were coming to the station for further questioning that after-noon. They had been asked to bring in their driving ledgers for the work done on *Gaslight*. The production company had also been contacted for details of the payments to the unit drivers.

It was hours of tedious work, gathering information and tracking down the individuals. It took half an hour, for instance, to confirm that Lester James had indeed, as he had stated, left his car in a friend's garage. When they finally managed to contact the friend, he said that he'd given Lester a key and let him come and go as he pleased. His car may have been parked for the dates in question, he thought, but he couldn't be absolutely sure as he had been away on business, and the garage was out of sight, round the corner from the house.

Anna was in her office fending one call after another and having real problems with the Amsterdam numbers. They were either engaged or no longer connected. It was looking likely that someone, she hoped not her, would have to travel over there. They still had no confirmation that any drug dealer known to them had met with Lester James, but were still making enquiries.

Josh Lyons was now settled in his new office complex and calming down from the upheaval of moving, but had still not been contacted by Jeannie Bale. Nor had the service used by Jeannie to pick up her hoped-for messages about auditions had any recent contact from her. Her agent had still not heard from her. Anna's concern for Jeannie's safety was mounting. No sighting and no contact for almost a week; even after the press requests for her to come forward, they had heard nothing.

It was now nine-thirty. Returning to her office, Anna put in yet another call to a number for a Rick 'Skull' Matheson, one of the names on Lester James's list. This time her call was answered, and by a throaty, growling male voice.

'Skull's Ink.'

'Mr Matheson?' she asked.

'This is him,' the thick voice replied. It turned out that 'Skull's Ink' was a well-known tattoo parlour in Amsterdam run by Matheson, who was originally from Huddersfield. Anna explained who she was and that she was making enquiries regarding his association with Lester James.

'Association?'

'I believe you know him?'

'I wouldn't say that, but I done work on him.'

It was over a week ago since Matheson had seen Lester; he'd wanted some part of his tattoo filled in. Anna learned that Lester had been a regular customer.

Before she could ask Matheson where the tattoo was, Joan knocked and entered; there was a call for Anna on line two. Anna thanked Matheson, made a note of the date Lester had last been in his parlour and switched lines. It was Jeannie Bale's agent Sylvia, breathless in her eagerness to talk to Anna.

'She just called in. I couldn't believe it, she just called in! I was having my breakfast and I didn't expect her to ring at that time and I got all flustered because you told me to tape it and I was in the kitchen, so I didn't have my machine there.'

Anna told her to take a deep breath, and then repeat the exact details of the conversation.

'I said "hello", and she said, "Sylvia, it's Jeannie, I just called my message service".'

Anna listened.

'I tried to keep calm. I told her we'd been hoping she'd call in, and that we'd left a message on her service about the audition at midday today, and she swore –

"Oh shit" or something like that. She didn't think she'd be able to make it on time. I got very nervous as I know you want to talk to her.'

'Where was she calling from?'

'I don't know where, but I did redial so I've got the number.'

'Sylvia, did she say she wouldn't go to the audition?'

'No, she said she couldn't make that time, so I said I would talk to the producer and see if he could change it. I stressed that it was a hurried recall and she might lose out again, but she said it was impossible for her to get to the theatre until about tea-time. I said I would call her back after I'd spoken to the producer to see if he could see her this afternoon. When I asked for the number she was calling from, she said she'd call in again later. She wouldn't give it to me.'

'What happened when you dialled the number?' Anna asked.

'It rang and there was no answer.'

As Anna jotted down the number, Sylvia asked what she should do next when Jeannie called back. Anna asked her to hold on while she checked out the location of the phone number.

'But what if she calls and I'm engaged?'

'I won't be long.'

Joan was quickly back with the information as Anna put Sylvia on hold.

'It's from a call box in Bristol.'

Anna asked her to arrange a patrol car to stand by.

'OK, Sylvia. When she calls back, give her a four o'clock audition at the theatre to give her enough time to get there. It's only just over an hour and a half by train to Paddington, and then it's a taxi ride to Kilburn High

Road. Don't let on that you know where she is – act like she's still in London.'

'Right, yes, four o'clock at the Tricycle Theatre . . . Should I say I'll meet her there?'

'No, that will be taken care of. You don't usually meet her at her auditions, do you?'

'No, but what if she doesn't call back?'

'I think she will. Stay calm, Sylvia, and don't give anything away, will you?'

'I was an actress, you know, before I became an agent.'

Anna raised her eyes to the ceiling.

'Ah yes, I thought you might have been, so I am depending on you, Sylvia. We really need to talk to Jeannie.'

Her heart was thudding when she replaced the receiver. So much for Langton and his dismissive response to her plan to ensnare Jeannie.

After two hours of waiting and still no call, however, Anna's confidence that she had pulled it off was lessening. At 12.45, Barolli returned from Lester James's flat, and went straight into Anna's office, bearing the video of Lester's showcase at Crystal Palace.

'We got this video, but bugger all else. If he had the hots for Amanda Delany, wouldn't you think he'd have photographs of her, magazine pictures, but there's nothing.'

Just as they were about to slot the video into the machine in the monitor room, Joan interrupted. There was another call from Sylvia. Jeannie had called her back and agreed to be at the audition for 4 p.m.

Anna and Barolli sped across London in a patrol car and parked up in a side street a few yards from the Tricycle

Theatre, from where they were able to monitor the coming and goings through theatre reception.

'What time do you have?'

Anna smiled. Barolli had checked the time over and over again.

'Two-thirty. We just wait. From Bristol to here takes nearly a couple of hours by train.'

'Busy theatre, isn't it?'

'Yeah, they do great shows.' Anna looked at her watch, and then at the clock on the dashboard. The waiting was now getting to her as much as Barolli.

Josh Lyons was eating a Chinese takeaway lunch at his desk when his phone rang. He wiped his hands with a paper napkin and picked it up.

'Josh, you said to put her straight through if she called.'

'Who?'

'Jeannie Bale – the diary girl. Want to speak to her?'

'Christ, yes!' He took a gulp of his Starbucks coffee, and waited.

'Mr Lyons?'

'Speaking.'

'It's Jeannie Bale. I'm back in London.'

Lyons kept it casual, asking if she'd been on a holiday. She laughed, then said in a singsong voice, 'I've got the diary, I've got the diary.'

'Have you? What do you want me to do about it?'

'Gimme a price. How much is it worth to you?'

'Well, Miss Bale, I'd have to take a look at it. Why don't you come in and talk to me about it?'

'OK. I got an appointment at four o'clock not far from you.'

'I've moved offices, my dear. Let me give you the new address. What time can you get here? We're in St John's Wood.'

She said she would get to him as soon as she'd finished an audition.

'You'll bring the diary with you?'

'Yeah, but we have to talk money, right?'

'Can you give me a contact number?'

'No. I'll see you later.'

Before he could say anything else she'd hung up. He wouldn't talk to Skidmore, he'd make the decision about the diary himself. And also, if it was worth diddlysquat, he'd be a helpful citizen and call Detective Travis.

At ten to four, Barolli and Anna moved from the patrol car and walked across the street. Barolli went to the theatre reception and Anna, with a radio contact, stood a short distance up the road from the theatre's advertisements. When Jeannie arrived, Barolli would make his approach from the front and Anna from the rear.

It was ten past four, still no show. Anna walked down a small alley by the side of the theatre, fearful that there might be another stage door. There wasn't. Then, just as she was heading back up the alley, she saw a cab draw up. Jeannie got out, wearing her black dress with big mutton-chop sleeves and full skirt down to her ankles with black cowboy boots. Her blonde hair looked as if she had dyed it a shade lighter; it was caught up on either side of her face with bright pink butterfly grips. Anna radioed Barolli.

'On her way into the theatre, wearing black, pink hair-slides and I'm right behind her.'

Jeannie, carrying a large leather bag in her hand and another over her shoulder, walked into the theatre after paying off the taxi.

'Miss Bale, Jeannie Bale?' Barolli showed her his ID and she froze, stepping back as Anna took her arm. She put up little resistance and seemed more concerned that she would miss her audition. Anna took her leather bag, and put one hand on Jeannie's elbow, Barolli at her other side. Jeannie became more frightened than obstreperous, and asked where they were taking her, what had she done?

'You not read the papers, love?' Barolli steered her towards the patrol car. Anna got into the front seat; he sat with Jeannie in the back as the driver pulled out into the main road, heading for the station.

'I've not done anything.'

'We just need you to answer some questions,' Barolli said calmly, not wanting to unnerve her. Jeannie sat back, biting her nails, and then caught Anna's eye in the rearview mirror.

'I was up for a big part. You just ruined it.'

Anna turned to her and said that there was no part; they had been trying to contact her for days.

'I don't fucking believe it! You're telling me there *was* no audition?'

'That's right. We had to do what we could to trace you. We've been very concerned about you.'

'I've not done anything, you've got no right to trick me like this. My agent was in on it, was she?'

'Where've you been, Jeannie?'

'I got a commercial.'

'How come your agent didn't know about it?'

''Cos that silly bitch couldn't get me a job. I got it for myself, I was in Bristol.'

'Why haven't you come forward? It's been in the papers and—'

'I was working, OK?'

'Fine.' Anna stared out of the window. She found Jeannie's patchouli-oil perfume sickening. She was tempted to tip out the contents of the bag she was holding there and then, but knew she would have to wait.

Josh Lyons waited, and when it got to after five-thirty he began to get impatient, wondering where Jeannie Bale was. He could hardly voice his irritation to anyone else, as he had told no one about her proposed visit.

Jeannie was taken into the station and led to an interview room for questioning about the death of Felicity Turner and the murder of Amanda Delany. Her leather bag was placed on a table in front of her. Anna was surprised how little emotion Jeannie showed over Felicity's death; she only became tearful when they began to take out and make a note of all the items in her bag. There was a Ziploc bag full of dirty panties, two rather grey brassières, hairspray and make-up, then, wrapped in a brown paper bag, a pink diary. Its lock had been broken and its pink velvet cover was filthy. On the front of it, written in smudged black felt-tipped pen, was the name Amanda Delany. Jeannie sat stony-faced. She turned away when they showed her the diary.

'I ain't done nothing,' she said angrily.

Anna held up the diary.

'Yes, you have, Jeannie. You have withheld evidence,

you have perverted the course of justice and that is an offence, one that could, if it went to trial, put you in prison.'

'But I ain't done nothing! It was in me flat, you can't get me for having it.'

Barolli notified Jeannie that she was entitled to a solicitor to be present at the interview. As he and Anna removed items from her shoulder bag – her mobile phone and a wallet containing a substantial amount of cash, Amanda Delany's BlackBerry in a leather case – Jeannie began to realise the seriousness of her situation. The Duty Sergeant was brought in to list all the items and, seeing a uniformed officer, Jeannie started to panic.

'You are in possession of stolen items, Miss Bale,' Barolli informed her. 'This BlackBerry belongs to Amanda Delany.'

'Oh fuck, she left it at the flat and I was gonna give it back, but then she died. I never nicked it, and I couldn't use it 'cos it's locked or somethin'.'

Mike Lewis was interviewing Amanda Delany's accountant, Ronnie Hodgson, who had brought in various backdated files. Amongst the papers was the account for the BlackBerry service, but as the BlackBerry was now in their possession, they would be able to access the calls and text messages made shortly before her death. It was usual that anyone using a BlackBerry would have it connected to a computer, but Amanda's laptop did not contain any such file. They now needed to find out if she might have used another computer.

Harry and Anthony James were brought in for questioning late that afternoon. Mike Lewis interviewed an

agitated Harry, who repeated over and over again that
he had nothing to add to his previous statements. He
brought with him a detailed dossier of the unit drivers'
times, pick-ups and collections. The names of the drivers
who had picked up Amanda for filming on the days
and nights before her murder were all noted; they were
either Harry himself, or his brother Tony. On the night
of her murder, Harry had been her driver, on the previous night, Tony. He denied that Lester had ever driven
Amanda during the filming of *Gaslight*. Mike asked if
Lester had turned up to eat at the unit caterers.

'Free dinner? Yeah, now I come to think about it, he
did come to the set that evening. I just forgot.'

'This would be the night before her murder. Did you
see him enter Amanda Delany's trailer that night?'

'No, he wouldn't do that.'

'He's admitted it.'

'Oh well, then he did. She must have asked to see him
because we never go near the artists' trailers – we're just
the drivers.'

'This would be the day after Miss Delany had heard
screams in the night and woken up frightened. Apparently she told everyone about it.'

'Yeah, she did, but nobody took much notice.'

'Maybe your brother Lester did?'

Harry became evasive, saying that even if Lester had,
there was nothing he could have done about it as she was
working on the night shoot. Harry had driven her home
that night. He was certain that Lester had left long before
Amanda was released for the evening.

The two older brothers had virtually the same spiel, still
refusing to admit that Lester could have been involved.

They both denied that he had driven Amanda on any of the night filming schedules, and continued to refute that there was any kind of relationship between him and Amanda Delany. In fact, Anthony eventually became truculent, accusing them of harassing the three of them. He was 100 per cent certain, he said adamantly, that his brother Lester wouldn't have harmed Amanda.

'Why are you so certain?' Mike Lewis asked.

''Cos I know. It'd be more than his job's worth. We're just drivers,' was the now familiar mantra.

The two James brothers were released and by 8 p.m. the team at last got their hands on the photocopied pages of the diary. As time was against them, they split the entries between Barolli and Anna, Joan and Barbara. The four of them were grouped in the incident room so that they could pass any significant information straight over to Anna, who was making notes.

Barbara was the first to initiate a break.

'I've got something. It's hard to decipher but it's to do with her stay at her parents' house in France.'

In her barely legible, childish scrawl, Amanda had written that while visiting her parents, she had gone to see someone she described as 'the creeper'. She wrote that she had wanted to make him crawl; she was old enough now to deal with his sick attentions. She had sat on his knee and allowed him to fondle her breasts until he was begging her to take off her clothes.

Anna asked if 'the creeper' had a name. Was it her father? Barbara thought not, as the diary revealed that she had kicked him so hard between his legs he had howled in anguish and she had run to her father with her shirt torn, screaming that he had done it again.

'Hang on a moment. Here we go.' Barbara read aloud. '"*This time he believed me, and he said I was to go to my bedroom and he would make sure Grandpa never touched me again*".'

The next day she had flown back to London. She added that her father had not given her any money.

Barolli was next to put up his hand.

'She's using just initials, but I've got quite a lot of references to LJ. It's got to be Lester James.'

He quoted an entry: '"*LJ stayed over and brought the goods. He said it was high quality, and we would cut it with something and make more money*". Next entry says she has been sick, nothing else, then two more entries about feeling ill, and LJ went to get a pregnancy test.'

He held up two blank pages, blank apart from one word underlined: *positive.*

'Could be a reference to her being pregnant. Anything else?' Anna asked.

Barolli read out how LJ had no money so she went back to France.

'"*I told Daddy that I was pregnant, and he would have to pay for me to have an abortion. I said that if he didn't, the baby could be deformed as he knew why, and he slapped me. I spat at him and called him a piece of shit, but he refused to believe 'the creeper' had got me pregnant*".'

Anna interrupted. 'Hang on. This LJ gets her pregnant and she's telling her father that it was as a result of her grandfather's assault on her?'

Joan was next up with detailed pages describing how Amanda had tried to find someone who could help

439

her. By now Amanda had to be at least four months' pregnant. She read out a short scrawled page.

'"*LJ drove me to the Asian, and it was done. I felt really sick but he was terrific, he carried me back to the car and drove me home*".'

Mike Lewis looked up from his pages.

'Christ, she put it about. There's hardly a night she's not screwing someone or other. She keeps up the reference to LJ and now I've got random numbers. It could be money, there's no pound sign next to the numbers, but they're five hundred, two hundred, eighty . . . on every page.'

'You think she was dealing drugs?' Anna asked.

'Not enough money. I'd say she was supplying to her friends. She's even got down Colin O'Dell owing her two grand, so . . .'

They ploughed on. The diary made sickening reading, veering between childlike tittle-tattle about some of the actresses to lists of male stars with ticks beside them. Sometimes she had noted ten out of ten scores for their sexual prowess. The initials LJ featured constantly, picking her up, driving her home and then getting a blow job as thanks. It was relentless and sordid.

'She was going down on every man she met!' Barbara exclaimed.

Anna was getting a throbbing headache. She had the pages covering the last year of Amanda's life, which were mostly filled with work commitments; the girl seemed to be focusing strongly on her career. There were enthusiastic entries describing the new house, and long entries about its furniture and fittings, then an entry about being interviewed about *Gaslight*.

She wrote of her excitement at working with Rupert

Mitchell, how she couldn't wait to make his stuck-up bitch of a wife cry; she was going to fuck his brains out. There were a couple of abusive paragraphs about Fiona, Scott Myers's wife, and then a long, badly-written section about Scott's prowess in bed. There were some empty pages, no further references to LJ, then again figures of between two hundred to five hundred listed. Anna presumed it was drugs; sometimes there were initials beside them, but they were as haphazard as the writing. There was a reference to her agent and to money and then, underlined, the words *something is wrong*. Beneath that was a scrawled note about wanting a puppy.

Anna looked up. 'I'm almost done and I don't have any reference to LJ. Anyone got anything else?'

'It's hard to believe, isn't it?' Joan said. 'I mean, she's had more sex than I've had hot dinners. It's almost every night! I wouldn't have the energy, or to be honest the inclination. I mean, she seems to get her rocks off doing it in the back of the car.'

'Does she say who's driving?' Anna queried.

'No, but apparently Colin O'Dell has a very small dick!'

Barbara gave her a slap. 'Joan! Wash your mouth out!'

'I'm only telling you what I'm reading and, for your information, the most well-endowed is Scott Myers.'

Everyone turned as Langton walked in; he made a gesture of disbelief.

'What the fuck is going on?'

Mike explained.

'And it takes all of you to do it?'

'It's five years' worth, Guv, and we've come across a lot that we can use.'

Langton looked furious. 'Meanwhile, you've got that

girl waiting around. She's in with a solicitor, and I want her interviewed again as she might have vital information. Put pressure on her, put the fear of God into her, and tell her she'll be charged with perverting the course of justice and add blackmail to that.'

Barolli stood up. 'I'll go. I'm nearly through.'

Langton nodded and then looked at Mike, demanding, 'We got enough to arrest Lester James?'

'We've got the initials LJ all over the diary. We can only assume it has to be him. He was lying about not having sex with her; it looks like it was an ongoing scene for years.'

'We're also pretty certain he was dealing drugs,' Barbara added.

'"Pretty certain" isn't fucking good enough. Anna, get in with Barolli and see if you can make it more than just "pretty certain".'

Anna nodded, and she gathered sections of the diary, putting them into her briefcase with the notes. As she bent down, she felt a wave of nausea and had to sit back in her chair. Joan saw her face drain of colour and went to her side.

'You all right?'

'Yes, just got a bit dizzy.'

Langton slammed the door of Mike's office shut with the heel of his shoe.

'This is fuck-all use, Mike. I want a detailed report of what Lester James is doing. We have surveillance on our prime suspect that is costing. Have the guys called in?'

'Yes, sir. He's keeping quite a low profile, stays at home, goes to a gym early morning, then to a dojo in Marshall Street in the West End, but he's not doing much driving or work that we know of.'

'Let him see he's being tailed. I want to put pressure on him now, and if you are getting material we can use from the diary, specifically the last few weeks before her murder . . .'

'Travis is on that section.'

'Terrific, and she's in with Jeannie Bale.' Langton sighed and yanked open the door. 'Have you watched the video taken from Lester's flat?'

Mike looked confused.

'The film of his exhibition at Crystal Palace karate nights.'

Mike hesitated. 'I'll get onto it.'

'No – *I'll* do it, and then after that I'll be in the viewing room. Pull your finger out, Mike, and start fucking leading this enquiry.'

Mike sat at his desk, deflated and tired, as was everyone else. He found Langton impossible to deal with at times. He came in like a whirlwind and cast aspersions left, right and centre, even though they were all working round the clock with no weekend leave on the cards. He looked at his watch; it was already 10.15. He hadn't even had time to call home to tell his wife that he would be late yet again.

Langton banged out a chair after turning on the monitor; he looked up at the smoke alarm, wanting a cigarette, but knew it would go off if he lit up. Instead he opened a bottle of water and then leaned forward, concentrating on the DVD he'd inserted. He watched as Lester James took to the mat for an exhibition in martial arts weapons. Wearing a white Gi with a black belt, Lester bowed and, acknowledging his opponent, moved to the centre of the mat. The two man began a display of part karate and

443

part self-defence, each with a new weapon which was described by the narrator. Lester held them up from a tray carried by a young boy at the side of the mat. The crowds cheered. Langton fast-forwarded; it was starting to get tedious. Then he straightened, pressed reverse and froze the frame. Lester was strapping on a bodyguard's sheath knife and let it rest at his left side. His opponent attempted to attack him from the rear. Langton let the film wind on in slow motion as Lester did a fast half-turn, used his left arm to block, kicked the man's legs from under him and unsheathed the knife in one fluid movement to lean over him with the knife held to his neck.

The knife he was using for the demonstration was a six-inch blade with a handle and bridge, virtually identical to the one described by forensics as the possible murder weapon.

Mike whipped round as Langton barked out his name. Langton thrust the DVD at him, his face set with anger.

'Look at this – the section I've stopped the film at. Lester James is only fucking using a knife described by the pathologist and forensic as being the type of weapon used to kill Amanda Delany.'

Mike blinked. He flushed.

'I want it found, and I want Lester James arrested for the murder of Amanda Delany. Tonight, Mike. Bring the son of a bitch in.'

Chapter Twenty-Three

Jeannie sat with her hands in her lap, head bowed. Anna went for her.

'You have lied to me. You had to have had that diary in your possession when I was in your flat, interviewing you. Why did you lie?'

Jeannie mumbled that she didn't know it was there until after Anna had left. Felicity had had it, she'd found it in Dan Hutchins's room. Jeannie had taken it into her bedroom for safekeeping, and had had every intention of calling the station to say that she had found it.

'Then why didn't you?'

Jeannie tearfully explained that Mr Delany had phoned and she had told him.

'He was very angry. He said to me that it was his property, right? He wanted it, and I had to give it to him.'

'But you didn't.'

'It was Felicity's idea. She said that if he was so anxious to have it, then maybe he would give us some money for it. We were both broke and she was having trouble with Social Security 'cos she'd been unemployed for so long and she really needed money. I think she'd been cashing money that belonged to Dan – you know, his cheques kept on coming after he was dead and she got scared and so she thought up the idea of asking Mr Delany for some cash.'

There was a pause, and she scratched her arms and then started biting her nails.

'But he didn't get given the diary, did he?'

'No.'

'Why not?'

Jeannie wriggled in her chair. Felicity had arranged to meet him and get the money, then he could pick the diary up from the flat. Jeannie was concerned that if Felicity got the cash, she'd go off and score drugs.

'I went looking for her, with the diary. I called her and she said she was over at Waterloo Bridge, so I got a taxi to meet her.'

'With the diary?'

'Yeah. We did intend giving it to Mr Delany, honestly. It was just she was acting all crazy.'

'So did she score?'

'No. He wasn't answering his phone and she didn't know anyone else to call.'

'Who did she get her drugs from?'

'Mostly Amanda, but she was going through a detox programme, and she wasn't bringing any gear around, especially not for Felicity 'cos she never paid her for the cocaine she'd got the last time.'

Barolli interrupted, saying Jeannie was talking as if Amanda was still alive.

'We knew where she got them from,' Jeannie said, 'and after she died, we called him. I mean, I didn't. Felicity did.'

'Who did she call?'

'Amanda's contact – her driver Lester James – but he wasn't around.'

'So then what did you do?'

'Well, Felicity got this idea about holding onto the diary to get more money out of Mr Delany. She even came up with the idea of contacting the publisher who come round to meet Amanda, and as she'd said her story was worth a lot, Felicity reckoned we'd get a big pay-off.'

It was obvious that Jeannie was placing all the blame on Felicity, who Anna considered too stoned to have an idea in her head. It was lie upon lie. Anna was certain that it was Jeannie manipulating the entire scenario with Mr Delany and Josh Lyons.

'Go on. After you met Felicity at Waterloo, what happened?'

Jeannie was biting her nails down to the quick; two pink spots had appeared on her cheeks.

'It was a sunny day, right, and we were by the pleasure boats, and Felicity'd bought a bottle of cider, so she decided we'd go for a trip up the river. I didn't want to go as she was getting drunk and she could get real nasty. I gave her a few hundred and said we'd try getting some coke for her later when she got home, and so she got a ticket and went on the boat.'

'So when did you decide to pack up and leave your flat?'

'When I read about Felicity in the papers. It scared me, I sort of blamed myself, you know. I shouldn't have let her go on the boat by herself as she was well on the way to getting pissed, and she could get into real fights with people. She was a nice girl, but when she was drunk she was a right fucking cow.'

Anna tapped her notebook.

'Doesn't work, Jeannie. You see, Felicity's death was

447

not in the press until three days after she died. You had already left your flat. We paid a visit there with your landlord. Why don't you stop spinning a pack of lies and start telling us the truth. You were on that boat, weren't you? Do you think we haven't made any enquiries, haven't talked to witnesses?'

Anna was spinning her own lies now, and Jeannie was shaking with nerves.

'Did you push her into the river? You think we are going to believe that she would just go off with a few hundred pounds when you were given five thousand for the diary, which you never had any intention of giving to Mr Delany, *did you*?'

Jeannie started to cry.

'You keep putting all the blame for everything you have done on a dead girl, but it's not going to wash with us. We know you tried to sell the diary to the publishers, we know you've been running around with it, and if, as you say, you only knew about Felicity's death from the newspapers, then you must also have known that we wanted to talk to you.'

'I never. I told you the truth, I swear before God.'

Langton, watching the interview, loosened his tie. He liked the way Anna was goading her. Suddenly the solicitor intervened.

'My client denies having any responsibility for the death of Miss Felicity Turner. She was never with her on the boat and, as she has explained, she read about her demise in the press.'

'That's right, I'm telling you the truth.' Jeannie nodded her head.

'Your friend was drowned, but from blood tests we

know she had injected a substantial amount of heroin. Where did that come from?'

'I don't know.'

'But you can understand our confusion with your statement?'

'Maybe she got some of Dan's gear; he died of an overdose, and he used to keep a stash hidden in the fireplace. She could have found it, you know, probably needed something to give her confidence to meet with Mr Delany. And I tell you something, we didn't mind ripping him off because we knew Amanda hated him. He'd molested her when she was a kid, and her grandfather, they'd both abused her so what we did was for her really.'

'That's enough crap, Jeannie. I think *you* were the one to find the drugs, *you* took them to Felicity, and that was the only way she would part with the five thousand pounds. You have been sitting here lying to us.'

'I haven't. I swear before God I have been telling you the truth.'

Anna gave Barolli a tap on his knee beneath the table, indicating for him to change the subject. He kept his voice calm and friendly.

'Tell us about Dan Hutchins, Jeannie. He overdosed on heroin, yet he'd been on methadone, trying to get clean, hadn't he?'

'Yeah. Amanda got him into a rehab programme, paid for him and he promised he'd get clean, and he did for a while.'

'But then he scored heroin?'

'Yeah, he sold her computer, that's how he got the money.'

'Who did he score the heroin from?'

'No idea. He had contacts, not just Amanda's bloke. And he wouldn't go to him as he'd have told Amanda, and she would maybe have stopped looking after him.'

'She was already dead, Jeannie.'

'Oh right, yeah, I forget. But I know he sold her computer, 'cos she kept it at the flat in his room for him to play internet games. She'd bought herself a laptop so she didn't really need it, but it was hers and he got some cash.'

'Who did he sell it to?'

'I dunno. He left the party we was at, and then when we come home he was dead on the floor in his bedroom.'

Jeannie dug into her pocket and took out a tissue.

'He never got over her being murdered. He really loved her, and she was very good to him, and often when she was at the flat she'd be in his room with him. They were once an item, you know, she and him, and they still sometimes slept together, but he was impotent 'cos he'd been injecting into his groin for a couple of years and it done something to his deckhand. By this time she wasn't that interested in him 'cos she had this thing with Scott Myers and a few others . . .'

'So Dan left this party, was able to sell the computer and score heroin in just a couple of hours from when you had last seen him?'

'No, he'd sold it before the party 'cos Amanda found out and she told him that she wasn't ever going to see him any more. If you ask me, that is why he OD'd, 'cos she wasn't going to be his friend any more.'

Anna sighed; her head was aching.

Jeannie clicked her fingers.

'At the funeral, I think he scored or arranged to get a

fix after that, so it might have been Lester what passed him the gear.'

'By Lester, you mean Lester James, Amanda's driver?'

'Yeah, he was there. In fact, maybe he got the computer, I dunno.'

'Take me through what happened when you returned to the flat and found Dan's body.'

'It was terrible. I mean, I looked into his room and I thought he was sleeping as he was in his bed, all wrapped up in the duvet.'

'On the bed?'

'Yeah, that's right. So I shut the door, and I made some scrambled eggs as we reckoned he might be hungry.'

'But Dan was found on the floor of his bedroom – not, as you have just stated, in his bed. Did you move him?'

Jeannie sat back in her chair, looked to her solicitor and then shrugged her shoulders.

'Felicity tried to revive him, I think, and he fell off the bed, and that's when we knew he was dead.'

Anna tapped the tabletop with her pencil. 'How much heroin did you find?'

Jeannie was offguard for only a beat, then was quick to implicate Felicity once again. She thought that Felicity had found some tinfoil wraps and cocaine.

'She hid it because we were scared the police would be called and we'd be involved in his death for scoring drugs. I'm an actress, right, and I didn't want to get any shit thrown at me. I mean, I have to think of my career.'

'So if Felicity had hidden it, why didn't she go and use the hidden stash taken from Dan's room when, as you said, she needed drugs?'

'She couldn't remember nothing.'

'But you remembered?'

She had a whispered conversation with her solicitor and then Jeannie nodded and sat stiffly in the chair.

'No comment.'

'Did you take drugs to give to Felicity when you met her at Waterloo?'

Jeannie looked to her solicitor and back to Anna.

'No comment.'

Barolli glared at the smirking solicitor, as Anna quickly defused the situation.

'Jeannie, you may be acting on the advice of your solicitor right now not to answer any further questions, but you do not have to take his advice. It may even damage your defence if you don't mention something now which you may rely on later in court. This, Jeannie, is your opportunity to give your side of the story. We can retain you here until tomorrow morning, especially as it is now eleven-thirty at night.'

'You can't do that,' Jeannie said angrily.

'Yes, we can. You see, up till now we have not pressed any charges and you have been simply assisting our enquiry. However, I consider you to have been implicated in the death of Felicity Turner and that you supplied her with Class A drugs. This will be a charge we will level at you. There could even be other matters we wish to interview you about, such as blackmail. We will take a statement from Mr Delany regarding the five thousand pounds.'

'You can't do this!' Jeannie was half out of her chair.

Her solicitor intervened. 'You are interviewing my client on matters about which I do not even have an evidence statement. To threaten to retain her in order to persuade a witness to give a statement is illegal.'

Anna ignored him. 'What isn't right, Miss Bale, is that we have been fed a stream of lies from the moment this interview began. We will give you one more opportunity to answer the questions truthfully. Now: *did you give heroin to Felicity Turner?*'

Jeannie started to cry. 'I only gave her what she wanted. She'd been desperate and she had the shakes. I never touch the stuff so I wouldn't know what I gave her. I don't do drugs.'

'Where did you pass this heroin to Miss Turner?'

'On the boat. She went into the toilets and took it in there. I stayed up on deck; we were going to Greenwich.'

'So you now admit that you *were* on the boat with Miss Turner?'

At last, between the sobs, they got the facts.

'I came back with some coffee to try to sober her up. We were near Tower Bridge, and she was at the front of the boat acting crazy, she could hardly stand up, and I got the money off her because she was so out of it, and then she stood on the seats. I told her not to, and she told me to fuck off. I went and left her 'cos I didn't want people coming up and seeing her. It was raining and they was all inside.'

She broke down sobbing. After a while she had gone back up on deck to find Felicity, but she had disappeared. She had searched the boat, but by this time they were docking at Greenwich.

'Didn't you tell anyone that you couldn't find her?'

She shook her head. Her nose was running and her black eye-make-up had smeared down her cheeks.

'I got off the boat, an' I got the tube home. I thought she'd just crashed out somewhere under one of the benches. I was scared about what would happen so I packed my bags and went to see some friends in Bristol.'

'With all the money?' Anna asked.

Jeannie nodded.

'Felicity drowned, Jeannie. You knew that was a possibility and you never told anyone who might have stopped the boat and turned it round to search for her.'

'No, that's not true. I just thought she'd passed out. I swear to God I didn't know she'd fallen overboard, I really didn't.'

She rested her head in her hands, as her solicitor seemed to shrink back from her. Clearing his throat, he asked what charges they intended passing against his client.

Anna spoke. 'We'll consider charging Jeannie for withholding evidence. She'll be released but we'll be keeping an eye on her. She mustn't leave the country, as we'll want to question her again.'

The girl's mouth dropped open as she looked from Anna to her solicitor. 'You mean I can go?'

'We'll prepare a report for the CPS to decide if you'll be charged with gross negligence or the manslaughter of Felicity Turner. You will be released, Miss Bale, on police bail pending further enquiries. We will need a statement from you to confirm that Lester James was supplying drugs.'

Anna and Barolli both knew that for Jeannie's evidence against Lester James to stand up in court, she would have had to witness a transaction and to know that it was heroin that he had passed to Dan Hutchins. Langton congratulated them and then, to their astonishment, told

454

them he had given the go-ahead to arrest Lester James. Having watched the video of his karate exhibition, he felt they had enough evidence to charge him with dealing and perverting the course of justice. He would kick off the interview the next morning; Anna and Barolli could sit in the viewing room and watch him at work. In the meantime he wanted Lester's weapon and suggested they search his lockers at the karate dojo he worked out in. Anna watched Langton, his arrogance grating on her nerves, and fully aware that they should have watched Lester's show as soon as the video had been removed from their suspect's flat.

'I include every one of you. To date this has been a shoddy investigation. Now is the time to pull your socks up. I want that bastard charged . . .'

Langton then swept out almost theatrically, leaving them drained and at the same time angry at the way he had spoken to them.

'Who the fuck does he think he is?' muttered Barolli. Anna was too tired to argue. 'What right has he got to speak down to us after we've been schlepping our arses off.'

Barbara wheeled in the television set and caught Barolli's remark.

'Reason could be that he is Detective Chief Superintendent and you are just Detective Sergeant. He's rubbed Mike Lewis up the wrong way as well.'

'Where is Mike?'

Barbara switched on the television.

'He's gone to pick up Lester James. OK, are we ready to watch this sodding video because I don't know about anyone else, but I want to go home.'

★

Lester James was arrested at three o'clock the next morning. He had been woken by Mike Lewis and two officers, and warned that he was to be questioned with regard to the murder of Amanda Delany. He was allowed one phone call; he made it to his oldest brother Harry to arrange for a solicitor. Lester had hardly spoken to anyone else, remaining subdued as he rested back on the bunk bed in his cell. After breakfast he would be given access to his solicitor before being interrogated.

With time to spare before she needed to be at the station, Anna skimmed over the pages of her section of Amanda's diary. It appeared that the girl had indeed attempted to straighten out her life. There were several entries about the filming of *Gaslight*. She described the director, Julian Pike, as a 'closet' queen and wrote that she was looking forward to working with Rupert Mitchell. The fact that he had virtually ignored her had really pissed her off. The make-up department were boring old gossips and her corset was so tight it made her feel sick. There were also references to her staying clean, how hard she found it to concentrate on the difficult dialogue, and how her interaction with the director was not going well.

Anna was running out of time. She still had a quarter of the diary pages to finish and knew she should be getting ready to leave for the station. She turned a page and came across a rough drawing that looked like the sketch of a woman. Underneath Amanda had written:

It doesn't really even look like me, and some of it isn't filled in, and it was just sad. But I couldn't tell him as he was like a kid showing it off to me. I feel sorry for him, he's such a loser and with no class. He's getting over-protective, and he's going to have to leave me alone, especially now I don't need him.

Anna closed her eyes. *Filled in* . . . Wasn't that what the tattooist had said when she had spoken to him, something about Lester James wanting his tattoo filled in? She turned over the page and found a list of numbers and words: *Need a lawyer, the fucking bitch has not paid me my money. I feel used and betrayed and I trusted her.*

Next came references to Josh Lyons and Golden Arrow, then details of the lunch at Le Caprice and the words, underlined in red pen: *I will make them all pay.*

She mentioned that Josh Lyons wanted to see her diary. *He's worried about the legal aspect . . . Can't see why – I am only gonna tell the truth.*

Then, three days before her death, Amanda had noted that she was not required for filming and had the night off. She had written down Colin O'Dell and Scott Myers's names and then one word – *party*. There was no mention of Lester James driving the two of them away from the house. There was, however, mention of LJ a couple of pages further on.

> *For all the times he is a pain in the butt, he was the only one who really listened to me. He was very sweet and gave me some tabs to help me through the night filming; he said he would check out the house. It's a relief, to have someone strong looking after me. He might be a bit of an idiot but he's still the only person who protects me.*

It looked as if something had been spilled over a section of the page and been wiped away, as there was an odd discolouration over the paper. The next entry was in a different pen, a thicker one, but it was still recognisably Amanda's childish scrawl.

I am fucking out of it and I've still got two scenes to do. I hate this movie. I fucking HATE it.

    I told the director to go stuff himself when he was rude to me, fucking wanker. They had me drenched with water half the night, and the horse-drawn carriage was smelly inside. I feel like getting onto my agent but it's too late, so I'm gonna really have a go at her in the morning and I am going to leave her and go to someone else, but first I WANT MY MONEY and I'll get onto the cops about it if she doesn't hand it over. I wish filming would end, I feel like I am drowning inside all the time.

There was a scribbled section as if the pen was running out and then a thick blob of ink. The paper was oddly creased as if it had been folded.

Anna frowned. Something didn't add up. If Jeannie Bale had been telling the truth, how could Amanda have written up her diary if she had left it in the flat in Maida Vale after her meeting with Josh Lyons? That meeting had taken place several days earlier, and yet there she was, writing in the diary the night before she was murdered.

The last page of the diary was blank. It appeared that Amanda wrote up her diary in the mornings and evenings. Would she have taken it with her to the film unit? Not only had she left her mobile phone on the set and the stand-in had found it, but according to Jeannie Bale, she had also lost her BlackBerry. Jeannie said she had found it in the flat after Amanda's meeting with Josh Lyons. It had to mean that Jeannie was still lying to them. Was it possible that she had gone to Amanda's house and taken the diary, along with the BlackBerry? If this was correct, Jeannie Bale would now have to be a suspect in the murder.

Anna knew she should go straight to the station, but instead she drove across Tower Bridge and through the West End. It took her over half an hour before she turned onto the Edgware Road towards Maida Vale. She parked a short distance from the flat and walked down the basement steps. The front door had been prised open: the temporary locks fitted by the landlord were broken and a padlock was hanging loose. Anna was able to push open the front door with ease, and she edged cautiously into the dark, dank hall. The single low-wattage light bulb in the hall gave a yellowish hue and she could hear dragging sounds, then a dull banging and the next moment Jeannie Bale walked into the hallway, pulling a large suitcase behind her.

'Jeannie,' Anna said softly and the girl whipped round in shock. 'We need to talk.'

'I got every right to be here, I'm just clearing out my things.'

'I'm sure you don't have the right, as the landlord has—' Anna was interrupted.

'He's talking a load of shit. We paid rent for this stink-hole for years, and if I wanted, I could stay on as a sitting tenant. All I'm doing is taking what's mine and then I'm getting out for good.'

Anna moved closer as Jeannie dragged the heavy case further into the hall, swearing because the strap was broken. She was holding a thick wide leather belt with a brass buckle, which she was clearly intending to strap round the case.

'When did you take Amanda's diary?'

Jeannie straightened and pushed her thick blonde hair from her face. She began to wind the strap around her hand.

'I never. She left it here, I told you. Felicity found it in Dan's room.'

'Yes, you said, after she had the meeting with the publisher.'

'Right. Happened like I said.'

'So when did you take it back to her, and then get your hands on it again?'

'I don't know what you're talking about.'

Anna edged still closer. 'Jeannie, you had better tell me the truth, because we have the diary now, and we've read it.'

Jeannie stared at Anna, tossing her head.

'You see, Amanda had to have got it back because she'd written in it. In fact, she'd continued to write it up until the day before she was murdered.'

'What?'

'So you lied. If you'd had it in your possession since the meeting with her publisher, then that was several days before her death. You see my problem?'

'No.'

'You took it, didn't you?'

'No, I fucking didn't.'

'Then who did?'

'Listen, you've got no right to come in here and start having a go at me. I was released and I've done nothing wrong.'

'Just answer the question,' Anna said calmly, 'because you could now be implicated in her murder. This is very serious, Jeannie, and you had better level with me because I am beginning to lose patience with you.'

'You really scare me,' the girl sneered.

'Don't push your luck. Start talking, Jeannie.'

The heavy suitcase was between them, as Jeannie took a step backwards, her face twisted with anger.

'I am sick to fucking death of hearing that bitch's name. She stole my part – I was told I'd have got it, if it wasn't for her. It would have been *me* with a diary worth a fortune, it would have been *me* starring in one movie after another. All I needed was a break and she took it from me – she took everything from me. And it wasn't just me – look what she did to Dan! He worshipped the ground she walked on, and all she did was feed him drugs and make him dependent on her like a wretched dog. But he wouldn't listen. She'd fuck his brains out and then dump him over and over again. She'd come here with her wads of money and dole it out to us, give us her cast-off clothes as compensation for robbing me of my chance. I hated her guts, *I fucking hated her . . .*'

The rage on Jeannie's face made her look freakish, with her long blonde hair flying and the spit forming at the corners of her mouth. She stepped over the case and, with the strap curled around her fist, lunged forwards. The edge of the buckle caught Anna on the side of her face, and the next moment Jeannie was on top of her, screaming and punching.

Using all her strength and training, Anna rolled side-ways and grabbed a fistful of Jeannie's hair. She brought the girl's head down hard on the edge of the suitcase, and sat astride her, gripping her wrists.

'I am arresting you . . .'

Jeannie spat at her, and this time Anna released her right hand to grip Jeannie's face and bang her head down

461

hard, once, twice. She then flipped her onto her stomach and hauled her arm behind her back, almost snapping her thumb out of joint. Jeannie howled in agony as Anna slowly got to her feet, still gripping the girl's arm and, yanking it even higher behind her back, forced her to stand with her face pressed against the wall. She grabbed the leather belt and tied it around Jeannie's arms, then pushed her into a kneeling position. Bleeding heavily from the gash to her forehead, Anna fumbled for her mobile phone and rang through to the incident room for back-up.

Then she cautioned the sobbing girl and, trying to stem the flow of blood down her face, made Jeannie sit down in the hallway to wait.

Langton could hardly contain his anger.

'Just let me get this straight,' he let rip at Barolli. 'Are you telling me that Travis, without any back-up or discussion with the team, made an arrest? What the fuck has she come up with?'

'I dunno all the facts, sir, just that she is bringing Jeannie Bale in and needed officers' assistance, and that whatever she's uncovered regarding this girl has to have connections to Lester James and the murder. That's all I know. The surveillance were pulled off from the flat two nights ago. She wants us to hold off Lester James's interrogation.'

'Well, let's use the time and see if we have completed the simplest task of unlocking our victim's BlackBerry . . . Have we?'

Barolli looked sheepish. 'Not yet. The tech support team are still working on it.'

'What about tracing the other computer?'

'No luck, but we're still making enquiries.'

'And the weapon?'

'We have officers going over to the dojo used by Lester James, but we haven't found any trace of it yet.'

Langton gave a brusque nod of his head, trying to contain his mounting fury.

'As soon as DI Travis makes an appearance, let me know.'

Lester James knew by now that he was being held on suspicion of murder. The waiting unnerved him and he couldn't keep still. Another hour passed, and he began slowly pacing up and down the cell like a caged animal. He banged on his cell door. A uniformed officer opened the flap and peered in.

'How long do I have to wait in here?'

'As long as it takes, pal. You're talking now, are you?'

'Fuck off.'

The flap was slammed shut. Lester cracked his knuckles, sat on the bed, got up, and began walking up and down again.

Anna looked dreadful. She had a deep cut to her forehead and her hair was caked in dried blood. Some of it had run down to her collar and stained her shirt-front. Her face was chalk-white, and around the abrasion a dark reddish bruise was beginning to form. Only in the safety of her own car, did she really react to Jeannie's attack. Although she had insisted she was perfectly fit to drive, she had to pull over. It took a while for her to calm down enough to continue the drive back to the station without shaking.

★

Langton stared at Anna as she walked into Mike's office. He pinched her chin with his fingers, tilting her head up.

'What happened?'

'I arrested Jeannie Bale and she didn't like it.'

He released his hold and gestured for her to sit down.

'She's not the only one. What in Christ's name were you doing, going to see her alone?'

'I was on my way into the station, and I just wanted to make sure she was still around.'

'On your way in?' Langton growled. 'You think I'm stupid? That was some fucking circuitous route. Why didn't you call for back-up straight away if you thought she was involved?' He threw his arms up in a gesture of amazement. 'Get to the reason we also have Jeannie Bale in the cells. You suspect her of Amanda Delany's murder?'

'It's the diary, sir.' She started to explain.

When she had finished, Langton stood up and went to perch on the corner of Mike's desk.

'Right now, I don't have the time to lecture you about unprofessional conduct. What you have unearthed does put a very different slant on things. Maybe Lester James didn't act alone. You think they could be in it together?'

'I don't know, but the diary had to have been returned to Amanda and she continued to write it up until the night before she was murdered. That would mean it was taken from her house on the night of her murder, perhaps along with her BlackBerry. Up till now, we've been assuming that it was missing several days prior to her death.'

Langton did a slow intake of breath, saying, 'So

Jeannie could have been at Amanda's house on the night she was murdered and took the diary, along with the other missing items. Either that or she was with Lester James, and they killed her together – that is to say, if we still have James in the frame for the murder.'

Langton stared at the ground, stuffing his hands into his pockets.

'We've still not found the murder weapon, nor unlocked her fucking BlackBerry, nor traced the missing computer.'

'Jeannie said that Dan Hutchins sold her computer. Whoever he sold it to must have access to her Black-Berry back-up system.'

'Did she know who he sold it to?'

'No. Apparently he sold it because he needed money for drugs. If these drugs were supplied by Lester James, then maybe *he* has the computer.'

Langton looked at Mike, who said straight away that they had not found one in his flat. By now they had accessed his private bank account but there was no evidence of any large cash sums that could have come from drug dealing. Only his wages from unit driving on various projects had been paid into his current account and any withdrawals covered his mortgage and personal items such as clothing and groceries. He had five thousand pounds in a savings account and eight hundred in his current account.

Langton gave a low tuneless whistle, and then straightened up and looked at the time.

'Right. Who do we go for first – Miss Lyin' Through Her Teeth Bale or our very own Bruce Lee?'

Anna opted for Jeannie. Half the time she didn't know if the girl was telling the truth, but now she had been arrested, she might be scared enough to give them some evidence they could use against Lester.

Langton looked at Anna. Her face was still white and the bruise to her forehead and cheek had taken on a purple hue.

'How are you feeling?'

'I'm fine.'

'Mike and I'll take Jeannie,' Langton decided. 'She might be less co-operative, seeing you again, and we can also use the attack as further reason for holding her in the cells and piling on the charges. Come on, let's get the ball rolling.'

By the time Anna had cleaned herself up and joined Barolli in the viewing room, Langton and Mike had been questioning Jeannie for half an hour. Jeannie looked in as bad shape as Anna had done, and she was agitated.

'Done a lot of howling, but she's quieter now. Langton so far hasn't said a word,' Barolli murmured.

Mike Lewis was conducting the interview in a quiet, calm voice, as he repeated the claim that Jeannie had made: that the diary was in her possession after the publisher had left.

'You also maintain that you found Miss Delany's BlackBerry behind some cushions – at the same time as you found the diary.'

'Yeah.'

Langton moved in now. He slapped the pages of her statement with the flat of his hand, making Jeannie physically jump.

'So now we've had all your lies, this isn't worth the paper it's written on, is it? *Is it?* I'm sick and tired of listening to you and I don't think you understand the seriousness of your position one bit. You want me to explain it?'

'I never did anything wrong.'

'*You never did anything wrong?* You walk away with five thousand pounds that you blackmailed Amanda Delany's father to give you for the diary, you let your friend fall off a boat and drown, you don't call anyone to help search for her. I don't think Felicity did fall, I think you pushed her overboard and as soon as the boat docked, you were off home to pack up and leave.'

'*I didn't do that!*'

'And we are expected to believe you? When you've lied about everything else? How was Miss Delany able to write in her diary up until the night she died when you claim you had it in your possession? Explain that!'

Jeannie bit her nails, head bowed. Langton was in full flow.

'Let me tell you what I think. You maybe did find it at your flat, it may have been left there by Miss Delany, along with her BlackBerry. But I think between the time she left it, you contacted her, you took it back to her, so that she was able to continue writing . . . with me so far? Doesn't quite add up, does it? The other possibility is that you were at Miss Delany's house, and you took both these items from there.'

'She left it at the flat and Felicity found it,' Jeannie insisted.

'So did Felicity take it back to Amanda?' Langton demanded. 'She had to be in possession of it, Jeannie, and then it somehow gets back to your flat. Tell us how it happened!'

'I don't know.'

'You don't know, but you have to know – unless

these lies are to cover up the fact that you killed Amanda Delany.'

'No, no, I didn't.'

'Why should we believe you? You were there! Why don't you admit you were there on the night of her death?'

'I wasn't.'

'Yes, you were – and you will be charged with her murder unless you have something to say that really makes sense of this entire fiasco.'

'I didn't do it.'

'Didn't do what?'

'I didn't kill Amanda, I swear to God I didn't.'

Langton pushed his chair back as if he was about to stand. Jeannie reached across the table to stop him leaving.

'Listen to me. I didn't do it. I wouldn't have hurt her, I cared for her – she was good to me.'

Langton pushed his face towards her.

'She stole your part, didn't she? You believe that it could have been you, the movie star – not her. You were jealous, bitterly envious of all she had, and you couldn't stand it because you had to know that you didn't really stand a chance against her. You didn't have the talent *or* the looks!'

Jeannie's mouth dropped open as Langton pointed at her solicitor.

'What's your name?'

'Sinclair, Rodney Sinclair.'

'Well, do your client a favour. Maybe you should have another consultation with her as she is digging herself into a deeper and deeper hole.'

Langton made as if to walk away from the table as

Jeannie bent forward, resting her head in her hands, sobbing. Sinclair tried to comfort her, but she pushed his hand away.

'I didn't kill her, I swear I didn't do it.'

Mike Lewis now moved in.

'Do you know who did? It's in your best interest to tell us the truth, Jeannie.' He turned to Langton. 'Give her a chance. She wants to tell us the truth – you do, don't you, Jeannie? Get it off your chest, love.'

When Sinclair piped up, asking for time out with his client, Langton was at the ready.

'I gave you the opportunity to talk to her and I'm sick of wasting time. I will now approach the CPS so Jeannie Bale can be charged with murder.'

'I didn't do it!' Jeannie said again.

'Then who did kill her, Jeannie? Who stabbed Amanda Delany to death?'

She closed her eyes, and her solicitor passed her a tissue. She blew her nose and wiped her face.

'I just dunno how to tell you things that will get me into trouble.'

'Try us, Jeannie.' Mike Lewis poured her a glass of water while leaning back from the table.

Anna turned to Barolli.

'Here it comes.'

He nodded, watching as Jeannie blew her nose again and began to shred the tissue in her hands.

'Felicity did find the diary. Well, she went into Dan's room looking for drugs and found it.'

Jeannie told them how Felicity had taken the diary into her own room and had started to read it. When Jeannie came home, she showed it to her. She told her about Amanda's meeting with the publisher that she'd overheard, that he was talking about paying Amanda a lot of money for the diary. Dan came in and they read out the sections referring to him, and he became very distressed. They had teased him, saying it was all going to be in a book she was writing and everyone would know that he was impotent. Felicity had laughed, saying that Dan wasn't the only one: they should read what she'd written about Lester! This was the first indication that Jeannie did know who Lester was, that he was more than just Amanda's driver and that she had scored drugs from him.

Dan tried to get the diary away from them, but before he could wrestle it away, Lester James himself walked in. He had Amanda's keys to the flat; she had asked him to pick up the diary and BlackBerry that she had inadvertently left behind. Lester had grabbed the diary and threatened them all, but Jeannie said he did not get the BlackBerry.

'I told him I hadn't got it and that she must have left it at the film unit, so he just took the diary and walked out.'

It was a while before Jeannie could admit to what had happened next. All she knew was that Lester had taken the diary later the same day that Josh Lyons had been to their flat. Two days later, she reckoned, they had received a phone call from Mr Delany asking about the diary and Jeannie had lied to him, saying that she had it and would want money for it.

'So when did you get the diary back?' Langton asked.

Lester had returned to the flat to have another look for Amanda's BlackBerry; it must have been a day or so before she was murdered. When he turned nasty, they told him that if anyone should be worried about what Amanda was going to write in her book, he should. He was in it all the way through; he'd find plenty of details of his drug dealing and his sexual problems.

'He hit me then – said I should wash out my mouth.'

He told them that he was going to be staying over at Amanda's house because she was frightened by hearing a woman screaming the night before.

'I said to him that she didn't hear anything as she was always having nightmares when she lived with us, waking us all up screaming, and if he didn't believe us about what she'd written, he should read the fucking thing for himself.'

Lester had taken Jeannie with him to the mews. This was the night before the murder, and he was in a strange mood.

'I think he was in love with her, but she treated him like shit. On the drive over there, he told me that she'd had a threesome the other night with Scott Myers and Colin O'Dell. I said that she was a slag and he shouldn't let her treat him so badly.'

Lester had parked not in the mews but in a side street. He knew a back way to the cottage that Amanda had shown him, to keep him out of sight of the press. As soon as they were in the house, he had begun searching for the diary.

'He was in a right old state. I helped him look for it, but it took ages to find as he wouldn't put the lights on.'

Jeannie took a gulp of water and sat, staring ahead. 'It was inside her toy rabbit, on her bed. I found it while he was looking in the lounge. I told him that I had to go home, and he just ignored me, so I left.'

'With the diary?'

'Yeah, and then when Mr Delany called, I was telling him the truth. I did have it, I never lied about it. Delany was a right bastard.'

'What did you do with the rabbit?'

She shrugged her shoulders. 'Tossed it into a skip and got the bus home.'

Anna turned to Barolli, shaking her head in disgust. All the hours they had spent searching for the toy, even asking Jeannie herself, and all the while she knew she'd thrown it away.

'The net's closing in on Lester James after what Jeannie's said,' Barolli observed as they watched the interview wind down.

'If she was telling the truth,' Anna commented.

'You think she's still lying?'

Anna couldn't really tell. It was Jeannie's word against that of Lester James.

Chapter Twenty-Four

Lester James was finally brought up from the cells. He had worked himself up into a state, hating being confined in such a small space. Jeannie was locked up next to him; he could hear her sobbing. They had made sure he had no chance to even have eye-contact with her; all he knew was, she was under arrest.

Lester's solicitor was waiting in the interview room as his client was led in. Lester complained about being held all night, then went quiet as Langton and Anna entered and took up their seats opposite him. Having cautioned him, Langton kicked off in a quiet but authoritative voice.

'Mr James, we are now privy to further information that places you inside Miss Delany's mews house on the night she was murdered. You have every opportunity to explain why you previously lied. The allegations against you are very serious and I suggest you start telling the truth.'

Langton paused as he opened up the file and poured himself a beaker of water.

'Did you kill Amanda Delany, Mr James?'

Lester sat with his head bowed and his big hands clasped together, refusing to look up at either Langton or Anna.

'From a statement given to us by Jeannie Bale, we know you were with Miss Bale shortly before Miss Delany returned home in the early hours of the morning. What have you got to say?'

Lester remained silent.

Anna spoke next, copying Langton's calm delivery.

'We know that you've been lying about your relationship with Miss Delany, that you were not, as you have maintained, merely her driver, but had sexual contact with her over a period of more than five years. Do you now admit that you have lied consistently and, contrary to what you have maintained, you also supplied drugs not only to Miss Delany but to her flatmates, Felicity Turner, Dan Hutchins and Jeannie Bale.'

Lester James finally spoke. 'You got no evidence that I was dealing 'cos I know two of them are dead, so they couldn't say nothing about any drugs, and Jeannie Bale is a pathological liar.'

'Perhaps she is, Lester, but we are also in possession of Miss Delany's diary, and she makes clear reference not only to your sexual relationship, but to the fact that you supplied drugs — cocaine, heroin, crack cocaine, amphetamines, Ecstasy . . .'

'Lies.'

Langton glanced at Anna, encouraging her to continue.

'I think, Lester, you were deeply involved with Amanda, and reading about how she felt about you must have torn you apart.'

'I was just her driver, nothing more.' His face was set with anger.

'Miss Delany makes many references to your sexual prowess, or rather, to your lack of it. That must have been really difficult for you to come to terms with, knowing she used you, laughed at you behind your back.'

'It wouldn't matter to me. As I keep on telling you, I was just her driver and she could write whatever she wanted because it's not true.'

'Isn't it? Isn't that why, when Jeannie Bale told you about the diary, you took her to the mews and you went in search of it.'

'I never did.'

'You couldn't find it, but Jeannie Bale did and she took it, leaving you at the mews alone, waiting for Miss Delany to come home.'

Lester clenched and unclenched his hands.

'I admit I lied,' he said gruffly. 'I *was* there, but I had reason to be. Amanda asked me to check out the place as she was scared because the previous night she'd heard screaming. She wanted me to make sure there was nothing to worry about. I do a lot of work as a body-guard and security, and that's all I was there to do – to see it was all locked up and safe for when she got home.'

Langton nodded, and leaned back in his chair.

'So Jeannie Bale had left – taking with her the diary as we now know – leaving you alone waiting for Miss Delany – correct?'

'Yes.'

'Take me through what happened when Miss Delany returned.'

Lester coughed and straightened in his seat.

'She got back about four-thirty in the morning. She was very tired and I said to her that I'd checked over the house and locked up and I'd not found anything worrying, so I left.'

'How did you leave?'

'Back way. Used the alley along the gardens and went to pick up my car, then I drove home.'

'So did Amanda lock up the door into her garden?'

'Yeah, she did. Well, if you found it locked then she must have.'

Langton sifted through the files, as Anna sat staring at Lester. His control was admirable.

'You have stated that you were just her driver and that you never had any interest or interaction of a sexual nature with Miss Delany?'

'Yes, that's right.'

'I believe you are lying. Not only do we have confirmation in her diary that you were very much Miss Delany's sex toy, someone she could use whenever she felt like it, but also someone she felt was becoming over-protective and she didn't want to continue the arrangements you had for either drugs or sex.'

'Not true. I was just her driver and she depended on me. That's why she asked me to check out the mews.'

Anna passed a note to Langton. He read it and gave her a small nod and she gave a smile to Lester.

'You were just her driver,' she said. 'Someone Miss Delany used on private jobs as well as working for various film units.'

'Correct.'

'So as *just her driver*, it didn't anger you when she asked you to drive Colin O'Dell and Scott Myers from her house after they had spent the night with her?'

'I admitted I drove them last time I was interviewed. Didn't bother me who she saw. Like I keep on telling you, it was just a job for me. I had no other feelings like you keep on suggesting.'

Anna raised her voice. 'She would give you a blow job in your car, wouldn't she? She certainly made a lot of notes about the size of your penis and the fact that you were unable to keep an erection for long. It must have really grated on you to have to listen to these two men who had just had a sexually active threesome with her. Then shortly after that night, you were told by Jeannie Bale that Amanda Delany had recorded all your inept sexual approaches in her diary and only did what she had to do to score drugs from you so she wouldn't have to pay you.'

Lester looked stunned by her accusations.

'All right, I admit she occasionally went down on me. I couldn't refuse her, as she was very insistent and, like I said, I depended on her for my income. That was the only reason. Whether or not I was not up to scratch, according to her, is neither here nor there. I got paid, that's what it was all about.'

'So you admit you dealt drugs?'

'No, I'm not admitting that at all. What I do admit is that occasionally she would want to have oral sex, that's all. And why refuse? It made her happy, if not me. I never liked it, to be honest. I just let it happen so I would get paid.'

Both Anna and Langton rested back in their chairs, as if what he was saying made total sense to them, which gave him confidence.

'I could tell you some stories about who she picked up at clubs, and if you think it bothered me, then you're wrong. I didn't have any emotional ties to her. I was only, like I keep on saying, her driver. Whatever you're trying to make out, how I felt because of some stupid stuff in her diary, it didn't make me get uptight.'

'Not even if it was to be published and your name—'
Anna was interrupted.

'She never had the deal, I know that. After she come
out from that publisher's lunch meeting she was pissed
out of her head, and the next time she met with him at
her flat she was coked up. She told me she would never
be able to write anything, it was all in her head; she
was also back on the crack cocaine, so she'd never have
held it together to write a fucking book. It's all bullshit
and if that Jeannie Bale told you anything different, she's
lying. All she ever wanted was to put Miss Delany down
because she was so jealous of her success.'

'Why didn't you tell us this when you were last
interviewed?'

Lester sighed, then made an expansive gesture with his
big hands.

'She was dead, I didn't want to rub salt in open
wounds. A lot of people will come out of the woodwork
and say bad things about her, and I just didn't want to be
one of them.'

'Because you cared for her?'

'I was her driver. Whether I cared about her is immaterial. We had a professional relationship, nothing more.'

'Did you kill Amanda Delany?'

'No, I did not. When I left her house that morning,
she was alive and I went home.'

'How did you feel when you were told she had been
murdered?'

'Terrible. It was a shock. Also, it would mean a big
loss of earnings for me. I had to get away – went to stay
with friends in Amsterdam. I was very depressed about it,
partly because I should have been more protective,
maybe not left the house but stayed with her.'

'If you had, she would still be alive?'

He nodded. Anna sifted through the files and statements, and Langton closed his folder, resting his hands
on top of it. Lester took it as an encouraging sign, and
leaned forward.

'I told you the honest to God truth. If that bitch
Jeannie Bale has tried to make out that I was anything
other than a good friend to Amanda, then she's crazy.
You've not got a shred of evidence against me, I know
that.'

'So did Jeannie leave the mews house before you?'

'Yeah. I was talking to her from the lounge and the
next minute, I realised she'd run off.'

'So she couldn't have been involved in the murder?'

He hesitated. 'Suppose not.'

Langton took over again.

'That still leaves you, so take us through exactly what
happened when Miss Delany returned home early that
morning.'

Lester wiped his face.

'I told you. I said to her I'd checked everything out
and nothing seemed to be of concern, so I left.'

'So both you and Jeannie Bale went out of the
garden doors and then down the alley back to the main
road?'

'Yeah, 'cos my car was parked up there.'

Langton opened his file again and made a note.

'Why didn't you park in the mews?'

'Ah well, there is a reason. My brother Harry would
be driving her back from the film unit, right? And I
didn't want him to know I was there waiting for her.'

'Why not?'

'He wouldn't have approved. Both he and Tony are

sticklers for keeping artists at arm's length, very professional they are.'

Langton closed his folder again, and picked up his pen
and replaced the cap. Anna followed suit. Their ploy
worked. It appeared that they were finishing the interview, which made Lester relax. He smiled.

'I'm sorry if I've wasted your time. I should have said
some of this to you before in my first interview, but I've
explained my reasons.'

Langton nodded and thanked him. It was Anna's turn.

'Do you have any tattoos?' She asked pleasantly.

He jerked with surprise. 'No.'

'Would you please take your shirt off, Mr James?'
She spoke quietly and Lester looked at his solicitor in
confusion.

'Is there a reason you wish my client to remove his
clothes?' the solicitor asked.

'Yes,' Anna replied. 'If Mr James refuses, then we'll
have to stop the interview for now and get the necessary
authority to strip-search him.'

Lester glanced once more at his solicitor, who gave
him a small shrug of his shoulders as if to say it was up
to him. First Lester undid the buttons on his cuffs and
then slowly, button by button, he opened his shirt. He
stretched it wide for them to see his bare chest.

'Take the shirt off, please,' Anna said firmly.

'Why? You looking for scratches or something?' Lester
glared at her. 'There won't be any 'cos I never was
involved. This is stupid.'

'Just take your shirt off, and then stand up and turn
around.'

Langton looked at Anna, frowning. Lester pushed back
his chair to stand in front of the table. His muscles stood

out, as did his six-pack and small waist, as he inched the shirt away from his trousers and took it off. He held it in one hand, staring at both of them.

'Satisfied? Or do you want my pants off as well?'

'Turn around, please.'

Slowly Lester turned. Even his solicitor peered at his back with interest and then with shock.

Over almost his entire back Lester had a tattoo of Amanda Delany's face. It was a good if rather exaggerated likeness, with her blue eyes and blonde hair and wide lips parted in a sexual pout.

'You can put your shirt back on now, Mr James,' Anna instructed.

Lester remained standing as he drew on his shirt, carefully buttoning up the front, leaving the sleeves loose.

'Sit down, please.'

Langton looked at Anna, raising his eyebrows.

'It must have hurt a lot when she laughed at your tattoo. Maybe not to your face, but she wrote about it in her diary, said it wasn't a good likeness. I disagree, it's very good – pity she didn't see the finished tattoo. You had it completed in Amsterdam, didn't you?'

Lester nodded. It was as if all the fight had drained out of him.

'Do you turn to see it in your mirror? Or is just knowing she's there enough?'

He swallowed. It was almost painful to watch the many expressions passing across his face, hurt being uppermost.

'You loved her, didn't you?' Anna asked gently.

He gave a small nod and his eyes welled up with tears.

'What did she say to you that made you so angry you made sure no one else could have her?'

He remained silent. Anna continued in the same low tone of voice, not wanting to break the mood. She suggested that after Jeannie Bale left him in the lounge at Amanda's house, something must have happened for him to lose control, wanting perhaps to hurt Amanda Delany the way she had hurt him. She got no reaction; Lester remained sitting like a block of wood in front of them. Now Langton leaned forward.

'Come on, Lester, give it up. You stabbed Amanda Delany over and over again and then you combed her hair and spread it over the pillow, never touching her face so she looked perfect, just like she looks on your body.'

'No,' he said softly, and then his body shook as he took a deep breath.

'Stabbed her repeatedly, didn't you? Neat fast incisions, one after the other. Did she cry out? Beg you to stop?'

'No.' It sounded like a low moan.

'Unless the first stab silenced her, and you knew what you were doing, one, two. Did she shudder, beg you to stop, or did she—?'

'The first stab killed her. I'm a professional. I'm not sure how many other times I stabbed her, but she didn't cry out, she didn't feel any pain.'

Lester gradually became more composed. Looking at his solicitor, he said quietly that he had done it. There was no point in pretending any more, he was admitting it.

'That's best for you, Lester,' Langton urged him. 'Tell us what exactly happened to make you do it . . . Come on, you'll feel better if you let it all out.'

'I loved her, I'd have done anything for her,' Lester said, almost dreamily. 'Five years I'd taken care of her, five years or more she'd depended on me. I never liked her taking drugs, but she insisted. I only got the drugs for her to keep her happy, and when she wanted gear for her friends I did that too, but I've never touched them myself – I value my health too much. She needed them to function, used to say that unless she had them, unless I got them for her, she'd go to some street dealer and get shit given to her, and then the press would find out. So I did it, always made sure it was good quality stuff, and I never let her use heroin. But she got into crack cocaine and that was her undoing. That movie actor Colin O'Dell was the first to give it to her, and then she used to get real nasty with me if I didn't score it for her, so I did.'

It took a long time for Lester to retrace the events that drove him to commit murder. It was when Amanda made him score for her friends that he became angry. But the biggest insult had come when she insisted he drive Colin O'Dell and Scott Myers and he had had to listen to the two of them laughing and talking about their threesome and what a slag Amanda was. He had wanted to stop his car and get out and beat the living daylights out of the pair of them, but he had controlled himself. He had rarely had full consensual sex with her and never in her bed, but he had always believed that one day she would realise that he was the only person who really cared about her.

'She told me her grandfather had sexually abused her from when she was only six years old, that her parents would never believe her because her grandfather paid for everything, and even when she had told her mother that he was molesting her, all she had said was it didn't matter because he had done the same to her.'

Lester passed a hand over his eyes.

'What kind of a mother is that, to allow it to go on, simply to maintain their luxurious lifestyle? Sick people – sick, perverted people – they never knew what they had done to her. Amanda was damaged goods and that's what made me so protective of her. She always said that without me there was no one else.'

Lester described how he had tried to persuade her to get help, but even at the worst time of her life, her parents had let her down again.

'She was pregnant, and she'd spent all the money she'd earned on her film on that bunch of no-hopers she shared a flat with. She fed them, paid the rent, gave them money and drugs and they were always wanting more, especially that parasite Jeannie Bale. Amanda felt guilty about her losing the part to her, so she was constantly trying to make up for it by giving her clothes and stuff.'

Anna asked if it was true that Amanda was pregnant by her grandfather and he shook his head.

'No, it was one of them she was seeing, Scott Myers or Colin O'Dell, but she didn't know which one, and they wouldn't admit it. She was so desperate she went back to her parents wanting an abortion, but they wouldn't give her the money. So she came back and by this time she was four months gone, and I said to her that it was dangerous to have it terminated. I told her that I'd marry her and look after her and the kid, that's how much I loved her, but that piece of shit Jeannie Bale got the address of some abortionist over in Wandsworth, and Amanda made me drive her there and wait while she had it done.'

Langton gave a covert look at his watch, as Lester told them about how he had driven her for the next two years, as she became more famous and more dependent on drugs. By now she was fodder for the media and she loved it. Sometimes she would call the paparazzi herself to make sure they were outside a club or party to see her falling over and having one sexual affair after another.

'But she always came back to me.'

He described how he'd picked up Amanda's diary from the Maida Vale flat and had given it back to her straight away.

'Did you read it?' Anna asked.

'No, it was private, and I knew Jeannie was lying about what was in it as she just wanted to get me all riled up.'

'What did Amanda say when you returned it?'

'She hugged me and then began to act all crazy, dancing around with it, saying she was gonna make a lot of people sorry for treating her like shit. I assumed she was talking about her parents.'

'When did you know what it contained? That it had lots of references to you?'

Lester closed his eyes to think. They could almost see the wheels in his brain turning.

'I wanted to find her BlackBerry – you know, get back in her good books because she believed that I'd taken it – and that was when I went back to that horrible flat.'

Jeannie Bale had been at home, and she had sneered at Lester, told him again that if he had any sense he would walk away from Amanda as she was using him and laughing about him behind his back. Jeannie repeated things that she'd read in the diary, and as she knew about the tattoo, he started believing her and became very upset. She said that Amanda was going to make a lot of money, millions, by selling her life story to a publisher.

'Then I got a call from Amanda, in a right state as she'd heard someone screaming the night before and it had woken her up. She said she was scared to go home and wanted me to check the place out and act as a body-guard for her.'

Lester said that he had gone to the film unit as Amanda was filming on nights. She said that she wouldn't be released until around five in the morning and would be scared to be alone in her house. She gave him her own set of keys, and instructed him to wait in the house until she got home.

'I didn't like the way she ordered me around and kept on asking me if I was sure no one had seen me entering her trailer as she didn't want any gossip about it. I honest to God intended doing just what she asked me to do, but then I thought I had enough time as it was only about twelve. I could pick up Jeannie and we'd both go over there. It was 'cos I was pissed off at the way I'd been spoken to, know what I mean?'

'Why would you do that? Take Jeannie Bale to the mews?'

Lester paused, then looked at his solicitor, who said, 'Just tell them the truth, Lester.'

'In enough shit, am I?' He gave a rueful smile.

Anna repeated the question.

'All right, Jeannie kept on at me about the diary, and she said I should read it 'cos of all the stuff Amanda had written about me, and to be honest, I was starting to believe her, especially as she was going on and on about how much money it was worth. She kept on saying I had a right to a cut of the money.'

'She wanted to get her hands on it, did she?' Langton asked, and Lester nodded.

Langton directed Lester to give them the details of exactly what happened when he and Jeannie were at Amanda's house, this time the truth.

'The diary, that was all I was there for.'

'Did you find out what was written about you?'

He nodded. Anna jotted a note and passed it to Langton, reminding him that Jeannie had stated that she had found the diary hidden in the toy rabbit and had taken it, leaving Lester alone. But if, as he said, he had read it, then Jeannie was lying.

'I couldn't find it, and we was careful we both put gloves on, and kept the lights off. We searched everywhere, in all the cupboards. It took ages and I had to keep my eye on Jeannie because I was worried she'd nick something. Anyways, I finally found it. It was on Amanda's bed inside this fluffy rabbit she carried around with her. It had a zip up the back, and she always kept her stash of cocaine in it.'

'So you then read it?'

'Yeah, I started it. I couldn't believe the stuff she'd written about me, it made me sick to my stomach. This was when Jeannie said we should just take it if it was worth money, and I told her to put it back where we found it, but she wouldn't and we were pulling at it between us when we heard the car driving into the mews. I got panic-stricken and I knew if Amanda found Jeannie there she'd go crazy so I told Jeannie to get in the kitchen and let me do the talking.'

Lester had looked out of the window, seen his brother's car and stayed in the bedroom, waiting for her to let herself in.

'For a second, I thought Harry was coming in with her, but he just waited until she'd shut the front door and then he reversed and drove out of the mews. She called out my name, and I said to her I was in the bedroom. I was worried she was going to go into the kitchen and find Jeannie in there, so I opened the door and she was switching on the lights in the hall.'

Amanda had gone upstairs to the bedroom, and he had told her that he'd checked everything out and there was nothing to worry about. She said that she was tired and wanted to go straight to bed. She waved Lester away as if he was annoying her.

Lester reached for a bottle of water and unscrewed the cap. No one spoke, waiting for him to continue, while he gulped two mouthfuls down. Then he told them how he had confronted her with the diary.

'I held it up. I'd got the fucking rabbit in one hand and the diary in the other, and she went for me, scream-ing at me to give it to her. She was like a crazy rat scratching at me, and I pushed her down on the bed, said to her that I'd read it, and I was disgusted with her, as all I had ever done was look out for her.'

He was close to tears as he described how Amanda had started to undress, teasing him, saying that she had only written the truth, that he was useless in bed and all he had ever really wanted was to fuck her. Now he could if he wanted to, she didn't care – he could take his kit off, see if he could get it up, and she was laughing cruelly as he threw the diary at her.

'She picked it up and flicked through the pages until she came to something about me, and she was doin' a funny voice, and I went closer to the bed. She could see I was getting into a real rage with her and she kept on telling me to undress. I pulled at the belt and I had my Commando knife there. You know, I was there to see if there were any problems, so I'd come prepared, and I unsheathed it and . . . I stabbed her. It was so fast, and she sort of flopped back with her mouth open, and she just looked at me, so I did it again. She didn't move or cry out, she did nothing to try and stop me, so I did it again, and again, and again . . .'

He began to sob, and Anna passed him the water, as he tried to get his handkerchief out of his trouser pocket.

'I think the second stab killed her because there was so little blood, nothing spurted out, and I just stood there, staring down at her, and then I heard screaming. It freaked me out. It was Jeannie standing in the doorway, screaming her head off, asking me over and over what had I done . . .'

'So Jeannie Bale was still in the house?' Anna asked.

Lester nodded. They had cleaned up the bedroom, and Jeannie had shouted at him when she saw him combing Amanda's hair. They had to get out, she said. He noticed that the rabbit and the diary were gone. Jeannie had said that she would keep silent if he let her take them; she said she would destroy them, but only if he never told anyone about her being there that night. She left the back way, as he stayed on, clearing up anything that might show he had been there.

Lester went on to describe how he had been the one to pass heroin to Dan Hutchins, and the part Jeannie had played when she called Lester to say he should buy the computer from Dan, as Dan needed the money, in case there was anything about the diary on it. Lester had taken the computer home and smashed it up, then left for Amsterdam. He had no idea that Jeannie had attempted to sell the diary to Amanda's father or had approached the publishers. He too suspected Jeannie of pushing Felicity Turner overboard; she was a real piece of work, and if she had stuck to their deal, he would have never implicated her in covering up the murder.

'Jeannie Bale only ever wanted to be Amanda. She was obsessed by her and felt that everything she had should have been hers.'

Chillingly, Lester described how Jeannie had helped him stretch out Amanda's body to lie as if sleeping on the bed, the way she had cut up a black plastic binliner to cover her clothes so as not to get any bloodstains on them. Only when he had combed Amanda's hair had she become hysterical.

Lester's last words to Langton and Anna before he was taken down to the cells were wretchedly sad.

'First time I had ever seen her naked was that night, first time I had ever held her body. It was like holding a fragile doll, so thin, her ribs stuck out, her hipbones, her legs were like a skinny child's. The stab wounds must have cut right through her, she was so tiny, and all that was perfect was her face, and now I have her with me for ever. If she'd seen my tattoo completed she wouldn't have laughed, she'd have been proud.'

Anna and Langton sat side by side after Lester and his solicitor had been led out, the thick stack of files in front of them.

'Tell me,' he said quietly. 'When did you know about the tattoo?'

'Reading the diary. I contacted a number in Amsterdam that was a tattoo parlour. Some man called "Skull" told me that Lester had been in recently, to have it "filled in". He made no mention of what the tattoo was and I didn't ask. I didn't actually piece it together until I read that Amanda had seen it on his back and laughed, said it was ridiculous. To be honest, I doubt she would have been proud of it even when it was finished.'

'Maybe not, but it cracked him open to talk.'

'Yes.'

Langton waved his hand over the files. 'I didn't read it in the reports.'

'Er, I hadn't got around to it.'

Langton stood up and stretched his arms.

'Really? Well, we got the result we wanted and now we'll also be able to charge Jeannie Bale with accessory to murder.'

Anna stood up and stacked her files.

'She's certainly a better actress than I gave her credit for. She's consistently lied from the very start. This case would have been over weeks ago if she'd told the truth.'

Langton walked to the door and swung it open. He stopped and gave her a long, unfathomable stare.

'Maybe if we'd all been privy to what you knew, it would also have cut a lot of wasted time. You haven't learned yet, have you? If you don't share information and don't stop acting like a one-man show, you'll never get ahead. I won't put you on report this time, but as from now, Anna, I am warning you. Work with the team, be a team member, and get respect more than congratulations.'

Anna didn't say anything. She was stunned. Langton constantly pulled the carpet from beneath her, but she hadn't expected it this time. If it hadn't been for her persistence in finding the diary, they would never have placed Lester as their prime suspect.

★

Anna did feel some sense of achievement from the team in the incident room as they gave her a round of applause when she walked in; even Barolli was smiling at her. It was over. Another case closed. They would still have a lengthy pre-trial wind-up, but with Lester admitting to the murder, it would move quickly. Mike Lewis would take him before the magistrates along with Jeannie Bale the following morning. Neither on their recommendation would be granted bail, as the charges against them both were so strong.

Lester James would be charged with murder, Jeannie Bale for perverting the course of justice and accessory to murder. Both would receive lengthy sentences, but no one felt compassion for either. They had cut short a life, albeit one with a diverse and dysfunctional history, of a movie star who had had a great future ahead of her.

Anna was glad to get home; she could still smell the awful shampoo that Barbara had given her to wash out her blood from her hair. All she felt like doing was having a long hot shower, and then an even longer sleep. The only thing that marred Anna's feeling of satisfaction after her eventful day was Langton's dressing down. It was as if he had really wanted to belittle her. Yet she was confident that she had almost singlehandedly secured the conviction, and she was certain the team felt the same way.

Since her one-night stand with Gordon Berry, Langton had been distant; Anna could sense his animosity towards her. The more the hot-water jets from the shower calmed and relaxed her, the more she felt it was a case of personal jealousy. Even though their affair was over and done with, Langton didn't like her forming any new relationship, especially not with someone he knew. There was, she suspected, even a tad of professional envy, and she was not going to let him put her down.

Wrapped in a clean white towelling robe, and with a chilled glass of wine, Anna watched the late-night news. The first item was the revelation that Lester James, one of Amanda Delany's unit drivers, had been arrested and charged with her murder. The long enquiry was finally over.

Chapter Twenty-Five

Anna's first call the following morning was from Gordon to congratulate her. She was pleased to hear from him. Although her intentions had been to stop seeing him, she readily agreed to meet him for dinner that evening. After being under such time pressure for so many weeks, she relished the prospect of being able to chill out. In the post that same morning came confirmation of her promotion interview. While it meant that she had considerable preparation to do, the letter had come at a perfect time. The run-up to Lester James's trial would afford her the break she needed before getting involved in another case. It felt good – *she* felt good. She booked a hair appointment, a pedicure and a manicure, in readiness for her dinner with Gordon.

The press were out in force to watch the prisoners being taken from the station to court. Lester James had a blanket over his head and shoulders, while Jeannie Bale, on the other hand, gave a creditable performance of a woman wrongfully arrested. Anna watched their departure from the station's rear exit before she left. Whether or not they would re-open the case of Felicity Turner's drowning would no doubt be a bone of contention and one without sufficient evidence to really press charges.

Gordon was prompt. At exactly seven-thirty, he rang Anna's doorbell. There was a slight moment of embarrassment when they approached each other, but he soon made light of it, opening the door of his car for her to get inside. He had chosen a small Italian restaurant across the river and by the time they were sitting opposite each other, they were more at ease.

'You look lovely,' he said.

'Thank you. I had an afternoon off and took advantage of it – hair, massage . . .'

'Oh, not needing me then?'

She smiled and shook her head. 'I don't think it is a good idea, do you? But if I get whiplash again, I'll be on your couch right away. It's amazing that I only needed one session.'

It felt like a perfect dinner. Yet again Anna found Gordon easy to talk to, and his interest in her work and the arrest of Lester James was genuine. She talked about the two brothers, Tony and Harry, what they must be feeling after the arrest of their brother Lester.

'Do you think they had any idea he was guilty?'

Anna wasn't 100 per cent sure. She believed they had covered for him, maybe even lied for him, but she doubted they knew the extent of his infatuation with Amanda Delany.

When she described the tattoo on Lester's back, Gordon looked puzzled.

'Why did he have it done on his back?'

'He knew it was there, and he would be able to see it in a mirror, I suppose.'

'But if he went swimming, everyone would see it.'

'Mmm, never thought of that. Unless he can't swim?'

'How big was it?'

Anna made a gesture with her hands to show that it was almost lifesize, just her head and neck with a fraction of one shoulder.

'Do you feel sorry for him?' Gordon asked.

Anna looked surprised by the question. 'Sorry for him?' she repeated.

'Yeah. Poor guy is treated as a sex toy, used to run Amanda's errands and then made a fool of in her diary. I feel sorry for him, what he must have been put through – you know, loving someone who's always just out of reach and yet so close, plus having to listen to the two actors who had screwed her. He must have been in torment for years.'

He took a careful sip of wine. 'Have you ever loved anyone like that?' he asked her.

She didn't answer, as at that moment their food arrived.

'*Buon appetito.*' Gordon tucked his napkin into his shirt, and joked about always spilling his food down his clothes. 'My mother used to say I didn't know what side of my face my mouth was!'

'Are your parents still alive?'

'My mother is, yes, but my father died a long time ago, of lung cancer. I honestly thought she'd go soon after, since they were a doting couple. But she's very feisty and lives in Dorset, seventy-eight and has a live-in companion.'

'Do you see her often?'

'Yeah, once a month. What about yours?'

Anna explained that both her parents were dead, that her father had been a police officer and her mother an artist. She described how proud her father had been when she had chosen to join the Metropolitan Police. She told Gordon about her prospects of promotion, and how it saddened her that her father wouldn't be there to see her moving ahead in her career.

'I think my mother would have preferred another choice of career, but I was determined. It also meant that with my education – I was at Oxford – I went straight into the Graduate Accelerated Promotion Scheme.'

'Unlike old Jimmy Langton.'

'Pardon?'

'He worked his way up, didn't he? From uniform into plainclothes.'

Anna felt a twinge of irritation that Langton's name had somehow intruded on their easy conversation.

'I believe he did,' she said, 'and rumour has it he's still climbing – probably aiming for Commissioner.'

'You reckon he'll get that high up?' Gordon asked.

'Possibly. He certainly has the right track record.' Anna didn't want to continue discussing Langton, and suddenly she didn't feel like finishing her meal.

'You didn't answer my question,' Gordon said, pouring more wine.

'You mean, did I feel sorry for Lester James? No. I maybe could understand his fury, but you don't see a victim stabbed to death like that and then feel any real compassion for their killer. If every case involved you emotionally, you couldn't really do your job. You have to learn to stand back.'

'I wasn't referring to a case, Anna.'

'I'm sorry, you've lost me.'

'I asked if you had ever loved anyone with as much passion as your suspect did.'

'Oh, sorry. What you call passion I would call obsession. Lester James was obsessed by Amanda Delany and, thankfully, to answer your question, have I ever felt that kind of obsession then the answer is no, I haven't. Have you?'

She leaned back in her chair with her wine glass and drained it. And when he didn't reply: 'Now *you* aren't answering *my* question.'

'Hard to say. I've thought I've been in love many times, but then it didn't work out. I just wonder what it would be like, to feel such a powerful passion.'

'I think it would be destructive.'

'Why?'

Anna sighed. 'I just do. If this passion was so strong, it would interfere with your life, especially if you had a career and all you could think about was the person you couldn't live without. And if they didn't reciprocate, it would be demoralising as well dysfunctional.'

'Did you love *him*?'

Anna was becoming tense, and her foot started tapping. 'Love whom?'

'James Langton.'

She carefully placed her glass down on the table.

'Is this why you've asked me out – to pry into my private life? Well – is it? It's none of your business how I felt about him, Gordon. He's no longer a factor in my life. It is over and has been for months. In fact, it is so much over that he's back with his ex-wife, and he has a child by her, his son Tommy. He's also, I think, adopted his stepdaughter Kitty.'

'Do you think it's over for him?'

'Christ, you're starting to really get me annoyed. Why are you so interested in my previous relationship with

James Langton? Like I said, it has nothing at all to do with you, and I don't want to continue this conversation, so can we change the subject?'

'Maybe I am trying to get round to saying something.'

'About me and Langton?'

'No, about me. I don't know if I should or shouldn't tell you the truth.'

'Well, go on. What shouldn't you tell me?'

'I'm bisexual.'

'I'm sorry?'

'I think you heard.'

She couldn't help smiling. 'Are you joking?'

'No, I'm very serious, although I sometimes wonder if there are any real bisexual tendencies, as I—'

'You really are bisexual?' Anna interrupted.

'Yes, and I am sort of obsessed by James Langton and have been for almost six months, ever since he came to me for treatment.'

She sat with her mouth open, scarcely believing what she was hearing. She could feel herself wanting to laugh.

'You're obsessed by James Langton?'

'Yes.'

'You're kidding me. I don't believe you.'

'Well, I'm telling you the truth. I haven't done anything about it, obviously, and to be honest I don't think I would dare, but I find him the most attractive and sexual man, and I don't seem to be able to just ignore it.'

Anna was stunned.

'It isn't funny,' he said quietly.

'I'm sure it isn't, but forgive me for not being able to have a heart-to-heart conversation about it, because all I can think of is the pair of us in the sack. Now you're telling me that not only are you gay, but the person you have feelings for is none other than my ex-lover, James Langton. Did you screw me because of this infatuation?'

'Don't start using words like "screw" and "sack", it doesn't suit you.'

'It's nevertheless the fucking truth. Is that why you screwed me? I'm so very sorry if it sounds uncouth, but from what you are saying, you have used me. For what? To get closer to him?'

'Yes.'

'I don't believe this.' Anna slapped her napkin down on the table. Gordon looked suitably sheepish. She picked up her bag.

'I'm going. I suggest you order some strong black coffee as you are way over the drink-drive limit.'

'I've just told you the truth. I'm sorry, but I couldn't keep up the pretence, and—'

Anna stood up, and leaned across the table.

'I suggest you keep it to yourself. If Langton were to know your true feelings for him, I think he'd punch the living daylights out of you. And, to be honest, I feel like giving you a hard smack across the face myself.'

Anna paid off the cab and went into her block of flats. Letting herself in through the front door, she tossed her handbag aside. So much for going to such lengths dressing for dinner. She stripped off her dress, throwing it onto the floor. How could she have been so inept at interpreting the real situation? She was certain that Langton had no idea and now looked forward to imparting the information and seeing his reaction.

As the team prepared for the forthcoming trials, Anna spent only mornings at the station. She then went home to swot for her promotion interviews. Langton had not shown up on any morning to oversee the presentation of their evidence for the prosecution, and she was not prepared to call him. She'd wait.

Anna had completed her application form for promotion and sent it to her former boss, DCI Vince Mathews, who had recommended her. It was then passed to the selection panel who would sift through all the applicants and select the nine who would go forward to the next stage, to appear before the Assessment Centre in Earl's Court.

Anna was one of the nine. She would now have to prepare for a whole day when she would be put through her paces in front of a panel consisting of a uniformed Superintendent, a Higher Executive Officer and a Detective Chief Superintendent.

She was very nervous, and had read up on the numerous policy case files; she knew, too, that she might be asked to reflect on actual cases she had been involved with. Her brain churned over and she had hardly slept. The night before the interviews, she went over and over in her mind all the cases she had worked on, and all the case files she had researched. But, having had her application approved, she was confident that it would not be too daunting a prospect, and it was with confidence that she drove to the Assessment Centre. She was there fifteen minutes early.

In the waiting room, Anna helped herself to coffee, and checked her watch. It was 8.45 and she sat down at a large table, waiting to be called. It was another hour before anyone else arrived, and she turned expectantly to see a heavy-set, bull-necked man at least fifteen years older than herself. He carried a green folder and dumped it down onto the table.

'Morning,' she said brightly.

He gave a curt nod of his head and crossed to pour himself a coffee.

'Have you been before the panel?'

'Yes.' He sat down and reached for a biscuit.

'I'm Anna Travis,' she said, trying to be pleasant.

'DI Frank Duggan,' he said tersely, and then swivelled around to stare at her. 'You up before the board?'

'Yes.'

'Huh.' He looked disapprovingly at her, and she blushed. 'Bit young, aren't you?'

Anna got herself a refill of coffee. 'Maybe I'm older than I look,' she said coolly.

Duggan munched on a digestive biscuit, then dipped it into his coffee and sucked it.

'How was it?' she asked.

'Not easy, and I'm not through yet. I have to write up this and then I've got to wait to go before the trick cyclists for the next interview.'

Anna knew he was referring to the psychological assessment, but by now she felt that whatever she said to him would get the same blunt response. He opened the file and took out a pen.

'Not bloody easy,' he muttered.

'I didn't think it would be.'

'Really? Well, get ready. They've got a panel of hard-nosed officers in there, one especially. He didn't like me, and made it obvious, but there's a female that's pleasant. I'd aim at getting her on your side.'

Before Anna could get any further details, a uniformed officer opened the door and looked at her.

'DI Travis?'

'Yes.' She stood up quickly, and he gestured for her to follow him out of the room.

At the end of the corridor, he paused, turning towards her. 'One moment.'

He knocked and stood in the open doorway. 'DI Anna Travis.'

There was a long trestle table with a green cloth and three chairs behind it, but only two occupants. Anna sat down on the chair provided opposite them. They introduced themselves: Superintendent Henry Smith and Sheila Cox, a Higher Executive Officer. They were just waiting for the third member of the panel to join them.

Sheila Cox was calm and spoke softly, saying encouragingly how impressed they had been by Anna's application form. The meeting would be an opportunity for the three of them to assess Anna's competency in answering questions, and they would be asking her about the case examples she had written up in her application.

'You will be given a folder, and you will leave the meeting to prepare a fifteen-minute oral presentation on how you would deal with the situation described on the pages inside. Then you'll be given a written exercise which is a report on how you would deal with that same situation. Is that all clear?'

'Yes, thank you.'

A small side door opened and Anna's heart stopped.

'Detective Chief Superintendent James Langton,' Miss Cox said, gesturing towards him.

Anna now knew who the hardnosed one was. He gave her barely a glimmer of recognition, merely nodding his head as he took his seat.

'Sorry to keep you waiting,' Langton said to the panel, again pointedly ignoring Anna.

Miss Cox waited for him to open his file. She then glanced to her right and received a nod from Superintendent Smith.

'Right, I think we should begin.'

It was almost an hour later, and Anna felt drained. Both Cox and Smith had questioned her case examples in detail. Langton appeared to be almost bored, leaning back in his chair, clicking his ballpoint pen on and off. He said not a word until she finished discussing her part in her second murder enquiry, and then he remarked abruptly, 'There was a very worrying leakage to the press during this enquiry. What do you have to say about that?'

Anna explained nervously that, to her knowledge, the leaks had helped garner information that the murder team were able to use to their advantage, especially as the killer was manipulating the press himself.

On every one of Anna's application cases that had involved her working alongside Langton, he brought up specific areas she knew he had queried at the time and even warned her about. Eventually she was excused to return to the waiting room and prepare for the next session.

'Shit!' she muttered as she began to read the folder. *Can you really sleepwalk into a crime* was the heading. The file highlighted the case of a murder which had been committed by a suspect who claimed he had been asleep at the time. It showed how worrying the concept was to the police, how difficult a task they faced to distinguish legitimate sleepwalkers from those using it as an excuse for their behaviour. One expert claimed that sleep-walking, once seen as an eccentric and harmless activity, was rapidly taking on an altogether more sinister aspect. Anna started to make copious notes.

It was almost midday when she was called back into the hot seat to embark on her oral presentation. She was allowed to refer to her notes, but knew it would make a better impression to keep her head up and show confidence.

'I believe that family history plays an important part in the truth of a suspect's claim to have been sleepwalking while committing a crime. So if there is a history of sleep-walking in childhood, then it's possible it can continue into adulthood, but the reality is that it would also require a hereditary disposition. Triggers such as stress, lack of sleep and alcohol can set off a sleepwalking incident, but the controversial element is . . .' She hesitated. She couldn't remember what she was going to discuss next. There was a long pause as they waited. She tried to recall some of the most pertinent facts she had just read, but she couldn't think. Her mind had gone blank.

Langton leaned back in his chair clicking his pen again, while Smith tapped the table with his fingers as if bored.

'So, Detective Travis, explain to us how you would deal with a perpetrator who had killed his mother and then pleaded sleepwalking as his defence . . .'

It was only 3 p.m. when Anna handed in her written report but it felt much later. She waited to be interviewed by the psychologist. By this time she had consumed too much coffee and felt bloated, and her nerves were ragged.

In the ladies' room, she washed her face in cold water, but felt no calmer. On the contrary, she was anxious about her performance. She was certain that Langton would be giving her a bad report. He had appeared distracted throughout, and had hardly asked any questions about her presentation. He had made plenty of notes, but whether they had anything to do with the process, she had no idea.

The next session did little to boost Anna's confidence. The psychologist took so long in between asking her questions, she sensed that there was a hidden agenda. She wondered whether or not his slow delivery was designed to make her more nervous than she already was, or more paranoid because he kept on repeating one specific query.

'Explain to me what you want to achieve.'

'Promotion,' she said rather sharply. 'That's why I am here.'

After another lengthy pause, he came up with another question.

'Can you explain to me why, on numerous past cases, you have been reprimanded for perhaps appearing to be an over-achiever?'

'I don't understand your question.'

As he slowly repeated it, Anna knew that Langton had to have given, in his report, details of the times he had reprimanded her regarding her continual habit of working alone. She became so enraged that she clenched her hands into fists.

'If by over-achieving you mean getting a result in a case, then I still don't understand your question. I have never, on any case, considered achievement to be an objective. I love my work, I only want to give the best of myself and to gain the best possible result – that is, the arrest of a perpetrator.'

'Do you think that is what you have done?' This time, his question came hot on the heels of her last answer.

'Yes, I believe so.'

'What about working as a team member? Do you find that difficult?'

'No.'

'Can you give me a more expansive answer?'

'Well, I am here to gain promotion. That would make me a leader of a team, rather than a sheep, and I think that I have all the right qualities for that position.'

'Do you find it difficult to impart information that you have uncovered to others in your team?'

'Not at all. If at any time I've appeared to be working alone, then it has been purely down to circumstances.'

'Would you call yourself a risk-taker?'

Anna was getting increasingly angry. 'Risk to whom? Myself or losing the case? As a police officer one is constantly at risk, and I am prepared to put myself in that position if necessary.'

'Is that why, in the past, you have not always brought your whereabouts to the attention of your team?'

This was Langton, it had to be. It was a waste of time remaining in the room. She pushed back her chair.

'I haven't finished yet, Travis.'

'Well, I have, sir. I can't see the point of answering any further questions. I believe the examiners have already made up their minds whether or not I am suitable for promotion.'

'That is your mistake,' said the psychologist. 'I am simply reading through your files. We will not be making any decision regarding promotion until we've had time to digest everything that has taken place today.'

She was in two minds whether or not to believe him, and then decided she'd blown it anyway. She stood up and, as a parting shot, suggested that at the next promotional board she would prefer not to have to face someone with whom she had had a close personal relationship.

She missed the psychologist's look of stunned amazement.

Anna didn't want to go home; instead she stopped at the station. Mike Lewis greeted her warmly and asked how it had gone.

'I blew it. I don't think for one moment Detective Chief Superintendent Langton would have agreed to my promotion, so I walked out.'

'Well, they'll let you know in a few weeks' time.'

'I already know,' she snapped and then apologised. 'Sorry, it's been a long day, and thanks for being supportive.'

Mike was reassuring, reminding her that it had taken him two attempts. There were so few places available and she was young, she would have plenty of opportunity.

'Now for some good news.' He took an envelope out of his pocket, and showed Anna two tickets. 'We've been sent them by the director for a cast and crew screening of *Gaslight* in Leicester Square on Sunday evening.'

'You are joking.'

'Nope. It appears they have pulled out all the stops to get it ready, probably on the tailwind of the arrest of

Lester James – you know, for the publicity. We're all going.'

There was a loud gasp from the audience when Amanda Delany made her first appearance. She was so beautiful, and the Victorian costume suited her delicate figure. The wig with its blonde ringlets and coiled bun at the nape of her neck enhanced her bare slim shoulders. She played the frightened heroine in *Gaslight* to perfection.

Mike, sitting next to Anna in the audience, whispered that he had had no idea of just how beautiful she was. It was her beauty that got to them all, yet it was almost impossible to block out the tragic, skeleton-thin victim lying on the gurney. Whether or not the murder became entwined with Amanda's performance was immaterial; there was still a sense of terrible loss. Amanda Delany was a star; she burned so brightly in front of them all and when the film ended, there was a moment of silence. Then the entire audience rose to their feet to applaud.

Langton must have come in when the movie had started, because Anna saw him at the end of their row. He wasn't clapping like everyone else but stood quietly, head tilted downwards so Anna couldn't see the expression on his face. As soon as the applause died down, and everyone began moving out from their seats, Anna went in the opposite direction. Some groups of the crew stayed chatting and laughing, but hurrying out, heads bowed, were the two James brothers, Harry and Tony. Anna was one of the first to leave the cinema and took off up the road to hail a taxi. She stood on the pavement in pouring rain. A taxi pulled up beside her and the passenger door opened.

'Get in,' Langton said abruptly.

Anna hesitated and then stepped inside.

'That was a hideous event,' he said, as the taxi moved off.

'Depends. I think the film will be very successful. I was surprised to see you there.'

'I got your spare ticket.'

She pressed herself back in the seat, and they remained silent. She wondered if he was, like her, trying to think of what to say.

'I know I won't get the promotion,' she finally said quietly.

'Correct. You're not ready for it, Anna, but you won't know officially for a few weeks.'

'Thanks to you!'

'Not just my decision.'

'Bullshit. You really primed that psychologist, and I knew by the questions he was asking that you'd put your oar in.'

He shrugged, and it made her furious.

'If I'd known you were going to be on the board of examiners, I wouldn't have even bothered going in for the day. As soon as I saw you, I knew it would be a waste of time.'

'That depended on you. What you should do is learn from it, and refrain from constantly acting as a one-man band. Until you understand the logistics of teamwork, you will never be a suitable candidate for promotion.'

She glared at him.

'Also, implying that one of the reasons you walked out of the psychological assessment was that you had a personal relationship with a member of the board was very childish. I wouldn't be surprised if the gossipmongers have you and Miss Cox forming a liaison.'

511

'*What?*'

He grinned. 'She's gay,' he said, as if there was a need for an explanation.

'Really? Well, I can tell you someone else who is also gay.'

He turned to face her, inching around in his seat.

'Your dear friend and massage guru, Gordon. And in case you are not aware of it, he has the hots for you.'

She didn't expect Langton to burst into laughter.

'It's the truth,' she said angrily.

'I'm sure it is. I always thought he was a bit light on his feet!'

'Is that all you have to say?'

He was smiling as he nodded, and then leaned forwards to tap on the window of the taxi driver.

'Tower Bridge, sorry.'

She sat back, arms folded.

'Unless you're hungry and we could grab a bite to eat?'

Anna shook her head.

'Sad tonight, didn't you think?' Langton went on.

She made no reply.

'Mind you, if she'd carried on sniffing coke and using crack cocaine she probably would have destroyed herself. That's the saddest thing – so beautiful, so talented, and if she'd lived, this movie would have made her an even bigger star. Instead she ends up with multiple stab-wounds and a body that was ready to cave in.'

Anna looked out of the window. The rain was still pouring down. She jumped when Langton took her hand.

'Don't get angry, Anna, get smart. I believe in you and I sincerely think you have a big career ahead of you.'

Relieved to be giving the driver directions to her block of flats, she nonetheless felt awkward as Langton held onto her hand. Not until the taxi had pulled up did she try to release her hand from his. Langton pulled shut the window between them and the driver.

'I love you, Anna.' His voice was low. 'You know that, don't you? I want to look out for you. Don't get into a situation where you can't come to me, talk to me. I'll always be here for you.'

She faced him. His dark eyes bore into her and for the first time she really took on board what he was saying, how much older he looked, how perhaps he was being kindly rather than having any ulterior motive.

'Goodnight,' she said softly.

'No, don't get out yet. Talk to me.'

'I don't think there's anything more to say.'

'Of course there is. You think I don't know how disappointed you must feel? Never mind how much you've been bottling up inside you about me.'

'I haven't bottled anything up,' she snapped.

'Of course you have. You think after all this time I don't know you? And bringing up that crap about Gordon – how did you expect me to react?'

'I just thought you should know.'

'Really? Well, his private life is his own business, but yours is important to me. I don't want us to part with any grudges against each other, Anna. Like I said, I care for you and it's quite possible we'll work together again.'

'Don't worry, I won't embarrass you.'

'For Christ's sake, stop this. You're acting like a child, when I am trying to be as positive as I can be about us.'

She faced him. Said hotly, '*Us*? It seems to me that you feel like you have the right to call in and see me at

513

all hours of the day and night. You turned up uninvited when Gordon was there, and you knew we had slept together. You couldn't have made it more obvious that you felt you had the right to interfere in my private business!'

Langton laughed gently. 'Well, as it turned out, I needn't have worried.'

'You think it's funny?' Her voice sounded shrill and she wished she didn't feel like bursting into tears.

'I was jealous as hell, all right? Is that what you want to hear?' He sighed. 'There you have it. And you are right — I shouldn't still feel that I can call on you when I choose. To be honest, I never thought about it until now. Maybe the hardest thing for me is to let you go.'

What he was saying confused her to such an extent that she closed her eyes. She was even more confused when he put his arm around her.

'Anna, you took good care of me when I needed you. Sometimes, I feel that I never really showed you how much I appreciated all your patience and, if it wasn't for you, I doubt if I would have ever got myself back together — well, not physically anyway. I'm still emotionally screwed up.'

'About me?' she whispered.

'Of course about you. I meant it when I said I loved you. I do, and I can't help feeling jealous when I think I'm losing the one person I feel so protective of. But this is not me wanting us to get back together. I don't want you to think that is what I want.'

'Why not?'

He slowly moved his arm from around her.

'Anna, I'm married and have two kids. Whether or not I got into this for the wrong reasons, it's my life now.

I am going to make it work, just as much as I want you to know how special you are. I want you to trust me and know that what I did at the promotion meeting was because I want you to succeed – and I believe you will, given time.'

'Can I go now?' She needed to be on her own.

He sighed, then cupped her face in his hands and kissed her. 'Yes, you can go, sweetheart. No hard feelings?'

'No hard feelings. I really appreciate everything you've told me. You're right, I'm still young, there'll be another opportunity. I'll show them!'

Langton gave her a lopsided smile as she got out, and waved to her as the taxi drove off. Then he sat back, wishing he could light a cigarette because no matter what he had said, all he wanted to do was to stop the taxi, run back to her and kiss her again. Anna represented youth and freshness and, beside her, he felt jaded and old, too old to continue their relationship even when it had been a possibility. For once though, he told himself, he was behaving responsibly.

Until the next time, at least.